We hope you e̶ [barcode] SHE rn or
renew it by the

You can renew ....norfolk.gov.uk/libraries or
by using our free library app.

Otherwise you can phone 0344 800 8020 -
please have your library card and PIN ready.

You can sign up for email reminders too.

**NORFOLK COUNTY COUNCIL
LIBRARY AND INFORMATION SERVICE**

# ANNA JACOBS

# Pride of Lancashire

**HODDER**

First published in Great Britain in 2005 by Hodder and Stoughton
This paperback edition published in 2006 by Hodder and Stoughton
A division of Hodder Headline

A Hodder paperback

11

A CIP catalogue record for this title is
available from the British Library

ISBN 978 0 340 84072 6

Typeset in Plantin Light by Palimpsest Book Production Limited,
Polmont, Stirlingshire

Printed and bound in the UK by
CPI Group (UK) Ltd, Croydon, CRO 4YY

Hodder Headline's policy is to use papers that are natural,
renewable and recyclable products and made from wood grown
in sustainable forests. The logging and manufacturing processes
are expected to conform to the environmental regulations
of the country of origin.

Hodder and Stoughton Ltd
A division of Hodder Headline
338 Euston Road
London NW1 3BH

# Pride of Lancashire

# 1

Carrie Preston watched stony-faced as the midwife helped her mother give birth to her ninth live child. After Lily's birth four years ago, she'd hoped her mother wouldn't have any more children. At twenty-two she was sick of caring for babies and small children. But her father only had to talk lovingly and her mother would do anything for him, then before you knew it there'd be another baby on the way.

'Eh! Come over here quick an' give us a hand, lass.'

As Carrie stepped closer to the bed, Granny Gates thrust the squirming baby into her arms, with a terse, 'There's another babby in there.'

'What? There can't be!' But Granny knew about these things because she acted as midwife at most of the births in the Lanes, as the poorer part of Hedderby Bridge was called.

'Didn't any of you guess it might be twins? Your mam must have been bigger than usual.'

'She doesn't go round showing us her belly and she allus looks fat when she's expecting! She just said this one was livelier than usual.' As Carrie cradled the tiny body against her, her mother gave a strangled scream and pushed out a second baby, then lay limply on the stained mattress while Granny cleaned her up.

Carrie groaned softly. Twins! Two babies to look after! That'd make seven sisters she had now and two brothers. How would they ever manage to feed and clothe the new ones? There wasn't enough food to go round as it was, not with her father spending half his wages at the pub. If only Stott's didn't pay their men at the Dragon! So many of them started drinking there as soon as the coins were clinking in their pockets.

Carrie held the first baby carefully, not wanting it to do anything that would mess up her clothes. She only had one set and they were so ragged she was ashamed to go to her work at the new laundry that was replacing washerwomen for some of the richer families in town. She had a good job there, helping with the box mangle, earning twelve shillings a week, but she'd have to find a way to get some more clothes because her skirt was torn and frayed at the hem and her bodice was nearly worn through under the arms.

'They're healthy enough for all they're so small,' the old woman said. 'Listen to 'em skriking. Here, give me that babby.' Deftly she wrapped up the tiny creatures and laid them top to tail in the wooden box that was to have been the cradle for one.

Carrie stepped back, wincing as her new sisters continued to let out those thin wails that nearly drove you mad sometimes. She turned to look at her mother. The afterbirth had come away, just one for the pair of them, but surely there was more bleeding than there had been the other times?

Jane Preston groaned and twisted her legs as if in pain.

After a few more minutes, Granny turned to Carrie and said in a low voice, 'Better fetch Dr Latimer to her. I can't stop this bleeding. I reckon she's tore hersen inside.'

For a minute Carrie could only stare, then she ran down to tell her dad. Only he wasn't in the kitchen.

'Where's he gone?' she asked Marjorie, who was sitting in their father's chair near the fire, gazing dreamily into the flames.

'Dad? Gone down the Dragon. He said he couldn't stand the noise Mam was making.'

Carrie glanced towards the pot on the mantelpiece. It had been moved. 'He didn't take any of the money, did he?'

Marjorie stared into the fire, not meeting her eyes.

Edith, always the quiet one but the most observant, said in her soft voice, 'I think he took it all, our Carrie.'

'Oh, no! How are we to pay Granny now? And how will we buy food? Why didn't you stop him, Marjorie?'

''Cos he'd have give me a backhander if I'd tried.'

Carrie bit back more hot words. Marjorie, her next eldest sister, would do anything, say anything, to avoid a belting. And lately their father had become more violent. It was the drink, she reckoned, twisting his brain.

'I'll have to go after him. I hope he's got some money left. Granny says we need to fetch the doctor to Mam.'

Marjorie's eyes filled with the easy tears she seemed able to produce for the slightest thing. 'She's not dying, is she?'

'She's bleeding too much. Go up and see if Granny needs help.'

'You know I can't stand the sight of blood.'

Carrie dragged her sister to her feet and shoved her towards the stairs. '*Go up!* Else it's me who'll be giving you a backhander. An' you, Edith, make sure you don't let that fire go out.' The others were in bed already. She could hear Dora, Grace and Lily whispering in the girls' bedroom and knew Ted was fast asleep in the boys' room upstairs. That boy could sleep through anything. Robbie was out drinking with his friends. Trust men to avoid being there for a birth. He was only a year younger than Carrie, but she felt many years older than him.

She left her brothers and sisters to it. Time enough to wake them if their mother . . . No, Carrie wouldn't *let* her die! She'd get the doctor to see her if she had to drag him here.

She snatched her matted grey shawl from the hook in the hall and rushed out into the night.

It took only a couple of minutes for her to make her way down the narrow streets to the Dragon. Taking a deep breath to give herself the courage to confront her father, Carrie pushed her way into the warmth of the pub, wrinkling her nose in disgust at the smelly haze of smoke from the men's pipes, her eyes dazzled by the light from the gas burners set around the walls. She was tall enough to see over most folk's heads, but still couldn't spot her father so reckoned he must be sitting down at the far side, which was his favourite spot. Sighing, she began to move across the crowded room. He had to be here. He always came to this pub because it was so close, right at the foot of the Lanes on Market Street.

She stopped for a minute, feeling uneasy. It seemed as if the mood in here tonight was angry: men scowling, thumping tables, gesticulating. Had something happened?

A drunken man stepped backwards suddenly and bumped into her, grabbing her as she tried to avoid him. But though Carrie tried to pull away, he wouldn't let go of her arm. Instead he smiled and said, 'Come an' have a drink wi' us, love,' in a slurred voice.

'No, thanks.'

'Go on. Have a drink. I'll pay.'

The men round them began to call, 'Have a drink! Have a drink!' some banging their pots on the tables or stamping their feet in time to the words.

Carrie tried to shake him off, but he was too drunk to listen to reason. When a younger man pushed through the onlookers and came up to them she tensed, hoping he wasn't going to join in the baiting.

'Let the lass go,' he said in a sharp voice.

'Not till she's had a drink wi' us.'

As the drunkard reached out his free hand and tried to feel Carrie's breast, she slapped him away angrily, but still couldn't manage to break his tight grip on her arm.

The newcomer grabbed the man's wrist and

squeezed it hard. '*Let go, I said.*' His voice was loud enough to cut through the noise and make everyone nearby turn and stare at them.

The drunk yelped and let go, rubbing his hand. 'What d'you do that for? I were only havin' a bit o' fun.'

'The lass didn't like it.'

'Thanks.' Carrie tried to step back, but the other men around them didn't move.

Her rescuer studied her, then said quietly, 'A decent lass like you shouldn't be in here at this time of night.'

Carrie rubbed her wrist. 'I wouldn't normally but I have to fetch our dad. Mam's just had twins and she needs the doctor. Only Dad's taken all the money.'

'I'll help you look for him. What's his name?'

'Arthur Preston.'

Her rescuer put two fingers to his mouth and blew a piercing whistle, then called out in the sudden silence, 'Where's Arthur Preston?' He had the loudest voice Carrie had ever heard and, for all he was still quite young, he had a presence that said he stood no nonsense from anyone. He was tall, looked sturdy and well fed. His brown wavy hair framed a rugged face and he had the bluest eyes she'd ever seen.

A chorus of voices in the far corner called out that Arthur was over there, so the two of them made their way in that direction. As they walked, the noise in the big public room gradually built up again so that they had to speak loudly to make themselves heard.

'Can you see him, lass?'

'Not yet – oh, yes. There he is. Thanks.' Carrie pushed her way through the last group of men. 'Dad!'

Arthur Preston turned and blinked at her owlishly and she realised with a sinking heart that he was very drunk indeed. 'Oh, Dad, how could you? Tonight of all nights.'

'Is it born yet? I hope it's a boy this time.'

'It's two girls. Twins.'

It took Arthur a minute to take this in, then he smiled. 'Gorra have another drink for that. Two, eh? Takes a real man to get two at once. You hear that, lads? I've got twin daughters.'

Carrie shook his arm. 'Mam's really bad and Granny Gates says we've to send for the doctor, only there's no money left. You took everything from the pot.' Not that there was ever much left in it by Wednesday.

He fumbled in his pockets and brought out a few coins, holding them on the flat of one hand and poking them with his fingertip. 'There y'are. Take it.'

She felt like bursting into tears, but what good would that do? 'Oh, Dad, is this all you have left? How are we going to buy food if you spend the money on drink?'

His foolish smile changed to a scowl. 'Don't you tell y'father what to do or I'll leather your backside, big as you are.'

'Just you try to touch me and I'll take a stick to you!' She stared down at the coins. 'How am I going to pay the doctor?'

'Go an' ask our Bill for help.'

'Uncle Bill's already told you he won't lend you any money. Haven't you any more coins at all?'

As Arthur fumbled through his pockets again, she saw people laughing at him. Was it any wonder? He was drunk as an owl. His clothes were as ragged as you could get without being indecent and he smelled sour because he rarely washed these days. His own brother didn't come round to see them now, because her father always tried to cadge money off him. Her aunt Sadie was a staunch Methodist and very much against drink, not allowing it into her own house. She would no longer speak to her drunken brother-in-law in the street.

Her father produced one penny more from his trouser pocket. Carrie added it to the coins in her hand and turned to leave, smearing away tears with the back of one arm. As she walked towards the front door, she found the young man who'd come to her aid still walking beside her, but she didn't look at him, didn't look at anyone.

When she reached the entrance, her companion put out his hand to bar her way. She looked at him warily. Now what?

'How much?'

She might have known that was what he wanted. They were all alike, men. Kept their brains in their trousers. 'I don't go with men.'

His face grew grim. 'I meant: how much money do you need for the doctor?'

She shrugged. 'Five shillings.'

He felt in his pocket and brought out half a sovereign. 'Here, take this. And get some food with the rest of the money. You look hungry.'

Carrie thrust her hands behind her back. If she took it, he'd want something from her later. 'I don't even know you.'

'Eli. Eli Beckett, at your service.' He gave a mocking flourish towards the big room behind them. 'I've come to help my uncle run this pub now my cousin's dead.'

He held out his hand and Carrie shook it briefly, reluctant to touch him, she didn't know why. The hand was warm and felt strong. For a moment they stared at one another and it felt almost as if they were the only ones there, then she pulled her hand away. She'd heard about Peter Beckett dying suddenly and had been sorry. He'd been well liked, a thin young man who'd never looked well, for all he ate good food every day.

She looked at the coin Eli was still holding out and was tempted to take it. It'd solve a lot of her present problems, including buying food the next day. 'It'll be a while before we can pay you back. *He* drinks more than ever when there's a new baby.'

'I don't want paying back. It's my first month working here, and this,' he closed her fingers round the coin, 'is for luck. Maybe if I do someone a good turn, fate will smile on me and I'll get what I want.'

Carrie didn't know about fate smiling on anyone round here. Most of the folk she knew thought themselves lucky if they could set bread on the table for their families every day, and didn't try to think beyond that.

'What's your first name, love?'

'Carrie.'

'Well, Carrie Preston, you nip off and fetch that doctor to your mother, then one day you can show me your new sisters. If they have brown eyes as pretty as yours, they'll be lucky.'

For a minute she stared at him, then remembered her mother and muttered, 'Thanks!' before hurrying off into the night.

Eli watched her go: thin and all eyes, with that look people got when they didn't have enough to eat and were working too hard. She was taller than most folk round here, nearly the same height as he was, and there was something decent and honest that shone from her, for all she was wearing clothes that were little more than rags.

That damned father of hers ought to be taken out and given a good thrashing. Eli had had to watch it many a time in his parents' alehouse: men drinking away their money on wage day while their wives and children stood outside, hoping there'd be enough left over to buy food. It was no different in this pub, even if it was bigger and sold wines and spirits as well as beer.

Well, there wasn't much he could do about that because selling drink was his living, but he didn't have to like how some men behaved, did he? One day he'd have a place of his own, a better one than this, some-where for the more respectable folk to enjoy them-selves, one with a proper music room attached. And he'd not let anyone get falling down drunk there, by hell he wouldn't!

He went back to Arthur Preston, found him arranging to have another drink 'on the slate', and caught the potman's eye. 'No more credit for this one, Jim.'

The potman frowned at him. 'But Arthur's a regular. He'll pay up later. He allus does.'

'I mean it. No more drinks on the slate for him. Not today and not any other day, either.'

With a shrug Jim turned away and went to serve someone else.

Arthur sat frowning, as if having difficulty under-standing what was happening.

Eli looked down at him, not bothering to hide his scorn. 'Get away home now, Preston. You've got two new daughters and a wife who need you, and you'll be served no more beer tonight.'

For a moment anger darkened Arthur's face, then something about the other man made him bite back the hot words of protest. He heaved himself to his feet, scowling at the tall young fellow eye to eye, for they were the same height. But even so, something held him back from lashing out and he spat on the floor instead to show his disgust. As he made his way out of the pub, swaying and unsteady, he grumbled under his breath and rubbed the place behind his ear that seemed always to be sore these days.

Eli followed him and stood in the doorway for a minute or two to make sure Preston didn't try to double back.

The other men at the table looked down into their pots until Beckett had moved away, then exchanged glances.

'What dost think of that new chap?' the oldest asked.

After grimacing as he considered it, the man next to him said slowly, 'Wouldn't like to cross him. Looks like he can handle hissen in a fight.'

'Never heard of 'em *stopping* folk drinking in a pub afore,' another commented. 'Not regulars, any road.'

'Aye.' They were all silent for a minute, contemplating this shocking state of affairs.

'What dost think of Arthur's lass?' one asked after a minute or two.

'She'd be bonny if she were better turned out. Most lasses make more effort than that.'

'She's too busy lookin' after all them kids. Eh, he's a wick 'un, yon Arthur is. Two more daughters!'

They raised their pots and drank to the new babies, then forgot about them as they got into an argument about which pub in town sold the best beer.

When Eli next went into the kitchen behind the bar for a break, his uncle was waiting for him, looking angry.

'Jim says you stopped Preston from putting a drink on the slate. That man's credit is perfectly good. Don't do that again without asking me.'

'Preston's wife's just had twins.'

'There! He'd have celebrated in style if you hadn't stopped him. And he allus clears the slate in the end. He's all right, Preston is. Doesn't start fights, drinks nice and steady. I only wish there were more like him.'

Eli folded his arms and leaned against the door frame. His uncle was one of the old-fashioned sort who just wanted to get as much money as he could out of his customers without thinking about tomorrow or the sort of pub he ran. He didn't even provide food, though you could make a decent profit on it, just encouraged pie and cake sellers to come in and sell to his customers. It'd take a while to change things here, so Eli had to tread carefully. 'It won't win you friends on the town council, Uncle, to have men reeling home drunk, spending all they earn on booze while their families go hungry. You told me yourself the new Mayor's a Holy Joe. He's already stopped pubs opening on Sunday mornings till church is over. If we want that music licence, I reckon things'll have to change round here.'

'*We* don't want a music licence, *you* do.' Frank Beckett stared at his nephew before adding sharply, 'Now, don't stop any more customers from drinking their fill. I'll tell Jim to put Arthur's name back on the slate.'

Eli used the only argument his uncle would understand, 'Look, Preston has a pretty daughter. She'll go hungry if he spends all his money on booze.'

Frank frowned 'Found yoursen a lass, have you? Well, you can have your way about Preston, I suppose, as long as you don't stop Jim serving any of my other regulars.'

Eli knew when to push and when to hold back. 'All right. Now, you promised me when you brought me here that you'd let me start up a music room. How about using the back of the big public area for a free and easy on Saturday nights? That'd be a start, bring more people into the pub. Then later we can make a proper music room. They're all the thing nowadays. If you leave it to me to arrange, I'll have partitions put round the back part of the pub and it'll earn you ten times what it does now.'

'What, shut the back part away? Nay, I'm not doing that! It's the biggest room in any pub in town and I'm not having it changed! It's because of that room Stott's pay their men here, and *that* brings us in customers every single week. We don't want Stott's going to another pub to pay out. That big public room earns our bread and butter for us, an' don't you ever forget that. And besides, it'd cost too much to put partitions in and buy that new furniture you were talking about. No, we'll wait a bit, save our money then decide what to do.'

Eli had already noticed that his uncle was trying to wriggle out of his promise to let him have a music room if he came to work here. Well, Eli's father had said as much when warning him not to take up the job offer. His father had no time for his younger brother and was bitterly jealous of the way an old uncle had left Frank's wife some money and enabled him to buy the Dragon outright.

Knowing he had to make a stand now, Eli folded his arms and said, slowly and loudly, 'If there's to be no music room then I'll not be staying. I told you that when you offered me this job, and I meant it.'

'I didn't say there wasn't to be one, just not *yet*.'

'We make a start on it right away or I leave.'

His uncle's voice became coaxing. 'You know you don't mean that.'

Eli leaned forward, resting his hands on the table at which his uncle was sitting. 'I *do* mean it. I can allus find myself another job because I'm good at what I do.'

'But we *can't* close down the back part. Think of the money we'll lose. Look, we'll do what you suggested and set things up for a free and easy on Saturday nights. I'll have the piano brought in from the parlour and we'll find someone to play it so that folk can have a sing-song. I daresay there'll be one or two who can recite a poem too.' Frank smiled at his nephew. 'There, how does that sound?'

'It'll do for a start, but only till we can set up a proper music room.' Eli had been here long enough to consider all the options and had already come to the conclusion that he needed somewhere larger and with a separate entrance if he was to attract enough customers, especially those of the better sort. 'What about the old stables at the side, then?'

Frank stared at him. 'The old stables? The place is in a right old mess, only good for storage. It'd cost a fortune to set that to rights.'

'But when it was finished, we'd have *extra* money coming in. Think of that.'

His uncle began chewing his lower lip. 'Extra money, you say?'

Eli pressed his advantage. 'It wouldn't take that much to clean it up. The roof's still watertight. I checked that yesterday when it rained. It'd make a nice big space if we knocked the stalls down – most of them only have wooden partitions, not walls. It needn't be too fancy, but it would need gas lights putting in there as well and—'

'More gas lights! Do you think I'm made of money? Do you know what the gas lights in the big room and the house cost me? The Hedderby Gas Company charges for each burner, you know.'

'But gas lights don't need cleaning and trimming every day like oil lamps do. Gas is the modern way to light a business.' Eli gestured towards the noisy, crowded public room. 'It's a regular goldmine, this place. I reckon you can easily afford to put in a proper music room.' He folded his arms. 'I mean it, Uncle Frank. If you give me half a chance, I'll make you rich. If you don't give me a chance, I'm leaving.'

'But I don't know owt about music rooms!' Frank looked at his nephew, read implacable determination in every line of his muscular young body, and tried desperately to work out how to avoid spending money while still keeping Eli here. He wasn't so steady on his own feet these days and knew he couldn't manage this place without help, but he didn't like to spend good money unless he absolutely had to. He earned as much as he needed, enjoyed being a publican, just wanted things to go on as they were.

'I'll *rent* you the stables and you can turn them into a music room,' he offered.

Eli walked across to where he'd hung his jacket.

'Can you make my wages up tonight? I'll leave first thing in the morning.'

His uncle's voice rose to a higher pitch. 'Now, hold on. Let's be sensible. You can't expect me to risk that much of my money without knowing how it'll turn out!'

'You promised. If I had enough money of my own to rent the space and fancy it up, I'd not ask you to do it. But I don't. And I only came to work here because of your promise.'

Frank saw his opportunity. 'I'll *lend* you the money, then.'

'Goodbye.'

'Come back!' He sighed and glared at his nephew. 'We'll talk about it in the morning, eh? Now's not the time. And we'll do a free and easy on Saturday night, see how that works, eh?'

Eli hesitated.

There was a sudden roar outside.

'Hell, someone's started a fight!' He threw his jacket on the nearest chair and ran out into the public room, heading for the circle of men in the middle, shoving them aside when they didn't budge. He was followed by the two potmen who'd been hired for their muscles as well as their skill in serving customers.

It took a while to calm everything down, by which time his uncle was calling 'Last orders, per-lease, gentlemen!'

Eli didn't return to the kitchen until the doors had been closed behind the last customer and the potmen had cleared all the tables and washed the pots.

His cousin Joanna joined them there, looking even angrier than usual. 'They were in a funny mood tonight. Even the folk in the snug were edgy.'

Her father nodded agreement. 'Aye. Stott's have cut wages by a bob a week and the men don't like it. Well, I don't myself! It'll reduce our profits, with most of Stott's men doing their drinking here.'

Eli looked from one to the other. 'I thought Stott's were doing well? They're the only light engineering works in town.'

'They are doing well, never better, but the father died last year and the son inherited. He's a mean sod, is Athol Stott. I wish the cousin had inherited, yon Edmund. He's an easier man, doesn't look down his nose at you like that Athol does.' There was an angry roar from outside the pub and Frank grimaced. 'They're still fighting one another out there.'

As he turned, he noticed his daughter, whose hair was falling down around her narrow face and who looked a bit dishevelled generally. 'What happened to you, our Joanna? You look like you've been dragged through a hedge backwards. There's no *need* for you to go out on the floor at all now that your cousin's here. You should stay behind the bar in the snug from now on, as you did when our Peter was alive.'

'You'd like to keep me caged up, wouldn't you?' She glared at her father then turned her scowl on her cousin. 'And I think there's every need for me to keep on top of things out there.' She gestured to the big room. 'This pub is *my* inheritance now my brother's dead and I'm not letting you set me aside for Eli.'

Her father's fond expression turned angry. 'Your mother didn't like you going out on the floor, you know she didn't. You only started doing it after she died.'

'*She* used to do it.'

'She had to when we were starting up and every farthing counted. She didn't go out on the floor once we'd bettered ourselves, an' neither should you. It's not *necessary*. Some of those men don't know how to treat a decent woman.'

'Just let any man treat me less than respectfully and he'll be out on his ear! Besides, I'm not on the floor much with the snug to run. Where else would the women and better folk drink if I didn't keep that nice?'

'Aye, and you stick to the snug, my lass.' He could see the anger on her face still, so said placatingly, 'I'll see you looked after in my will, you know that, but a woman *can't* run a big pub like this on her own, especially with most of our customers coming from the Lanes. It's too rough round here, an' well you know it.'

'You're quite happy for me to go out there in the mornings, though, when someone has to clear up the mess those dirty devils leave behind. I'm not too good for that, am I?'

Eli watched with interest, wondering if he could turn this to his advantage. His cousin Joanna had been hostile towards him from the day he'd arrived. She was three years younger than him, twenty-five and still unwed, with her hair screwed back unflatteringly into a tight knot at the nape of her neck. She dressed plainly in dark clothes because she worked hard in the pub from dawn till dusk, and he had to admit she kept the place nice, cleaner than you'd think possible.

He reckoned her plainness came from the anger that seemed to emanate from her, not from her features which weren't bad. But from what his uncle had said when he persuaded Eli to join him here, she'd own a major share in this pub when her father died and he, as nephew, would get only a minor one, so it'd be better to keep on her good side. He hadn't managed to make friends with her yet, but he would.

He'd never seen Joanna smile, not really. She wore a slightly more pleasant expression when greeting a few favoured regulars, mostly women and elderly men, who sat in the snug and caused no one any trouble, but when she was at rest the corners of her mouth turned down and her dark eyes had a brooding look to them.

No, now he came to think of it, there was one other person she smiled at – Bonny, who cleaned the pub, a moon-faced woman whom others would dismiss as an idiot, but who had enough sense to do the cleaning and who talked perfectly sensibly, if slowly and simply.

He'd find a way to get Joanna on his side, he vowed. He knew what he wanted, which was to run a music room, and no one was going to stop him from getting it. No one! Though he'd make a start by running a free and easy here on Saturdays.

Later he'd get his uncle to agree to turning the old stables into a music room. If he didn't, Eli really would leave. He wasn't wasting himself here for years on a vague promise of being left a share in the pub when his uncle died. It was now that things were happening, with music rooms opening all over the place, and Eli wanted to be part of it.

Anyway, if his uncle broke one promise, he'd probably break the other and leave everything to Joanna.

# 2

Gerald Latimer answered the door because he happened to be passing through the hall when the knocker sounded. The girl standing on the step was clearly from the Lanes.

'Mam's just had twins an' she's bleeding badly, Dr Latimer. Granny Gates said to fetch you.'

His wife had come into the hall, listening, ready to help as always. 'Shall I come with you, dear?'

He knew Lydia was even more tired than he was because she'd been working at the mother and baby clinic she'd opened at the far end of the Lanes and been run off her feet by women coming in for the free bread and milk she offered all those who attended. In a fairer world Lydia would have been a doctor as well because she had a gift for healing. As it was, she knew more than most doctors and he often allowed her to help him.

He sighed. He could have done without a call-out tonight himself, because he'd had a hard day too, but there was no other doctor in the town who'd answer calls from the Lanes at night. Indeed the town had grown so much in the past two decades that it badly needed another doctor who would work in the poorer districts as he did, even though most folk there had trouble paying his fees.

He studied the girl. She had a steady look to her, and though she was stick-thin, probably because she was underfed like most of the residents of the Lanes, her eyes were bright with intelligence and life. 'I think this young lady will be able to help me, Lydia, but perhaps you could find her a piece of that delicious fruit cake while I'm fetching my bag?'

His wife nodded. 'Come with me, dear.'

Carrie followed willingly because she hadn't eaten since morning and wasn't too proud to accept any offer of food. She stared round her in fascination. They said the doctor lived like a king and it was true. Soft carpets on the floor, everything shining clean and a faint smell of flowers.

In the kitchen another woman was sitting by the fire, a cat in her lap. She was plump and rosy from the heat, was wearing a big apron and had screwed her faded brown hair into a bun on top of her head from which wisps were escaping. She made to stand up. 'Can I get you something, ma'am?'

'Stay where you are, Essie. I'm just finding this girl a piece of your fruit cake and perhaps a glass of milk. We have to be quick, though. Her mother's had a difficult birth and Gerald's just getting his things together.'

But Essie had shooed the cat off and was already on her feet. 'I'll get the milk. You'd better drink it first, love, then you can eat the cake as you walk along.'

Carrie was overwhelmed by everything and wanted to stare and stare, but did as the second lady had suggested, drinking the milk and sighing with delight at the creamy taste of it. And no dirty bits floating in it at all, like the stuff they bought sometimes. As she moved her arm incautiously, her bodice ripped still further and she looked down at it with a cry of dismay to see her ragged chemise exposed. Tears of embarrassment filled her eyes.

'Do you have anything else to wear?' Lydia asked, knowing that expression.

Carrie shook her head.

'If you come back tomorrow morning, I'll find you some clothes.'

'I don't have any money to pay for them.'

'You don't need to pay, dear. These are collected by a group of ladies who want to help women less fortunate than themselves.'

Carrie couldn't hold back a sigh of relief. 'Thank you, Mrs Latimer. I'm that grateful.' She wrapped the shawl round her in such a way as to hide the gap in her bodice.

'I'll be here all morning. If you come to the back door, Essie will let you in.'

When the girl had left Lydia looked at her cook, who was her ally and as near a friend as was possible for two women of such different stations in life. 'She has a weary look to her for one so young.'

Essie nodded. 'An honest face, though. And pretty eyes with those long lashes. Now, you don't know how long the doctor will be so you should get yourself to bed, ma'am. You look weary too.'

★

Carrie walked back to the Lanes beside the thin, grey-haired doctor who was a couple of inches shorter than she was. She munched the piece of cake with relish because it was sweet and full of fruit. She ought to save some of it for the others but there wasn't enough to go round so many of them, and for once she ate the whole piece herself.

As they turned into Throstle Lane, which was near the top of a small hill, she pointed. 'That's our house at the far end, doctor.'

He followed her inside the narrow passageway that led past the front room to the kitchen at the rear, with the stairs leading up between the two rooms. He paused at the foot of the stairs to say 'Good evening' to the man sitting slumped in the chair near the kitchen fire, but didn't get a response.

'Dad's drunk,' Carrie whispered. 'Mam's upstairs.'

She stood in the bedroom doorway as the doctor conferred with Granny, then examined her mother and pressed his fist down firmly on her belly.

'Has the bleeding slowed down at all, Mrs Gates?'

'Aye. I thought I was losing her at one time, but then it started to ease. You said to call you if I had a case with complications.' She pronounced the last word carefully, for it was one of the long ones he'd taught her. 'She'll need building up after losing so much blood.'

'I'll put her on my wife's list for beef tea and extras.'

Carrie knew about that list. 'Excuse me, doctor, but you'd better tell them to give the food to me and no one else. There are a lot of mouths to feed here an' kids'll pinch owt when they're hungry.'

Gerald looked at her. 'Bad, is it?'

She shrugged. 'We're allus short of food, if that's what you mean.' They ought to have been all right, with several of them in work, but her father didn't hand over much of his money these days, her brother Robbie spent most of his wages on himself, and her mother wasted what money she did get from Carrie and her sisters' earnings. Not that girls earned nearly as much as lads, but Carrie knew *she* could have managed quite well on what was coming in.

'Is your father not in work?'

'Yes, but he drinks.'

'Ah. How many of you are there?'

'Those two new 'uns will make ten of us childer, an' there's Mam an' Dad too, of course.'

The doctor stayed for an hour, talking gently to Jane, bringing a faint smile to her face as he praised her tiny new daughters, then making her yelp as he sewed up a tear in her soft flesh. He asked to have the foot of the bed raised and Granny sent Carrie out for some old broken bricks from the brickyard just along from Throstle Lane.

She was exhausted when she got back with them, but relieved when the doctor eventually pronounced her mother out of danger and left.

'He's a saint, that one,' Granny said when Carrie came back upstairs.

'His wife's nice too. She gave me a piece of cake. I've never tasted owt as good in my life. I didn't save any for the others, though, so don't tell them. There wasn't enough to go round.'

Granny's expression softened. 'You did the right thing, love. You're going to need all your strength to help with these two.'

'Um – I can't pay you tonight. I'm really sorry, but *he* took the money Mam had put by for you.'

Granny's eyes flashed with anger. 'I'll have a word with your father tomorrow mysen, then. I'll give him a right earful, *an'* I'll be waiting for him in the Dragon when he gets paid on Friday.'

Carrie sighed wearily as she closed the door behind Granny. Running the house would fall on her shoulders until her mother recovered and she'd have to send word to the laundry that she couldn't go in for a day or two. She reckoned she'd lose her place for sure this time. They'd warned her last time her mother was ill that they weren't running a charity and said if she wasn't so good a worker, she'd not have been kept on this long.

Well, at least Marjorie and Dora were still bringing home wages from the spinning mill, while Edith worked in the little shop on the corner. As soon as Mam was better, Carrie would go and look for another job. But not in the mill. She hated that place. The air was so full of fluff you felt as if you were choking, and the overlooker thumped you as soon as look at you. No one was going to thump her. Her dad had tried once or twice lately when something upset him and she'd thrown the nearest thing at him last time. He was getting really foul-tempered lately. And he hadn't drunk so much in the past, either. It was only lately.

It was then that she remembered the half-guinea Eli Beckett had given her. How could she have forgotten something so important? She could have paid Granny Gates out of that. And why hadn't the doctor asked for payment, too? He'd more than earned it. She felt guilty but knew she wouldn't volunteer to give Dr Latimer anything unless he asked for it. He was rich compared to them.

As she reached into her pocket for the precious coin, the front door banged and her brother Robbie came in. She left the coin where it was and turned to face him. 'Where've you been till this hour?'

He grinned and laid one finger on the side of his nose, making a shushing noise at the same time and swaying on his feet. Her heart sank as she realised he'd been drinking. She looked at her father, snoring gently in front of the fire, and thought her heart would break if Robbie went down the same path.

'You've been with that Declan Heegan again, haven't you?'

He scowled at her. 'You're my sister, not my keeper. What's it got to do with you?'

'I'm the one who has to scrape together the money for food and there won't be much to eat for the rest of the week, I can tell you.'

'Declan says the children aren't *my* responsibility!'

'So you'll see your brothers and sisters starve because of what that lout says?' She folded her arms across her chest to hold her anger in. 'You know we need your wages if we're to manage. Well, if you can't pay for your keep, don't ask me for any food, an' Dad had better not, either. If I can get hold of owt it'll go to Mam and the children.'

'I've enough left to pay for my keep.' He fumbled in his right pocket, then in the others, standing frowning. 'I know I should have some left.'

'Well, if you haven't, see how you like going hungry till wage day.'

Robbie subsided suddenly in their mother's chair and looked at her pleadingly, then jumped in shock as he heard wailing from upstairs. 'Oh, hell! I'd forgotten about Mam. Is she all right?'

'Not really. She bled a lot and we had to get the doctor in, so she'll not be doing much for a while.' Carrie sank down on the stool. 'I'll have to stay off work and look after her, so I won't be bringing any money in.'

'What did she have? I hope it isn't another girl.'

'No, it's two. Twin girls.'

'Hell, how long is she going to go on having children? She's forty-three, for goodness' sake.'

'Who knows? She and Dad are always at it.' Carrie felt weary and depressed at the mere thought of more mouths to feed, more months where her mother would be too sickly to cope – but not too sickly to lie with her father and start another baby.

Robbie looked across at her. 'I'm really sorry about the money. I'll see Declan tomorrow. He was holding the kitty.'

Carrie shrugged, not feeling very hopeful. She was fond of Robbie, who was often kinder than most young fellows, but he was soft underneath that kindness, he and Marjorie both, which left Carrie having to take charge. She'd expected him to wed by now, or at least have started courting like most other lads. But he and she had talked about that one day and it turned out they had one thing in common: neither of them wanted to marry and be burdened with kids.

She gave him a half-smile. 'I'm sorry if I sounded unkind but Dad took the food money from the pot and I only got a shilling or two back from him. I don't know how I'm going to manage this week. We've nothing left to pawn, can't even redeem the stuff he pledged last time. An' just look at him!' She pointed scornfully across the room to where their father lay snoring, mouth open, the gaps in his teeth showing clearly. 'It's a wonder he could even find his way home tonight. I'm sick of it.'

It was at that moment Carrie decided she was going to keep the half-guinea Eli Beckett had given her and not tell anyone about it. Her dad would only take it from her and spend it on booze. Her mother would spend lavishly on a feast, after which they'd be without food for the rest of the week, and even Robbie would try to cadge some of the money to spend on his wonderful new friend Declan Heegan, one of three brothers of whom Carrie was a bit wary because they were all so big and exuberantly male.

If she kept the half-guinea, she'd have something to fall back on, but she'd have to make sure no one saw it.

She'd try to get some food from the charitable ladies of the town this week, something she hated doing. It'd mean being prayed over and acting humble, but she'd do what was necessary to feed Ted, Grace and Lily, the 'little 'uns' who were still at school. She'd take Lily along with her when she went to see the ladies. At four, Lily had a fragile appearance which always softened their hearts, though Carrie knew her youngest sister was tough underneath. Eh, she was forgetting! Lily wasn't her youngest sister now. She had two others.

One day Carrie was going to get away from all this. If she didn't, her family would use her till there was nothing left of her, the way life and child-bearing had worn out her mother who wasn't much use for anything these days. But if there was some way other than marriage to secure her escape, Carrie would choose that. She didn't want to spend her life having one child after another and being dependent on a man who might or might not treat her well. Men changed after they'd married, whatever they said to you when they were courting. Everyone knew that.

She didn't know what she wanted in life, not exactly, only to be clean, wear decent clothes, and have something interesting to do with her time. Working at the laundry was hard, and it was boring too, because you weren't allowed to talk while you worked. The box mangle was full of stones to press the clothes flat and get the water out as it was run over them. It took both Carrie and a man to work it.

She'd be sorry to lose a steady job, but you had to look after your family. If you didn't, who would look after you when you needed it?

In the morning Eli Beckett got up early and checked the barrels of beer in the cellars. They had one of the new hydraulic beer engines at the Dragon – nothing was too good for the beer his uncle loved so much. Afterwards he went to find his cousin who he found wearing her rough sacking apron and working with Bonny to clean the big room.

Joanna looked as bad-tempered as ever, which made him hesitate in the doorway. But he'd lain awake till the small hours thinking about everything and had come to the conclusion that the only way to pin down his slippery uncle was to enlist his cousin's support.

He watched her for a minute, noting how she was working alongside Bonny even as she chatted, doing the dirty jobs as well as the lighter work. He didn't think it necessary for his cousin to do the menial work. The pub brought in a lot of money and his uncle could well afford to get other help. But as he'd noticed, Frank Beckett hated spending money on anything but his own comforts.

He walked across to the two women. 'Can you spare me a few minutes, Joanna?'

She didn't even turn round. 'Not really. As you can see, we're busy. We need another woman in here, but I can't get Dad to agree to that. He's a mean old devil.'

Bonny sniggered, repeated 'mean old devil' and continued wiping tables.

Eli moved a little closer to his cousin and spoke in a low voice. 'Aye. He's too tight-fisted to spend a shilling to save his own life, my uncle is. That's why I'm thinking of leaving.'

Joanna gave him a quick, assessing glance, as if

checking that he meant what he said, then put down the cloth and wiped her hands on her apron. Putting her hands on her hips, she eased her back, bending to and fro, then saying, 'Come into the snug.'

He followed her into her special territory. The potman had once told him that street walkers wouldn't even dare look through the doorway of this room, so afraid were they of Joanna, though Mr Beckett let them come into the far side of the main room as long as they behaved themselves. Eli wouldn't even have allowed that.

He looked round. Everything here was sparkling clean because Joanna always did the snug first. The wooden furniture was polished, the gleaming brass fender set neatly in place round the hearth and the horse brasses on the wall were shining brightly. Though the room was only about seven yards square, it was different from the rest of the pub, more cheerful. 'You've got it really nice in here.'

'Much you care. Or *him*.'

Eli kept his tone mild. 'I appreciate hard work when I see it.'

Joanna folded her arms. 'I haven't got all day to exchange compliments, so get to the point.'

'As you know, my uncle promised I could have a music room, which was the main reason I came to work here.'

'Dad's good at making promises, not so good at carrying them out.'

'As I'm finding. I thought I'd ask your help.'

'Ha! Why should I help *you*? You're trying to steal

my inheritance. I know he's promised you a part share in the pub when he dies, so don't try to deny it.'

'I won't. But I'm prepared to earn my share. You and I should work together because *you* would like to improve the tone of this place and *I* would like to run a music room. We might do better at achieving our aims together – given the obstacles.'

'Oh?'

'And if we succeed, the value of your inheritance will be trebled in the end, or more, even if I do get a part share in the Dragon.'

Joanna looked at him, her brow wrinkled in thought. 'How can you be so *sure* of that? I've heard that music rooms can be rowdy places.'

'They don't have to be. My parents' beerhouse isn't big enough to provide more than a bare living for them, and it'll go to my brother Tom when they die, so I started working for other folk as soon as I could. I know about music rooms because I've worked in them in Manchester and seen the money they can rake in if they're run properly. I've been to London, too – they're opening up really big places there. They're starting to call the fancy new ones theatres of variety or music halls, an' they're like theatres. That's what I really want one day, my own music hall, built proper for it, not a makeshift place. Before I'm through I'm going to own one, an' it'll be my pride and joy. That's what I'm going to call it: The Pride of Lancashire. I know you think I'm talking through the back of my head, but you'll see.' Eli looked at her assessingly. 'Have you ever been to a music room or saloon theatre?'

Joanna shook her head. 'When would I get the chance to do that? There isn't one in Hedderby. Any road, I never get a day off.'

'I'll take you one evening, if you like, then you'll see what I'm talking about. We could catch a train into Manchester. They've got a few nice places there. We might have to leave before the end of the show, though, to catch the last train back, but we'd see most of it. And, more important, *you* would see what the places are like.' He could tell she was astonished by his suggestion and added in a coaxing tone, 'Go on, Joanna. Give it a try, at least. I'm not your enemy. We'd make good allies, you and me, because you've got your head screwed on right.'

'Well . . . I would like to see a show, I must admit.' His cousin sighed. 'But we'd never persuade Dad to manage without both of us, even for one night.'

'Leave that to me. I'll get someone in to help out here in the big room and make sure things stay peaceful. Do you know a woman who could serve in your place in the snug?'

Joanna nodded, but still looked doubtful. 'Dad'll kick up a fuss at the mere idea.'

'Ah, you enjoy ruffling his feathers, you know you do.' When he saw a tight little smile creep across her face, he grinned at her. 'But if you tell him you've persuaded me to stay on until you've looked into things, he'll maybe come round more easily to us going.'

The frown was back. 'You've got it all worked out, haven't you?'

Eli shook his head. 'Not really. I knew I was taking a risk coming here. But it seemed worth a go, at least.'

She was silent then said, slowly and distinctly, 'Let's get one thing straight before we start. If you think you'll win the pub by wooing me, you can think again. I don't intend to get married, and if I did, it wouldn't be to you.'

'That's good, because I don't intend to marry anyone till later, after I've made something of myself. Besides, cousins marrying isn't a good thing. Too much inbreeding and you get sickly offspring, whether it's beasts or people. Everyone knows that.'

Her voice had an even sharper edge to it than usual. 'You'd better make it plain to Father that you won't marry me, then. He's been trying to buy me husbands for the past five years because he doesn't believe a woman can run a pub on her own. I reckon that's the main reason he brought you in. I've seen him looking at us in that calculating way he has.'

'I'll set him straight about that, but can I ask – why don't you want to get wed? Most women do.'

The frown returned. 'Because I'm not having a man ordering me around, expecting me to wait on him. Anyway, men don't find me attractive, so who's likely to ask me?'

'You scowl too much. You'd look better if you smiled occasionally and fussed with your hair a bit.'

'I've got too much to do to worry about that sort of thing.'

Eli smiled. 'Well, that's your choice. Any road, are you coming into Manchester with me or not?'

'All right then, I will. I must admit, I'd like to see one of these music places.'

She went back to work without another word and he went to find his uncle, weathering Frank's anger at his wanting a night off by simply staying stubborn.

Later Joanna also spent some time with her father and came looking for Eli afterwards. 'It has to be on a Thursday. He says he can't manage without us on Fridays or Saturdays, and he's probably right.'

'I'll find out about train times. And you'd better decide what to wear. The ladies dress up, you know. Not evening dress, but nice clothes.'

Which brought a different sort of frown to Joanna's face as she looked down at herself.

# 3

As soon as she could take a break from looking after her mother and the twins, Carrie washed her hands and face and went round to see the doctor's wife about the offer of new clothes. Her little brother and sisters were at school, but only because some of the ladies in town paid the school pence for poorer children. Ted grumbled about this, because he'd rather be out and about, earning a penny here and there by running errands for folk, but Grace and Lily loved school. Carrie had told the teacher that Lily was five to get her in early and she was a clever little thing, so nobody questioned that, thank goodness.

She was relieved to get out of the house. Her mother was feeling a lot better today and hadn't stopped talking all morning, mostly about the babies' names. Jane always chose these because her husband didn't care. She liked fancy double names that no one ever used, like Carrie's own Carolyn Mary, and Dora's Theodora Jane. Her mother made such a fuss about it while she was waiting for the birth that it nearly drove you mad. She'd change almost daily from one name to the other and expected you to get excited all over again about her latest choice. This morning she had at last decided that these two were to be called May Elizabeth and Nora Frances.

Well, however pretty their names, the babies would still cry and wake everyone in the night, not to mention messing in their clouts! Carrie breathed deeply and took her time walking across to the better part of town, enjoying the clean tang of the fresh air. She wasn't looking forward to the next few months.

She tapped on the back door of the doctor's house and a voice called, 'Come in!' Pushing it open, she found Essie standing at the table with her hands covered in dough.

'There you are. Shut the door, love. I won't be a minute then I'll set this bread to rise. It's my day for baking. Sit down over there, why don't you?'

Carrie sat on the edge of a wooden chair, watching the cook squeeze and pull the huge white mass. 'I thought the doctor would buy his bread from the baker's.'

'I make good bread and I enjoy doing it. Homemade is best.'

'We buy the broken or stale loaves usually, whatever's cheapest.'

'Well, you would, wouldn't you? It makes the money go further.' Essie gave the dough a final pummelling and set the wooden trough down on a stool near the big black stove with a damp cloth over it. She washed her hands quickly in a bowl and dried them on a towel that looked soft and pretty, then asked, 'Would you like to wash your hands and face before I throw this water away?'

Carrie flushed, knowing perfectly well why Essie had suggested this. She would have liked to keep herself cleaner but there was no way of doing that where they lived. There were just two standpipes to serve the Lanes and the water was switched on only for two hours in the morning and the same in the evening. When folk had to carry all their water home in a bucket they used as little as possible. She always told the children to drink as much as they could at school, where there was a proper tap with running water all the time.

Essie's voice was warm with understanding. 'Don't be ashamed, love. I grew up in a place like the Lanes and I know what life's like there. They should leave the water switched on all day. The doctor's always telling the fools at the Town Hall that.'

Carrie nodded. What a difference that would make! She didn't usually get home from the laundry till after the water pipe had been switched off, so anyone in the family who saw an empty bucket had to go and fill it – well, they did if they wanted something to drink – and a few nights without soon taught even the young ones to keep an eye on the buckets. The Prestons owned three and these were among the few possessions that never got pawned. Even with three, by the time everyone had drunk their fill there was very little water left for washing, though Carrie did try to keep her hands and face clean, at least.

She had more trouble keeping her clothes clean because she didn't have any spares. And now she'd have to keep the babies' clouts clean somehow, as well as all the girls' monthly rags. She always felt it was unfair of the laundry owner to charge his employees for washing their own clothes there, when it would have cost him nothing to let them put things to soak in the hot, soapy water that was poured away several times a day. But he wanted to use every second of the time he paid his workers for, and never thought of their needs. Carrie realised Essie was smiling at her and pulled her attention back to the present.

'Just carry that bowl through into the scullery and you can have a wash in private. There's no hurry.'

The water was still warm, which was a real treat for Carrie. There was a bowl of soft, home-made soap to scoop up and a small piece of cloth to rub yourself with. Then there was the towel – soft and clean, a proper towel, not a piece of rag or sacking. She breathed in deeply, enjoying the smell of soapy water and the sheer luxury of it all, with no one calling to her to do something, or bursting through the door when she'd rather be private. After a minute's hesitation and a worried glance towards the kitchen, she pulled off her clothes and washed her whole body. She even tried to wash her hair, though by that time the water in the bowl was dirty – so grey she was ashamed. Her skin felt wonderful and she hated putting on her soiled, ragged clothes again, especially the torn top.

When she peeped out, Essie was chopping vegetables, humming away to herself.

'Could I pump some more water, please, to rinse my hair?'

'Of course. Here, I'll come and help you. Put your head over the slopstone and I'll fill the jug and pour it over you.'

Carrie was shivering by now and the water was cold but she didn't care because her whole body was glowing with cleanliness and it felt lovely.

'There you are. I've got another towel here. Rub your hair then come and sit near the kitchen fire to dry it. I'll see if I can find you a hairbrush. And would you like a butty while you're waiting?'

Carrie nodded. Of course she would. She was always hungry. She couldn't help asking, 'Why are you being so kind to me?'

Essie patted her shoulder. 'I used to be poor myself, so if I can ever help a lass like you then I do. Not men, just lasses. I don't like men much, except for the good doctor.'

The butty was huge and the bread so thickly spread with butter that Carrie spent a few seconds staring at it, anticipating the taste. She closed her eyes in ecstasy as she took her first bite, chewing slowly because there was no fear here of her father snatching it from her. Even her younger brother Ted stole food from his little sisters if he thought he could get away with it, and no matter how often she slapped him, hunger always won and he'd pinch anything he could, whining that he was famished.

When she'd finished eating Carrie stayed where she was, basking in the warmth of the fire, feeling so relaxed that Essie's voice made her jump.

'Don't you look nice and rosy? Here, give me that

towel and I'll put it in the wash basket while you brush your hair with this. Then I'd better go and tell Mrs Latimer you're here.'

The doctor's wife came through to the kitchen almost at once, smiling at Carrie. She was much younger than her husband with rosy cheeks and neat, light brown hair. 'I'm so glad you came. Goodness, you've got pretty hair, haven't you? I never realised. Let me take you up to the attic and we'll find you something to wear.'

The attic held so many piles of clothes Carrie couldn't hide her surprise.

'We collect these to give to those who need them,' Mrs Latimer explained, adding in a brisk voice, 'Now, take those clothes off and don't be shy with me, dear, because I'm a doctor's wife and I've seen many human bodies before.'

It hadn't occurred to Carrie to be shy about her body with another woman because there was no such thing as privacy in a big family like theirs. Wide-eyed, she let the doctor's wife pick out clothes for her, trying on a chemise and petticoat, both of which showed hardly any wear.

'That's good. Now you need a spare chemise and petticoat so that you can wash your underclothes.' Mrs Latimer began piling new items in front of her. 'Let me see . . . there was a skirt . . . yes, here it is.' She pulled out a black skirt that showed no tears or fraying round the hem and held it up against Carrie. 'What a pity! It's not long enough. You're nice and tall, aren't you?' She put the skirt back and went to another pile of clothes, taking out a blue skirt with matching jacket. 'Here, try these on.'

With fingers that trembled, Carrie tried on the clothes. And, oh, they were so beautiful! But the skirt reached right to the ground and she could see that the material was too loosely woven to wear well, besides which the colour was so light it would soon show the dirt. 'It's lovely, but have you got anything darker, Mrs Latimer? I need a shorter skirt really, or I'll get the hem dirty, and it has to be something that'll take a lot of hard wear. I work at the laundry – at least, I used to do, but they've turned me off for staying home and looking after my mother. I'll have to find another job as soon as she's on her feet again.'

'You're right to be practical, but it's a pity because the blue does suit you. Let me have another look.'

Carrie went home the proud possessor of two dark serge skirts, one grey and one brown, and two cotton blouses, high-necked, thank goodness. There was also a dark jacket to wear when going out but that was too fine to use for work. Her old shawl would do for that. She also had a spare set of underwear, so wouldn't need to stay in the house wearing only her skirt and top while she washed and dried her under-garments.

'I don't think your old clothes will be much use to you now,' Mrs Latimer said as they went downstairs again. 'Shall I get Essie to throw them away?'

Carrie clutched her ragged old clothes to her bosom. 'No, please don't. I'll give the skirt to my sister Dora. Marjorie's nearly as tall as me, but Dora's shorter, so

we can borrow a needle and thread from our neighbour and shorten the ragged hem. Dora's skirt can go
to our Edith. And we can make some clouts out of
the top for the new babies.'

'Borrow a needle . . . Dear Lord, I forget sometimes how much I have,' Mrs Latimer murmured.
'Wait here.' She left Carrie in the hall and went across
to the parlour, removing a needle from her work-
basket, together with some dark and light sewing
thread. She wrapped the thread round a piece of
paper and stuck the needle into it. 'Here. Take this.
And just a minute . . .' She went back up the stairs
and came down with a bundle of baby clothes. 'Give
these to your mother and tell her to bring the twins
to my mother and baby clinic. We'll provide her with
food every time she comes to see us.'

'Thank you, I will.' Though whether her mother
would bother to go to the clinic, Carrie didn't know.
All her mother wanted to do nowadays was stay at
home. She said it tired her to walk far, didn't even like
going to the market because it was uphill all the way
back. 'I don't know how to thank you.'

'It's thanks enough to know that I'm helping people.
Now, I really must get on. And Carrie dear . . .'

'Yes, Mrs Latimer?'

'If you ever need help again, *with anything*, come
to me.'

'I will. I'm really grateful.' The doctor's wife was
so matter-of-fact about things that it didn't make
you feel bad to accept clothes from her and she
hadn't once asked Carrie to pray, which was a relief,

because Carrie wasn't at all sure she believed praying did any good.

As the girl passed through the kitchen, Essie beckoned her. 'Here, love. I've wrapped up a bit of cake that was left and some stale bread. Don't tell me you can't use them. And if you come round on Monday afternoon, I'll have something else for you.'

She watched Carrie walk off down the garden path, wondering why she was taking a greater interest than usual in this particular girl? They saw many poor folk at the doctor's house and, while she helped them when she could, she didn't usually make any effort to keep on helping them. Perhaps it was the way this lass had seized the opportunity to wash herself so thoroughly? Or the way her hair had come up when clean? Just like Essie's sister's, it was, really pretty with waves rippling through it and red glints in the brown when the sun shone on it.

Poor Mary had died twenty years ago and there was only Essie left to remember her now.

When Carrie got home she found her mother lying in bed feeding one of the babies while the other lay on the mattress beside her, staring round with that blurred look new-born babies had. You had to admit they were a healthy pair and already showing signs of being sunny-natured.

Jane gaped at her. 'Eh, look at you! Wherever did you get them new clothes from?'

'The doctor's wife gave them to me. Two sets of everything.'

'That's good. We can pawn one set an' buy some extra food. I could fancy—'

Carrie took an involuntary step backwards, clutching her new clothes to her bosom. 'No! You're not having them. They're mine.'

'But you can't wear two lots of clothes at once! Only rich folk can afford to leave clothes lying round doing nothing.'

'You're not pawning them. If you do, I'll leave home. I mean it!'

Tears began to roll down Jane's face. 'I never thought a daughter of mine would be so selfish. How are we to eat if we don't pawn what we can?'

'You could tell Dad not to drink so much.' And, she thought, *you* could stop frittering money away when you do get it. But she didn't say that because it'd do no good. Her mother was incapable of making money last. Whatever came in, she'd spend straight away.

'My Arthur works hard. A man needs a bit of relaxation.'

'And we need more food!' Carrie had been so excited about her new clothes she hadn't thought about her family's reaction to them. She didn't move from the doorway. 'Besides, I can get better jobs if I look decent and keep myself cleaner.'

'I still think you're being selfish.'

'Well, just remember how selfish I am. These are mine and you'd better not touch them. I meant what I said about leaving.'

Carrie went downstairs and put the bundle of spare

clothes under the straw mattress she shared with Marjorie and Dora, her next two sisters. Better out of sight, she felt, so that her mother wasn't tempted. The six girls all slept on two scratchy, lumpy mattresses in the front room, while Robbie and Ted slept upstairs, a whole room for just the two of them, the lucky creatures.

What would her family say, Carrie wondered, if they knew she had a whole half-guinea hidden in the pocket of her new skirt, wrapped in a bit of rag and pinned there for safety? They'd take it from her, that was sure.

In the kitchen she got out the loaf she'd bought on the way home with some of her father's remaining coins. It'd have to be dry bread for tonight's meal, but there was quite a big piece of cake and if she cut it up carefully, they could all have a taste. Like the cake she'd had yesterday, it had currants in it, but it was paler in colour and looked rather dried out. She smiled wryly. As if they cared whether food was stale or not! They'd eat anything, her family would, and glad of it.

Robbie bumped into Bram Heegan after he finished work at Stott's.

'Coming for a drink, lad?'

'I can't. I've got no money. Bram, do you know where Declan is? I'm trying to find out what happened to my wages. I think he put them in the pot, but I can't have spent all my money surely?'

Bram frowned at him. 'You've been drinking a fair

bit lately. But I'm sure there'll still be some of your money left. I'll have a word with Declan for you.'

'I'd be right grateful to you, Bram. My sister needs it for food.' Robbie was a bit in awe of his companion and still marvelled that a man who was a cut above him in many ways would sit and drink with him. Though actually Bram didn't drink much, now he came to think of it. Declan was the boozer in that family.

Just then Carrie came marching up and planted herself in front of them, so that both men had to stop walking. She glared at Bram. 'I want the rest of Robbie's wage money back from your brother. He can't have drunk it all and the kids are hungry. We need whatever's left for food, not beer.'

Bram looked at her in surprise. He'd seen her before but never with her hair gleaming and her skin looking so rosy. Who'd have thought Robbie's scrawny sister could look this pretty? Or have so much spirit? Not many lasses in the Lanes would dare confront him like this.

'What makes you think I've got his money?' he asked, enjoying teasing her.

'Not you, but Declan. He's took Robbie's money before, too. He's soft as horse muck, my fool of a brother is, but I'm not, an' I'm not moving till you've said you'll get it back for me. Your Declan might not listen to Robbie, but he'll listen to you.'

Bram sighed. 'You're a daft ha'porth putting all your money in the pot, lad. You should never do that.'

Robbie shrugged. 'There was a hole in my pocket. I meant to get it back.'

Bram smiled at Carrie. 'I'll get it for you if you'll have a drink with me at the Dragon.'

She drew herself up, shocked. 'I can't do that! People will think I'm on the streets.'

He looked at her, head on one side. 'You've never been with a man, have you?'

She was shocked by his frankness and flushed scarlet, unable to speak for a moment. Then she pulled herself together and threw more words at him. 'No. And I shan't go with a man unless I marry – which I don't intend to do.'

Bram liked the way her eyes sparkled, the way she smelled of soap and sunshine. 'Walk along the street with me then, as far as the Town Hall and back. It's a lovely evening and I'll settle for that.' He liked teasing lasses.

Carrie hesitated. 'You'll get me the money if I do?'

'Yes.'

'How much is left?'

He turned to Robbie. 'How much did you put in the pot, lad?'

'Fifteen shilling.'

'Then there'll be a few bob left. I know where Declan keeps it.' He didn't, but he'd supply the money himself then get it out of his middle brother later. He turned back to Carrie, unable to resist teasing her. 'Well? Do you want me to get you the money or not?'

She looked at him scornfully. 'All right. I'll walk along the street with you. But it's only because we need to eat, and I think you're mean to make it a condition.'

He held out his arm, keeping the grin from his face.

She put her hands behind her back. 'I can walk on my own, thank you.'

'If you don't take my arm, I'm not getting you the money back.'

'People will think we're walking out. I can't—' She broke off, scarlet-faced again.

'Let them think what they want.' Again he extended his arm. 'See you later, lad.'

Robbie hesitated, then stepped backwards.

With a furious look at her brother, Carrie laid her hand on Bram's arm and they began to stroll along the street. When she tried to walk faster, he slowed her down.

'Where do you work, Carrie?'

'I used to work at the laundry, but I had to stay at home to look after Mam so they turned me off. She's just had twins.'

'Aye, I heard, but you don't sound happy about that.'

'I'm not. One baby's bad enough. With two, you've never a minute to yourself.'

'It's for your mother to look after the babies, surely, not you?'

'She's sickly. If I didn't take charge, nothing would get done.' Carrie couldn't help sighing at the thought. She got so tired sometimes and though the twins looked like being good babies, they still gave you a lot of extra work – and cost you your sleep.

Bram walked along in silence, amused by the way

Carrie's back was rigid and her answers were snapped out, as if he was dirt and she the Queen. He couldn't hold back a chuckle.

'What are you laughing at?'

'You.'

She stopped dead, so stiff she might have been carved out of wood. 'What is there to laugh at?'

'You're hating this, aren't you?'

'Yes, I am.'

They began walking again.

'I'm not hurting you,' he said mildly.

'Yes, you are. You're hurting my reputation by making me walk with you. You've got a bad name where women are concerned.'

He could see tears in her eyes and that surprised him. 'Does it matter that much?'

She nodded, biting her bottom lip, sniffing to clear away tears.

That sniff touched him. 'Why?'

'It's all I've got, my respectability. If Dad doesn't waste our money, Mam fritters it away, so we've no food half the time.' She gestured to herself. 'These clothes were given me out of charity or I'd be wearing rags. But I've kept myself decent in spite of everything, only now *you're* trying to spoil it.'

He felt guilty. On a sudden impulse he turned round and started walking back, though they hadn't quite reached the Town Hall. 'Come on, then. Declan will have the money at home and if you send Robbie round to our house, I'll get it back for him.'

'Thanks.'

This time, when she tried to walk faster he let her.

Once they got back to where they'd started, Bram held on to her arm for a minute as he said, 'And Carrie . . .'

'What?'

'I'll make sure your Robbie doesn't drink all he earns from now on.'

She cast a doubtful look at him and ran off up the hill, not stopping till she got to the Lanes. She half expected him to follow, but he didn't.

She didn't know what to think of Bram. If it were any other man, she'd think he was being kind. But with a Heegan, you never knew. The men of the family were brawlers . . . She frowned. At least, some of them were. This one wasn't noted for fighting but for his easy charm. The Heegans nearly all worked for themselves and didn't give a toss for anyone else. They'd never actually been in trouble with the law, but there were whispers that they'd been lucky to stay clear of trouble for so long, especially the middle brother, Declan.

When Carrie got home, Dora and Edith were each rocking a crying baby and Robbie was keeping Ted away from the food, something the older ones all did regularly. She cast a quick glance at the babies, saw they were all right and turned to her older brother. 'Bram says if you go round to his place, he'll give you the rest of the money back.'

Robbie's face brightened, but as Ted tried to get past him, he grabbed his brother's shoulder. 'I won't tell you again, my lad. If you don't leave that food alone till our Carrie shares it out, I'll give you a belting you won't forget.'

'But I'm hungry! Why can't I have mine now?'

'Because you'd eat yours and then pinch Lily's. You'd take the last mouthful off our plates if we let you. You an' our Dad are a pair of greedy sods. Come with me and you can eat when we get home.'

'Get another loaf from the baker's with some of your money, Robbie!' Carrie called, pulling the ragged old pinny off a hook and fastening it round her to protect her new clothes.

Marjorie came in looking white and tired.

'You're late.'

'The overlooker was in a foul mood today. Kept some of the girls back an' made us clean up all over again, just because Jen and Clara skimped on their corner. I'd cleaned my part properly the first time, so that wasn't fair. And when he's not bad-tempered, he's touching you. I hate that.' She looked round. 'Is there owt to eat? I'm fair famished. Surely Mam has *some* money left? She took all my wages this week, didn't even leave me a penny.'

'Robbie's got some money left and he's fetching a loaf.' Carrie heard footsteps and quickly whisked the parcel Essie had given her out of sight.

Her father came in, looked at the bare table and scowled at them. 'Where's my tea?'

'You drank it at the Dragon again last night. If you keep emptying the money pot, how do you expect me to buy any food?'

Arthur jerked a head at his younger daughters, who'd also come in from their various jobs. 'What's happened to their money?'

'That was in the pot, so you took it.'

'You usually manage better than this, Carrie. You usually keep *your* money back till it's needed.'

'Well, I don't have any this week. I've been turned off for staying at home to help Mam, an' the laundry refused to pay me for the work I already did.' It wasn't fair, but what could you do?

They locked gazes but she didn't look away or say anything to calm him down. Why should she always have to keep the peace? When he lashed out suddenly she ducked back and Arthur only caught her a glancing blow, but it was the final straw. Carrie snatched up the frying pan and went for him, making him roar as she clouted him on the shoulder with it.

Marjorie and the other girls ran along the hall to their bedroom, leaving Carrie facing their father alone. For once she was so angry she shouted, 'Every time you hit me, I'll hit you back!' She brandished the frying pan. 'I've had enough of you thumping folk for nowt. What's got into you lately? You never used to hit us.'

He was open-mouthed with astonishment, didn't seem to know what to do, but she was sure he'd go for her again in a minute.

'Put that down, Carrie. You shouldn't threaten your own father.'

They all turned to see Jane standing at the foot of the stairs, looking white and strained.

'I'm not letting him hit me, Mam. Not *ever* again.'

Jane turned to her husband. 'Why are you so angry with her?'

'There's no food on the table.'

'No one can buy food without money.'

Even as she spoke, she swayed dizzily and he was the one to run across and catch her before she fell.

'What are you doing out of bed?' he scolded, his voice softer as it always was with her. He swung her into his arms and carried her up the stairs.

Carrie let out a long, shuddering breath. Her dad was a strong man still and she knew she couldn't best him if he decided to give her a beating, but she was tired of his selfishness, tired of the struggle to put bread on the table, just plain tired.

She sank onto a stool, put her head down on her arms and couldn't help crying. The other girls came out of the bedroom and gathered round her, shocked by her tears because she rarely wept. They patted her shoulders and made soothing noises.

'I'm s-sorry. I'll be all right in a minute. I'm just – so tired, bein' up at night with the twins on top of everything else.'

Robbie came in just then, followed by Bram Heegan. 'Eh, what's up?' He put a loaf down on the table and came across to her.

'Dad hit her an' she hit him back with the frying pan,' Dora said. 'He wanted something to eat. If Mam hadn't stopped him, he'd have give our Carrie a thumping. He's in a rotten mood tonight.'

Carrie made an effort and stood up, brushing away

the tears. She frowned to see Bram standing there. 'We're not in a fit state for visitors.'

'I walked back with your Robbie, had a parcel to deliver down the street.' He looked round the room, which was bare and comfortless with no sign of food other than the loaf Robbie had bought. He didn't like to think of that poor lass going hungry. 'Is that all you've got for tea?'

She shrugged. 'It'll fill our bellies.'

'Do you like tripe?'

'We like anything,' Ted said, licking his lips at the thought.

'We can't afford to buy tripe,' Carrie said, keeping the loaf in front of her, with her arms round it so Ted couldn't pick at the crust.

Bram surprised himself. 'I'm going round to my uncle's. He'll let me have the leftovers from yesterday's boiling. I'll fetch a bowl of 'em back for you.' He went out as quietly as he'd come in.

Carrie was too tired to protest, though she didn't like to accept any more favours from him. It seemed this week her family was the object of everyone's pity, but if that brought extra food into the house, she wasn't going to protest.

Her father came downstairs and looked at the loaf.

'I'm not cutting it till everyone's here,' she said, her eyes challenging him.

He breathed deeply then reached for his jacket. 'I'm going down the Dragon for a wet. Make sure you keep some for me.'

He was back five minutes later, bursting into the

house looking furious. 'They won't even put one lousy pot of beer on the slate for me! Can you believe that? Regular customer I am, allus paid up afore, and suddenly that new fellow won't let me have any credit. Uppity young sod! Who does he think he is?' He threw himself into his chair. 'Pass us some bread, then?'

'Robbie's fetching some tripe, Dad,' Edith said, keeping her distance from him.

'You'll enjoy it more if you have some bread to dip into your gravy,' Carrie said, slicing the loaf carefully into ten pieces, one larger for their father. She'd send Dora out later for some broken bits of bread for the morning.

Her father slumped back in his chair. 'Well, he'd better hurry up then. Me belly's touching me backbone.'

A few minutes later Robbie came in, again accompanied by Bram who grinned at Carrie and said, 'I'll have to wait because I need to take the bowl back.'

The smell of the tripe wafted round the room and everyone stared at the steaming bowl.

Arthur brightened. 'Get me a spoon and a dish,' he ordered.

Bram watched in amazement as the man started to ladle out far more than his share of the food, nearly half the bowl's contents. He knew he shouldn't interfere, but he'd brought that tripe back for his friend and Carrie, and at this rate there'd be no more than a mouthful each left for everyone else. No wonder she was so thin. He stepped across the room, took the dish from Arthur and tipped its contents back into the big bowl, acting so quickly he took the older man by surprise. 'I brought that for the children,' he said.

'*I'm* the wage earner. I need me food.'

'An' you're the wage drinker too, from what I hear,' Bram said. '*I* bought this, not you, and it's for them.' He jerked his head towards the row of children. 'They're hungry.'

Arthur stood up, 'If that's how it is, I'll tell you to your face, this is my house an' you're not welcome in it.'

'If I leave, I'll take my bowl of tripe and onions with me. Now sit down, old man.'

For a minute the two men stared at one another and Carrie started to worry that there would be a fight. Then Bram set the bowl on the table again and leaned forward till his face was close to Arthur's. 'We're rough sorts, us Heegans, an' I know what folk round here think about the Irish, but we look after one another an' we adults don't eat all the food an' let our kids go hungry.'

There was a moment's silence, then Bram turned and said, 'Pass me the plates, Carrie, an' I'll serve everyone since it's my treat.'

She was ashamed to have to set out such a set of cracked and chipped plates and dishes, but as long as they held food, they'd do.

'You pass out the bread, lass.' Bram began to share out the pieces of tripe, warm still and glistening with the pale yellowish gravy they'd been cooked in, with pieces of onion clinging to them.

Carrie got to her feet. 'I'll just take up a dish for Mam.'

'You're tired. One of your sisters can do that.' He looked at Marjorie.

Without a word she picked up a dish, spoon and slice of bread and carried them up the stairs.

When the food had been shared out, Bram beckoned to the children standing round. 'There don't seem to be enough chairs, but I daresay you can eat just as well standing up.' He took a dish and the largest slice of bread, dumped them in front of Arthur, then went to lean against the wall, arms folded, watching them eat.

There was silence, except for sucking sounds and the smacking of lips as the children began to shovel down the food as quickly as possible.

As usual Ted tried to pinch a piece of tripe from Grace but Bram was across the room before he could put it in his mouth, slapping the lad's hand away. 'Did no one ever teach you not to steal your sister's food?'

'Thank you, mister.' Grace picked up the tasty morsel from where it had fallen on the table and crammed it quickly into her mouth.

Carrie looked across the table at him, tears in her eyes. 'Thanks, Bram.'

He felt like a king as he took the empty bowl back to his uncle. Then, as he walked home with the bowl filled again for his own tea, he grew angry with himself. What was he doing, interfering in other people's lives? Hadn't he vowed never to be trapped by any woman? He'd better stay away from Carrie Preston in future! She was too nice a lass for what he wanted.

And he'd stay away from children with hungry eyes, too. That's what had got to him most of all. What if folk found out what he'd done tonight? They'd laugh themselves silly at the idea of him playing benefactor.

# 4

Eli walked across the pub to where a group of younger men stood drinking. He'd watched them before, especially the leader who never got drunk himself but observed the others doing so with faint amusement and kept them in order if they got a bit unruly. He tapped the leader on the shoulder. 'Could I have a word, please?'

Bram Heegan swung round quickly. 'What's wrong?'

'Nothing. I want to discuss a small business matter, if you have time.'

The whole group had fallen silent and the men were watching him warily, as if expecting trouble.

'Sure, I'm always interested in doing business.' Bram got to his feet.

He's about the same height as me, Eli thought. I reckon it'd be a toss-up which of us would win in a fight. There weren't many men who were as strong as him, he knew. 'We'll go into the back and talk privately, if that's all right by you?' At Heegan's nod he led the way, not going into the kitchen where his uncle was taking one of his many breaks with a glass of beer beside him as usual but into the small parlour that was rarely used. He'd already lit the gas lamps in there. 'Take a seat.'

Bram walked round the room first, openly studying the furniture and ornaments. 'Nice.'

'It's hardly ever used.'

'What's the point in having it then? I'd use it if it were mine.'

'I haven't time to sit around in here. Too busy with that lot.' Eli gestured towards the noisy public room, waited until Heegan had taken one of the armchairs then sat down opposite him and got to the point. 'People tell me if anyone wants a job doing in the Lanes, they come to you. They say you're a versatile fellow.'

'What is it you want doing?'

'I need someone to take my place here on Thursday of next week because I'll be out all evening – someone who knows the pub and can keep order, if necessary. Are you interested in the job?'

Bram didn't hide his surprise. 'Why did you think of me?'

'Because you don't get drunk. I know all the heavy boozers by sight now, but you're not one of them. You sip your drinks, watch what's happening around you, and what's more you keep your brothers and friends in order if they get too lively, even the one who drinks more heavily.'

'I don't know how to run a pub, though.'

'You won't need to. My uncle will be here to do that. But he's getting on, not quick on his feet any more, so I need someone to keep order out there while I'm away. The fellows from Stott's are still a bit touchy and I've had to break up a few arguments this week before they turned into fights.'

'Aye, I've seen you doing it. How much are you paying?'

'Five bob for the evening. It'll probably be easy money, but if there are any fights or trouble, I'll make good any damage to your clothes as well.'

Bram considered this, then nodded. 'Why not?'

'You'd better come in tomorrow night to work with me and make sure you understand what I want doing. I'll pay you for that as well. I may need you from time to time from then on – *if* you're interested, that is?' Eli waited and, when the other man nodded, leaned forward and stuck his hand out.

As Bram shook it, he said with a smile, 'I'm *always* interested in making extra money.'

'Good. You'll get free drinks within reason, but I don't expect you to get drunk on the job.'

Bram grinned. 'I don't like being drunk, so I'll not abuse the privilege – though don't tell anyone else that. It might damage my reputation.'

'I don't like getting drunk, either. I've seen too many men make fools of themselves when the beer takes over.'

Later, when Eli told his uncle what he'd arranged, Frank turned dark red and sputtered indignantly, 'That Irish sod! Do you know what a name he's got in the Lanes? He's a womaniser and he'll do anything for money. I'm not having a man like him behind the counter. He'll probably steal the takings.'

'Actually he has a reputation as an honest man. And if you don't get help, how will you keep order while Joanna and I are out on Thursday?'

Frank fell silent. 'Perhaps you'd better not go. We've a business to run here. That has to come first.'

'You can't stop us going.'

'Oh, can't I?'

'No. Because if you do, I'll leave. I'm that far from leaving already.' Eli held up his hand, forefinger almost touching the thumb. 'That far,' he repeated slowly, and waited.

His uncle scowled and said no more.

When Eli told Joanna what he'd arranged, she too seemed surprised.

'I don't know if you've done the right thing. I've heard a few things about the Heegans.'

'You haven't heard that anyone pushes them around, though. I want someone here who'll be able to keep order, and Bram's the most suitable person I've seen.'

'Maybe Dad's right and we shouldn't go.'

'You don't mean that.'

She sighed. 'No, I don't. I can't wait to get away from here for an evening.' Then, as if annoyed with herself for betraying her feelings, she whisked back into the snug.

He stood for a moment or two thinking about that till his uncle popped his head through the doorway and asked him if he intended to stand there all night when there was work to be done. With a smile, Eli sauntered back into the big public room.

He'd been wondering for several days whether he'd still be here the following week. He hadn't fully made up his mind about staying, even if they did start having free and easy nights. His uncle's meanness and hatred of change were getting on Eli's nerves, and a night of singing in the pub was nothing like a music room with proper paid performers.

But on the other hand he liked the Dragon. It had potential, if only his uncle would see it, because it straddled the border between the respectable parts of town and the Lanes, and was on Market Street just before it grew narrow and led out of town. This pub could become anything you wanted, he reckoned, but his uncle was too old and tired to embark on improvements.

Joanna kept an eye on Bram Heegan that evening and the next, watching as he made himself part of running the pub. He chatted easily with her customers in the snug, broke up fights before they started and came to the bar twice for pots of beer, but that was all.

The second time she served him herself. 'You don't drink much.'

He smiled, his green eyes full of amusement. 'I drink enough to quench my thirst.'

She had never spoken directly to him before or had him address her and she liked the lilting sound of his voice, his direct and friendly gaze. Before she could stop herself Joanna found herself smiling back at him. 'Quite enough for anyone, I'd agree, but don't tell my father I said that.'

'I promise I won't.'

She watched him walk away. How tall and strong he was!

Bram could feel her watching him, but he didn't turn back. The landlord's daughter had surprised him tonight. She was famous for her sharp tongue and scowls, but tonight when she'd smiled she'd looked like a different woman.

He blinked in surprise and stopped walking for a moment. That was the second time in a week he'd found a respectable woman attractive. Joanna Beckett wasn't as obviously pretty as Carrie Preston because she screwed her hair back into a hard little knot and had a watchful expression on her face, but she couldn't hide the fact that she had beautiful skin, clear and creamily smooth, and a fine pair of eyes, blue as the summer sky at dawn. And he'd bet her legs were as shapely as her wrists and forearms, which were showing because her sleeves were rolled up for work.

What had got into him? Stop it, you fool! he told himself.

But when he thought about the young widow in the next street, who had made a point of telling him how lonely she was feeling, he couldn't bring himself to go and visit her. Somehow, after Carrie and Joanna, the widow seemed blowsy and too free with her body. Well, he'd never gone with women who'd sleep with just anyone. He smiled. He'd not actually slept with a quarter as many women as rumour would have it, he just enjoyed talking to them and flirting a little.

Bram, me boy, he thought, if you don't watch out, you'll be caught in parson's mousetrap!

No, not him. He knew what he wanted and it wasn't a wife and house full of squalling children.

He took good care not to look in Joanna Beckett's direction again.

At the other side of the room she took equal care not to look at him.

But neither could resist stealing quick glances at the other from time to time.

Nev Linney walked slowly along Market Street, having ordered his supplies for today, some food for himself and some bread and dripping to sell to the customers of his common lodging house, who slept there on a day-to-day basis, so that he never knew how many to expect. He suddenly remembered what the house had been like when his mother had been alive. He'd had no need to do the chores then or hire a woman to clean the place because his mother had done everything.

After years of quarrels, his father had left them to go and live with Nev's brother, and Nev and his mother had lived happily enough together after that. She hadn't liked the stigma of being a deserted wife, but in fact she'd been glad to see the back of her husband and Nev had been glad to be rid of the quarrels that had become an almost daily occurrence between them. Eh, were ever two people so ill-suited as his parents?

When she'd realised she was dying his mother had

told him to get himself a wife. Ha! Nev scowled as he walked. The only lass he'd ever fancied had married someone else, and after that he'd found he liked earning money and didn't want a wife and children eating him out of house and home.

A smirk replaced the frown. He was quite good with money, had never gone hungry even in the bad times, and had saved up enough to buy his present house in the old part of town. It was a rambling place, quite large, and earned him a nice steady income. He had two big rooms on the ground floor at the back where homeless folk could sleep for threepence a night. There was also a little kitchen where they could make food or hot drinks. He'd not have bothered to provide that, but the town council had recently set up regulations about common lodging houses and you couldn't be licensed if you didn't have a kitchen. Stupid regulations they were, too!

Still, not many folk used the kitchen. Most of his lodgers had trouble scraping the money together for the night's lodging, and made do with a piece of bread and dripping which he sold to them at a penny a slice. That gave him a nice profit of a halfpenny a slice if you cut up the four-pound loaf carefully, which Nev always did.

Before he got back he met a fellow he knew quite well and stopped to chat, enjoying the morning sun on his face. 'How's it going, Charlie? New babby arrived yet?'

His young friend smiled at him. 'Aye, arrived an' gone.'

'It died? Eh, I'm sorry, lad.'

'Nay, it were fine and healthy. Pam was give extra food while she was carrying.'

'Then what do you mean, "gone"?'

Charlie looked at Nev, opened his mouth, shut it for a moment, then asked in a low voice, 'Can you keep a secret, old friend? I'm fair burstin' to tell someone.'

'Aye. You know I can.'

'Well, there were a farmer as wanted a son an' couldn't get one. His wife quickened all right but she allus lost 'em after a few months. So he decided to adopt a baby. Paid us good money for ours, he did, an' it'll inherit his farm one day. My son, a well-to-do farmer! I like to think of that.'

'You *sold* your baby?'

'Aye. An' I'd do it again, too, though the wife's a bit unhappy like. She'll get over it, though. After all, we have six others.'

'How did you find out about this farmer?'

'Through the doctor.'

'Dr Latimer?'

'Nay. That one wouldn't help a fellow get shut of a babby. It were the other doctor, the fellow as looks down his nose at folk like us. Barlow, he's called. I heard a whisper so I went to see him. He talked to me like I were a maggot in his cheese, but he can sneer at me as much as he likes – it didn't stop him payin' me fifty pound for the babby if it were a son. Eh, I were biting my nails about that. The farmer weren't interested if it were a lass, you see.'

'I never heard of anyone doing that before.'

'Well, Dr Barlow doesn't like it being known, an' the families as buy the babies don't want it known either, do they? But if my wife has another babby, I'll do it again like a shot. Let alone it's more money than I've ever had in my hands in my whole life, they don't pay enough wages at Stott's to feed big families. He's a mean sod, that Athol Stott is, worse than his father by far. Any road, I'm glad to see you to say goodbye. I've give notice on the house an' left my job. We're movin' to Bury where her family lives, an' they're goin' to help us start up a little shop. Her brother has one an' he says if you do it right, you can make decent money. Bugger working at Stott's when I can work for myself!'

When Nev walked on, he was very thoughtful. To think of making fifty pounds just from having a baby. Most folks got poorer when they had a lot of children, not richer. He'd allus been glad he didn't have any, but now he could see that you could turn anything to your advantage if you kept your eyes and ears open. No wonder he and Charlie had always got on well. The man had a bit of sense between his ears.

Nev had had to make his money gradually, in ha'pennies and pennies, and he knew folk thought him mean because he still kept an eye on every detail of what he spent. Well, he was only mean with other people. He bought himself what he wanted these days, and ate well too. He'd just bought a piano, though he'd got it at a bargain price because the woodwork was battered but that didn't stop him playing it. He

could only pick out tunes with one finger, but he
enjoyed doing that of an evening. One day he might
pay for piano lessons and learn to play it properly.
His dad had played the piano, played it well, too, but
his mother had sold the instrument to Frank Beckett
at the Dragon when his dad left them, saying she
couldn't abide the sight of it.

When Joanna came down into the kitchen on
Thursday afternoon, ready for her outing, Eli studied
her and nodded approval. She was wearing her
Sunday church-going outfit, the material a light-
weight, navy blue merino wool and the skirt fuller
than her workaday garments, though nothing like as
wide as the skirts of the well-to-do ladies in town.
He thought those ridiculous. There was silky-looking
braid trimming the front of the skirt in an inverted
V-shape and the braid continued round the hem.
That braid was new. It definitely hadn't been there
last Sunday. She must have trimmed the dress
'specially for tonight. Its plainness was further softened by small frills of creamy lace at wrists and neck-
line.

The matching jacket came halfway down her skirt,
and on her head sat a bonnet, as neat as everything
else about her but now sporting a bit of lace and
ribbon to match her dress. Her hair was parted in the
middle and looped smoothly over her forehead instead
of being drawn tightly back into a small, screwed up
bun. It suited her. As did the half-smile on her face.

'You look nice,' said Eli.

'So do you.' She studied his outfit. 'I haven't seen you wearing that before.'

'I'd not wear my best clothes for working in the pub, now would I? And since I don't go to church, I've not had any reason to pull this out of the cupboard.' He looked down at his dark grey trousers and pilot jacket, with a good linen shirt and maroon silk waistcoat worn underneath, then smiled at her and picked up his mechanic's cap, a square head covering of soft dark cloth sewn in four sections with a hard peak at the front. One day he'd be rich and wear a top hat and frock coat, but until then this mechanic's cap was more suited to his station in life. All the clothes were of good quality, something which pleased him greatly. He'd bought them piece by piece from the better second-hand shops, though he wasn't going to tell anyone that.

Frank came out of the back room to stare at them as they walked down the stairs, his frown turning into a knowing smile. 'You make a handsome couple.'

Joanna's expression instantly changed back to her old scowl. 'I've told you before, Dad: we're *not* a couple. This outing is for business purposes only, so that I can look at music rooms and understand what my cousin's on about.'

Frank shrugged, but his sly grin didn't fade.

Eli gave Joanna a little push. 'Wait for me outside.' When she'd gone through into the public room, he said quietly but emphatically, 'I'd never marry a cousin. Never. Not even if you put it in your will as a condition of my inheriting something. I want strong, healthy children one day, and plenty of them, so don't get any ideas in your head about me and Joanna.'

The older man swung round and slammed the door of the office behind him.

As Eli went out into the public room he saw Bram Heegan chatting to Joanna near the door. Her expression was animated but as her cousin came up to them, she fell silent and her smile faded.

'Everything all right?' he asked.

Bram answered for her. 'Everything's fine. And if I need any help tonight, I've got my brothers and Robbie Preston coming in.'

'Right then. Let's get off to the station.'

As they started walking, he asked, 'What was Bram Heegan saying to make you blush?'

'Just that I looked nice.'

Eli wasn't sure he liked the idea of Heegan making personal remarks to his cousin. Or the way she had blushed at the compliment.

Try as she might, Joanna couldn't maintain her usual calm expression when she was enjoying herself so much. She even enjoyed the train journey into Manchester, a means of travel she'd only used a couple of times before. Well, their branch line hadn't long been open.

They went second class because the third-class compartments were open to the wind and smuts. As the train rattled towards Manchester, the rhythmic sound made by its wheels reverberated through Joanna's body and she could feel excitement rising within her.

Victoria Station in Manchester was bigger than she'd expected, with a great circular carriage sweep in front of the main entrance to the imposing stone edifice. Eli offered her his arm and led her along Market Street, which wasn't strictly on their route, to show her how elegant it looked since it had been widened and how bright the gas lights were in the shops and street lamps.

'Manchester is much bigger than I'd expected,' she commented. 'And this is wider and grander than *our* Market Street.'

'You can keep London. To me, Manchester is the best city in all England. It's so alive, and growing all the time. Look at how those folk are bustling to and fro.'

Joanna knew what he meant by saying Manchester was 'alive', though it was a strange word to use to describe a city. The streets in this part were thronged with people and vehicles of all sorts, and the shops had all sorts of goods on display. That was part of what made it alive. But the main thing was the feel in the air, a kind of energy crackling around you.

They turned off down a side street and arrived at last at the music room Eli wanted to show her. It was attached to a pub and was blazing with gas lights, both outside and in.

'It's huge!' Joanna gasped once they were inside.

'Aye. It can seat four hundred comfortably. Ours won't be nearly as big, seating two hundred at most, I reckon. But then Hedderby's much smaller.'

Eli paid for their seats and led her over to some long tables set at right angles to the stage.

Above them was a balcony for the better class of client with small tables and comfortable chairs. To the right side of the stage, set slightly lower down, was a piano and drums and several empty chairs. To the left was a table and chair.

Eli followed his cousin's wondering glance and pointed to the left. 'That's where the Chairman sits. He runs the show and introduces the acts.' He pointed behind them. 'We'll not be able to have a balcony in our music room, not even a small one. Pity. It gives a nice feel to a place, a balcony does, and it attracts a better class of customer who'll pay more to sit away from the common folk. I'm sorry you and I aren't sitting up there tonight. One day we will be, but for the moment I have to watch my pennies.'

She nodded, too overwhelmed by it all to do more than follow his lead, though she could usually speak up for herself.

'If you want to relieve yourself, there's places out the back,' he said and when she nodded, he beckoned to a woman selling flowers. 'Threepence to show my cousin where the ladies' necessary is,' he said. 'Twopence now and a penny when you bring her back.'

The woman's eyes brightened. 'This way, love.'

Joanna looked round the women's necessary with interest. It was clean and you could even wash your hands for a penny extra, with a towel provided. If they did open a music room, she'd insist on such places being provided for both men and women. She hated the way men pissed up the walls round the

Dragon and was always glad when it rained and cleaned the pungent smell away. When it didn't rain she got Bonny to throw buckets of water over the favourite pissing spots every day or two.

When she got back inside the music room, Joanna found that Eli had bought them both a glass of gooseberry cordial, which had a nice green colour to it.

'I knew you wouldn't want a glass of beer,' he teased, raising his to her in a toast.

'Thank you.'

The musicians filed in, five of them: a pianist, two fiddlers, a flautist and a drummer. Joanna had to clasp her hands together tightly in her lap to contain her excitement as she waited for the show to begin. She hoped there would be a lot of music because she loved singing, absolutely loved it. She took after her mother there, because her father could produce only a tuneless bass growl which made her wince.

In the mornings she would sometimes stop cleaning to listen if a ballad singer passed by in the street, though there were fewer of them around these days than in her girlhood. When a good one came she sometimes went outside to ask for another tune and give the singer a penny. When she could be sure her father wasn't around, she hummed or sang as she went about her work, and then Bonny would sway in time to her singing.

On Sundays Joanna went to the parish church instead of the Methodist Chapel, which was closer and had been her mother's place of worship, because the choir at the parish church was the best in town.

She loved singing the hymns, though she took care not to let her voice rise and single her out because it was so powerful it embarrassed her at times.

Something made her look sideways and she saw Eli watching her with an indulgent smile, which made her worry about betraying her feelings to him.

'I love these music rooms,' he said suddenly. 'This is one of the fancier ones in Manchester, or saloon theatres some call them.'

'It's . . . very pleasant here.'

He chuckled. 'You know you're enjoying it. Stop holding yourself in so tightly and let out a smile.'

So she did.

The musicians played a flourish and Joanna turned to see a man in evening dress come out and take his place at the table near the stage. When he was seated he banged a gavel on a piece of wood till the audience fell silent.

'Good evening, ladies and gentlemen!'

'Good evening, Mr Chairman,' they chorused back.

'Are you all ready to enjoy yourselves?'

'Yes, we are!' the audience replied, so promptly that it was clearly a ritual here.

'Then let's have a round of applause for our stalwart musicians and encourage them to give us the overture.'

After the applause the group of men began to play a lilting tune that had the audience tapping its feet and moving their bodies in time to the music.

From that moment Joanna forgot about everything except what was happening on the stage. A man came

on and played the flute. The audience barely toler-
ated him and only gave him faint applause, though
he was a good musician. He was followed by The
Manchester Songbird, a lady past the first flush of
youth but with a glorious soprano voice. She sang
three sentimental songs. The audience joined in the
choruses as she walked to and fro on the stage, gesticulating and conducting them as she sang. At first
Joanna didn't know the words, but joined in on the
repetition of the first chorus because it was a simple
enough tune. She heard Eli singing beside her and
his voice surprised her. It was a tuneful baritone, not
remarkable but pleasant enough to listen to.

When The Manchester Songbird left the stage, Eli
turned and looked at Joanna thoughtfully. 'You've got
a beautiful voice. Why have I never heard you singing?'

She could feel herself flushing. 'Oh – well – Dad
doesn't like it. He says it's common.'

'Not with a voice like yours, it's not.'

She was embarrassed by his praise, relieved when
the next act cut their conversation short. This was a
pair of acrobats, men wearing long white tights and
white tops, and above the tights colourful short
trousers that came nearly to their knees. Their wiry
bodies seemed to move more easily and bend further
than normal people's, so that the audience gasped in
surprise at their feats, applauding vigorously when
they finished.

Then came a comedian who surprised a laugh or
two out of Joanna and finished his act with a comic
song about his mother's greedy cat. The audience

sang the catch phrase at the end of each chorus with their usual gusto.

> *No wonder that cat was fat!*
> *Oh, my!*
> *No wonder that cat was fat!!*

During the interval Eli said softly, 'You're enjoying it, aren't you?'

The words were out before Joanna could stop them. 'Yes. Yes, I am.'

'Bit different from the Dragon here, isn't it?'

She nodded, turning her head from side to side to study the people near them. 'But we couldn't do anything like this. Let alone the Dragon isn't big enough, it'd take a fortune to set up such a big place.'

'We can start small. Even smaller places draw the crowds because folk love music and singing. I want to run a proper music hall one day, in a real theatre building. That's what I want more than anything in the world, and I mean to get it. Our little music room will be just a start.' He stared hard at her. 'We could be partners. Such places are usually run by families. Would you be interested? We'll not get the money out of your father unless we become allies.'

The noise around them seemed to recede into the distance as Joanna thought this through and slowly nodded. 'All right.'

'Good. I'm pleased about that.'

Eli held out his hand as if she were a man, and they shook hands gravely. She didn't speak again but studied the other members of the audience, both those above them and those nearby, avid to learn as much as she could about this world that was familiar to him, but new to her. She felt comfortable here, though, and very happy.

So did other people. Up on the balcony there was a man with rosy cheeks and side whiskers who had his wife and family around him, all of them plump like him, and clearly enjoying themselves. There were several young couples nearby, holding hands surreptitiously and exchanging fond smiles with one another. What must it be like to have someone who loved you? Joanna wondered. Then there were cheeky, ill-dressed folk of all ages, both men and women, who called out to the performers and joined in the choruses lustily. They were clearly there to enjoy themselves, not cause trouble. And no one was drunk, no one spewing up or spitting. It seemed like a different world from the Dragon, a world worth fighting for.

The two of them had to leave before the final act in order to catch the last train to Hedderby. When Eli took out his pocket watch and nudged her, Joanna was so disappointed that for a moment she couldn't move and wanted to protest. Then common sense took over and she nodded, standing up and following her cousin outside.

And, oh, they walked away into a world that was so bleak and dull after the brightness, colour and cheerful noise inside the music hall! She could have wept for disappointment!

Eli seemed to understand and didn't say much as they walked briskly to the station, merely tucked her arm through his. Only as the train pulled away did he say abruptly, 'Now you know.'

And she did. She knew exactly what he wanted and why.

And, heaven help her, she wanted it too now.

'What are you going to tell your father?' Eli asked as they left the station in Hedderby and walked back to the pub.

'That your ideas bear thinking about. That people are prepared to spend a lot of money in such places. That we could maybe start in a small way and see how we go.'

He laughed so softly she thought at first she was imagining it, then he stopped to say earnestly, 'Don't worry, Joanna love. I'm not stupid enough to over-reach myself. All we can hope for at the moment will be a fairly simple music room, and that only if we persuade your father to shell out some money and let us redo the old stables. In the meantime we'll do free and easies on Saturdays to show him there's money to be made in giving folk music as well as drink.'

'Yes. And food. I've wanted to serve food at the pub for a while now, but he won't let me, says it's more trouble than it's worth.' Joanna stopped just before they got to the door and stood looking at the Dragon. Her prison, she'd always thought. Now perhaps she could pull down some of the bars and make her life there more interesting, even if she couldn't escape. Perhaps she wouldn't even want to escape if things changed. Strange how she'd resented

Eli when he arrived and now she didn't, because he'd given her hope for the future.

Eli kept a close eye on Joanna, not trying to hurry her into the side entrance of the now dark pub. He could understand her emotions perfectly well. He'd felt stunned, too, the first time he'd been inside a well set up music saloon.

Then, as they walked along the side of the pub into the light shining from the kitchen and scullery windows, he saw the old anger settle on her face again, the tightness return to the way she held herself. The attractive woman who had slipped out from beneath the mask that evening vanished even before they went inside.

Eh, lass, he thought, you're an unhappy soul. But I wonder if you've the guts to stick it out against that old sod? My uncle won't give in easily.

But nor would Eli. He squared his shoulders as they entered the quiet pub, thinking: Well, let battle commence.

Bram enjoyed his new role keeping order in the Dragon, but then he enjoyed most things he did. If not, he didn't do them because he had enough ways of earning money to pick and choose what he took on, and wasn't greedy. People said he was lucky. He didn't believe in that sort of thing. You made your own luck, to his mind, by working hard and not letting opportunities escape.

Two years ago, at the age of twenty-five, he had

come back to Hedderby, having worked in London and other towns. Once he'd even gone to Ireland to see if all his father's tales of 'the ould country' were true. They weren't. It was so quiet in the village where his aunt and uncle still lived that he'd have died of boredom if he'd had to live there. The main focus of everyone's lives there seemed to be the church, and that didn't suit Bram at all.

He was fond of his family, still living with his parents in the Lanes because it was convenient to have his mother look after him. His two brothers had married young, more fools they, though Michael at least seemed happy with his bustling little wife Biddy. He came to the pub less often than the other two because of her, but Bram didn't mind. He rather liked Biddy and was fond of his two small nephews.

Declan was less happy in his marriage, which didn't surprise Bram at all. Ruth was a fool and a shrew, always nagging and complaining. But then, Declan often made bad choices, and sometimes you could stop him rushing headlong into things, other times you just had to stand back and afterwards try to help him out of the mess he'd made. He was lucky he hadn't landed in prison a couple of times.

When people asked Bram how exactly he made a living, he would shrug and say, 'A job here, a job there, whatever comes along.' They didn't press the point because he knew how to make folk nervous, had always had that ability, laughed at himself because of it. Actually, most of his money these days came from the markets. Thanks to the railways he could go round to nearby towns and villages, buying things cheaply, anything he thought might sell. He was quite good at choosing stuff, if he said so himself.

Michael and his wife ran the stall for him. He wouldn't have trusted Declan to keep his temper and jolly the customers into buying, so his middle brother continued to work at Stott's, a job he hated and which he'd surely lose if he didn't learn to hold his tongue and appear more respectful. The new owner wasn't the sort to take impudence from anyone.

Bram also did all sorts of little jobs on commission. In the summer he set up fights when the fairs were on, betting modestly, winning modestly. It seemed to him it was the greedy folk who lost out in the end. Small profits mounted up if you didn't drink them away. Folk would be surprised if they knew he had money saved in the bank – as well as hidden away here and there, because he couldn't bear to put all his eggs in one basket.

He'd started his working life at Stott's, too, but had got sacked when he grew big enough to thump the foreman back. Hell, what a fight that had been! Bram grinned at the memory. He'd won the fight – just! – but lost his job.

After that he'd been desperate for money for a while and had fought a summer season or two in the booths, winning enough to set himself up in the markets. He still had a scar on his temple to prove it. During his last fight he'd been knocked out, they told him. He still didn't remember what had happened during that fight or for several days before it. That had settled the matter of what he did with his strong body. Bram was no fool, could see the danger of a fighter's life and how some of the older men seemed to have their wits addled, so he'd left that sort of risk to others from then on.

Sometimes he helped his uncle in the tripe shop or his father in his second-hand clothes shop, and occasionally he lent a hand to his mother's cousin who had a small ironmongery. Bram also gave business advice to his family, and those who took it prospered in a modest way.

But he'd been growing restless lately, wanted something more from life, some new challenge. And damned if he knew what, except that he wanted a house with a fancy parlour like the one at the Dragon, now he'd seen it. He laughed at himself for that. Silly sort of ambition for a fellow to have, wasn't it?

It wasn't the parlour itself, but what it stood for. Maybe that was why he was finding respectable women more attractive these days. Well, one especially. Joanna Beckett. He'd been surprised how good she'd looked tonight when she was setting off for Manchester. And when she'd blushed at his compliment, he'd wanted to clip her up in his arms and give her a big hug, tell her to let go of her anger and be happy.

Ah, he was getting some silly thoughts lately, he was indeed.

# 5

For two weeks the Preston family managed to survive without Carrie's wages, but only just. Her mother was so slow to recover that Carrie still couldn't look for another job. She was worried about her father's wages being spent mainly on beer and the way he even took part of what the others were earning. She planned to make sure that this week she got all the money her sisters brought home before their father came back from work, and would hide it carefully about her person.

She warned her sisters to get back quickly after work and Marjorie did. But there was no sign of sixteen-year-old Dora, who often dawdled to chat to her friends. Edith came home much later from the shop where she worked, but Carrie had arranged to take her wages in food, so that money at least was safe. Mrs Debbin at the shop understood the situation perfectly. She had had similar problems till her own husband died. Now she ruled the roost with her only child, a son of twenty or so who was still unmarried, and the shop was thriving.

Marjorie fidgeted to and fro. 'Dad'll be home soon.'

'You should give some of your wages to him,' their

mother grumbled, rocking May on her knee. 'He'll not like it, you know he won't. Pick up Nora, someone. I can only hold one of 'em at a time.'

'Don't you care whether we go hungry or not?' Carrie demanded, leaving Marjorie to pick up their tiny sister.

'We allus manage somehow,' Jane said.

'*I* allus manage,' Carrie snapped. 'An' I'm sick of making the pennies stretch out. I want—' She broke off as Dora burst through the front door, sobbing, and flung herself into her oldest sister's arms. 'Nay, then, nay. What's wrong, love?'

'Dad were waiting for me outside work. He took my money, all of it!'

'Oh, dear, he shouldn't have done that,' their mother said. 'He should have left you some for food.'

Carrie patted Dora's heaving shoulders and looked across the room. 'Will you go down to the pub and ask him for some money back, Mam?' she pleaded. 'We really need it and he'll listen to you.'

'Me? I can hardly walk to the end of the street. Besides, it wouldn't do no good now he's there. He'd not give up the money in front of his friends. He's had such a bad head lately, aching all the time, an' he says the drink helps. You surely don't begrudge him a little comfort?'

'Yes, I do! Especially when I'm hungry. And any road, he's got his own wages. You'd think that'd be enough, but no, he has to treat his mates when they're short. They're more important than us, it seems.'

'Eh, you're a real hard one, our Carrie.'

'Aye, an' it's a good job for everyone that I am. Now, let's eat before he gets back.'

Arthur came home much later in high good humour. 'Where's my tea?'

Carrie glared at him. 'You drank it. There's nothing left.'

'What do you mean, nothing left? You had Marjorie's money.' He went to search the shelf where they kept their food, looking for the loaf that usually stood there waiting for breakfast.

Carrie folded her arms and watched him. She only kept that loaf safe by threatening to kill the children if they so much as breathed on it and by taking it into the bedroom with her at night. It was hidden there now. When her mother opened her mouth to tell Arthur there was a loaf, Carrie glared across the room at her. She'd still got the half-sovereign and had already threatened to go out and find a job if her mother betrayed where the food was. Yes, and move into lodgings, too. Jane was terrified of her doing that, knowing she wouldn't be able to manage without her.

'It's a poor lookout when a man can't get a bite to eat after a hard week's work,' Arthur grumbled. 'An' you're a poor housewife, Carrie Preston, if you haven't even got food in for breakfast. How am I to do a day's work without owt to eat?'

'You should have thought of that when you drank the food money. If you'll give me some of your wages, there's still time to send Dora out for a loaf.'

'I'm giving you nowt! I need beer money for tomorrow. You've got Robbie and Marjorie's wages, an' you get stuff at the shop with Edith's money, so let that be enough. An' make sure you save summat for me in future.'

'If you want food, you'll need to give me money.'

'If you don't stop giving me lip, young woman, I'll belt you one.'

'An' I'll hit you right back!' Carrie yelled.

'One of these days . . .' he threatened, as he had so often lately, then made his way up to bed.

'You'll push him too far,' Jane said with a sigh. 'Men don't like being defied by their children. And he's having a hard time of it lately, the way things are at Stott's.'

'I'd like to push him right out of the house,' Carrie muttered, but didn't speak loudly enough for her mother to hear what she said. She was daft where their father was concerned. How a woman could go on loving a man whose boozing kept her and her children hungry, Carrie would never understand. Never!

Athol Stott watched his employees leave at the end of the day. Lazy sods! You had to be on top of them every minute to make sure they didn't waste the time you were paying them for. And his cousin Edmund, who was the firm's engineer, was too lax with them, only you couldn't get him to see that. What's more, Edmund had his pets among the employees, Robbie Preston for one. There was something about that young man that Athol didn't like. He was keeping an eye on him, whatever his cousin said, and if he didn't do exactly as he was told, he'd be fired.

He frowned as Arthur Preston shambled past. One of the worst, that one was these days. If he didn't pull his socks up, he'd be out of a job too. By the time Athol had finished, he'd have an obedient workforce and those who wouldn't toe the line would not only be out of work but out of the firm's houses, too.

When the workers had all left, including his cousin who was probably off seeing his mistress, Athol checked that everything was in order. He enjoyed his nightly stroll round the large, quiet space which was starting to cool down, relished the fact that it all belonged to him now. He nodded goodnight to his deputy engineer, Turner, one of the better employees who didn't rush off as soon as the day was over, and told the night watchman to be on guard for stones hurled at the place and to be sure to remember who did it if it happened again. There had been several such incidents since Athol had reduced the men's wages and he was keeping an eye on those he thought to be the main trouble-makers. If he ever caught them lingering near the factory after work, he'd want to know why.

He went home, a brisk walk up the hill to where his family home stood looking over the town. He was a big believer in taking a daily constitutional, so didn't use his carriage to go to the works except in the most inclement of weather. He had a strong body and was proud of it. When he'd washed and changed his clothes, he presided over his family's evening meal with Edmund sitting halfway down the table, lost in thought as usual, and Athol's wife Maria sitting at the other end, as quiet as ever. She was a good, obedient woman who didn't nag him and who kept his house and children in order.

After the meal, he and Edmund sat at opposite sides of the fireplace and in a leisurely way discussed the day's work and a new order they'd obtained for some smaller pieces of machinery, while Maria worked on her damned embroidery. It was useful having Edmund living with them because if something needed discussing he was always to hand. His cousin had spoken of buying a house of his own but Athol had persuaded him to stay in the family home. After all, it didn't look as if he was going to marry in the near future, though Maria kept introducing him to young women. But Edmund seemed impervious to their charms, probably because he kept a mistress in one of the firm's cottages at the upper end of the Lanes. Well, a man had his needs, didn't he? It was good to see Edmund had some faults, wasn't Mr Perfect all the time.

However, their conversation turned once again to the steam engine at the works and Athol was tired of hearing Edmund harping on about that. 'The situation hasn't changed since last week. We can't spend all we earn. No, that engine will have to do for another year or two, at least – and I don't want you bringing the subject up again. What we really need is a new warehouse, that's much more important.'

'That's easily found. Or we could build one.'

'Just shows how much you understand about business. I've studied the town and the only land cheap enough is out on the far side, too far away from the works and railway station to be practical. I suppose I could knock down a row or two of houses near the works, but if I did, where would our men live? Anyway, my workers' cottages are rather scattered and I can't get Chas Turner to sell me any of his.'

'Well, the storage situation is getting critical, I admit, but the engine—'

'Do you never come home without some new demand for me to spend money on that damned thing?'

'Sometimes you have to spend money to make money.'

'The discussion is closed. I'm *not* buying a new steam engine yet. We've only just recovered from a few bad years. We need to consolidate, not spend.' He waited for Edmund to respond and when his cousin didn't, said in a more genial tone, 'Let's talk about something more pleasant. I think I'll take another glass of port. What about you, old fellow?'

'No, I think I'll retire and read my new book.'

Athol shook his head as the door closed behind Edmund. 'It's a good job my cousin has me to attend to the business side of things. He's not very practical about money.'

Maria paused in her embroidering, needle held away from the canvas. 'You're so clever, Athol. I'm sure I don't understand half of what you say.'

He smiled benignly. 'To each his own. I shouldn't like a learned wife. A woman's sphere is in the home.'

She nodded, and when he didn't continue the

conversation, bent her head over her embroidery again.

He sipped his port and stared into the fire, wondering if he too should set himself up with a regular mistress. There were enough nubile young women around town. You couldn't walk out without tripping over one, and he'd had a few casual encounters. A man had more robust needs than a gently bred lady could satisfy and what Maria didn't know wouldn't hurt her.

The following week Carrie didn't wait for her sisters to come home on wage day but went to meet them. Marjorie came out of the mill first and handed over her money, then just as Dora was leaving the mill yard their father turned up, ready to take her wages again.

He stopped dead at the sight of the three of them. 'I know what your game is,' he shouted at Carrie.

'That's right. Because I'm the one who has to buy the food and make sure your children get summat to eat.'

He backed off, muttering 'ungrateful' and 'no respect for parents these days', rubbing his head.

It made her feel sad that things had come to a state of permanent hostility between them because once he'd been fun and had played with his children sometimes. But she was angry too at the way she now had to spend all her time doing what should have been her mother's job. She seemed to grow more tired every day because she was the one who had to get up in the night to help her mother with the twins if the whole household was not to be woken.

And Robbie only handed over part of his wages nowadays, even though he knew how short of money they were. He spent nearly every evening in the Dragon. Was he too turning to drink? If so, heaven help the woman he eventually married.

In fact, heaven help all married women, because they had a far harder lot in life than married men did, from what Carrie had seen. She'd never marry, never!

One afternoon a few days later Carrie came home from buying some potatoes for their evening meal to find her mother looking anxious and tearful. 'What's happened now?' she demanded at once.

'Nothing.'

Her mother was avoiding meeting her eyes. 'I can see something's wrong, so you might as well tell me.'

Jane began to sob and that woke one of the babies.

'See to May for me, will you, love?'

'Not till you've told me what the matter is.'

Nora woke up then and added more lusty wails to her sister's. Carrie folded her arms and went to stand by the fire, refusing to help. The others were out. Her younger brothers and sisters spent as much time as they could away from home these days, what with their father's moods, the crying of the twins, and the baby clouts drying everywhere that made the kitchen permanently steamy.

After a minute, during which her mother tried in vain to pacify both infants, Carrie asked her again what was wrong.

Jane turned on her eldest daughter, yelling above the howls, 'They finished early at Stott's. Trouble wi' the main boiler. Your dad come home and he – well, he took your spare clothes. Just to the pawn shop, not to sell. And it's not as if you really need them so—'

'And you let him?'

'How could I stop him? He *is* the man of the house.'

Carrie ran into her bedroom to check under the mattress and found that every last piece of her spare clothing had been taken. Ignoring her mother's cries to come back, she rushed out of the house and ran headlong down the street, not caring who she pushed aside. Her father couldn't have been gone long because she'd only been away for a few minutes. She knew he always took the short cut through a narrow passageway known locally as Crookit Walk, because it twisted between buildings, so turned off into that.

She caught him in the middle stretch of the narrow ginnel, out of sight of the road. He'd stopped to piss against the wall and she snatched the bundle lying behind his feet. Arthur turned and tried to grab it back but Carrie wouldn't let go, shouting at him and calling him a thief.

As her shrill voice echoed from the walls, Arthur's face grew red with anger and he clouted her so hard she fell over. But that meant he had to let go of the bundle and Carrie immediately rolled on top of it, ignoring her stinging cheek. He tried to pull it away from her and she fought back, scratching his face and yelling at him, 'You're a thief! Them are my clothes. You're *not* havin' 'em.'

'I'm your father an' I've a right to do what I want with everythin' in my own house!' he roared. When she wouldn't give in, he kicked out at her, catching her on the arm.

Carrie screamed in pain and tried to roll away, but he kicked her again and this time the heavy boot hit her on the temple. The world exploded into pain and darkness.

As she fell back, Arthur leaned over her and reached for the bundle. This time she didn't move and he hesitated. Her eyes were closed and there was a bruise on her forehead. He shook her but still she didn't move and her head lolled to one side.

'She asked for it, defying me like that,' he muttered. He picked up the clothes, adding, 'A man has a *right* t'punish his childer.'

Drops of water on his face made him realise it had started to rain. He hesitated, then rolled Carrie into a doorway. Hurrying off down the Walk, he was smugly conscious that he had more than done his duty by keeping his unconscious daughter dry till she woke up.

Turning left at the bottom of Crookit Walk, he made his way to the pawn shop and handed over the clothes, arguing half-heartedly over the amount allowed on them. His head was bad today and he couldn't seem to think straight, but he was clear about one thing. 'Man has a right t'punish his children,' he repeated as he walked back towards the Dragon, finding it hard to keep his steps straight and lurching into the wall a couple of times. 'An' a right to what they earn, too.'

He needed a beer. It was the only thing that made him forget the pain.

Arthur got so drunk that night his friends had to carry him back to Throstle Lane. By that time the money had all gone.

Marjorie and Dora got home from work to find both babies wailing and their mother sitting weeping beside them. Grace and Lily trailed into the house soon afterwards because the rain had grown heavier.

'Where's our Carrie?' Marjorie asked at once.

'Gone out.'

'She never goes out at this time of day.' She stared at her mother and, like her elder sister before her, guessed something was wrong. Being soft-hearted, she went across to put an arm round her mother. 'What's the matter, Mam? Don't cry. Eeh, don't cry, love.'

So it all came out.

'The town hall clock's chimed twice since then, so it must be over an hour since she went out,' Jane finished. 'She's not come back an' neither has he. She'll have upset him an' he'll be in the pub, but where's she?'

'I'll go out an' look for her.'

But Marjorie could find no sign of her sister. Carrie hadn't been to the baker's, though she'd been to the shop where Edith worked. But further questioning of her younger sister revealed that Carrie had been buying potatoes, and Marjorie had seen those potatoes at home.

She met Robbie and he helped her search the streets, but they found no sign of their sister. When it started to pour down heavily, they made their way home.

'She'll have got back afore us,' Robbie said comfortingly.

But there was no sign of Carrie in Throstle Lane, nor was there anything for tea except a few uncooked potatoes. And all their mother could do was weep and say it wasn't her fault.

Robbie fumbled in his pocket and pulled out his beer money with a sigh, thrusting it into his sister's hand. 'Here. Go an' get us summat else to eat. It's a hungry sort of day.'

Marjorie took the coins and went along to the baker's, begging a bag of broken crusts for a penny as well as a loaf with one corner crushed for breakfast the next day. They were selling off the dregs of the milk at the corner shop, so she rushed home for a bucket and came back triumphantly with milk sloshing around in it.

Dora sieved the milk through a piece of cloth to get the muck out of it, because the churn stood at the door of the shop and people dipped out their milk with any container they happened to bring along. By the time it got to the bottom few inches, it contained all sorts of bits and pieces. 'It's not gone sour,' she said triumphantly. 'Eh, we were lucky tonight.'

They enjoyed a meal of crusts in warm milk, the younger children standing at the table to eat, Marjorie and Robbie taking the rickety stools, and after a minute Dora taking Carrie's stool.

'I can't think where she's got to,' Jane said as the girls cleared the table and washed the dishes as best they could in the last few inches of cold water in one of the buckets, then tipped the dirty liquid out through the back door and stood the bucket in the rain to catch some more water. 'It's not like her to stay out after dark. Now, save the food that's left for your father an' don't let our Ted get hold of it.'

Dora nodded, setting the bowl of soggy crusts on the mantelpiece.

Marjorie looked at Robbie. 'Maybe we should go and have another look round the Rows?'

'It's dark now. We won't be able to see anything. Is there owt left from that money I gave you?'

'We need that for tomorrow.'

'Well, I need a pint tonight. Give us some back, love, just threepence for one pot of beer. You can keep the rest.'

'You're getting as bad as Dad. The children will go hungry tomorrow if you spend it on beer tonight, Robbie.' She watched his face, the way his brow wrinkled, the way he chewed his lip, saw him sigh and let his shoulders sag. Knew she'd won. She usually left that sort of thing to Carrie. It felt strange to be the one coaxing money out of someone. Even stranger to succeed.

Their sister still hadn't returned by bedtime and

by then they were so worried that Robbie was talking of going to see whichever of the new policemen was on duty that night.

'Don't do that,' Jane pleaded. 'People will know she's been out an' she'll lose her good name. She'll be all right. She can look after herself, our Carrie can. I expect she'll just have gone to a friend's to stay out of your dad's way.'

'Carrie hasn't got any close friends.' Marjorie hesitated then asked, 'Could she have gone to Uncle Bill's, do you think? He doesn't have owt to do with us lot, but he'd help if Carrie was in trouble, I'm sure he would. We're still family, after all.'

There was silence, then Jane shook her head in bafflement. 'I don't think she'd turn to him, but where else could she be? Robbie, will you go and see if she's there? An' if she is, bring her straight back. I need her.'

'I'll go with him,' Marjorie said.

They walked along towards the better terraces. 'I wish we lived in this part of town,' she said wistfully as they turned into Perseus Street. 'Even the names are fancy here.'

Robbie put one arm round his sister's shoulders and gave her a quick hug. 'Maybe you'll marry a well-to-do fellow one day an' live in a place like this. You're pretty enough.'

She smiled. 'I don't know any well-to-do fellows an' if I did, they wouldn't look at me twice, dressed like this.' She looked down at her ragged skirt and grimaced.

'Here we are.' Robbie knocked on the door, and was relieved when his uncle opened it because he was a bit afraid of his aunt, with her sharp tongue. 'I'm sorry to disturb you so late, Uncle Bill, but our Carrie's gone missing and we wondered if you'd seen her?'

His uncle shook his head. 'No. I saw her in town the other day and thought she was looking tired, but I haven't seen her since.'

Robbie sighed. 'We don't know where else to look. She's never stayed out so late before. We're really worried about her.'

'I'm sorry. I can't think what to suggest. Have you been to the constable, asked him?'

'No. Mam says if we did that, everyone would know she'd been out all night.'

Their aunt Sadie came out of the front room to join them. She had obviously been listening to what they were saying. 'Maybe she's got a fellow.'

Marjorie knew what their aunt was suggesting and anger overcame her nervousness. 'Even if she had – an' I know she hasn't – she wouldn't stay out this late.' She stared the other woman in the eyes. 'We may be poor, but we're respectable.'

Aunt Sadie sniffed loudly but didn't say anything more.

Robbie took a step backwards. 'Thank you anyway. We'll just go on looking.'

'If you need any help . . .'

'Thanks, Uncle. If we do need owt, we'll come to you.'

When they'd gone, Bill shut the door and looked

hard at his wife. 'You didn't need to say that. Carrie's a good lass.'

'Good lasses don't stay out till this hour. Ours have been in bed for over an hour, an' if I hadn't wanted to finish my sewing, I'd be there too.'

He sighed as he watched her go. Sharp-tongued, she was, and you had to tread carefully with her. He knew she didn't like Arthur and his family, but she'd had no need to say that. He'd never heard a bad word said about his nieces.

Eh, he hoped Carrie was safe.

A voice floated down the stairs. 'Are you coming to bed, Bill, or are you going to stand there all night? I need some sleep even if you don't.'

He hurried to fold his newspaper and break up the coals so that they didn't burn through. Then he checked again that the doors were bolted and climbed the stairs.

When Robbie and Marjorie got home they met their father's friends carrying his unconscious body back from the pub.

'Eh, he had a good few tonight, old Arthur did,' one of them said, laughing in a silly way that showed he'd drunk his share too. 'He were in the money an' were treating us.'

'That's because he stole my sister's clothes and pawned them,' Robbie said.

'Eh? Nay, you're fair an' wrong there. That weren't stealing. A man has a right to owt there is in his own home,' one of them said at once.

Robbie didn't bother to argue. They were all too drunk to make sense. For the first time he wondered if he looked this silly when he'd drunk too much and didn't like the thought of it. He helped the two men carry his father up to the front bedroom, where his mother and the twins were, then followed the men back down. 'You haven't seen our Carrie tonight, have you?'

'No, not her.' One of them sniggered. 'She doesn't usually come into the Dragon, your sister. Too good for us lot, she is.'

'Your dad saw her afore he come into the boozer,' the other man said.

'He didn't say *where* he saw her, did he?'

'Nay, just that she were trying to get her clothes back when he were pawning 'em. Kept goin' on about it, he did, till we shut him up. He can be a right old grumbler sometimes, Arthur can.'

'Thanks.' Robbie shut the door behind them, then opened it again, deciding that dark or not, he'd take a final walk round the streets which weren't safe for decent women at turning out time from the pubs. He didn't like to think of anyone attacking his sister.

But he didn't see any sign of her and came back more worried than when he'd left. Only Marjorie was still up and he shook his head in answer to the question in her eyes. 'We'll have another look round in the morning. Best get to bed now.'

'I shan't sleep a wink for worrying about her.'

Carrie woke up shivering with cold. When she moved pain stabbed through her head. She groaned and tried to sit up but couldn't manage it. As she lay there she realised she was on the ground outside, though she didn't know where, and that her feet and the lower edges of her skirt were soaking wet. Not knowing where she was frightened her so much she did manage to sit up, but had to lean her head against the wall until everything stopped spinning around her.

It gradually came to her that she was in a doorway. Had she fallen? Had an accident? Her head was hurting so much it took a long time for each thought to form.

Eventually she realised she couldn't stay here and tried to stand up, managing to get to her knees, then use the wall to help her stand up fully. That brought nausea roiling up her throat and she had to lean over to vomit, stepping back from the mess, shivering and dizzy.

*I can't stay here*, she decided after what seemed a very long time, so stepped out of the doorway, still uncertain where she was. Everything was dark around her so she kept her hand on the wall to guide herself along. It was sheer chance that led her downhill. She hesitated at the end of the alley, unable to think where to go next because everything seemed blurred and hard to recognise.

There was a light in the next building, so she stumbled along to try the door. It was locked. She knocked on it, but couldn't summon up enough strength to hit hard. When no one came to answer it she followed the building round, turning into a narrow passageway at the side.

Eventually she came to another door and slumped against it. The door gave way and she let out a cry as she felt herself falling . . .

Eli was making the rounds of the outer doors, checking that each one was locked for the night, when he heard a noise in the kitchen and went rushing towards it. If someone was trying to break in . . . He could feel the draught before he got there. Who had come in and left the door open? Then he saw the body on the floor and hurried forward, expecting it to be a drunk. He was about to haul the figure to its feet and carry it outside, because they didn't allow drunks to stay here overnight, when he paused. It was a young woman, not one of the old soaks!

As he turned her over he recognised Carrie Preston and saw that she was injured. It looked as if someone had hit her over the head. It must have been a hard blow because she was only partly conscious, groaning as he moved her then murmuring something he couldn't make out.

He went to look out of the door, but saw no sign of her attacker, so came back in and locked it. Picking her up, he carried her along to the kitchen. It was still warm there and he set her down in the big rocking chair his uncle used, murmuring in sympathy as he examined her temple and saw how bad the bruising was. He sniffed but couldn't smell any booze on her person or breath. Unsure what to do next, he went up to knock on his cousin's bedroom door.

'Joanna, can you help me? I've found an unconscious woman in the scullery. She must have come along the alley and fallen through the door.'

'Well, take her outside again. We don't offer beds to drunks.'

'She's not drunk. I think she's been attacked. Can you come down and help me?'

'You're sure she's not drunk?'

'Absolutely certain. It's Carrie Preston an' she's not the sort to be out on the streets. She's a decent lass.'

'All right. I'll be down in a minute.'

He went back to find Carrie staring round, looking terrified. She didn't seem to recognise him and shrank back when he went over to her. Eli knelt beside her. 'You're all right now, Carrie. Someone's hit you on the head, but we'll look after you.'

Joanna came in and made a soft sound of distress when she saw Carrie's injury. 'Did she tell you what happened?'

'She isn't properly conscious.'

'We'd better have the doctor to look at her. She's as white as a sheet and that's a bad bump. You go and get him. I'll stay with her.'

So Eli ran through the empty streets and hammered on Dr Latimer's front door until someone answered. When he explained, the doctor sighed but agreed to come and see the injured woman.

By the time they got back to the Dragon, Carrie was making a bit more sense and was trying to remember what had happened.

'I think someone – hit me. I don't remember . . .' Her voice trailed away.

Gerald examined her, smelled her breath and stood up again. 'She's not had anything to drink, as far as I can tell. If you'll leave us alone, Mr Beckett, I'll check whether she's been tampered with.'

Eli stood stock still, amazed at the anger that had welled up in him at the thought of someone doing *that* to a decent lass. If they had, he'd find them and make sure they couldn't hurt another woman in that way ever again, by hell he would!

Joanna gave him a shove. Once he'd left, she helped the doctor examine Carrie, impressed by how gentle he was.

'No one's touched her in that way, thank goodness, but it was a violent blow. I wonder why someone would attack her? The family's so poor there'd only be pennies to be gained, if that.' He studied her again, then turned to Joanna. 'Can she stay here tonight? I'd rather not move her further than we have to and she's in no state to walk anywhere.'

She nodded and went to summon Eli. 'Carrie's not been touched in that way.'

Relief made him unable to say more than, 'Good, good.'

'Will you bring her upstairs? There's a bedroom in the attic she can have.'

Gerald cleared his throat to get their attention. 'It'd be better if someone stayed with her tonight, just in case she wakes and is confused. And she should be kept warm. I know it's a lot of trouble for you, but if we can't help our fellow creatures . . . and head wounds can be tricky.'

Joanna sighed. 'She can sleep in my bedroom, then. It's over the kitchen, so it's always warm. Go and bring a mattress down from the attic, Eli.'

When they'd taken Carrie upstairs and settled her, he looked at his cousin. 'Had I better go and tell her family where she is?'

Joanna yawned. 'I'd wait till morning. It's gone one o'clock. They'll all be asleep by now.'

'They might not.'

'Do as you please, then. I'm not going anywhere but back to bed.'

'The father was carried out of here drunk tonight. Uncle Frank said to let him drink as long as he could pay, but I'd have stopped serving him before he got to that stage.'

'Dad would have a fit at you for saying that. He only thinks about taking money off them.' She gave a short sniff of annoyance. 'I'd like the pub to have a better reputation than as a place for men to get roaring drunk, but who am I to decide anything?'

'One day we'll change things here,' Eli said quietly. Since their visit to the music saloon he'd felt a lot closer to her, as if she were his sister, and although she still spoke sharply to him, and to everyone else for that matter, he sensed that the edge of venom she'd shown towards him before was gone. At least he hoped it was, it felt as if it had.

Joanna gestured towards the door. 'Right then. I want to get to bed even if you don't. Turn that lamp low and leave it here so I can check her during the night.'

When Eli had left, Joanna stared at the girl on the mattress, wondering why anyone would want to attack someone as poor as her. Then a huge yawn overtook her and she huddled down in the warm bed.

# 6

Before it was light the next morning Jane was woken by the babies crying and got up to feed them. They were soaking wet and she'd forgotten to bring up fresh clouts without Carrie there to remind her, so she carried the wailing infants downstairs one at a time, grumbling under her breath. No use asking Arthur to help. It was hard enough waking him in the mornings, near impossible during the night. The house could burn down around him when he first went to bed and he'd not stir.

Should she call Marjorie to help? No, her daughter had to go to work in the morning, and if she didn't they'd not eat, so Jane would have to manage on her own.

When she'd finished feeding the babies she decided the rest of the family could get themselves off to work without her help. She was exhausted and was going back to bed to get some more sleep. Two babies gave you no rest and it was wrong of Carrie to stay out overnight when she knew she was needed at home. Downright selfish, it was. She was probably sulking because of losing the clothes. Likely she'd be staying with one of her friends from the laundry but she'd have to come home sometime and then Jane would give her what for. It wasn't right, staying out all night wasn't. She'd brought up her girls to be respectable, however poor they were.

Blowing out the candle, she carried the second baby upstairs in the darkness. She knew every tread of the stairs and the box where the babies still slept was next to the window so it was easy to find. Relieved that they'd both gone straight off to sleep again, she got into bed. The knocker-up was coming down the street, banging his long pole with its wires on the tip on the windows, and she turned over to poke her husband in the ribs and tell him to get up.

Arthur didn't move, not even to give his usual sleepy grumble. The knocker-up rapped again, this time rattling the wires against the window more loudly. He wouldn't move on until someone showed a light inside the house or called to him.

Annoyed, Jane poked Arthur again, but he still didn't stir, not an inch, so she went to bang on the window, which sent the knocker-up on his way, then turned back to give her husband a good shake. It was then that she noticed he was breathing funny, sort of snoring, only he wasn't usually a snorer.

'Arthur? Arthur, wake up!' Her voice quavered in the darkness and that soft snoring noise went on and on. She ran down the stairs, feeling suddenly afraid, poked a spill into the embers to light the candle again and with a shaking hand carried it back up and bent to look at her husband.

What she saw made her drop the candle and screech

loudly. She went on screeching in the darkness, which woke the rest of the family who came rushing into the bedroom.

Robbie got to her first. 'What's wrong? Mam, stop screaming and tell me.'

Jane clung to him, shivering and weeping. 'It's your dad. Look at his face! It's all slack at one side an' I can't wake him.'

'Go an' light a candle,' he told Ted. 'I can't see a thing.'

'The candle's on the floor. I dropped it.'

Robbie had to break his mother's grip on him before he could fumble around for the candle. 'Here, Ted. Go an' light it.' Cursing the darkness, he bent over the figure on the bed and shook his father's shoulder tentatively.

'Listen to that breathing,' his mother whispered.

So they all fell silent, hearing that strange rasping sound that wasn't like any breathing they'd ever heard.

A flickering light showed as Ted came back up the stairs. Robbie took the candle from him and held it near his father's face.

'What's wrong with him, Mam? He was all right yesterday.'

'No, he wasn't. His head was really bad yesterday.' Jane bent closer to her husband. 'Look at his face, how it's dropped at one side. He's had a seizure, that's what. My father died that way.' She began to sob. 'What am I going to do now? We'll all wind up in the workhouse. Two new babbies an' no breadwinner to look after us. What am I going to *do*?'

Robbie looked round and found everyone staring at him. He wished Carrie were here to take charge. She'd have known exactly what to do, but now everyone was looking to him. 'Go and fetch the doctor, Dora. Perhaps he'll be able to tell us what to do for Dad. He isn't dead, so if we look after him, he may recover.'

Dora clutched Edith. 'Come with me. It's still dark outside.' They slipped down the stairs.

Jane stopped sobbing for long enough to say, 'Even if your dad does recover, he'll be no use to anyone. I've seen it afore. Oh, Arthur! Come back to me!' She threw herself across her husband's body in a paroxysm of grief.

The babies woke and added their cries to hers.

Robbie moved closer to Marjorie. 'Can you stay with her while the rest of us get dressed?'

She nodded and went to sit next to their mother on the bed, comforting her as best she could while stealing the occasional glance towards her father's still body. He looked like one of the figures on the edge of the church roof, the ones with twisted faces that water from the roof gutters poured through. Was he going to die? She shivered at the thought.

Robbie came back. 'I'll stay with her now while you get dressed. Should we go to work, do you think, or should we stay at home? You know. In case he dies.'

'Mam, what should we do?' Marjorie looked at her mother, but got no help. When she turned back to Robbie he was still waiting for her answer. 'I'd better stay home to look after Mam and the babies. The rest of you should go to work because there's nothing you can do here. Grace and Lily can stay off school and run errands for me. I'll send for you if . . .' her voice faltered and she had to take a deep breath before she could continue '. . . if the worst happens. Tell the overlooker Dad's really bad, then maybe he won't fine me.' He wouldn't fine her at all if she let him touch her breasts, but she wasn't going to do that. He was a horrible man.

After a pause, she looked at her brother again. 'Where's our Carrie? We really need her.'

Robbie shook his head.

Dr Latimer arrived a short time later, examined Mr Preston and asked the family about his health. He found the swelling behind the dead man's ear and said gently, 'He has a growth. See? It's probably spread into the brain. That'll have caused the seizure.'

Jane began sobbing again and repeating, 'How shall we manage without a breadwinner? An' me with two new babbies.'

Gerald didn't attempt to answer, though he felt sorry for this woman. It wasn't that he didn't care, but he saw all too many families struck by tragedy and had learned that he couldn't help them all. 'Has Carrie come home yet? Is she feeling better now?'

Robbie stepped forward. 'Carrie? Do you know where she is? She didn't come back at all last night. We looked for her everywhere but couldn't find her. There's been no sign of her this morning, either.'

'She was hurt, hit on the head, must have been lying unconscious for some time. She managed to

*Anna Jacobs*

reach the Dragon and on my advice they kept her there overnight. I thought they were going to let you know.'

Jane stopped sobbing. Her voice changed from a pitiful whine to an indignant tone. 'They should ha' sent someone to tell us. We've been worried sick about her. Grace, you get down to the Dragon an' fetch our Carrie back this minute!'

'She may not have recovered fully yet,' Dr Latimer said. 'It was a hard blow.'

'She can do her recovering here, thank you very much, doctor. I need her.'

Carrie woke to find herself in a strange room and jerked upright in shock – or tried to, only the minute she raised her head, it started spinning so she fell back.

'How are you feeling?' a voice asked, and she turned her head to see Miss Beckett standing beside her mattress.

'Where am I?'

'In the Dragon.'

'I don't understand. Why am I here?'

'You were attacked and knocked unconscious last night. When you came to, you somehow found your way to our back door and fell through it. We took you in because you still weren't able to think properly and the doctor said it would be wiser not to move you.'

Carrie felt the bump on her forehead and winced.

'Do you remember what happened?'

She sat there for a minute as it all came rushing

back to her, then said in a low voice that wobbled, 'Yes.' She couldn't help it, she began to cry. Her father had kicked her unconscious, her own father! She realised Miss Beckett was kneeling beside her, rubbing her shoulder, making soothing noises, and for a moment clung to that kind hand because she felt so hurt, so lost. But Carrie wasn't the sort to go on weeping and managed to stop, whispering, 'Sorry.'

'That's all right. It must have been dreadful.'

'It was. I still can't believe what happened.'

'What did happen? Eli wants to complain to the police. If we know who your attacker is, they can go after him.'

'It was my father who did it.'

Joanna stared at her in horror. *'Your own father did that to you?'*

Carrie nodded and winced as her head throbbed a protest.

'Why?'

So she explained about her clothes. 'He'll have pawned them and drunk the money.'

'I'm afraid he did. He was drinking more heavily than usual last night, treating all his friends. They had to carry him home. He couldn't even walk by the time he left here.'

Tears came into Carrie's eyes. 'There'll be no money left, then. I'm definitely going to leave home. I'm not staying there for him to steal my things. I don't have any spare clothes now. How can I keep myself clean?' She had felt it such a step up in the world to be able to do that.

Joanna felt an unwilling sympathy for the girl. Imagine having so little. 'It sounds as if you'd be a lot better away from him. You could go into lodgings or find a live-in job and . . .' She broke off as an idea came to her. 'Stay there. I'll fetch you a cup of tea and something to eat.'

'You needn't wait on me. I'll be all right.' Carrie tried again to sit up but the room spun round her and she gasped and fell back on the pillow.

'Stay there, I said!'

Carrie didn't move because to do so made her feel like being sick. Instead she tried to work out how to get away from her father. She felt in her petticoat and there it was, her precious half-sovereign, wrapped in the rag and sewn safely in place. That was the key to escaping. She'd been tempted to use the money several times when they'd been short of food, but something had always stopped her. Just having it made her feel safer. Her hand went up to her forehead. Anger filled her, and sadness that he'd do that to her.

When there were footsteps on the stairs she didn't look up, thinking it was Miss Beckett coming back. It came as a shock to hear a man's voice ask, 'How are you feeling now, Carrie?'

With a gasp she opened her eyes to see Eli standing in the doorway, looking healthy and strong, his face ruddy with soap and water – she could smell the soap from where she lay, a lovely smell it was. 'Ooh, you made me jump. I thought it was Miss Beckett coming back.'

'She said you were awake. I'm just going to let your family know you're all right. They must be worried about you. Only she said . . . well, that your father did this to you.'

'Yes.'

'Do you still want me to tell them where you are?'

'I suppose you'll have to. We live at the end house in Throstle Lane.' Carrie frowned, trying to work it all out. 'What time is it?'

'Nearly nine o'clock.'

'*Nine!* Eh, I'm usually awake by five.' But at least her father would be out at work now. She definitely didn't want to meet him till she'd got her thoughts in order and planned what to do. 'If you wait a few minutes, I'll come with you.'

She tried again to stand up but the room began to spin round her and the most she could manage was to sit up, leaning against the wall. Tears of frustration welled in her eyes. 'I'm still dizzy.'

Without realising she was doing it, Carrie spoke her thoughts aloud. 'I'm tired of it all. I don't want to go back. There are too many of us. Mam can't manage, but it's not fair to expect me to do everything. I can't go on like this, I just can't. I'm going to find somewhere else to stay before *he* comes home from work.' She closed her eyes and sighed.

Eli's voice was gentle. 'You could stay here for a day or two. Just until you get something sorted out. There's a room in the attic that's not being used.'

'That's very kind of you.' She tried to think whether to accept this offer, but her mind wouldn't work properly. 'I can't seem to decide what best to do,' she confessed.

Joanna came back into the room then, speaking briskly because she could see poor Carrie was near to tears, and who could blame her? 'What you're going to do is drink this cup of tea and eat some toast. It'll put new heart into you, then we'll think how to help you. Eli, go and see her family. Let them know she's all right. Tell them she's not well enough to go home yet.'

'She definitely isn't well enough. She gets dizzy if she tries to sit up. Do we even have to tell them yet where she is?'

'Yes, we do, so go and get it over with.'

When Joanna spoke like that, you didn't argue, he thought wryly as he went slowly down the stairs.

His uncle was in the kitchen, finishing his breakfast. 'That public room still needs cleaning. When's our Joanna going to make a start? We're not here to take in waifs and strays. I dare say that girl got what she deserved. If they will walk the streets, they must expect to be beaten up now and then.'

For some reason, Eli felt angry at his uncle for implying Carrie Preston was like that. He went to lean on the table, shoving his face close to the older man's. 'That is a decent lass who got attacked, not a street walker, and if we can't help someone in trouble, we're not worth much ourselves.' He swung round quickly and left before he said something he'd regret. His uncle was getting on his nerves more than ever lately.

Well, first things first. He'd better go and see Carrie's family.

★

The old man was limping badly and looking exhausted as he made his way along the narrow moorland road that led down to Hedderby. Bram clicked to his donkey to slow down and it ambled to a halt beside the stumbling figure. 'Need a ride into town?' he called.

The man's face lit up. 'Eh, that'd be a big help, lad.'

Bram laughed. 'I'm hardly a lad any more.'

'You look like a lad to me.' The old man looked at the cart and shook his head. 'I can't get up there on my own. Will't give me a boost up?'

'Aye.' Bram told the animal to stand still and leaped down. He'd lifted the old man up on to the bench seat before his companion could do more than squeak in shock, then bent to pick up the pitifully small bundle he was carrying, which had fallen open.

Tears came into the old man's eyes and he held out one hand as if he expected the younger man to drop his precious bits and pieces.

'I've got it safe. I'll just tie up your bundle again. There you are.' Bram handed it up and went round to his side of the cart again, swinging himself up easily and calling to the patient creature to 'Walk on'.

After a few minutes' silence, he asked, 'What are you doing out here in the middle of nowhere?'

'Tryin' to get to Hedderby Bridge.'

'Got family there, have you?'

'Could have. I've got none anywhere else now, that's for sure.'

'Maybe I know them?'

'There's just one, a fellow called Nev Linney.' He saw Bram pull a face. 'He hasn't changed, then?'

'No. Still as close-fisted as ever, if that's what you mean?'

'Aye, I do. But I'm his dad, Raife's my name, an' he may be close-fisted but I'm hoping he won't want me puttin' in the poorhouse.' As well as loving money, his elder son had always worried about how he appeared to the world, especially after he'd started to make something of himself. Raife sighed again, gazing into the distance. 'I lived with my younger boy.' He gave a rather sad smile. 'He were a lot easier to get on with than Nev. But he were killed a few months ago in a mine accident.'

He paused for a moment, his mouth working in his efforts not to weep, then continued quietly, 'Such a kind lad, our Paul were. Never got wed, never wanted to, but he looked after me and I looked after him. I tried to manage after he'd gone, but I fell ill. I sold off his things one by one to pay the rent, an' when the money were nearly gone I set off for Hedderby. Folk have been kind – given me rides, let me sleep in barns. Some have given me food, too.'

Bram nodded. It was all too common a tale. Old folk destitute and unable to help themselves. He'd make sure his parents never wanted for anything once they were too old to work, though they were doing all right still. He grinned suddenly at the thought of Nev Linney's face when his destitute father arrived at the lodging house everyone called Linney's.

Next to him Raife squinted at the setting sun and let out a rusty chuckle. 'At least I'll be sleeping indoors tonight, one way or another. If my son won't take me in, I'll have to go to the poorhouse.'

The old man seemed friendly and good-natured, and Bram found himself wondering how he could possibly have fathered a miser like Nev who made every farthing do the work of a ha'penny.

When they got into town, Bram went out of his way to drive to Linney's, which was partway up the hill just behind the Dragon. 'Here you are. This is your son's place.' There was a small group of people waiting outside the lodging house already, though they must have known they wouldn't be allowed in until six o'clock.

'Bigger than the old one. He must be doing well for himself.'

'Wait there. I'll go and fetch him.'

Bram banged on the door and, when no one answered, banged even harder.

'Not open till six!' a voice yelled.

'This is about something else.'

The door opened just a crack, held by a chain. 'Oh. It's you, Bram. What do you want?'

'I've brought your father to you.'

Nev stared beyond him. 'What the hell does *he* want?'

'A home.'

'Has my brother chucked him out?'

'Your brother's dead, mine accident. I met Raife walking across the moors.'

Nev cursed fluently.

'Are you going to turn him away? Surely you're

not that short of money?' When he didn't answer, Bram added slyly, 'If you can't afford to keep him, I'll take him to the poorhouse.'

Nev's plump features tightened and he drew himself up. 'Who says I can't afford to keep him? Bring him over here. I'll have to watch this lot or they'll be pushing inside. I don't allow anyone in before six.'

Bram looked at the sky. 'You could open a bit early today. It's coming on to rain and they'll get wet.'

'That's their lookout. I open at six and not before, and I turn 'em out at nine of a morning on the dot. They can think themselves lucky to find a safe place like this. I don't allow any thieves in here, you know, an' I keep the place clean. Cleaner than they deserve, that's for sure.'

Bram walked back to the cart.

'Is he refusing to take me in?' the old man quavered, looking suddenly older and anxious.

'No. He's keeping the door shut in case that lot try to push inside.' There was no mistaking the relief on Raife's face and Bram felt a strong surge of sympathy for him. 'Come on, lean on me.'

As he drove off he felt angry at the grudging welcome offered by Nev to his own father. The Heegans might be a rough lot, but at least they looked after one another. Aye, and cared about one another too, whatever their faults.

Inside the house Raife looked at his son and tears came into his eyes. 'Thank you for taking me in, Nev.'

'You're my father. Come this way. I spend most of my time in the kitchen during the day.'

Raife picked up his bundle and limped along the corridor. The kitchen was warm and he sighed with relief as he sank down on a chair. 'I'm not usually so feeble, but I've been ill. I can help around the place when I'm better, an' I'm quite a good cook.'

Nev looked at him and nodded.

'I'll try not to be a burden.'

'I can afford to keep you, whether you help or not.'

'Thanks, son.' Raife pushed himself off the chair and went to hug his son, and although Nev stiffened against him at first, he relaxed a bit and even gave a quick hug back.

'Be nice to have a bit of company, actually,' Nev said as they drew apart. Then, in case this should be taken as a sign of weakness, he added, 'Though I'll definitely expect you to do what you can about the place once you're better.'

Eli strode up to Throstle Lane and found a group of people standing outside Carrie's house. 'Is something wrong?'

'Arthur Preston's had a seizure,' one old woman told him. 'Doctor's in there now. He won't be able to do owt for him, though. Well, you can't with seizures, can you? Eh, an' Arthur's nobbut forty-five. I remember him bein' born.'

Eli pushed open the front door. 'Hello, there!'

Two little girls peered at him from the end of the corridor.

'Can I come in? I need to see your mam.'

They nodded, backing away as he entered the kitchen. Footsteps on the stairs made him turn round to see Dr Latimer come down, carrying his black bag. The two men stared solemnly at one another as more footsteps shuffled down the stairs and Jane appeared, carrying a baby. She walked past them and set the infant down on the floor in front of the fire, then went back up the stairs without a word.

As soon as she was out of hearing, Eli asked, 'How is he?'

The doctor shrugged. 'Unconscious. It's only a matter of time, I think, though you can never be absolutely sure in these cases. How's Carrie today?'

'Still not herself. My cousin wants to keep her in bed for a day or two.'

'It'd be best. That was a hard knock she got.'

Jane came down the stairs carrying a box with the other baby in it. 'What happened to our Carrie?'

'She was attacked last night, knocked unconscious. She's a bit better this morning, but—'

'Tell her we need her here. I can't manage on my own.'

Eli was suddenly impatient. 'She's not well enough yet, can barely stand up.'

'She'll come once she knows her dad's so poorly. She won't let us down.'

But you'll let *her* down, Eli thought. It didn't feel right for him to be the one to say who'd hit her, so he just added, 'I'll go and tell her about her father, see what she says. She may not be able to come back yet, even if she wants to. She's still very dizzy.'

He was angry as he walked back down the hill. Jane hadn't really been interested in how Carrie was, only how soon she could get back and take charge. He'd seen it before, families draining the capable members dry of all their energy, taking and taking from them until people collapsed under the strain. His own mother was a generous soul, always ready to help someone in distress, but his father kept her from overreaching herself. Who was there to help Carrie, though, and stop her wearing herself out?

He entered the pub and found Joanna in the big room cleaning up with Bonny. 'How is she?' he asked.

'Lying down. Still weak.'

'Carrie's father had a seizure last night and looks like dying. The doctor says there's nothing he can do. The rest of the family seem lost without her, but I don't think she's well enough to go back to them.'

Joanna sighed. 'She will when she hears what's happened.'

'Has she had anything to eat?'

'Just nibbled at some toast. Doesn't want to do anything but sleep.'

'Let's wait a bit to tell her, give her a chance to rest.'

Joanna glanced sideways. 'What concern is she of yours?'

'None. I just don't like seeing decent folk put upon.'

'Women like her are always put upon.' Joanna hesitated. 'I'll go and see if she's awake. If she isn't, we'll let her sleep a bit longer.'

But Carrie was awake. She turned her head as the door opened. 'It feels wrong to be lying abed in the daytime. I just can't settle.' She pushed back the covers and sat up slowly and carefully, wincing and rubbing her forehead in the centre.

Eli came into the room. 'Stay where you are for a moment, Carrie. There's something we have to tell you.'

She sat leaning against the wall, looking shocked when Eli told her about her father. After he'd finished speaking she pushed herself to her feet, steadying herself against a chair. Her face was chalk-white except for the massive blue and purple bruise on one temple. 'I'd better get back. They'll need me.'

'You're not well enough,' he protested.

She grimaced. 'I'll have to be. Mam's no use in an emergency.'

And nothing they said or did would convince her otherwise. So Joanna sent Eli away and helped Carrie tidy herself up. Before they went down, she said in her abrupt way, 'Look, I need someone to help out in the pub, with the cleaning that is. Early in the morning for a few hours every day, Saturdays and Sundays included, paying two shillings a day. Are you interested in the job?'

'Yes. Yes, I definitely am.'

'Come back in a day or two once you're better. Don't leave it too long. I really need someone now. And if you want, you can live in – if you're not happy at home, that is – though I'll have to pay you less if you do that.'

'Thanks.'

Joanna watched her go. She'd decided one thing last night. She wasn't wearing herself out any longer by managing the pub without proper help. Just let her father try to stop her employing another cleaner – or any other help they needed!

She didn't intend to wind up as Carrie Preston likely would, as dozens of other women did, worn out before she was thirty.

Eli watched Carrie walk out of the pub, clicking his tongue in exasperation at her stubbornness. She was moving very slowly, as if every step was an effort, and weaving from side to side. He couldn't let her go like that, so ran after her to offer her his arm. She hesitated then took it, leaning heavily on him.

'Thanks. I'm still a bit wobbly.'

When they got to the end of Crookit Walk she stopped, drawing back. At his questioning look she said, 'It was up there I was hit.'

'Ah. Well, we can go the long way round, if you prefer it.'

For a moment she hesitated, then shook her head. 'No. That'd be silly. It's a short cut everyone uses and I'm safe enough with you.'

But as they set off up the narrow ginnel, he could feel her hand trembling slightly as it rested on his arm and his heart went out to her. About halfway up she stopped. 'It was there, I think. Yes, it must have been. I was in a doorway when I came to and that's the only one there is in Crookit Walk.'

There was nothing to show that a man had kicked his daughter senseless here. Eli stole a quick glance at her bruised and battered face. If Arthur Preston hadn't had a seizure, he'd have been tempted to give the fellow a good thumping himself to teach him not to beat up women. He doubted it'd have done any good, though. Some men were violent by nature. But what sort of man left his own daughter lying unconscious like that? He heard Carrie sigh, saw her rub her forehead. 'Is your head hurting?'

'A bit.'

'More than a bit, I should think.'

She gave him a wry half-smile. 'Well, I'll mend. It sounds like my father won't, though. You won't tell them that he did it?'

'Not if you don't want me to.'

'It'd do no good now, just upset Mam more.'

'You really should have waited a day or two to go back. We'd have been happy to let you stay with us and they could manage without you if they had to.'

'No, they couldn't. Edith's going to be a sensible lass when she grows up, but she's too young now. Marjorie,' she shrugged and sought for words to explain her next sister, 'allus means well, but she can't bear to hurt anyone, or to be hurt herself. And Dora acts without thinking.'

'But you've a grown-up brother. Surely it's for him to take charge now?'

'Robbie?' Carrie smiled. 'He's a big softie an' usually turns to me for help.'

Eli didn't know what to say. He met many people in his line of work, but this lass stood out a mile from the others. She was brave and hard-working, and in his opinion her feckless family didn't deserve her. You had to wonder why she hadn't married. She'd make some man a fine wife.

When they got to Throstle Lane, Carrie stopped for a moment, looking along the narrow street. It was paved by irregular setts, the sort of square paving stones which had corners knocked off or were cracked, the ones the town council had left over after it paved the better streets of the town. Some of them had been laid carelessly and had sunk a little, and there were puddles in the hollows. Above them the sky was grey and overcast, promising more rain.

Two women were standing in a doorway partway along the street, heads close together. One exclaimed, 'Eh, what happened to you, Carrie lass?'

'I had a fall. I'm still a bit dizzy so Mr Beckett's had to lend me his arm. I'm working for Miss Beckett at the Dragon now, you know.'

'Sorry about your dad.'

At the end house Carrie pulled her arm out of Eli's. 'Thanks for helping me get home.'

'Just a minute. What did you mean, you're working at the Dragon?'

'Miss Beckett's offered me a job cleaning. I'm to start in a day or two.' Then she pushed open the door and went inside, calling, 'I'm back!'

She didn't turn round to wave goodbye or watch him go, but he stood and watched the door swing slowly shut and it was a minute before he moved away.

Eli spent the time it took to get back to the Dragon alternately telling himself to stay away from her from now on, and wondering how he could help her. Only he wouldn't be able to stay away from her if she was working at the pub, would he? And he didn't know whether to be glad or sorry about that.

Carrie closed the front door and took a couple of steps down the hallway, her feet feeling so heavy it was an effort to lift them. As she came to a halt, leaning against the wall, the kitchen door opened and Grace peeped out, holding a wriggling baby in her arms.

'It's our Carrie!' she yelled.

Immediately there were other voices and Marjorie came rushing towards her, gasping when she saw her sister's battered face.

Carrie nearly fell into her sister's arms. 'I'm not right yet,' she managed. There was silence and she could see several faces peering at her beyond Marjorie. 'Get me to bed – before I fall over.'

Footsteps followed them along to the bedroom and their mother came in behind them.

'Where have you been, Carrie Preston?' she demanded, her expression and voice both vicious. 'You've been brought up better than to stay out all night an' you should have come home to us if you were hurt.'

Marjorie rounded on her, for once roused out of

her gentle ways. 'What a way to talk when she can hardly stand! Go back into the kitchen and look after the babies, and leave me to look after our Carrie!'

Her sister sank down on to the nearest straw-filled mattress, which she shared with Marjorie and Dora, closing her eyes. 'Sorry. Won't be much help today, I'm afraid.' There was silence and she forced her eyes open to see Marjorie staring down at her.

'We all depend on you, don't we?' the other girl said suddenly. 'And now you're hurt so I'll look after you. I'll do my best, I promise. Carrie love, who did this to you?'

'Dad.'

'*No!*' Marjorie stared at her in horror. 'Why would he do that?'

'I was trying to get my spare clothes back off him an' when I fell over he kicked out at me. I've got nothing now but what I stand up in.' She felt her sister take her hand, felt Marjorie's tears drop on the back of it, and opened her eyes again to see her sister weeping over her.

'You've got us. We're not much use, but we do love you, Carrie. You don't need to do anything today but rest. I've stayed off work and I'll do whatever's needed.' She hesitated then added, 'But if you could just say *what* to do . . . Dad's upstairs dying, you see, and I don't know what to do about that. Mam's no help. Well, she never is, is she? Me and the little 'uns have to look after the babies while she sits with Dad, crying and calling his name. He doesn't answer, though. He just lies there breathing funny. It's awful to see him . . . awful.'

Carrie sighed. 'Mam loves him in her own way, so it'll be hard for her. Leave the babies to the little 'uns today as much as you can and just make sure Mam feeds them. You'll have enough on your plate seeing to the food for tonight an' taking care of Mam and Dad. Is there any money left at all?'

'Just a few pence.'

'It'll have to be dry bread again, then. There's nothing left to pawn now. He took it all.' The room was swirling round her now and she closed her eyes with a groan.

'You go to sleep, love.' Marjorie sat looking at Carrie for a minute or two, then took a deep breath and stood up, her expression more determined than usual.

When Carrie woke, she found Lily sitting on the end of the other mattress.

Her little sister stood up. 'I've to tell Marjorie when you wake up.'

As she was leaving the room, someone knocked on the front door. Carrie heard Lily open it and a voice she recognised ask for her.

Lily peeped round the bedroom door. 'It's a lady for you!' she whispered, so loudly that the visitor must have heard her.

'Ask her to come in.'

Essie entered the room. 'The doctor told me you'd been hurt so I came to see if I could help. I've got an hour or so to spare.' She came across to the mattress and knelt down to take Carrie's hand in her big, warm one. 'Eh, lass, you're in the wars, aren't you? Let's see what we can do to put things right.'

And Carrie let herself sob out her tale, holding tight to Essie's hand as she did so, weeping out her pain that her own father had done this to her, that he was dying and she'd never know now if he'd realised what he was doing. Her world was being turned upside down and for once she was too weak to help herself, let alone her family.

Essie heard her in grim silence, patting her hand from time to time and making soothing sounds. 'I doubt he'd even have remembered today what he did yesterday. They're like that, drunkards, as my sister found to her cost. Only it was her husband who killed *her*, beat her to death, he did. But you're not going to die. I'll make sure you're looked after properly.'

'You're so kind to me. Thanks, Essie.' She stretched out her arms and the two women hugged, then Essie pushed her away.

'Look at me, acting all soft!' she said in a scolding tone, trying to hide how moved she was by the gesture. 'Now, let's get you something to eat and drink. I've brought some food round, so you've no need to worry about your family, and I've brought your mother's beef tea while I'm at it, plus some for you. I'll make sure she drinks it all.'

Under Essie's gentle bullying, Carrie drank the beef tea and ate a piece of cake before sinking back into sleep. It felt so good to have the burdens lifted from her shoulders.

## 7

Carrie had expected to be all right by the next day, but she still felt dizzy. She didn't know what she'd have done without Essie, who came round the next afternoon as well, bearing further gifts of food. She wouldn't let Jane touch anything except the beef tea till the invalid had eaten the best of her offerings. She got her way in this by threatening not to bring any more food otherwise and Jane stopped protesting.

Since Carrie knew she had to get better if the family were to survive, she did as Essie told her and tried no more than to walk slowly to the kitchen and sit by the fire that first day, cuddling one of the babies for a while. Grace stayed home from school to help them because it wasn't possible for Marjorie to take more time off.

Arthur Preston lingered for three more days without regaining consciousness. Jane insisted that the children visit him every evening, but the younger ones didn't really want to. He'd had little to do with them during the past few years, because he'd spent most of his spare time at the pub.

Jane, however, spent every moment she could sitting with her husband, remembering the fine young man he had once been and wondering how he'd come to this. At forty-five he was old before his time, with sparse grey hair and a wrinkled face, while she, in spite of having all those children, knew she looked younger because she'd seen her face in shop windows. The only time she left her husband was to go down and feed the babies. Against all the odds both infants were thriving, but somehow she didn't care about them as she had about her other children. There were just too many of them now and she got so tired and breathless.

On the third day she realised suddenly that Arthur had slipped away without her noticing that the shallow breathing had at last stopped. Throwing herself on to his body, she began screaming and weeping in a mindless frenzy of grief.

Downstairs Carrie and Essie were having a cup of tea together. When they heard Jane they jumped to their feet, putting down the babies they were rocking before running upstairs.

'He's gone,' Essie said after one look at the man in the bed. She pulled the hysterical woman upright and shouted, 'Stop that!' When Jane continued to scream, Essie slapped her face. 'That's doing no good. You'll frighten them babbies of yours.'

'My Arthur's dead. He's dead!' Jane opened her mouth to scream again, saw the hand come up ready to slap her and gulped back the cry.

Essie didn't let go of her, shaking her slightly to emphasise what she was saying. 'I'm sorry about that, but you've still got your children to look after, so you can't give in to your grief.'

'Carrie's seeing to them.'

'Yes, and see how ill she still looks. She's in no fit state to do this, hasn't recovered fully from the attack yet.'

'Serve her right for walking the streets after dark,' Jane muttered, giving her daughter a dirty look.

Essie swelled visibly with anger. 'She's not told you, but I will—'

'Don't. Please.' Carrie tugged at her friend's arm.

'No. There's been too much shielding her.' Essie turned back to Jane, who was looking at them in puzzlement. 'It was your husband who attacked Carrie, kicked her in the head – his own daughter!'

'He never! He wouldn't . . .' She turned to Carrie. 'How could you make such a thing up?'

'He did it, Mam. I was trying to get my clothes back.'

'Well, there you are. You should ha' let him have them. He had a right to them! He was the man of the house.'

'No one has a right to steal,' Essie said loudly, 'and Mrs Latimer was very angry when she heard about it. *She* gave those clothes to Carrie, not him. I'm bringing Carrie some more things tomorrow and no one's to touch them or you'll have me to answer to.'

Jane glared at her daughter. 'It was probably you upsetting him as made your father ill in the first place. Ungrateful, that's what you are, ungrateful!'

'How can you say things like that?' demanded Essie. 'He had a growth inside his head and that's what killed him, Dr Latimer told me so himself. And if you ever say anything like that again to this lass, I'll come round and wash your mouth out with soap myself, see if I don't!'

Jane opened her mouth, then shut it again. 'What does it matter?' she asked dully. 'He won't never hit no one again.'

Carrie tugged Essie's arm. 'Leave it now. Please.' She turned to her mother. 'We'll have to lay him out and arrange for him to be buried.'

Jane immediately dissolved into tears again. 'It'll be a pauper's burial. Oh, how can I bear the shame?'

'We've no choice,' Carried said in her usual quiet way. 'Every penny that comes into this house is needed for food, and even then it's not enough. Now, let's lay him out properly. We can do that for him, at least.'

Essie took her arm. 'I'll help your mother do that. You go and tell the doctor. He'll have to sign you a death certificate. Then you can call in at the poorhouse to make the necessary arrangements for the funeral. Take your time, lass. You're not fit to be rushing round, but a bit of fresh air and sunshine will do you good.'

On the way back from the doctor's Carrie called in at her uncle's house. The two families might not have anything to do with one another, but her uncle would surely want to know that his brother had died.

Her aunt opened the door and stood there, arms folded, as if it were a stranger knocking on the door. 'Well?'

'I came to tell you that my father's just died. In

case Uncle Bill wants to attend the funeral, it's the day after tomorrow, at ten o'clock in the morning.'

Sadie scowled. 'Where is it?' She listened, her expression growing even more angry. '*A pauper's burial!* The shame of it. I'll let Bill know, but I doubt he'll want to attend one of those.'

The door closed before Carrie could say another word. Wearily, she turned and made her way back to Throstle Lane, feeling exhausted now. She was supposed to start work at the Dragon the next day and felt more like lying down and sleeping than doing a hard day's work. Still, a job was a job and they'd need every penny they could scrape together from now on, so she'd manage it somehow. She'd send Grace down after school to ask Miss Beckett what time they wanted her to start.

To Carrie's relief, Miss Beckett didn't want her till eight o'clock, so she'd not need to pay the knocker-up to wake her. She left the house the following morning soon after the others had gone to work, following a short, sharp argument with her mother who claimed to be too distraught to look after the twins. Carrie took Grace aside and said, 'You're to go to school, you and Lily. Don't let her keep you here. Say I told you to do it if she makes a fuss.'

Grace nodded.

It was a relief to get out of the house and Carrie took in deep gulps of the fresh early-morning air as she walked the long way down the hill to avoid Crookit Walk, the thought of which still gave her the shivers. It was going to be a lovely sunny autumn day.

At the Dragon she found the big front doors open and stepped inside, pulling a face at the stale smells of tobacco and spilled ale. The other woman who cleaned was there already, bringing out the cloths and buckets. She nodded to Carrie in a friendly way, then raised her voice to call, 'Miss Beckett! She's here.'

Joanna came out of the back room, looked at Carrie and said in her abrupt way, 'I've got a big sacking pinny for you to wear because it's dirty work. Come through.'

Eli was going up and down from the cellar preparing for a delivery of beer from the brewery. He stopped to greet Carrie, and when Joanna had set her to work, went across to his cousin and said, 'She doesn't look fit enough for heavy work.'

'I can't give her all the easy stuff, Eli. It wouldn't be fair to Bonny. But I'll make sure Carrie gets something to eat and a sit-down in the middle of the morning. Bonny too.'

She went out to keep an eye on things, pleased to see how thoroughly her new employee cleaned everything. Once or twice she saw the girl stand back and smile at a table she'd cleaned as if pleased to have got it really shiny again.

In the middle of the morning Joanna called the two women into the back for a cup of tea. Bonny looked surprised, so she said, 'With an extra pair of hands we can spare ten minutes, and I'm thirsty even if you two aren't. I'm hungry too and we have a bit of cake left, so how about we have some of that?'

Bonny beamed. 'Allus ready for a cup of tea, Miss Beckett. An' a piece of cake 'ud be lovely. I like cake, I do.'

Carrie sat with her hands round the warm cup and sipped her tea without saying a word.

As Joanna watched her eat every crumb of the cake, she felt that her guess had been right and the girl was hungry. How did you recover from an attack like that if you didn't even have proper food to eat?

When her father peered into the kitchen, he turned red with anger and opened his mouth to say something. Joanna glared at him so fiercely that in the end he didn't speak, but she knew he'd make up for that later. Well, let him. She was sick of his mean ways.

Eli came to the kitchen door just after her father had gone away. 'Is there another cup in that pot?'

'Of course. And you can take one out to Dad while you're at it. We're going to stop for ten minutes every morning from now on. I get thirsty and hungry by then, if no one else does.'

At the end of the morning Joanna gave her cleaners two shillings each, their morning's wages, and Bonny sat down to wait for someone to collect her.

'Why does someone have to come for her?' Carrie whispered. 'Surely she knows the way home? She seems sensible enough to me, even if she is a bit slow.'

'Folk torment her because they think she's an idiot. It's so cruel, I hate to see it. She's a Heegan, you know, so Bram or someone else always comes to fetch her. Are you all right? You look tired.'

'I'm fine, thank you.' Carrie clutched her coins,

relieved she'd managed to last the morning. Her family would be able to eat properly tonight now. 'I'm sorry, Miss Beckett, but it's my father's funeral tomorrow and . . .'

Joanna gave her a quick smile. 'You won't be able to come in. I know. See you the day after.'

Carrie waited till she was outside, then had to lean against the wall for a minute. She'd got through the work and now she had a little money.

'Are you all right?'

She opened her eyes to see Eli standing there and managed a quick nod. 'Yes, thanks. I was just – a bit tired.'

He watched her walk away slowly and wondered how she'd summoned up the strength to come to work that day. She was a battler, if ever he'd seen one. He admired that.

Joanna joined him at the front door. 'She's a good worker. I thought she would be, somehow.'

'She's exhausted. Couldn't you have waited to start her?'

'No, I couldn't. She desperately needed a job or they'd not have enough to eat, so I gave her one. It's a hard world and she knows that better than most.' She frowned at him, noting the way his eyes were following Carrie. 'You're not interested in her, are you?'

Eli straightened up and turned to go inside. 'I can't afford to be interested in anyone. I've got my way to make in the world.'

But Joanna wasn't convinced. He hadn't denied it,

had he? And there was something about the way he looked at Carrie . . . Well, that was his business. She'd better go and get something on the table. Her father loved his food. He'd no doubt nag her about feeding Carrie and Bonny, but she was less and less willing to do as he wanted. She had her own conscience to answer to as well.

Joanna saw Bram striding along Market Street towards her and found herself returning his smile. It was lovely the way he treated his auntie. In fact, folk could say what they liked about the Heegans. All she knew was they looked after their own, and that was something she admired. Her father only looked after himself.

It was a subdued group who attended Arthur Preston's funeral. Bram had volunteered to carry the coffin to church on his little two-wheeled donkey cart and the poorhouse had provided a crude coffin. Jane was helped up to sit beside Bram, somewhat consoled for the disgrace of a pauper's burial by the fact that her Arthur hadn't been pushed to the churchyard on a handcart. She kept weeping into an old rag at regular intervals and turning to look at the coffin.

The eight older children walked behind the cart and the twins were left behind in the care of Mrs Baxter next door.

When they got to the church, they found Bill Preston standing there with a black ribbon tied round his sleeve.

Jane began to weep loudly at the sight of him and

cry, 'Bill, he's gone! Oh, Bill, what am I going to do without him?'

He helped her off the cart and offered her his arm, looking round at the group of nephews and nieces and thinking what a thin, ragged bunch they were. 'Sadie sends her best, but she's not well today.'

'Kind of her,' said Jane.

He nodded. It was a lie. Sadie had told him he was a fool to take time off work today, but Bill remembered Arthur as the big brother who'd protected him from other lads' bullying and he wanted to be here to say a final farewell. He looked at the oldest daughter and thought what a strong face she had, then looked back at Jane and thought, as he'd thought when Arthur married her, what a weak creature she was. His Sadie might be sharp-tongued but she was a hard worker and together they'd made a better life for themselves and their four children. For most of their life together Jane had been a burden on Arthur, with her feckless ways.

Carrie followed her uncle and mother. *Kind* was the last thing you'd call her aunt Sadie. The kindness lay in her Uncle Bill pretending his wife had sent them her regards. It was strange, really. His face was very like her father's when you studied it, and yet it gave such a different impression, that of a man in charge of his life, a man who walked upright instead of slouching. Well, she'd seen her uncle's house, one of the new ones on the other side of town. She'd heard those houses had three bedrooms and their own water tap in the scullery, with water piped in from the new reservoir the Council had had built a couple of years ago. Just imagine that, having enough water in the house at the turn of a tap! It was the same at the Dragon. Miss Beckett said Carrie could go and fetch a bucket any time they ran out, which would make her life a little easier.

They went inside the church, which felt dusty and echoing. Carrie never went to church. She was usually too busy at home, and anyway was ashamed of her ragged clothes.

The curate held a very brief service and they all bowed their heads when he did, after which he nodded for the coffin to be carried outside and Jane began sobbing again.

At the sight of the big hole at the far end of the churchyard, where paupers' coffins were laid one on top of another, she cried hysterically, 'We shan't even have a proper grave to visit. Oh, the shame of it! The shame.'

Robbie tried to put his arm round her and she shook it off, shouting accusingly, 'You should ha' found the money for a proper grave. You could ha' borrowed it.'

'You know we couldn't afford to take on any debts, Mam,' Carrie said sharply. 'We'll be hard put to manage as it is.'

Jane rounded on her. 'You don't even care that he's dead, an' it's *your* fault he died! You made him angry. That's what did it, made him have a seizure . . . *you!*'

Marjorie saw Carrie's face turn white and stepped forward. 'That's not fair, Mam. And it's not true, either.'

'What do you mean?' Bill asked in bewilderment. 'How can it be Carrie's fault?'

'She made him angry, didn't give him any respect.'

Robbie took hold of her arm and shook her hard. 'Stop that, Mam. It isn't Carrie's fault. He was stealing her clothes.'

Bill turned to Marjorie, who was standing next to him, and she whispered a quick explanation. He looked at her in shock, then turned in pity to his eldest niece whose pallor was emphasised by the big purple bruise at her temple.

As Jane showed no signs of stopping weeping, the curate raised his voice. 'Will you *please* be quiet, Mrs Preston, and let me finish this funeral service?'

Jane fell silent, but her mouth was set in a stubborn line and as she threw a handful of dirt into the huge hole she cast an angry glance sideways at Carrie.

After the brief ceremony was over, Robbie took his mother away, pulling her forcibly when she moaned that she wanted to join her husband in the grave. As he hoisted her up on the cart again, she went on weeping. Bram rolled his eyes and told his donkey to walk on.

'You go with her,' Carrie whispered to her brother so he ran after the little cart. She and Marjorie waited to thank the curate and say goodbye to their uncle.

Bill pressed a coin into Carrie's hand. 'To help out,' he whispered.

She hated to take it, but they needed every penny they could get so she said, 'Thank you very much!' and forced a smile.

She turned to find the children and take them home.

'Can we go an' play out now?' Ted asked at once. 'It's too late to go to school.'

'Why not?' Carrie said dully. The funeral had been bad enough, but what had upset her most was her mother's unfair accusation that she had caused her father's death. Why did she keep saying that?

'Mam didn't mean it,' Marjorie said in her soft voice.

'She did, even though it isn't true.'

Dora came to put her arm round her eldest sister and give her a quick hug. 'Why don't you walk home along the river? Get a bit of sun on your face.'

Carrie nodded. 'Yes, I'd like that. We don't have to go straight home, do we?'

'Me an' Marjorie can't come with you. The over-looker said we was to get back to work as soon as the funeral was over. I'm that sorry, our Carrie, but he's a mean sod an' we don't want to lose our jobs.'

'An' Mrs Debbin said I was to get back to the shop as quick as I could, too,' Edith said. 'Sorry.'

Carrie hesitated, then took Dora's advice and headed for the river path. She walked slowly, glad of the warmth of the sun, dreading going home. Eh, she had to pull herself together. The family needed to make plans if they were not to end up in the work-house. And would Mr Stott let them stay in the house now that their father was dead? She hadn't said anything to the others, but she was worried about that. They'd been given the house because her father worked at Stott's. They might have to find somewhere else to live now and that wasn't easy in a town that was growing as fast as Hedderby. They were building some new rows of houses on the other side of the mill, but they were for men who worked there so her family would have no chance of one of those.

When she got to Throstle Lane Carrie hesitated, not wanting to go home, but what choice did she have? Straightening her shoulders, she walked quickly to the end of the street. Inside the house she found her mother on her own, sitting slumped in a chair by the fire.

'Robbie's gone back to work. No one cares that Arthur's dead but me,' she announced in a die-away voice.

'Where are the twins?'

Jane shrugged. 'Next door.'

'Didn't you even bring them back?'

'No, I didn't. A poor widow woman needs time to grieve.'

Tight-lipped, Carrie went next door and thanked Mrs Baxter for looking after the babies.

'They've been as good as gold, but they're getting a bit hungry now, poor mites.' She looked at her visitor's tense face. 'Taking it badly, is she?'

Carrie nodded.

'Allus did need a man to lean on, Jane. She'll find another one quick enough, you mark my words.'

Carrie stared at her in shock.

'And if she does, don't you try to stop her. You shouldn't let her put on you so much, lass. You've your own life to lead an' these babies aren't your responsibility. Oh, just one thing: everyone in the street's put a shovelful of coal in your back place. That'll see you through till wage day.'

'You're all very kind, more kind than she deserves.'

Mrs Baxter didn't mince her words. 'We did it mainly for you, lass, you an' the little 'uns. Is your head better now?'

'Getting better. Still a bit sore.'

'Is it true your father did it?'

'I don't want to talk about that.'

Mrs Baxter nodded and made a soothing sound, putting an arm round Carrie's shoulders and giving her a quick hug. 'You come round to me if you need any help. We've none of us got much, but if we can't help one another it's a poor look-out, it is that.'

Which warmed Carrie's heart and made her feel better able to cope with her mother's moaning and refusal to lift a finger in the house.

When she got back, she found Jane spooning tea generously into the pot. Carrie dumped the twins quickly on the rug and went to pick up the pot and the precious little twist of paper before her mother could carry the kettle across. 'What are you *doing*?'

'Making a cup of tea.'

'All those tea leaves, just for the two of us?'

'It's there for using, isn't it? Besides, I like it strong.'

'That tea was a present from Essie and we need to make it spin out.'

'Are you defying me, telling me what to do in my own home? First you drive your father to his death, then you defy your own mother! What sort of unnatural child are you?' Jane swung round and flung herself in the rocking chair that had been her husband's favourite seat, sobbing loudly.

Carrie took a deep breath before she spoke, 'So unnatural that if you go on at me like this, I'll leave home.'

Her mother fell silent, mouth open in shock.

Carrie decided it was more than time to make a stand. 'I'm not putting up with you saying such unkind and untrue things. I've a job now and I can manage on my own just fine. Miss Beckett said I could live in if I wanted to, so I've even got somewhere to go. See how you like that with two babies to look after, an' the rest of the family expecting meals to be on the table every day when they get back, not to mention all the washing and fetching water! You can't even make the money last out till Monday, so without me you'll all starve for half the week.'

Jane glared at her. 'You'd do it, too, leave a poor grieving widow on her own.'

'Only if you drive me to it.'

'It's your *duty* to stay.'

'Then mind what you say to me.'

Luckily one of the babies began to cry just then and Jane had to feed it. Carrie went to find her father's boots and took them round to the pawn shop to get some money while she could. Her mother had wanted him buried in them and they'd had a fight over that, too. Carrie knew if she didn't take them to be pawned, her mother would, and then all the money would be wasted on a single lavish meal.

★

Bram went to the lodging house and rapped on the front door. Some imp of mischief made him want to torment Nev Linney, though he'd rather taken to the old fellow and would be genuinely glad to know that he was all right.

There was no answer, so he knocked again.

'Not open till six!' someone called out.

'It's me, Bram Heegan! Come to see how you are, Raife.'

The door opened a crack and the old man peered out, then pulled the chain off and opened the door fully. 'Nev says not to let anyone in.'

'He would.' Bram walked inside anyway. 'How are you? Has your son offered you a home?'

'Aye. As long as I make myself useful.' The old man smiled. 'I can do that all right. And he's got a piano so I even get to play of an evening.'

'He has a piano?'

He nodded vigorously.

'And you can play it?'

'Aye. I can't read music, can't read words neither. But if I hear a tune I can play it, and properly, mind. There are better pianists nor me, but I don't play badly and I don't make wrong notes.' He tapped the side of his forehead. 'It'd hurt me here to make a wrong note.'

'I like to hear a piano played.'

'Aye. They're lovely instruments when they're treated proper. That one needs tuning, though.'

'Why don't you play it for me? Go on, give us a tune.'

Raife glanced up at the kitchen clock. 'All right. Just for a few minutes. I'm in need of a sit-down anyway.' He led the way into the parlour, opened the lid of the piano and sat down, his expression gentle and happy.

To Bram's astonishment the old man played really well and he listened with great pleasure. When Raife started playing a tune he knew, Bram couldn't resist singing.

'Eh, you've a nice voice there, lad.'

'I love singing.' He turned to see Nev leaning against the door frame, smiling. 'Your father's a good piano player.'

'Aye, he is. And you're a good singer.' He hesitated then said, 'You could come round one evening and have a sing-song, if you liked. There's nothing I like better than a sing-song.'

Bram hid his astonishment at this unexpected side of Nev Linney. 'I'll do that one day. I'd better go now, though.' He walked off, whistling. Who'd have thought Nev Linney loved music? But then, with a father who could play like that, maybe it was born in him.

It just showed you should never judge what someone was like till you knew more about them. He remembered the expression on Nev's face as he'd suggested Bram should come round again and realised suddenly that he had been nervous of making the offer, as if he half expected him to refuse.

Well, he would definitely go round. The Linneys weren't the only ones who loved music. When Bram got out on the moors he often sang, not having to keep his voice quiet for fear of disturbing others. He enjoyed his buying trips.

Athol Stott heard of Arthur Preston's death and pauper's burial and nodded in satisfaction. 'Good. I was going to dismiss him and turn them out of that house anyway because I reckon I can use that area for outdoor storage.'

Edmund frowned at him. 'You're going to turn the Preston family out? There are ten children, man!'

His cousin shrugged. 'That's their lookout. They're no concern of mine now.'

'The son still works here.'

'And he's another lazy sod. I've got my eye on him.'

'Robbie's not lazy. He's an excellent worker. I've been training him to work with me on the machinery.'

'Him? Are you mad? Anyway, our houses are for married men, not single ones.'

'You'll find the family another house, surely?'

'Why should I? The father doesn't work for me any more. I'm not running a charity here, you know.' He frowned, doodling on a piece of paper. 'It'll take me a week or two to sort things out, another month or two to build a storehouse. I'll let them stay till then. Which is more than fair of me. As long as they pay the rent on time, that is.'

Edmund gave a snort of indignation and marched out of the works office before he said something he'd regret. He wasn't ready yet for a confrontation with his cousin but it was brewing. Things couldn't go on like this.

And anyway, he had to repair some of the machinery driven by the wheezing old steam engine. Everything in the works was elderly and he had the devil's job to keep things running. The trouble was, his cousin refused to admit how bad things were.

Edmund wasn't staying for ever, was making plans for setting up on his own in a small way, doing repairs and making smaller pieces of equipment. That'd bring in enough money for him to live on, together with the small bequest he'd received from his uncle. He wasn't greedy like Athol, had no desire to ape the gentry.

That evening he went to visit his mistress, but he couldn't get the Prestons out of his mind. Imagine losing the breadwinner with ten children to feed. No, not ten. The older ones were working. But still, a father's death was a big loss to any family.

His own father's death had upset him, but not as much as his mother's had when he was twelve. Edmund had been all adrift for a while after she'd died and they'd brought him to live with his uncle, whom he'd grown to love. Athol had bullied him, though. He should have known he'd not get on with his cousin and left after his uncle's death. He definitely wasn't staying much longer, needed to build his own life.

# 8

Eli and Joanna waited to speak to Frank till he had finished his midday meal on Sunday. They weren't allowed to open the pub till after the morning church services were over, so this was as close as they got to a day off.

'About the music room . . .' Eli caught Joanna's eye and with difficulty kept his face straight while he waited for his uncle to stop spluttering and choking, a predictable reaction. 'You didn't think I'd forgotten about it, did you?'

Frank scowled at him. 'I hoped you'd come to your senses, yes. I'm not made of money an' there's no *need* for a fancy music room here. I've already said we can have free and easy nights, with singing in the back of the big room, so what more do you want?'

'A proper music room,' Eli said yet again.

'I think Eli's got the right idea,' Joanna said. 'I'd like a proper music room, too. And what's more, if you don't let us do it, Dad, I'm leaving here with him. I'm fed up of the way things are here. We can do better for ourselves than run a common pub where drunkards vomit under the tables.'

Frank darted quick glances from one to the other and

his scowl deepened. 'I never thought you'd side with him against me,' he said reproachfully to his daughter.

'I'm siding with myself.'

'I've spoken to Jem Harding about the old stables,' Eli said as his uncle opened his mouth. 'He's happy to clear the place out, make things good where they're damaged and rebuild the inside.' He grinned at the look of frozen shock which had replaced the scowl on his uncle's face.

'*Talked to a builder?*' Frank asked faintly.

'Yes, and he's coming tomorrow to find out exactly what we want doing.'

'You'll be the death of me. I'm getting palpitations just thinking of all the money that lot's going to cost.' He patted his chest and moaned.

'Then don't think about it,' Joanna said. 'Think of all the extra money it's going to make for us instead.'

There was silence, then Frank drew in a deep, shuddering breath. 'You give me no choice, but you two will have to do it. I can't spare the time. I shall want to know what each job is going to cost before you agree to it, though, large or small. I insist on approving everything.'

'No,' Eli said flatly. 'There won't be time. I've found out who the best builder is and—'

Joanna interrupted. 'If we leave it to you, you'll penny-pinch, Dad, I know you will. We're not having shoddy workmanship. We want to attract the better sort of people here, families and tradesmen, those with money to spend. And we can, because there's nowhere else for them to go in Hedderby.'

Frank moaned and clutched his chest again. 'To think of my own daughter going against me!'

'Working *for* you, rather. Don't worry. I'll keep an eye on costs.' Joanna patted his arm. 'Just as I'll be helping to run it for you.'

'Then who'll run the pub?'

'You'll be in charge there, as you are now, and we'll find someone to work for you when the time comes,' Eli said impatiently. 'Me and Joanna will still be able to do a fair amount. Now, I want to check that the new barrel of beer has settled all right. Shall I draw you a pint, Uncle Frank?'

'Aye, you'd better. I s'll need to keep my strength up.'

'Get on with you. You'll outlive us all.' Eli walked off whistling.

When Frank turned back to his daughter she was staring at him, arms folded, eyes challenging. 'This isn't just Eli who wants it, Dad. It's me, too. I *really* want a music room. Now, before we can start the free and easy nights, we have to move the piano into the pub and find someone to play it for us.'

Frank moaned and buried his head in his hands.

When Carrie arrived at work a couple of days later it was to find a man coming out of the left-hand side of the Dragon with a wheelbarrow full of rubble, which he tipped on to a pile in the street. That part of the pub wasn't normally used and the rickety wooden gates that had let in horse-drawn coaches were kept locked, but now they'd been removed from their hinges and the whole area stood wide open. Even the small side gate next to them had been removed. She wondered what was going on as she pushed open the main door.

She was getting used to her new job now and didn't need telling what to do. It was worse than working in the laundry in some ways, better in others, because at least the air wasn't full of steam even if it did smell of stale beer and tobacco. She was there before Bonny, for once, so tied on her big apron and began to get out the cleaning things.

Joanna came into the public room just as Carrie was starting work, and nodded approval. 'Good. I can't abide it when people wait around to be told what to do all the time. Where's Bonny?'

'She's not here yet. Miss Beckett, can I ask what's happening next door?'

'We're making the old stables into a music room. It's Eli's idea, and a good one, I think.'

Carrie hesitated, then asked it, even though it might make her look stupid: 'What do you mean, a music room? I thought we were going to have the music in here.' She jerked her head in the direction of the piano, which had been brought in the day before.

'They're starting music rooms all over the place now. There'll be a stage, with singing and dancing and acrobats, all sorts of entertainers. It'll be a place decent folk can come and enjoy themselves, women as well as men. Eli and I went to see one in Manchester.'

Carrie was amazed at the way Miss Beckett's face

softened as she talked about the new music room. 'It sounds lovely.'

'It will be. And I'm going to make sure it stays lovely.' Joanna's face took on a determined look. 'There'll be no spitting or smoking in there.'

'Eh, you'll never stop men spitting and smoking!'

'Oh, yes, I will! And their wives will help me, I'm sure. Women have nowhere to go in this town, except for the few older ones who come and drink in my snug. People look down their noses at them, but I don't see why men should have all the fun.'

Carrie had never thought about that before. 'Won't the women have children to look after?'

'Not all of them. If their children are older, they can come too, or the bigger ones can stay at home and look after the little ones.'

Imagine being able to sit and enjoy yourself watching such things, Carrie thought.

The door opened and Bram came in with his aunt, whose moon face was all smiles. Joanna became brisk again. 'Oh, good! I'm glad you're here, Bonny. We'd better get started.'

As his aunt went to get ready Bram looked at Joanna. 'So, have you found anyone to play the piano for your free and easies?'

'No. We've been asking around, but we haven't found anyone yet.'

'Nev Linney's father can play the piano really well. He knows all the old songs and some of the new ones as well.'

'Are you sure?'

'Yes, I've heard him myself.'

'Do you think he'd come and work for us? Would Nev mind?'

Bram smiled at her. 'I'm sure Raife would come if you paid him, and Nev always likes the thought of earning money. He's a nice old chap, Raife. I'm sure you'll like him.'

'I'll go and see him later, then.'

'I can take you if you want, and introduce you.'

She felt flustered all of a sudden, but tried not to show how Bram affected her. 'Right. Thanks. When you take Bonny home, perhaps?'

'My pleasure.'

Their glances caught for a minute and, though neither said anything, each was very conscious of the other. Then Bram took a deep breath and stepped backwards. 'All right if I go and have a look round the side?'

'Yes.'

Which made Carrie decide that she'd go and have a look, too, after work. Though she'd ask Miss Beckett first because she didn't want to upset anyone. It was exciting to think of having a music room. Maybe she would get a chance to go there one day, if she and her family could get their lives in order.

Before she went home she asked permission to peep into the side part where the workmen were knocking down the wooden stalls. Eli appeared from round the corner and Carrie took a quick step backwards. 'I just wanted to see what was happening here. Miss Beckett said it'd be all right.'

'Come and have a proper look.'

He had taken her arm before she knew it and was guiding her along one side to the far end. She was surprised to see how much space there was. 'I didn't realise it was so big out here.'

'No, a lot of people don't.'

Eli began pointing and explaining and she suddenly realised how excited he was, that he wanted to tell someone about it. And as he talked she could see it all come to life. She'd always been good at picturing things.

'Will it cost a lot to come here?' she asked. Not that she ever had any money to spare.

'When it opens I'll let you in free. After all, you work here now, don't you?'

Carrie stared at him. 'Really?'

'Really.'

She beamed at him. 'That'll be something to look forward to.'

He kicked at a piece of crumbling wood, trying to take his mind off her face, glowing with excitement, looking so pretty and alive. 'We're reusing the good bits of wood, but I'll have to pay someone to take these away.

Carrie stared at the pile of assorted pieces. 'Could I have some? We could use it instead of coal.'

'Aye, why not? We've a hand barrow you can borrow. Get your brother to come along and help you carry it away. He's a big fellow.'

As Carrie looked at the wood an idea blossomed. 'Are you going to get rid of all this?'

'Why?'

'Well, we could take it away for you, bit by bit, if you don't need that space straight away. We could sell it to people, you see, make a bit of extra money.'

Eli stole a quick glance sideways at her flushed face. 'Sounds like a good idea to me. You'll save me the cost of having it carted away, so you can have it free. But you'll have to get rid of it fairly quickly. I'll find some place to store it till then.'

She smiled all the way home. They could sell the wood for at least sixpence a barrow load. Folk would pay that quite happily, she was sure. And they could use the money they made to pay off everything that was still at the pawn shop, and then perhaps buy Mam and the children some better clothes.

The two shillings she had earned that morning sat in her pocket, bumping comfortingly against her leg as she walked. She felt guilty at even thinking it, but life without her father was a lot easier and the house already seemed a pleasanter place.

Carrie's smile faded the minute she walked into the kitchen at home. The table there was piled with food and her mother had clearly been drinking a cup of tea with Mrs Baxter from next door. She was now putting fresh tea leaves into the pot, spooning them in liberally, and when she saw her daughter watching her, she deliberately put in another heaped spoonful.

'Where did all this come from?' Carrie asked in shock.

'Mr Edmund Stott brought round some money.

They'd had a collection at the works for your father. So we can eat well this week.'

Carrie could feel the muscles in her face tightening. 'I need to speak to Mam privately, Mrs Baxter.' She took the teapot out of her mother's hands before she could tip boiling water into it, but waited till the neighbour had left before asking, 'What are you *doing*, using all this tea at once?'

'Making a fresh pot.'

'I thought we decided last time to use the tea leaves twice at least?'

'Why should I when there's plenty of new ones?'

Carrie set the teapot down and pushed her mother down into her father's old chair. 'How much money did Mr Stott bring you?'

A cunning look came into Jane's face. 'A pound or two.'

'Give me what's left.'

'No! They brought it for me, because I'm his widow. You're not having it.'

Anger overflowed in Carrie at the thought of this much-needed money being wasted because her mother couldn't bear to keep coins in her pocket for more than a day or two, always finding something to buy, whether she needed it or not. She felt in her mother's skirt pocket, feeling the lumpiness of coins there, but had to fight to get them out. Her mother began to scream and shout at her.

Mrs Grant from two doors away came running in through the back door, calling, 'Whatever's the matter? I can hear you from my kitchen.'

Without letting go of her mother Carrie turned to her and shouted, 'Get out! This is between Mam and me.'

'But—'

'*Get out, I said!*'

Carrie made sure her mother had no coins left then turned to look at the table. She could have wept to see so much food, far more than they needed.

'You're a thief, you are!' Jane shouted, pounding her daughter's back with both hands. 'And you called your father a thief! Why, you're worse than him, because you're robbing a poor widow woman.'

'We don't need all that food today. You should have kept some of the money back.'

'I'm not a miserable skinflint like you. I like to make folk happy. An' when Robbie comes home, he'll *force* you give me that money back. You see if he doesn't.'

Carrie stared at her, not sure her mother was right but knowing Robbie and the others would always be happy to eat more. And of course he'd like to keep the extra money from his wages instead of giving it to her for food. If Carrie let her mother handle the house-keeping money, they'd be back to the old feasting on wage day and going short the rest of the week. She had to find a way to keep their money safe. There were several pounds left still from the collection at Stott's.

'I'm going out,' she said abruptly.

Her mother rushed to bar the way. 'Give me my money back first!'

Carrie shook her head. 'No, Mam. I'm going to keep it somewhere safe.'

'Robbie won't let you do this.'

'I think he will. It's a chance to better ourselves, can't you see that? Remember what I said: either we live carefully from now on or I'm leaving home.'

'You can leave for all I care, but you're not taking my money with you.'

The two women looked at one another, then Carrie shoved her mother to one side and walked out, hearing one of the babies start to cry as she left. She knew her mother meant what she said at the moment, though it'd be a different story when she wanted help with the babies.

Outside the house she found a knot of women standing gossiping. They fell silent as she closed the front door, turning to stare at her.

'Eh, Carrie, you shouldn't treat your mother like that,' Mrs Grant said reproachfully.

'Should let her waste the money, do you mean?' Carrie snapped. 'Well, there are seven days in a week, and I mean to make sure there's food on the table every one of those seven days from now on. And if I get back and find any of you has been in our house eating that food or drinking tea with her, there'll be trouble.' She set her hands on her hips and glared round at them.

One or two of them took a step backwards at the sight of her fierce expression. Only Mrs Grant stood her ground. 'You're a hard lass, you are. No sympathy for a woman who's lost her husband. All you care about is money.'

'All I care about is making sure my brothers and

sisters are fed every single day. Is there summat wrong with that?'

As she walked away she heard an argument break out about the rights and wrongs of what she'd done; some, like Mrs Baxter, agreeing with her, the more feckless ones disagreeing. She didn't turn to answer those criticising her. As she walked, the money she'd tied up in the corner of her shawl banged against her hip, several pounds, riches to a family like theirs. She had to put it somewhere safe and keep it there, then make sure her brothers and sisters gave her their wages each week, not their mother.

If she didn't manage things, no one else in her family would, she knew that, but she hated always being the ogre.

At the doctor's house Essie opened the door and smiled to see her. 'Come in, lass.'

Carrie did but refused a cup of tea, explaining her dilemma. 'Can I leave the money with you, Essie, please? If *she* has it, she'll waste it all. I'll just take enough to get the rest of our stuff out of pawn.'

'Aye, of course you can leave it here. I'll get a special pot for you and put it on the mantelpiece – and I'll make sure Mrs Latimer knows what it's for.'

She watched the girl walk away and shook her head. It was going to be hard for Carrie. She seemed to be the only one in the family with any sense about money.

The mother was a fool, an absolute fool. She didn't deserve a daughter like that. Tears came into Essie's eyes. What she wouldn't have given for a child of her own! Too late now, of course, but still the longing hurt sometimes. She had no one left in the world, was the last of her family. And if anything happened to Dr Latimer, who was older than she was, she'd probably be too old to find herself another job. It was a chancy world. You never knew what was around the corner.

Bram accompanied Joanna to Linney's. He knocked on the front door and when Nev opened it, explained why they'd come.

'You'd pay my dad just to play the piano?' Nev asked, clearly finding this hard to believe.

'I'll need to hear him play first,' Joanna said.

'Come in, come in!' He showed them into the parlour and told them to be seated then rushed away to find his father.

Raife came in, smiling to see Bram and greeting Joanna with the open friendliness that always radiated from him.

'Could you play for us, please?' Bram asked. 'It's only fair to show Miss Beckett what you can do.'

'It's allus a pleasure to play,' the old man said, sitting down and opening the piano lid. He rubbed his hands together to warm them up, wiggled his fingers about in the air, then started playing.

Soon Bonny was swaying to and fro in time to the music and Joanna was smiling in pleasure. When Bram began singing one of the tunes and gestured to her, she joined in. She felt shy at first, then forgot her audience in the sheer pleasure of singing.

Afterwards it was a minute before she could speak,

because the music was still rippling through her, as it always did.

'You're good enough to go on the stage, lass,' Raife said, smiling at her.

She stared at him in surprise then shuddered. 'I couldn't do that. I'd be terrified to sing in front of a hall full of people.' She changed the subject quickly. 'What'd it be fair to pay you, Raife? I've never employed a pianist before.'

'Well, they used to give me ten bob for an evening at the first place I played at. I was living with our Paul then. But he moved to another village and they didn't want me playing at the pub there. Eh, I missed it. I like making folk happy.'

'Ten shillings it is then, for Saturday evenings. Perhaps you'd better come down and check the piano. I think it needs tuning, though Dad says it doesn't.' She hesitated, then added, 'You'd better see me about anything you need. Dad's not keen on the music, so he's being a bit – difficult. But I can manage him.'

When she'd gone Nev stared at his father in surprise. 'I never knew you'd played in a pub.'

'You don't know much about me, never have done, because your mother kept us apart as much as she could, even when I were still living with her. You were her favourite an' she didn't want to share you with anyone.'

Nev stared at the floor, not saying anything. On the one hand he'd loved his mother and didn't want to blacken her name now she was dead. On the other, he'd long suspected that she'd deliberately driven his father and Paul away, been glad to see the back of them. He hadn't been glad. He'd missed his brother and father. She'd also insisted they were lazy, but he'd seen for himself recently that his father wasn't in the least lazy. Why, Raife would turn his hand to anything that needed doing, whether it was women's work or not, and Nev respected that.

He looked up and grimaced. 'Yes, you're probably right. We didn't associate much with other folk, either. She said we had each other and that was enough.'

Raife held back stronger words about his wife and her behaviour. Water under the bridge now, all that. You couldn't change the past. 'Well, you've got me for good if you'll have me, lad, but it'd be nice for us to make a few other friends too.'

Nev was silent a moment then muttered, 'Folk don't like me.'

'Do you give them a chance to?'

Another shrug and Nev walked out into the kitchen.

Raife went back to the piano, played a few chords, then closed the lid gently. He was looking forward to playing in the pub, to meeting people, and he'd insist that Nev come too. It'd do the lad good to get out and about. Lad! He smiled. Nev was forty-six. Hardly a lad any more. Good with money, a lot to learn about people, though. Maybe he could help his son there. He could try, anyway.

Eli spent a lot of time in the old stables, even when there was no need for him to be there. He resented every minute he had to spend in the pub but knew better than to skimp on his work there or his uncle would become even angrier.

As the old divisions between stalls came down, they saved the good pieces of wood for reuse and made a pile of the fragments for Carrie.

When Joanna asked what the pile was for, he explained.

'She's got her head screwed on right, that one has,' Joanna said. 'And she's a hard worker. Bonny likes her, too.'

They stood side by side for a moment longer then each went off to carry on working. There was always something to be done in a busy pub like the Dragon, and Frank was contributing less and less these days.

As Carrie had expected, when Robbie came home he took their mother's side and said it'd be nice to spend the money on food. Ted snatched a piece of bread before she could stop him and she clouted him round the ears for that. Before they ate, she made everyone listen carefully as she told them about how they could use the money to make a better life for themselves if they spent it carefully.

'We'll have a special meal tonight so as not to waste this good food, and from now on, if you let me manage the money, we'll eat better than we have been doing. But I'll tell you straight, I'm not staying here if we're going back to the old ways of wasting stuff.' Carrie folded her arms.

Marjorie said hesitantly, 'But shouldn't it be down to Mam to say that?'

Jane smirked at her eldest daughter. ''Course it should. I'm the head of the house now your father's dead.'

'Then act like it!' Carrie yelled. 'Do some planning, make the money spin out, clean this place up! You leave everything to me and I'm sick of it!'

There was dead silence, with the younger children keeping very quiet and staring down at their plates.

'I would if I had the strength,' Jane said, forcing out a sob that convinced no one she was in tears.

'I'll leave tomorrow, then,' Carrie said, arms, still folded keeping her expression calm. 'I can live in at the Dragon. Miss Beckett has already offered.'

Lily hurled herself round the table and clung to her. 'No, don't go, our Carrie! Don't go!'

Grace followed her, both children sobbing and holding on to her. She put her arms round them, knowing she was far more of a mother to them than Jane was.

Dora and Edith looked at one another then Edith, who often spoke for the pair of them, said, 'I think our Carrie's right. I don't want my money wasting.'

'Me, neither,' Dora said.

Robbie said, 'There's no need to be mean, surely? We could all keep more of our wages for a week or two if we use what Stott's collected for Mam for our food.'

'You just want to spend it on drink like Dad did.' Carrie could hear how sharp her own voice was, hated the way she always had to fight to make them be sensible.

To her surprise it was Ted who asked, 'If you do

look after the money, Carrie, do you mean we'd have more to eat all the time?'

'Yes. I know I could manage it better than we have done before.'

He looked at his mother then back at his sister. 'I'm allus hungry an' I'm sick of it.'

Carrie watched Robbie, still frowning, and said in a loud voice, 'If you don't let me manage things, I'm definitely leaving. I'm not having people pawning my new clothes again. And I don't see why I should go hungry when I work so hard. I never stop when I get home from the Dragon. Mam doesn't do any of the shopping, and she doesn't do much of the cleaning either.'

Dead silence followed her words.

Jane glared at her, but didn't speak.

'Oh, dear,' Marjorie said, in her soft, breathless voice. 'I don't want you to go, either, Carrie love. I can't think what we'd do without you. Mam, wouldn't it be easier for you if you didn't have to worry about money?'

'It's not right if a woman isn't mistress in her own house! You should all give your wages to me now your father's dead.'

As Carrie opened her mouth to protest, Marjorie rushed in again. 'Yes, but you've got the twins to look after. You wait till they're walking, you'll be run off your feet. You can't do everything, no one can.'

After several minutes' arguing, it was agreed that they'd try things Carrie's way for a month. Robbie moved then as if to leave.

Carrie caught hold of his sleeve. 'Just a minute. There's something else.'

'What now? You've got your own way. What more do you want from us?'

She felt tears rise in her eyes at this and gave him a reproachful look, then pulled herself together. 'I've found a chance for us to earn some extra money.'

They fell silent again.

'How?' her brother asked. 'I'm tired enough when I get home. I don't want to work longer hours.'

'This is just for a short time. Couldn't you even manage half an hour after work?' She explained about the wood and how they could have it free to sell if they'd only take it away from the Dragon.

'For a few pence extra!' Robbie pulled a face. 'A man needs his rest after a hard day's work.'

'I suppose you think I sit around drinking tea all day! I suppose you think women don't work hard as well.' She held out her hands, reddened and chapped from scrubbing. 'How do you think I got these?'

His expression turned sulky. 'It's different for men.'

'No, it isn't! We all work hard, so we should all have a rest. But if you don't help us, you don't get any of the benefits. I want to use the money to buy everyone new clothes. You can buy your own.'

Again it was Ted who surprised her. 'I can help you and go out selling, too. But if I do that, our Carrie, can I keep some of the money for myself, just a little bit?'

She looked at him and he stared back at her, solemn-faced. She realised suddenly that he'd grown taller recently, but like her he was too thin, far too thin. No wonder he was always so hungry. 'Yes, you can. We'll get the wood free an' I reckon we can sell it for sixpence a barrow load. If you go out selling, you can keep a penny for every load you sell. The rest of the money you get goes into the family pot for clothes, though.'

'If there are any good pieces of wood, we could get hold of some wheels,' Ted said, 'then I could ask my friend's dad to help me make a box to push the twins out in. He made one for Sammy's little sister. Then Mam wouldn't have to stay at home all the time.'

'I'm too weak to go out walking. I need all my strength just to cope,' Jane said at once in a die-away voice.

'Oh, but Mam, you'd be able to look in the shop windows if you had the twins safe in a push cart,' Dora said with a quick wink at the others. 'You know you like doing that.'

'Well, I dare say if I walk slowly and don't try to do too much, I could manage to get into town some-times,' Jane allowed. 'If I had a little push cart, that is.'

'If there aren't any pieces of wood that are good enough,' Carrie promised rashly, 'I'll ask Mr Beckett if I can buy a few. I didn't realise you knew how to make things out of wood, Ted.'

He wriggled uncomfortably. 'Sammy's dad is showing me. I really like doing it. I like the smell of wood and how the grain runs. It's pretty sometimes.'

Carrie looked across at her mother. 'I'm hoping we

can make enough money to buy everyone new clothes. We'll need some warmer things for winter. You'd like a new dress, wouldn't you, Mam? And the babies will soon need new clothes, too. I never saw babies grow so fast as our May and Nora.' She smiled at her two tiny sisters, fast asleep on the rag rug. You couldn't look after them without growing fond of them, they were such happy little souls, always laughing and gurgling, crying only when they were hungry.

'I've no one to see me looking nice now,' Jane said, and wiped her eyes ostentatiously. Then she smoothed the skirt over her knees, studying it as if she'd never seen it before. However, the dirty look she gave Carrie when she raised her eyes again said she hadn't forgotten or forgiven her daughter for taking control of the money away from her.

The air was stiff with resentment between them for a minute or two then Marjorie, always the peace-maker, looked at Carrie and asked, 'Shall we really be able to earn enough to buy new clothes?'

'Yes. Well, not brand new, but decent things from Bram's father's shop perhaps.'

'I'd like that.' Marjorie looked down at her own faded clothes.

The other girls nodded. It hurt Carrie sometimes to see how ragged and worn their things all were. 'Two sets of clothes each if we get enough wood,' she promised rashly. 'Then we'll be able to keep ourselves cleaner.'

'It's not good to wash yourself too often,' Jane said at once. 'It takes the oil out of your skin.'

'Well, I like to be clean because dirty folk smell sour.' Carrie bit off any further reproaches. 'That's enough talking. Let's get on with our meal.' Going over to the table, she quickly removed one of the four-pound loaves and the cheese, setting them on the mantelshelf. 'We'll save some for breakfast and for taking to work tomorrow.'

This earned her another glare from Jane and Carrie knew that though she'd won a victory about the money, she'd upset both her mother and Robbie. Well, was it any wonder? He was just at the age when a young man wanted his independence, not a sister telling him what to do. But she didn't intend to stay dirt poor when they could manage a more decent way of life. The food tasted like sawdust in her mouth and she only forced it down because you had to eat to keep up your strength.

When they got to bed, Marjorie whispered, 'Mam will come round in a day or two.'

On the other side of her, Dora snuggled down and said sleepily, 'I don't think she will. She doesn't like being careful. And she misses Dad a lot. She allus cared more about him than about us.'

Carrie sighed. 'Go to sleep. I'll get up if the twins wake.'

'No, I will,' said Marjorie. 'You do too much. You get a good night's sleep for a change. And Carrie –'

'Yes?'

'– I think you're right. It'll be lovely to have better clothes an' keep ourselves cleaner.'

# 9

When Nev had turned all the lodgers out, he locked up carefully and walked down the main street to do his grocery shopping, enjoying the July sunshine. He called in at Marker's, which he considered the best grocer's in town, chose some food and arranged to have it delivered. Then he decided to carry on walking. They'd been a smelly lot of boarders last night and he'd welcome some fresh air.

He was feeling edgy, and no wonder. In many ways it was better than he'd expected having his father living with him, and now that Raife was feeling better he had taken over most of the cooking, was a good cook too. But there were some drawbacks, because now Nev couldn't occasionally take to bed one of the women who slept in his lodging house. It was silly, really. He had his own bedroom, so what he did there was between him and the doorpost, but having his father in the room next door embarrassed him so much that the one time he'd tried, he'd found himself unable to finish what he'd started.

He sometimes wished he was married. It'd make everything so much easier. Not that he'd wanted to marry when his mother was alive. Certainly not. As she had said, if he didn't lumber himself with a wife and children he could really make something of himself. And he had, hadn't he? He had a thriving little business now and one or two other irons in the fire.

As he turned a corner he tripped over a wooden trolley, nearly fell and found himself clutching a soft female body to keep his balance. He immediately recognised her. 'Jane Preston!' She smiled at him, making no attempt to push him away, so he didn't hurry to step back either. He liked the feel of a woman's body against his – especially this woman, the one he'd been fond of as a young man.

'Nev,' she said in the soft voice which had hardly changed since they'd been children together. 'I haven't seen you for a while. Well, I haven't been out much.' She looked down at the two babies lying in the rough trolley and sighed.

'I was sorry to hear your Arthur had died.' Nev wasn't really sorry but you had to say the right thing, didn't you? Arthur had taken Jane from him when they were all youngsters and Nev had hated the man ever since. Eh, she'd been so pretty then, still was in a faded sort of way.

She blinked and tears came into her eyes. 'I do miss him. I don't like sleeping on my own.'

Neither did he, Nev thought. Especially in winter. 'These your latest?'

They stared down at the twins.

'Yes.'

'You don't sound happy about that.'

'I've had enough of babies an' two at once is hard

work for a woman of my age. Still, I won't be having any more of them now, will I? There is that, at least.' She tidied her hair self-consciously, but made no attempt to walk on. 'It's nice to talk to old friends.'

Nev looked at her speculatively. She wasn't bad-looking for a woman of her age. Amazing really when you thought how many children she'd had. 'I'll walk along with you a bit, if you like,' he said. 'Wouldn't mind some company myself. Here, let me push that trolley. It's heavy for a woman.'

By the time they got back to the Lanes after walking as far as the Town Hall, she'd managed to let him know that she'd enjoyed his company greatly and that she often walked out of a morning.

Nev went home in a pensive mood, so lost in his thoughts that after the evening meal he asked his father to play the piano and then didn't even notice what tune he was playing.

Raife ran his fingers over the keyboard of his old piano, now installed at the Dragon, delighting in the feel of the keys. It did need tuning, but it was still a good piano. He played a few simple tunes, to warm his fingers up and get the feel of the instrument, then launched into some of his favourites.

After a while he became aware of Frank standing behind the counter, looking at him as if he'd grown two heads.

'The piano needs tuning!' Raife called.

Frank scowled. 'Why does everyone want me to spend my money?'

Joanna came up to her father then and threaded her arm under his. 'Because we'll make more money on Saturdays with our free and easies, but you need a good piano for that.' She raised her voice to call, 'Do play some more, Raife. It's lovely listening to you.'

She got on with her work, but when she looked up her father was still standing listening, a sad expression on his face. Remembering her mother, she supposed. For all his grumpy ways she'd never doubted that he'd loved her mother.

The following Saturday evening Raife turned up at the Dragon, more neatly dressed than usual, to find a big notice outside announcing that it was a Free and Easy Night. Men and women were invited to attend, respectably dressed people only to be allowed in the music room.

Inside the pub, the big room was divided into two by a line of wooden posts set on square stands, with a rope threaded through holes in the tops of them. He stood in the doorway, surprised by the way Eli and Joanna had been able to smarten up the back area. He was quite sure it wasn't Frank's doing.

He wished suddenly that Nev had come with him though he'd discouraged it this first time.

Feeling a little self-conscious, Raife walked forward to the barrier and found Joanna standing there with Eli beside her, turning away folk who weren't decently dressed. More signs read 'No Spitting in Music Room' and 'No Smoking in Music Room'.

The men who usually occupied the rear area were sitting in a big group near the rope barrier, grumbling.

Most of the women in the queue were with their husbands and were looking a little nervous, because they didn't usually come into the Dragon. A few older women, widows probably, were there in groups.

'Mr Linney! Do come through. The piano's waiting for you.'

Eli's voice boomed out so loudly that people turned to stare at Raife, shuffling aside to let him pass.

He walked forward and Eli took him to the piano, winking as he said loudly, 'Here you are, Mr Linney. I hope you'll be comfortable.' He lowered his voice to add, 'What can I get you to drink? Just start playing when you want. I'll ask for volunteers to sing or recite when the place is a bit more full. It's looking like being a good turn-out, though.'

Raife sat down, feeling more at home when he touched the piano which was now properly tuned. He played a few chords, letting his fingers make ripples of sound, then launched into some old favourites.

Eli stood watching not only Raife but the people in the fenced-off area of the room. He and Joanna had personally invited the more respectable drinkers to come along and bring their wives, and enough of them had done so to make a good showing. Frank was standing behind the bar, looking glum as his usual customers grumbled about being moved. All round the walls the fishtail-shaped gas lights were flaring brightly at the end of their pipes and already the place felt warm. More modern places had Argand burners with gas chimneys, which looked better, but Eli couldn't see his uncle spending money on fancy new gas lighting when simple flames would do the job. He was determined that when he got a proper music room it'd be bang up-to-date in every possible way, if he had to fight tooth and nail for each improvement.

He was pleased to see that the people near the piano were already looking happier, some moving their heads in time to the music, others tapping their feet.

From behind the barrier there was a sudden roar of voices raised in song and he turned to see the displaced regulars standing up and trying to drown out the sound of the piano with a different tune. Before he could get to them, Bram and his brother Michael were there. When the disruptive men continued singing, Bram picked out one of the ringleaders and force marched him to the door. For a minute there was an ugly feel to the place as Bram threw the man outside and shouted that he'd not be allowed in again that night. When he marched back to the group and asked who wanted to be thrown out next, the other men shuffled their feet then one by one sat down again.

Bram leaned over the table and said something which made them all laugh and settle back to their drinks again.

He was good, Bram was, knew how to handle crowds. Eli relaxed a little and went back to give Raife his pot of beer, able to assure him that the trouble had been taken care of.

When most of the tables inside the singing area were filled, Eli asked Raife to stop playing for a minute and announced that as this was a free and easy evening, they would soon be inviting people to step up and sing. Anyone judged a good singer would get a free pot of beer or, if a lady, whatever she chose to drink. They had ginger beer available for the ladies in the audience tonight or gooseberry cordial.

Anyone who couldn't sing well enough would be asked to sit down again. 'The judges have the final word on that,' he continued in that loud voice he could summon up at need. 'And the first singer is already booked. You might not know it but our own Bram Heegan has a wonderful voice and has agreed to give us some well-known folk songs, starting in ten minutes' time. So if you want fresh drinks, order them now. We shan't be serving during the songs.'

There was a rustle of surprise and everyone who knew him turned to stare at Bram. Those who didn't had him pointed out. Others were trying to attract the potmen's attention. Behind the bar, Frank brightened up a little at the interest being shown and the big crowd that had turned up and bought drinks.

A small man came up to Eli. 'Comic recitation,' he said gruffly. 'Name's Chas Benton.'

Eli wrote his name down, then found a young man and two young women offering to sing, the three bearing a marked resemblance to one another.

Just over ten minutes later he got Raife to play a few crashing chords and announced that the entertainment was about to start. By that time all the tables were full and there was a row of people standing along the back next to the ropes. He could see an occasional head bob up from the other side, trying to see what was going on, and smiled at that. He'd bet that next week some of them would be inside the ropes too.

Bram walked forward through the crowd and took up a position next to the piano. He began with 'My Love Is Like A Red Red Rose' and such was the power of his voice that he could be heard clearly all through the pub. People looked at one another in surprise, because even those who knew him hadn't realised he had quite such a beautiful voice. When he'd finished, there was a spontaneous round of applause.

He bowed his head and waited for it to subside, then gave them 'The Oak and the Ash' which everyone liked, because it was about a 'North Country maid'. Soon the audience was joining in the chorus.

When that ended they called for more songs from him but Eli stepped forward. 'I'll see if I can persuade him to sing again later.'

The comic recitation was audible only to those inside the ropes and the men outside looked at one another and scowled.

'Tell him to speak up,' one said to the potman.

'Sorry, sir. I'm only on this side of the rope, like you.'

When the trio of brother and sisters sang, the men outside quietened down again, because their voices carried clearly. They weren't as good as Bram, but were good enough to give people pleasure, make heads sway and feet tap in time to the music.

Then Eli shouted that they would now have a half-hour break, after which Bram would sing again and lead everyone in a sing-song, so they'd better wet their whistles while they could.

The new police constable, who'd been standing near the door, moved across to the bar to a chorus of ribald comments about his uniform, because the police force had only been set up at the beginning of the year and people were still amused by seeing the town's three policemen walking round in their distinctive black top hats and navy frock coats. 'It's quieter in here than usual,' he said to Frank. 'How's it going?'

'All right.'

'You've got a good big crowd. I was surprised to see how many there were inside. I'd have expected it to be noisier.'

Eli came up as he was speaking. 'They've brought their womenfolk, so they're on their best behaviour. Are you staying for the rest of the show, Constable? You'd be very welcome.'

'Wish I could,' the young man said. 'I've been told to look in once or twice to make sure you're not abusing your music licence and using it as an excuse for rowdiness, so I daresay I'll see you again.'

'You'll find no rowdiness here,' Eli said at once. 'We hire men ourselves to keep order, though the police are always welcome, of course. Doesn't hurt folk to see the law present.'

By the time Bram sang again the audience was very

mellow. For most it was the first evening's entertainment of this kind that they'd enjoyed, and from what the women said to Joanna when she made her way round the room during the interval, they wanted more opportunities to come out and enjoy themselves like this.

Bram waited till everyone was looking at him and began by singing 'Drink To Me Only With Thine Eyes' which had everyone in the pub listening in hushed appreciation, even those beyond the rope. He went on to a series of well-known songs and soon had the audience singing along with him. They were clearly enjoying themselves hugely.

When it was time to close, there were lots of appreciative comments made and the clients left the pub in a rather more orderly manner than usual.

Michael Heegan walked Raife home and Bram was the last to say goodbye.

'I loved your singing,' Joanna said. 'You have a beautiful voice.'

He smiled at her. 'Always good to be appreciated.'

Eli went into the kitchen where his uncle was counting the takings. He sat quietly and watched Frank frown over them. 'Well?' he prompted in the end.

'The money's up,' his uncle admitted.

'By how much?' Joanna asked, coming to join them.

'Enough to cover the cost of Raife Linney playing the piano, though I still say you could have got him for five shillings.'

'The takings are up by more than his wage,' she said, having counted the piles of coins quickly, because he always arranged each one in a pound's worth.

'Admit it, we've made more than usual and without any fights. The place was crowded out.'

But he wasn't prepared to give in so easily. 'It was a near thing at the beginning. I was worried then.'

'They'll all want to be behind the ropes next time,' Eli prophesied. He and Joanna exchanged smiles, then he went up to bed, feeling pleasantly weary not to mention triumphant. Surely now his uncle would stop complaining?

The week after the confrontation with her family, Carrie got home to find her mother in floods of tears. 'What's the matter?'

Jane held out a crumpled piece of paper. 'It's this. The rent man brought it today, read it out to me. It says we have to leave this house! We shall be homeless. What are we going to *do?*'

Carrie tried to read the paper, but it had too many long words and she wasn't very good at reading. She picked it up. 'I'll take it round to Essie. She'll tell me what it all means.'

'I've already told you!' Jane screeched, thumping one hand down on the table. 'It means we have to leave this house.'

'When by?'

Her mother's brow furrowed. 'The rent man says we can stay on till they knock it down. A few weeks maybe. Mrs Baxter will have to leave her house too, but they'll give her another one because her husband still works for them. They won't give us another house, though, not now my Arthur's dead.'

'Well, we'll find another place to rent, then.'

'There aren't any. You know there aren't! Only one-up, one-down places, and they aren't big enough for us all.' She began to weep again and repeat, 'What shall we *do*?'

Carrie left her sobbing and went round to see Essie, who read the piece of paper and explained it patiently to her. But it was just as her mother had said, they had to leave the house. And everyone knew there'd been so many incomers to the town now the mills were on full time again that there was a severe shortage of houses to rent.

'Just as I thought we were getting things sorted out!' Carrie whispered. 'I don't know what to do, Essie.'

'I'll ask the doctor and the mistress. Maybe they can help.'

'They can't find houses when there aren't any.'

She walked home feeling deeply upset. She should have thought of this when her father died, because it had happened to other families who'd lost their breadwinner. But at first she'd not been well and then she'd been busy trying to sort out the family's money arrangements.

When she went to work the next day she told her troubles to Miss Beckett, but although her employer repeated that she could live in, if she wanted, that was just Carrie. There was no way anyone could take in a family as big as hers.

Was nothing ever going to go right for them?

★

Every time Bram went to work at the Dragon he found his eyes drawn to Joanna. She was a puzzle to him. Mostly she seemed plain and rather bad-tempered, but occasionally when she was talking to someone she liked she seemed to relax. And when she smiled, really smiled, her face became quite different. Attractive in a quiet sort of way that he found very appealing.

She didn't change like that when she spoke to him, however, but stayed guarded as if wary of him. He was intrigued by that, especially when he saw her dealing with his aunt. Bonny loved working there and said Miss Beckett was kind to her. Not many people were. They not only called the poor woman an idiot to her face but some even treated her as if she was dangerous. She wasn't. She was slow and more like a child than a grown woman, but so happy-natured and willing that all the family loved her. She could cheer you up just by being in the room.

Carrie Preston was unfailingly kind to Bonny, too, and once, when he'd been unable to fetch her and could only send a lad with a message for his aunt to wait for him, Carrie had seen her home right to the door, though it was out of her way. Even his mother had spoken well of Carrie since then and said it was a pity she wasn't a Catholic, a very high accolade for her.

One evening, Eli came up to Bram when things were quiet. 'You did well on Saturday. If you'll sing for us every week, I'll double your money.'

Bram grinned at him. 'All right with me.'

'And would you be interested in working here full-time when the music room next door's open?'

'Depends what I'd be doing.' Bram gestured to the room. 'Maybe when you get paid entertainers in you won't want me singing, which I admit I like doing. I'm lucky that I can always find ways to earn money, but I prefer to do something that's interesting.' He waited for the other man to become angry about this, as most employers did, because Bram had been offered steady jobs several times before and had turned them all down.

'I reckon you've got a good brain,' Eli said unexpectedly.

'I'm not stupid,' Bram allowed.

'Have you ever been to a real music hall?'

Bram shook his head.

'We'd better send you to see one, then, if you want to keep performing. I'll take you to one in Manchester next week.'

But Frank threw a fit at the thought of being without both the men who could control potential trouble-makers, so Joanna offered to take Bram instead.

That upset her father just as much. 'I'm not having you going off on your own with that – that philandering Irishman!'

She drew herself up. 'Do you think I'm the sort of woman he treats in that way? Or that I'd behave loosely with any man?'

Joanna's voice was so icy her father looked at her apprehensively. 'No, of course not, love.'

'Then what's the harm in my going? This is a

business outing. If we give Bram a permanent job here, he'll need to know what we're aiming at.'

'Well, take another woman with you as well then.'

She rolled her eyes and made an exasperated sound in her throat. 'Who, for heaven's sake? I don't have any women friends.'

'Anyone. It doesn't matter who. I'm not having you going on your own with him, and that's flat.'

'I'll think about it.'

The first person she saw as she came out of the back room was Carrie so Joanna turned round and called to her father, 'I'll take Carrie with me. She needs cheering up at the moment.'

'Why does she need cheering up?' Eli asked, coming to stand in the doorway beside her.

'The Prestons have been given notice by Stott's to quit their house.'

He whistled. 'They'll not find somewhere else easily, not with that big a family.'

'I know. I feel sorry for Carrie. She works so hard, and from what she's told me never stops when she goes home from here, either.'

After a minute's silence Eli said abruptly, 'There's a problem with taking her to Manchester. She's not nearly well enough dressed.'

'Hmm.' Joanna studied Carrie, head on one side, not wanting anything to prevent their going to a music hall again, with its bright lights and happy atmosphere but above all the music she craved. 'I could lend her some of my old clothes. She won't mind if they're a bit worn.'

He looked sideways at her. 'Are you sure?'

Joanna smiled and confessed, 'I'd do anything for another night out.'

They were both smiling as they went back to work, she because she'd found a solution, he because he thought that poor lass deserved a treat.

After Carrie had finished work, Joanna asked her to stay behind for a minute. 'I want to go into Manchester to show Bram Heegan what it's like in a proper music saloon but my father insists I take another woman with me because he doesn't trust Bram alone with me. How would you like to go?'

Carrie stared at her, unable to speak for a moment, then stammered, 'Me? Me go with you?'

'Why not?'

For a moment Carrie allowed herself to dream, then shook her head reluctantly. 'I'd love to, Miss Beckett, but I don't have nice enough clothes. And it'd cost too much. I don't have any spare money.'

'I'd be paying for everything and I could lend you some clothes. You're a bit taller than me, but we're about the same size otherwise. Have you time now to come upstairs and try them on?'

Carrie couldn't speak for a moment, so excited did she feel. After swallowing hard, she nodded and scraped out, 'Yes, please.'

When she came down again she felt as if she was floating and she was clutching a bundle of clothes. They were to go the following week! She'd get to ride on a train, see Manchester, visit a music saloon . . . all in one evening! She kept waiting to wake up from a dream, but as the hours passed she didn't and it gradually sank in that this was real.

Her family were astounded and Marjorie made her try on the lovely new clothes that very night. They all exclaimed over how nice she looked, and it felt wonderful to be dressed like that, just wonderful. If only her hands weren't so red, she'd feel like a proper lady, but every time she saw them Carrie knew what she was: a scrubbing woman. But you couldn't have everything, could you? And she meant to enjoy every second of her outing.

Even finding a new house wasn't as urgent as she'd thought at first. She'd talked to the rent man herself and it seemed they had a few weeks more before their house was going to be knocked down.

A few days later Nev looked at his father across the dinner table. 'If I bring a friend back with me, will you play the piano for us?'

'Aye, of course. You know I love playing. Is he coming round tonight?'

Nev went a bit pink. 'It's a she, and no, she's busy at night. She's coming round tomorrow afternoon, if that's all right? Well, middle of the day, really. We can give her a bite to eat as well.'

What Raife hadn't expected was a plump, faded-looking woman pushing a crude cart with two squalling babies in it. He blinked and bit back an exclamation as he was introduced. He remembered Jane now. She'd been a bonny lass, the sort of soft, gentle creature that men rushed into marriage with then regretted it later after they found out how shift-less the woman was. He'd seen it time and again. But it wasn't his place to comment, so he smiled and talked a little about the old days, then left Nev to take his lady friend into the parlour while he sat in the kitchen.

It was bigger than kitchens usually were, with a place at one end for the lodgers to prepare their meals. He'd tidied it up after last night's lodgers had left and everything was clean now. The poor souls had such pitiful bits of food – if any – that they rarely used the cooking facilities Nev was obliged by law to provide. But they did buy the slices of bread and drip-ping he sold, and it was one of Raife's jobs to prepare these. Last night's lodgers had been soaking wet. He'd have let the poor creatures come in early in bad weather if it had been up to him, but Nev was adamant about keeping to the set hours.

When his son poked his head round the kitchen door and made a beckoning signal, Raife got up and went to play the piano for them. He started with a couple of old favourites and then turned to ask the visitor if she'd like any special tune. But she was clearly more interested in talking to his son so he went back to his playing, choosing songs he liked.

The babies seemed to appreciate the music anyway. They fell fast asleep. Bonny little lasses they were, as alike as peas in a pod.

After a while Nev said, 'Thanks, Dad. That was lovely. We'll – um – have a bite to eat now if you'll bring it through.'

Raife did so and then excused himself, saying he wasn't hungry. That won him an approving glance from his son.

He smiled as he sat down in the kitchen to his own food. At forty-six, his son was courting. What else could it be? Now, there was a turn-up for the books! Then Raife frowned. He couldn't see Nev being lumbered with another man's babies, or even small children. Too selfish and fond of his own creature comforts, his son. And that woman looked as soft and helpless as she had when she was a lass. Nev liked things doing properly round the house – he was his mother's son there. Raife couldn't see Jane keeping this place immaculate somehow, especially not with babies around.

He liked childer himself, though, often wished he'd had grandchildren when he saw little lasses or lads playing in the street. He'd enjoy having babies around the place.

After they'd eaten, Nev called goodbye to his father then walked back with Jane, leaving her with regret on Market Street because she didn't want any of her neighbours seeing them walking home together, which would have made things look a bit particular between them. He'd really enjoyed her company. She knew how to listen to a man, Jane did.

His smile turned thoughtful. Those babies were a nuisance, though, always needing attention. One would be bad enough, but two . . . he wasn't at all sure about taking on two of them.

Then he suddenly remembered his friend Charlie

who'd sold his baby for good money. Were there other people around wanting to buy babies? If so, he might be on to a good thing here, because Jane kept complaining about all the hard work they made for her.

As for her other children, if he became their step-father, it'd be for him to collect their wages each week and provide for them. Jane had never been good with money, but Nev knew he was. It might not be so bad. He liked having company round the place, he'd realised that after his father came back.

And since Jane said she couldn't have any more babies, he'd be all right in future. He'd have his bed play every night if he wanted.

If they sold the babies, that'd still leave eight children though some were grown up now. He went for a walk round the lodging house, not seeing his surroundings as he tried to work out what to do. Should he risk it? Jane was clearly willing. Or should he step back? No, he needed a woman, and it'd be most convenient of all to have one of his own.

And anyway, she was good company, Jane. After a lifetime of hard work he deserved to relax a little and enjoy the fruits of his labour.

It'd all depend on whether they could do something about those babies.

The following day when he met Jane, Nev persuaded her to walk out to the edge of town with him, though she complained about her aching feet.

'The hard work has only just started with those

two, I reckon.' He jerked his head towards the babies. 'What'll it be like when you've two of them running round and getting into everything?'

She looked down at them and said nothing, only sighed.

'Eh, you poor lass, you've spent too much of your life looking after babbies, you have that. You deserve to enjoy yourself a bit while you still can.'

Jane stared at him doubtfully.

'If you didn't have them two, I'd be courting you, asking you to marry me.' Nev looked at her soulfully. 'But I'm too old an' set in my ways to live with one babby, let alone two.'

Her lips began to quiver and her eyes filled with tears. 'Oh, Nev love, don't say that! I was hoping . . . We have to leave our house soon, you know, an' you have such a lovely place.'

'I don't want to lie to you, Jane love. I were awake half the night worrying about it all.' In fact, he'd slept as soundly as ever, but it sounded better for him to be worried.

A tear rolled down one of her cheeks.

'Mind you . . .' He paused, waiting for her to prompt him, and when she did told her about Charlie. 'I know a fellow as sold his babby. Fifty pound he got for it from some rich sod as couldn't get his own. An' it'll have a better life than he could ever give it, so he were happy enough to do it, didn't feel guilty.' He glanced quickly sideways. She was staring at him, not looking in the least upset, her expression thoughtful.

'I didn't know you could do that,' she said at last.

'I didn't either.' He was pleased that one of the babies started crying just then and the other soon joined in. 'Eh, they're a noisy pair.'

Jane scowled down at the twins. 'They can skrike all they like, I'm not picking them up again. I never have a minute to mysen these days.'

When she began to nibble her forefinger and frown, Nev could see she was thinking and kept quiet. He didn't want her to say he'd forced her into anything.

'Nev, can you find out about it? About whether anyone would pay good money for these two? They're healthy babbies, pretty too, but they're wearing me out. If I could know they were going to good homes, well, I'd let them go in a minute.' Jane looked at him then lowered her eyes as she added, 'For their own good, of course.'

Elation ran through him. 'You leave it to me, lass. If you're quite sure?'

She looked at him, then down at the yowling babies, and nodded. 'I'm very sure.'

'Now think on, I don't want you complaining afterwards that I forced you to do it against your will, because I'd never do that.'

She laid one hand on his arm. 'I won't. But I'd only do it if I were wed an' had someone to keep my thoughts off 'em.'

He looked at her hand, not in the least offended by this. He'd be the same in her place, making sure of what he was getting. 'I'd wed you in a minute if it weren't for them. You know I've allus been fond of you. I never found another lass to take your place after you wed Arthur.'

She sighed, a blissful sound this time. 'What a lovely thing to say!'

'It's the truth.' He nearly burst out laughing when it was obvious she believed him. He put his arm round her and gave her a hug, managing to squeeze her soft breast with one hand as he did so.

She gasped in pleasure and looked at him, saying simply, 'I miss having a man, Nev.'

'Do you?'

'Aye. I've allus liked the bed play. Mind, I'd not part with the twins till I were safely wed.'

'I'd not ask you to. Look, I'll go and see Dr Barlow and find out if what my friend said is true. If it is, you an' me will discuss – everything.'

They were quiet as they walked back towards the town centre, but when he looked sideways he could see Jane was smiling.

Eli whistled cheerfully as he went into the big empty space that had once been the inn stables. Dawn was just breaking and the builder's men would be here in a minute, but he wanted to stand and enjoy the scene first. He liked to fill the space in his imagination. Rows of happy customers eating and drinking, a little stage at one end, a bar at the other . . . he could see it all.

There was the sound of footsteps then and Carrie came in through the open hole that would be a proper double doorway soon. 'Oh, sorry, Mr Beckett. Me and Ted just came to get another load of wood before work.'

He smiled at her and her little brother. 'You go ahead.'

They began to load the little handcart, working quickly, not wasting their breath on chatting. He admired how hard she could work and it looked like the lad was the same. On a sudden impulse Eli went over to help them. 'Many hands make light work, and I'm sure this young fellow's got school later.'

Ted grinned at him. 'I don't mind being late.'

'You'll get there on time and do your lessons properly this week,' Carrie said sharply. 'If that teacher keeps you in after school, you'll not get any loads sold tonight.'

The lad's grin turned to a scowl.

'Don't you like school?' Eli enquired, though he could already guess the answer.

'No, I don't. An' I'm leavin' as soon as I turn twelve. I'll be eleven in a week or two, near the time Carrie has her birthday. Them ladies as pay my school pence said I had to stay on till twelve an' our Carrie agreed with 'em.' He threw a resentful look at his sister as he spoke.

Eli waited a minute then said, 'I didn't like school either, but I'm glad now that I learned to read an' write properly. As for arithmetic, why, I need it all the time if I'm not to be diddled by my customers.'

Ted frowned at him. 'What, even multiplication tables?'

'Oh, yes. Especially them. You have to know how

to divide, add and subtract. All of it. No use making money unless you can count it and keep it safe afterwards.'

Ted piled some more pieces of wood on the handcart. 'I don't mind arithmetic too much, but there's Bible study every day after school for those of us who have our school fees paid. I don't even understand the words they make us learn, they're that long. No one I know speaks words like them.'

'It's the price you pay for a free education, young fellow. The children of this town are lucky Mrs Latimer and the other ladies are paying their school pence. In other places, the young 'uns stay ignorant. *You* will be able to make something of yourself – and not be cheated out of your money. If I were you, I'd make the most of the opportunity.' Eli stepped back and dusted his hands together to get the crumbly pieces of wood off. 'There. That's a fine big load you've got.'

Carrie moved to take one of the handles and with a quick 'Thank you!' she and the lad set off, pushing the heavy handcart out through the opening in the wall.

Eli watched them go. Joanna said she wanted to put Carrie in charge of keeping the music room clean. Thought a lot of her, she did. It'd be interesting to see what Carrie made of her trip into Manchester. She was looking a lot better lately, less gaunt, as if she was eating more regularly, delicate colour glowing in her cheeks, her hair shining and clean. He knew Joanna fed both her scrubbing women mid-morning, and gathered Carrie had taken charge at home since her father's death so the Prestons weren't so pushed now to put bread on the table. He hoped they'd find another house soon. He'd heard Carrie talking to Joanna about one she'd been to look at which she said was damp and rat-infested, as well as having only two rooms.

Later he walked through the big public room and saw Carrie scrubbing away at a tabletop.

She straightened up as he approached, easing her aching back. 'I wanted to thank you, Mr Beckett.'

He looked at her in surprise. 'What for?'

'What you said to our Ted this morning. He'll listen when *you* tell him to learn what he can at school, though he won't pay much attention to me. Well, why should he? I've no book learning. I can read and write, but only just, because I was allus being kept off school to help Mam with the new babies or the washing, an' then later she couldn't find the school pence for all of us – that was before Mrs Latimer started helping poor children.'

'There's many a person learns to read and write properly later in life,' he said mildly. 'I learned at school because the teacher caned us hard if we didn't. He had a heavy hand, did that fellow, but I'm grateful to him for giving me a start. I've learned much more since I left school, though.'

He nodded and walked on because he'd been tempted to offer to help her with her reading and that wouldn't do. He really must stop talking to her. And watching her. He turned round on that thought and there she was, bent over the next table, scrubbing away, her hair twisted up on top of her head. Below it, her neck was bare and somehow vulnerable. It made you want to kiss it, that slender neck did.

Desire swelled in him and with a grunt of annoyance at his own weakness, Eli hurried down to the cellars and didn't go near her again that day.

# 10

For her big outing Carrie washed herself all over, then dressed carefully in her borrowed clothes with the help of Marjorie and Dora only, because the bedroom wouldn't hold anyone else. She let Marjorie put her hair up in a softer style than usual, which added to the strangeness of everything. When she was ready, she walked into the kitchen where the rest of her family were waiting to see her.

There was complete silence as she entered and she looked from one to the other, seeing mainly astonishment on their faces. 'Don't I look right?'

'You look lovely,' her mother said, blinking away a tear. 'I never saw you look so nice. I was pretty, too, when I was a girl. Had lots of fellows wanting me, but I only wanted your father.' She heaved a dramatic sigh and clasped one hand to her breast. 'You'll be wed afore we know it.

'I'm not even walking out with anyone,' Carrie protested. 'Nor I don't want to. I'd like to wear clothes like this all the time, though, an' be clean. Not have to scrimp and scrape to put bread on the table.' She saw her mother's face crinkle up, as if she were going to cry, so said hastily to Robbie,

'Walk down with me to the station, will you? I don't want to be late.'

When they got there, they looked at the big station clock.

'We're early,' said her brother. 'Come on, let's sit on that bench and wait for them.'

'Thanks for coming with me. I'm a bit nervous about going on the train.'

He smiled at her. 'It's perfectly safe, you know. But I'd snap up the chance to go, whether I was nervous or not. Besides, you deserve it.'

Carrie gaped at him. 'What do you mean by that?'

'You work hard, hold the family together. Why shouldn't you have a bit of fun? And Mam's right, you should get yoursen a fellow. I know a few as'd be interested.'

'Well, I'm not interested in fellows because I don't want to get married.'

'Why not?'

She didn't need to answer because Miss Beckett came walking along towards the station just then, accompanied by Bram Heegan.

They too stopped and stared at her as if they didn't recognise her.

'What's the matter?' Carrie asked in dismay. 'Don't I look right?'

'You look lovely,' Joanna said. 'Surely you can see that?'

'We haven't got a big mirror only a broken piece, so I don't know what I look like. My sisters said I looked nice, though.'

'Come with me.' Joanna led the way into the Ladies' Waiting Room where there was a big mirror over the fireplace and a gas light flaring, making the place bright as day. 'There. Take a look at yourself.'

Carrie stared at the stranger in the mirror, a pretty young woman wearing a neat bonnet with her shining hair showing at the front. The bodice of her dress showed off her trim figure and the full skirts swayed as she moved because underneath she was wearing two frilled petticoats Miss Beckett had lent her. 'Is that me?' she asked faintly. 'Eh, I can't believe it.'

The memory of that vision in the mirror – not only pretty but looking highly respectable – gave Carrie the courage to face the evening with her head held high.

The train came in with a cloud of sour-smelling smoke, as Carrie had seen it come in many times before. But this time she was actually going to ride on it. Her heart did a little hippety-hop at the thought of that.

They waited for a porter to open the door to a second-class carriage and then got inside where there was space with lots of seats in it. The two women sat facing forward, with Bram opposite them. Someone blew a whistle then the porter shut the door with a great thump that made Carrie jump.

With a hissing sound, accompanied by clanking metallic noises, the train left the station, going faster and faster through the darkness so that houses with lights in their windows seemed to whizz past, alternating with dark fields and once a horse, standing so close to a fence that Carrie could see it briefly in the lights from the train. There were two oil lamps burning in their compartment, so it was bright enough for her to see Bram watching her with an indulgent smile.

'Enjoy it, lass,' he said. 'There's nothing like your first train ride.'

'I wish it was daylight, then I'd be able to see more.'

Joanna was smiling at her too. 'Wait till you get to Manchester. It'll be so bright there you'll see plenty, even at this time of the evening.'

They saw the city before they ever arrived at the station. So many big well-lit buildings, Carrie couldn't believe it. And then Bram helped her out on to a very long platform – as if she couldn't have jumped down herself! – and offered each woman an arm. Shyly she linked hers with his and he led them forward into the station itself, which was full of bustling people. Where were they all going at this time of the evening? she wondered.

'We'll catch a cab to the music hall,' Joanna said. 'Could you get us one, please, Bram?'

He hurried off and Carrie edged closer to her companion, terrified of getting separated and lost in such a busy place.

Bram reappeared almost immediately, smiling. 'This way, ladies.'

And so Carrie had her first ride in a cab as well, feeling like the Queen sitting there being driven through the streets in style. One street had so many splendid shops in it she was speechless, could only stare and stare again at them. There were gaslights there, so it was as bright as anything, and she wished she could stop the cab and go and look into the windows which were full of lovely things. The shops in Hedderby were nothing compared to these.

There were so many people here she wondered what it would be like to walk down a street and know no one at all. She ran her fingers over the upholstery of the cab and stared from side to side, trying to remember every single detail of this magical night to tell her family later.

When they arrived at the music hall, Bram helped the ladies down and Carrie carefully followed Miss Beckett's example, gathering her skirts together so that she didn't show her legs and giving him her hand. The outside of the building took her breath away, it was so brightly lit, with even more gas street lights than in the city centre. She'd never seen any place as bright at night before, not even the Dragon. Why, it could have been daylight, and a sunny day at that.

Bram purchased the tickets, then they went inside, sitting on chairs at long tables set at right angles to the stage, which was at the far end of the room. There was a table and chair next to it, but lower down on its own little platform. Up above them was a balcony with rich people sitting there smiling down as if they had no troubles at all. Carrie knew they were rich because they were so well dressed and quietly polite, murmuring to one another, while the folk in the body of the hall weren't nearly as well dressed and kept calling out to one another across the tables and even across the room.

When someone put a glass in front of her Carrie looked at it in bewilderment because she didn't know what it was.

'It's lemonade,' Joanna said. 'I didn't think you'd want beer or wine. I'm having lemonade too.'

Carrie shuddered at the thought of drinking beer and took a sip of the cloudy liquid, closing her eyes in ecstasy at the sweet and yet tart taste of the lemonade. 'I've never tasted anything as delicious!'

Bram winked at Joanna and she smiled back at him. She was enjoying her second visit even more than her first because of Carrie's naïve delight in all these new experiences. Suddenly she was glad her father had insisted on another woman going with her. It was definitely much easier with three of them present. Bram on his own might have been – overpowering. He was so very male and exuberant.

And yet, in some ways it was as if she and Bram were together in a rather special way tonight, two adults looking after a child. She studied him covertly, surprised to see how well dressed he was, even smarter than Eli had been, though he too wore a mechanic's cap not a top hat like the men up in the balcony.

When the show started with the Chairman greeting the audience, then introducing the small orchestra, Joanna found her eyes straying to Carrie from time to time. The show was excellent, for her much better than the one she'd seen with Eli because of two top-class singers who formed part of it. A man with roguish eyes came on early in the show and sang four songs, one sad, two lilting and one rather suggestive. The audience loved him and applauded so loudly the Chairman asked him for another song.

But his voice was no better than Bram's, Joanna decided.

Later on in the show The Manchester Songbird once again came on stage. She was a regular turn, it seemed. Her songs tonight were new to Joanna. They had glorious melodies and simple yet pretty words, but it was her voice that carried them, not they her, a soaring soprano that easily reached the high notes and could be heard clearly across the whole hall. The audience knew her songs, and were soon joining in the choruses, swaying to and fro in time to the music.

Joanna couldn't resist joining in too, raising her voice instead of keeping it subdued as she did in church. Among so many she surely wouldn't be noticed?

But Bram did notice her and he was singing loudly, too, in a resonant tenor. After the first chorus he even sang in harmony, melding his voice with Joanna's, so that people nearby turned to stare at them.

After they'd finished applauding the singer, the man on the other side of Bram leaned across to say, 'You've got a beautiful voice, lass, near as good as Miss Nelly was tonight. I reckon you an' your young man are good enough to make a turn yourselves. Have you never thought of it? There's nice money to be earned singing. I've a cousin as does it, though he has to travel around all the time an' I shouldn't like that.'

Joanna could feel herself blushing and didn't know what to say.

'We've not long known one another,' Bram said, all solemn-faced. 'We're still practising.'

'Well, keep it up. I'd come to hear you, that I would.'

Carrie looked from one to the other in awe. 'It must be wonderful to be able to sing like that. I can't sing at all. The tune comes out wrong if I try and people laugh at me.'

Bram smiled at her. 'Never mind. We can't all be good at everything we do.'

'I'd be grateful if you didn't mention my singing to my father,' Joanna begged.

'Why ever not?' Bram asked.

'He doesn't like me to sing, says I have too loud a voice.'

'We'll not say anything,' Carrie said quietly. 'I wouldn't want to make your father angry with you. It still upsets me that mine died angry with me.'

Joanna squeezed her hand in sympathy. 'That wasn't your fault.'

'It feels like my fault. Mam says it is.' She looked down, annoyed with herself for letting that out when she'd decided to try to forget it and to ignore her mother's spiteful jibes.

Luckily the next act was a comedian, who told jokes that had all three of them laughing, and then finished with a comic song whose refrain, 'I'm just her little lodger', soon had the audience joining in again, lustily roaring that rather suggestive line at the end of each verse.

When they left the music hall, Carrie couldn't speak, she was so full of the new sights and sounds. She let the other two discuss the show and argue about which turn they'd enjoyed most. She'd enjoyed it all.

In the train she sat mostly in silence, relieved that the others were still chatting and didn't need her to join in.

Once they were back in Hedderby she and Bram walked Joanna home, then he took Carrie up the hill behind the Dragon right to her front door.

Everyone had waited up for her so she had to tell them about her wonderful evening and it was well after midnight before they got to bed. Even then she couldn't sleep for reliving her magical night out.

When Nev knocked on Dr Barlow's back door and asked to see him, the maid looked down her nose at him. 'He doesn't see people like you till the afternoons. Come back after three o'clock.'

'I'm not sick. Tell him it's the same sort of business as he did with Charlie Hurst. The doctor will see me then, I'm sure.'

She came back and showed him into a bare little room where he was to take a seat and wait. 'My master's just finishing his breakfast.'

It was a while before Dr Barlow came in and, as Charlie had said, he looked down his long nose at his visitor.

'It's about babies, ones that aren't wanted,' Nev said, coming straight to the point.

'Oh?'

'You paid Charlie Hurst fifty pound for giving you his.'

'He told you?'

'In confidence, doctor, and I've told no one else. He's a close friend of mine, see. I miss him now he's left Hedderby.'

'Get to the point. I'm a busy man.'

'Well, I know of two babies as could do with a better home. The mother's got ten childer after the last one turned out to be twins. Then her husband died, so it's all too much for her.'

'They've been born already?'

Nev nodded.

'We don't usually take babies that have already been born. We like to give the mothers extra food while they're carrying. We only want healthy children.'

'Well, these are as healthy as you please. You should hear them skriking! They'd wake the dead, these two would.'

'Boys or girls?'

'Girls. Look as alike as two peas.'

'How old are they?'

'A few months, I don't know exactly. I'm a friend of the family, just helping out, the mother being a widow and all.'

'I'd have to see them before we discussed it further.'

'She can bring them round here whenever you say.'

'Tomorrow at this time.'

Nev whistled happily all the way home. Not only would he get himself a wife, the one he'd always wanted, but she'd bring him plenty of money. On the way he passed a mother carrying a baby and frowned. It was nicely dressed, while Jane's pair seemed to be wrapped in old rags. Have to do something about that.

He went along to Throstle Lane, not even trying to hide the fact that he was calling on Jane, and they had a rapid discussion that ended very satisfactorily with a quick trip to the second-hand clothes dealer so that the babies would look nice.

The following morning, as soon as everyone had left for work or school, Jane bathed the twins all over and dressed them in their new clothes. She looked at them fondly, thinking how bonny they were. Tears welled in her eyes but she sniffed them away. What Nev said made sense. It fair wore you down having so many childer and these two would have a far better future with someone else.

When he arrived she was ready so they loaded the twins into the wooden push cart and walked across town to Dr Barlow's. They were shown into the same back room and once again had to sit and wait until he could see them.

He came in finally and studied Jane. 'I believe your husband died recently, Mrs Preston?'

Tears welled in her eyes, as they always did at the mention of Arthur. 'Yes, sir. Dr Latimer said he had a growth in the brain.'

'And these two will make ten children. All living?'

'Oh, yes, sir. There were three others who died, but I have ten still living.'

'Fine children they are too, but a heavy burden for a poor widow,' Nev put in.

The doctor didn't answer, but went to the door and called, 'Mrs Lowson!'

The woman who acted as midwife to the town's better-off ladies came in then, looked at the two adults as if they were worms, as Jane complained to Nev later, and moved to pick up one of the babies. She laid it on a table and undid its clothes, examining the infant carefully and then standing back so that the doctor could make his own examination.

The procedure was repeated with the other baby, then Mrs Lowson nodded to the doctor and left the room.

'They are indeed a fine pair of infants,' the doctor said, smiling at Jane now. 'You are to be congratulated, my good woman.' He hesitated. 'I may know someone who would like to adopt your children. Leave it with me.'

'We're not giving them away for nothing,' Nev put in.

'If they take the children, which is not yet certain, you will be paid the same as your friend.'

'For each baby?'

The doctor sighed. 'Yes. For each baby. Now give me your address and I'll send word in a day or two.'

They gave him Nev's address.

As they strolled back he grinned at Jane. 'I think I'll be marrying a rich woman.'

She smiled back at him and parroted the words he'd said to her so often: 'It'll be for the best. They'll have a good start in life, better than I could ever give them.' She felt sad, though. It didn't seem right, giving your children away. But on the other hand she wouldn't be at the beck and call of two noisy and demanding infants, day and night, might stop feeling so tired all the time.

And if she wed Nev, she'd live in his big, comfortable house and feel safe, because if ever a man knew how to make and hold on to money, it was him. And he didn't drink, said it made him ill. That'd make life so much easier.

Carrie soon heard about her mother meeting Nev Linney because quite a few of the neighbours made it their business to tell her. As if she would be upset about that! It was quite the opposite as far as she was concerned. If her mother got married again, as most of the younger widows hereabouts did, it would be a burden off her eldest daughter's shoulders.

But there were one or two things about Jane's behaviour that puzzled her.

'Where did those new baby clothes come from, Mam?'

'A friend bought them for the twins. They look a real picture in them, don't they?'

'Which friend?'

Jane scowled at her. 'None of your business.'

Carrie inwardly debated whether to insist on being told what was going on, then decided not to press matters. She didn't want to upset her mother, whose mood had changed for the better over the past few days.

But when she got home after work one day and found

the house empty she went out again on a sudden impulse, wondering where they all were. Her mother wasn't one for long walks, didn't really like any exertion.

She couldn't see any sign of Jane near the little shop where they bought most of their food so went on into the town centre where she couldn't resist going to stand on the bridge that had given the town its name. It was solidly built of grey stone and there were two wider places on each side where pedestrians could stand and look down at the River Hedder. It'd rained quite a lot during the past month, so water was rushing and gurgling along over the stones, curling up the bottoms of the bridge supports and then hurrying away who knew where. It was ages since Carrie had had time to stand here and watch it but she'd done so regularly when she was younger. She loved the patterns the water made and unmade.

'I like to watch it, too,' said a voice so close to her that she jumped in shock.

Eli smiled and leaned on the parapet next to her. 'In the river near where my parents live, there's a place where you can catch trout sometimes. I used to go there with my father as a lad. He loved a bit of fried trout for tea.'

'I've never tasted it.' She sighed and added, more to herself than to him, 'There are so many things I've never done.'

'Well, you're not dead yet, there's still time.'

She smiled at him. 'I suppose so. You haven't seen my mother and the twins, have you? She isn't at home and that's not like her.'

'I saw her over the other side of town, walking along with Nev Linney.'

'I think they're courting. Well, I hope they are anyway.'

'It's a bit soon, isn't it?'

'Not for her. She's pining for a man, can't live without one to boss her around. I don't mind at all if she gets married again, the sooner the better. It's what'll happen to the children that worries me. Who'll want ten of us – or have room for us? We've only a week or two left now before we have to get out of the house and we haven't found anywhere else even halfway decent.' Carrie looked round, caught sight of the station clock and clicked her tongue in annoyance. She knew how to tell the time from it, unlike many of her neighbours, because she'd never forgotten what she'd learned in school, had loved going there while she could. 'Look at me, wasting my time staring at the river when there's work to be done.'

'You've a right to rest now and then.'

She let out a snort of laughter. 'Tell that to my family if they come home and find no food on the table! Even in these few weeks since Dad died they've got used to eating better.' She started walking back towards the Lanes and found to her surprise that Eli had come with her.

'I have to get back, too. If there's no rest for the wicked, you and I must be very bad folk.'

She chuckled. 'I've no time to do anything wicked. Is there any more wood ready for us?'

'Yes. But there won't be much more after this load.'

'I'll bring the barrow along later when Ted gets home from school.' Carrie stopped outside the shop and said, almost shyly, 'It was nice talking to you.'

'I enjoyed talking to you, too.' He stood for a minute staring at the doorway through which she'd disappeared, then shook his head and set off for the Dragon. There was a lot to be done and his uncle was still moaning and complaining about all the money that was being spent.

But he'd enjoyed talking to Carrie. Even the simplest conversation with her was so pleasant and easy. She might not be well schooled, but she was interested in everything and anything.

Exactly a week later Nev received word to go back to the doctor's and to bring the babies so that the interested parties could see them. He went round to Jane's early to make sure she washed the infants carefully and dressed them in their new clothes. She was relieved to be summoned because she'd been worried that something might go wrong. The thought of all that money made her feel dizzy. She felt a bit sad sometimes at the thought of losing the twins, but only on their good days. On their bad days, when their crying nearly drove her mad and the rain kept her indoors with them and a room full of steaming clouts, she could only long for release from this neverending toil.

They seemed to behave better for Carrie than anyone else, gurgling and laughing when their eldest sister picked them up. Ungrateful, that's what childer were, as Jane knew only too well.

Mrs Lowson greeted them at the back door of the doctor's house. 'If you leave them with me, you can come back at two o'clock and they'll be ready for you.'

'Don't you want me to stay and look after them?'

'I think I can be trusted to do that. Are they weaned?'

'No.'

'Then you'd better start weaning them. I'll bring you some special food every day for them.'

'I've never weaned babbies so early.'

'These are well grown, quite amazingly so for twins, and I think you'll have no trouble with them, especially with the food I'll bring to you.'

As Jane and Nev were about to leave, a carriage drew up outside the house and Mrs Lowson pulled them back. 'Wait here till they've gone inside.'

Jane stared at the carriage, which was old and creaky. She'd never seen it around Hedderby and the poor horses looked tired, as if they'd come a long way. A lady and gentleman got out of it. He was tall and a bit stooped, with a face like a sheep. She was thin and had a veil over her face, but a piece of curly red hair had escaped from one side. Jane heard her call the man Dudley as they waited for the door to open.

Nev put his arm round Jane. It was going to happen, he knew it. A hundred pounds they'd get, and without any need to work for it!

Only after the front door had closed behind the newcomers did Mrs Lowson let them leave, telling them to come back in two hours.

The time passed quickly and pleasantly. Nev took Jane back to his home, which was closer than hers, and for the first time showed her all over it, explaining how the lodgers were dealt with. She was awed by the size of the place and by the beautiful furniture in the parlour, stroking the piano and daring to press down a note or two.

As they came back down the stairs she gathered together her courage to mention something that had been worrying her. 'You haven't said what's to happen to the other childer after we're wed.'

'They'll come and live with us here, of course. The older ones are earning money and will hand their wages over to me once I'm their step-father, so they'll not cost me owt. I think you'll find I'm good with money. You'll never want for anything, Jane love, I can promise that. The younger ones can help around the place after school or do odd jobs for folk. I've seen your Ted selling wood lately. He seems a sensible lad, able to turn a penny or two.'

'Where will they sleep, though?'

'There's another room next to the common room. I only open it up in the winter – I get more customers in the winter, you see – and they can sleep there.'

'All of them in one room?'

'Why not? They're brothers and sisters, aren't they?'

'Arthur allus said lads an' lasses should sleep apart, and Carrie and Marjorie are a bit old now to be sharing with their brothers.'

His voice grew sharper. 'Well, there won't be room for them to sleep apart, I'm not putting children in the best bedrooms. And after all, you've no other home to offer them so I'd expect you and them to be grateful.'

'Oh, dear. I am grateful, Nev, really I am. It's just – well, I don't know what our Carrie will say to that. She's a bit bossy, I'm afraid.'

'So am I. Especially in my own home. She'll mind what I say or find somewhere else to live! Now stop worrying. It'll all work out, you'll see.' He had it all figured. Not only would the older ones' wages more than pay for their keep, but they'd be able to help around the place so that he wouldn't have to hire a scrubbing woman. You could turn a profit from anything if you tried.

But apart from the profit, he thought wistfully, it'd be nice to have company. It had surprised him how much he enjoyed having his father around. He wasn't good at making friends, never had been, but now there'd be all sorts of people to talk to. And if any of the children had decent voices they could have sing-songs in the evenings sometimes, with his father playing the piano.

When they got back to the doctor's house, they were let in by the back room and Barlow himself came to see them.

'The babies have proved satisfactory. We'll need to have adoption papers drawn up and you'll sign them before you hand the little girls over to their new parents.'

'And the money?' Nev asked.

'Will be paid on the day you hand over the chil-dren, and not until.'

'Who will they be going to?' Jane asked.

'That is none of your business, madam.'

Her face crumpled. 'I just want to know they'll be all right.'

'I can give you my word they'll live very comfortably indeed, but you're to say nothing of what's happened to them except that they've gone to live with relatives in Yorkshire. *Nothing!* Do you hear me? If I find out you've talked about this, I'll make sure you regret it.'

Jane was frightened by his fierce expression as much as by the threat, and nodded. 'Yes, sir. Whatever you say, sir.'

Nev smiled all the way home and didn't at all mind pushing the rickety wooden cart. They were worth a lot of money, these two babies.

Two weeks later Jane waited till everyone had left for work or school, then got ready for her wedding. She hadn't told any of her family what she was doing because she knew they'd try to stop her. She was especially afraid of what Carrie might say or do. Her elder daughter had been upset when the twins were born, but had grown fond of them now. Well, all the children had.

It was a bit soon for her to be marrying again, but a woman needed a man and if Jane didn't make sure of Nev, someone else might tempt him into marriage. He was lonely, she could tell that. She washed herself all over, since getting married was a momentous occasion, then put on the new clothes Carrie had bought her from the pawn shop. Her milk had dried up quickly, thank goodness, and the twins had taken happily to the mashed food and boiled goat's milk brought for them every day by Mrs Lowson.

As she smoothed her skirt down, Jane hoped she looked as nice as she felt. She even had a bonnet to wear today, instead of putting a shawl over her head, because Nev had bought it for her 'specially as a wedding present.

Feeling very self-conscious, she let Mrs Baxter in to look after the twins and when her friend exclaimed at her appearance, tried not to blush and failed. But she didn't say where she was going because Nev had told her not to, and when he spoke firmly with a certain look on his face Jane was a bit nervous of him. Arthur hadn't noticed much about what was going on around him, but Nev seemed to notice every single thing.

When she got to the church, she found him waiting for her, with his father for a witness.

'Where's your witness?' he asked at once.

'Oh, dear! I forgot to bring someone.'

He looked so annoyed she began to cry. He sighed and patted her shoulder, telling her not to worry, then went round the back of the church and found the gravedigger making a new hole. For a couple of shillings the man was happy to come and oblige them.

Then they all went inside and, just as easily as anything, the curate married them. Not till she'd signed her cross in the parish register and received her marriage lines did Jane relax. She couldn't read them, of course, but if the curate said that's what they were, she was sure he wouldn't lie. She'd lost the bit of paper she'd got when she married Arthur, but she didn't intend to lose this one.

'Come on, Mrs Linney,' Nev said, hurrying her out of the church. 'We've another job to do today. Two little parcels to dispose of. We have to be at the doctor's in an hour.'

'Oh, dear, I haven't washed them or anything yet.'

He held back his impatience. He knew Jane was a lazy sort, but was quite confident that he'd be able to train her out of that because unlike other men his line of work lay mainly at home so he would nearly always be there. And he'd not only have her company, he'd have the comfort of her in his bed without the worry of her belly swelling. Hadn't she told him herself that she couldn't have any more children? 'Then we'll go back and wash them now. Dad, you can go home – and take the marriage lines with you. We don't want to lose them.' He snatched the piece of paper out of Jane's grasp and passed it over, then turned back to offer her his arm.

Raife walked away. No use asking what was going on. Nev didn't tell you owt unless he wanted to. Whatever his son was up to, it would be something that brought in money, and good money too, because he had been gleeful this morning.

Still, Raife had a home again, good food every day and a piano to play. He didn't intend to lose that so kept his thoughts inside his own head and continued to make himself useful around the place, not to mention handing over half of what he earned at the pub to his son. Nev was really pleased about the money. Raife was more pleased about the enjoyment he found in playing for folk.

And as for Jane's family coming to live with them, he was looking forward to that enormously. He liked childer and they usually liked him.

# 11

Carrie got home from work to find her mother and Nev Linney sitting at the kitchen table, sharing a pot of tea and looking very cosy together. She wasn't surprised when he took charge, because everyone knew he was that sort of man, and her mother seemed to love having a fellow to tell her what to do.

Nev gestured to a stool. 'Sit down, Carrie. Your mother will pour you a cup of tea, then we have something to tell you.'

She did as he'd ordered and was surprised to see how her mother's hand was shaking as she passed her the cup. Only as she took it did Carrie see the wedding ring on her mother's finger. She stared at it, blinked, but it wasn't her imagination, there really was a ring. That shocked her and she looked from one to the other, her eyes asking the question her voice couldn't form yet.

'I see you've noticed,' said Nev with a smug smile. 'Your mother and I were married today.'

With an effort Carrie managed to say, 'That's good news. I hope you'll be very happy together.'

'Yes, indeed.' He patted his bride's hand then turned back to her daughter, his smile fading. 'It'll mean a lot of changes for you all. As you know, this house is to be knocked down –' his scornful glance said that'd be no loss '– so you were going to move anyway, but now you'll be able to move into my house with your mother.'

'Isn't that nice, love?' her mother put in, her eyes pleading for understanding and co-operation.

'Yes.' Carrie suddenly realised that the twins weren't to be seen or heard. 'Are the babies upstairs sleeping?'

Her mother gave a sob and put a hand across her mouth.

'Now, now!' Nev patted his bride's arm but his voice was sharper and he didn't turn back to Carrie till his new wife had calmed down. 'That's the other thing we have to tell you. Your baby sisters have been adopted by a rich couple who will be able to offer them a much better life than your mother could ever have done.'

Carrie felt sick. 'You've given the twins away?'

'For their own good,' her mother put in quickly.

'*How could you do that?*'

'Because it was best for everyone, not just them,' Nev said, his tone stern now. 'Your mother's not strong. It was wearing her out, trying to look after two lively babies, and it'd only have got worse as they grew older.'

'We were give a lot of money for them and—' Jane began, but her husband jabbed his elbow into her side and she broke off.

He breathed deeply then said in a carefully controlled voice, 'I told you not to tell anyone about that, Jane.'

'It's just our Carrie. She won't let it out to anyone else, will you, love?'

When his step-daughter didn't answer, Nev studied her, his eyes shrewdly assessing as if he could see into her mind.

Carrie could feel anger rising in her, overcoming the sick, frozen feeling. Selling her baby sisters was a shameful thing to do, and nothing they could say or do would convince her otherwise.

Before she could speak, Nev continued, still in that measured voice, 'The adoption papers have been signed and the children taken away. There's nothing you – or I – can do to change that now. We don't even know where they've gone and it's better for everyone that way.'

'Better,' Jane echoed, nodding like a puppet.

Carrie couldn't speak because tears were clogging her throat. She'd grumbled about the extra work the twins made, but when you looked after babies day in, day out, especially such bonny, happy-natured little creatures as her sisters, you grew fond of them. The way May loved to have her tummy tickled, the way Nora liked to be held up so that she could see more . . .

The thought that she'd never see them again, never play with them, made Carrie want to weep – only she didn't intend to break down in front of Nev Linney. When he raised his voice slightly, she forced herself to pay more careful attention to what he was saying.

'We'll not discuss that any more, Carrie, but we do need to talk about the move. I have certain conditions for anyone living in my house, and I want you to make sure your brothers and sisters understand them. For a start, you'll all hand your wages to me untouched. I don't like to see good money being wasted.'

'I don't waste money, Mr Linney.'

'She's allus very careful, Nev,' Jane put in. 'Too careful sometimes.'

'You can't be too careful with money.'

Carrie watched him pat his wife again, as if she were a dog, then turn back to her.

'If so, you're the only one in this family who is, but I like to make sure of things myself – *in my own household* – so I'd prefer you all to hand over your wages to me.'

She could hear the threat under his softly spoken words. 'Who'll buy the food, then?'

'I will.' He gave her a tight-lipped smile. 'You'll never go hungry in my house, I promise you.'

'I'm not giving you all my wages, only enough to cover my keep.'

Another of those looks that said he was sure of his power over her. 'If you want to live with me, you'll hand over everything – as will your brothers and sisters. Otherwise you can find yourself somewhere else to live. It's your choice. If I find you being sensible, I'll give you a few coppers every now and then to spend on yourself. That's only fair.'

Carrie looked at her mother reproachfully. Not only had the babies been sold, but it looked like the rest of them had too.

'It's not much to ask in return for a place to live,'

Jane said quickly. 'You should be grateful, all of you, that I've found you somewhere. It's a lovely house, just lovely, and my Nev's a good man. He'll be the head of the house, and this time *you* had better understand that. We don't want any more upsets about that sort of thing, do we?'

Her mother's expression was so triumphant Carrie felt sick to her soul. Don't say anything else, she told herself. Wait. Think about things. See how it all turns out. This would probably be better for the younger children, though she doubted it'd be better for her. She glanced round and sighed. It couldn't be much worse than this place, though. She was ashamed for him to see how little they possessed. 'When are we moving?'

'Your mother is moving today. The rest of you have to move out of here before Friday, so you can start going through the house and making sure it's spotless. We don't want the landlord trying to fine us, do we?'

'But it's going to be knocked down!'

'That doesn't matter. Mr Stott always insists that his houses be left spotless, so that's how it'll be done. We gave notice to the rent man last week and he'll be round to inspect everything on Friday morning.' Nev stood up and helped Jane to her feet, then glanced at Carrie again. 'I'll send a cart over for the furniture about nine on Friday. One of you girls will have to be here to see everything loaded and do the final cleaning. I don't mind which one of you it is. Whoever can most easily get the morning off work, I suppose. Jane, my dear?' He offered his bride his arm.

Stony-faced, Carrie followed them down the hall and watched her mother walk away without even calling farewell or turning to wave. She stood at the front door and couldn't for a minute think what to do next except turn her face up to the sunshine, close her eyes and let it warm the chill that had settled inside her.

'Excitin' news, isn't it?' Mrs Baxter called from next door.

Carrie nodded and went quickly inside again. She couldn't face their gossiping neighbour till she'd pulled herself together. She walked into her bedroom, then came out again, ending up in the kitchen where ragged, grey-looking baby clouts were still hanging up to dry. She blinked her eyes furiously at the sight of them, hoping May and Nora would be happy, hoping their new mother would love them – as their old mother hadn't.

It was no use. The tears wouldn't be held back. She covered her face with her hands and let the mois-ture run down her cheeks, not daring to release the sobs that had built up inside her or she'd have been howling as loudly as an infant.

Of course, she could go to the Dragon. Miss Beckett had already offered to let her live in and . . . No, she couldn't do that, not yet. There were the children to think about. She had to make sure they were all right before she did anything about her own life, so she'd need to go and live in Nev's house, at least at first. He wouldn't ill-treat them – would he? He didn't seem like a physically violent man, but everyone knew how he loved money, how careful he was with each halfpenny.

The front door opened again and she hurriedly brushed away the tears, turning to see her new step-father standing there in the kitchen doorway, breathing heavily as if he'd been hurrying.

'Your mother has just told me there's a pot of money somewhere. *Her* money. Given to her by the men at Stott's. Several pounds, I believe. Before you do anything else you'll hand that over to me.'

'It's not here.'

'Where is it?'

'At a friend's. I'll go and get it, bring it round to you later.'

'I'll come with you *now* to get it. I'm not having you cheat your mother out of a single penny.'

All desire to weep left her then and Carrie glared at him. 'I've never cheated anyone in my life! If I'd left the money here with Mam it'd have been spent within the week – wasted. If you don't know how bad she is with money now, you soon will.'

He stood for a minute, frowning, then nodded. 'You're probably right about that and I apologise for doubting your honesty. But it's still her money, and now that I'm her husband it's mine. Get your shawl. We'll tell your mother to go home, then we'll go and fetch the money together.'

'I've used some of it up on buying new clothes and food. We had nothing but what we stood up in when my father died.'

'But there is some left still?'

She nodded and followed him out, trying not to let her anger show at the way he clearly mistrusted her.

She led the way round to the back of Dr Latimer's house, explaining, 'The housekeeper's a friend of mine.'

When Essie opened the door she stared in surprise at the man standing there and looked at Carrie for an explanation.

'This is Mr Linney. He and my mother got wed today. He wants the money I left with you.'

Essie's lips tightened. She knew what she thought of men who took money off hard-working lasses like this one, and anyway, everyone in town knew about this fellow's love of money. What did *he* need with Carrie's hard-won savings? 'Wait there.' She closed the door and went inside, lifting down the pot. After a moment's hesitation she took half the money out of it and piled it quietly on the mantelpiece, taking care not to let the coins chink.

When she opened the back door she held the pot out, rattling it contemptuously. 'I'll tip it into your hand, shall I, Mr Linney? The pot's mine, you see.'

He held out one hand and when she'd poured the coins into it, he counted them straight away. Essie stood there with her arms folded, watching him, not even trying to hide her disgust.

'Two pounds, three shillings and fourpence,' he said. 'I'd expected more from what your mother said.'

Carrie kept her face straight because she knew there had been more and guessed her friend had kept some back. It was a relief because she didn't know what Nev Linney was really like and it'd feel better to have something behind her, just in case. 'I told you about that already. We had things to get out of pawn and we needed to buy clothes for everyone.'

He frowned. 'Well, you won't find me pawning anything. With a business like mine, I have a position to maintain in this town and you'll all need to do me credit from now on. I'll make sure you eat adequately and are dressed decently.' He gave the housekeeper a nod and took his step-daughter's arm, pulling her away. 'Come along then. You can come home with me now. I've decided to show you my house.'

Carrie didn't know what to think of him then. If he did feed and clothe them all properly, she'd be grateful and it'd be a load off her mind. She stole a glance or two sideways at him as they walked, but his expression gave away nothing so she didn't know what to expect. Rumour said he was tight with money, but it didn't say much else about him. It was as if no one really knew him.

Did her mother? Or had Jane just rushed into marriage because she couldn't bear to be without a man?

Essie watched them walk off, her face grim. When Carrie turned at the gate to wave, she raised her hand then shook her head in irritation and went back inside. Dr Latimer disapproved of the way Linney kept the daily lodgers waiting outside, whatever the weather, but he also said Nev kept the place as clean as he could in the circumstances and gave fair value for money, even in the food he provided for those who could afford it.

Would Linney be kind to Carrie and her brothers and sisters? Would he feed them properly?

She didn't like to see Carrie in someone's power, but at least her young friend would have a roof over her head now and the responsibility for her mother would be lifted from her. With a woman as silly as Jane Preston – no, Jane Linney now – that was a godsend.

In the meantime Essie would keep the money safe and continue to help the lass if she needed it. That at least she could do. She didn't know when she'd taken such a fancy to someone, she really didn't. Not since her sister died. Was she being foolish? What did it matter? When you were alone in the world, you could be as foolish as you wanted and no one would know or care.

In the meantime she was worried about Mrs Latimer, who had been doing too much and was looking distinctly peaky. She intended to ask the doctor to make sure his wife took things easier. The trouble was he was working too hard as well. And he was looking older, well he was much older than his wife, but he hadn't looked his age until recently.

Life was never easy, not for anyone.

A few minutes' brisk walk brought them to Linney's house. Carrie stopped to look at it as Nev fumbled for his key. She'd passed the place many times, of course, since it was just up the hill from the Dragon, but she'd never been inside. 'It's much bigger than our house!'

He smiled, clearly pleased by that remark. 'It's even bigger once you get inside, because there was a bit of land at the back and when I managed to buy the house, I bought that too. I had the common rooms built on it.' He opened the front door. 'We'll go in this way today, but normally you'll go round to the side door.' He locked the front door carefully behind him, to Carrie's surprise since no one else in the Lanes locked their doors. 'This way.'

She followed him along a narrow passageway which had a strip of carpet runner down the middle. Quite new carpet, too, with pretty colours. It felt lovely and soft beneath her feet. They passed three doors before they came to the kitchen. How many rooms were there, then?

Her mother was sitting at the table and the old man who played the piano at the Dragon was pouring water from the kettle into a big brown teapot.

Neville waved one hand in his direction. 'This is my father. Dad, this is Carrie, Jane's eldest.'

'Pleased to meet you, Mr Linney,' Carrie said.

Raife smiled at her. 'I'm pleased to meet you, too, lass. You don't favour your mother.'

'Arthur allus said she favoured *his* mother,' Jane put in.

Nev's mouth grew tight. 'I don't want to hear any more about what Arthur said or did, Jane. You're *my* wife now. As I've already told you.'

'Yes, Nev. Sorry, love. It just slipped out.'

Carrie was angry at that. He'd had no need to jump on her mother so sharply. It was only natural that she'd mention a first husband of so many years.

Raife pulled out a chair. 'Sit yoursen down, lass. You look like you could do with a bit of feeding up. What do you think, Nev? We don't want folk thinking we can't feed our family, do we?'

Nev studied her, his eyes half-closed. 'You're right. She does look as if she's not eating properly. Give her some bread and cheese.'

Raife moved across to a pantry, winking at Carrie as he passed, and brought out a fresh loaf and the biggest piece of cheese she'd ever seen outside a shop. The mere sight of the golden crust on the loaf made her mouth water.

'We'll all have something to eat,' Nev said abruptly. 'I missed my dinner and I don't want my new wife fainting on me on our wedding day.'

It was obviously an attempt to improve the mood. Jane laughed heartily, as she did at any simple joke, Raife let out a rusty chuckle and Carrie forced a smile.

They were served on matching crockery and Jane said comfortably, 'Eh, what lovely plates. Nev, I can't believe I'm really here, living in this beautiful house.'

Carrie watched in amazement as another man's expression softened at a word or two from her mother. Her father's had always done so, too, even when he grew bad-tempered with the rest of them. What was there about her mother that men liked so much?

As he started to eat, Nev studied his wife and said abruptly, 'We shall definitely have to get you some new clothes, Jane. You don't do me credit in that ragged thing. I'll take you into town tomorrow.'

She beamed at him. 'Eh, that'll be lovely. You're so kind to me!'

Then he turned to Carrie and studied her in turn. 'I suppose those clothes will do for cleaning at the Dragon, though I'll look for a better job for you than that.'

'I like working there and Miss Beckett is going to give me a better job when the music room opens.'

He considered this for a moment, then nodded. 'That may be all right then. I hear Frank Beckett's not best pleased with the idea of it, though. Are you sure it's going to happen?'

Carrie felt uncomfortable discussing her employers' private affairs. 'I wouldn't know about that, but the workmen are there every day so *something's* going to happen. *I* think it'd be a little gold mine. We haven't got anything like that in Hedderby.'

Nev leaned back, looking a bit scornful now. 'How can you possibly know that?'

'Miss Beckett took her into Manchester to see a music saloon,' Jane said. 'She took that Bram Heegan too, because he's going to work there as well. But old Mr Beckett sent our Carrie with them because he didn't want his daughter going out on her own with a man after dark.'

Nev pursed his lips. 'They're serious about the music room then, Carrie?'

'Mr Eli and Miss Beckett are very keen on it, yes.'

'Well, there's many a slip, 'twixt cup and lip.' He picked up his second piece of bread and cheese and took a large bite, chewing thoughtfully and eventually adding indistinctly, 'Yes, many a slip.'

After they'd eaten, he turned to Carrie. 'You get two shillings a day from the Dragon, your mother tells me. Till you move in here, I'll send your mother round for it and she'll bring you the food for the day. I can get stuff cheaper when I buy in bulk for the lodgers.' He held out his hand. 'Give me today's money.'

With great reluctance Carrie pulled out the florin coin and put it into his hand.

At a nod from his son, Raife went into the pantry and packed some food up.

'Show her the common room and the other one on the way out,' Nev ordered, then turned back to his new wife, whispering something that made her giggle.

Raife showed Carrie the common lodging room with its rows of coffin-like sleeping stalls and a neat pile of rough blankets by the door. 'They all sleep in here, men and women alike. I open the windows to air it, but it allus smells bad. Well, the poor sods have nowhere to wash theirsen, do they?'

He glanced over his shoulder to make sure they were alone, then lowered his voice and added quickly, 'When you come to live here, if you want to know owt, ask me first. Nev isn't a bad chap, not really, but there are things that upset him and I can mebbe give you a hint or two about how best to manage him. He does like to be in charge of the money, but he's good with it and generous about food and such.'

'I'd be grateful for any help you can give me, Mr Linney.'

He smiled and patted her arm. 'I'm looking forward to your family moving in because it'll be nice to have some company. No one ever comes here except on business. That's why Nev married your mam, I reckon. For the company. Folk don't seem to take to him and he gets lonely, but he's not a bad fellow, you know, not now his mother's not there to egg him on to be nasty. My wife was a strange woman. *Your* mother thinks a lot of him and that puts him in a better mood. We all need to be liked, you know.'

She'd never thought before how Nev might feel about the way people avoided him and looked at the old man with new respect, thinking how kindly and sensible he seemed. Perhaps with him here it wouldn't be so bad.

He showed her into a second room, which was not as big as the first. 'This is where you'll all be sleeping.'

Carrie stared round. 'All of us?'

He nodded.

'Some of us girls are too old to share a room with our brothers. We'll have no privacy and there are times when you need that.' She blushed.

'Nev wants you in here for the moment. He doesn't open this room in summer, because it's not usually needed, but he gets more customers in winter when folk'll do owt to spend a night indoors.'

'I'm not sleeping with strangers!' Carrie swung round. 'And I'm going to tell him so.'

Raife grabbed her arm. 'Don't do it now. Move in and then think what to do.' He winked at her. 'There are some nice big attics, only no one's ever done owt up there. If Nev thinks you're taking up beds the lodgers could *pay* for, he may change his mind about where you should sleep. Only don't tell him I said so. Say you've gone exploring and found the attics, and you're worried about stopping him earning money.'

She looked at him, thinking about this new idea.

'You seem like a clever lass,' he said. 'Use your brain and you'll live very comfortably here.'

On a sudden impulse Carrie gave him a hug. 'Thank you, Mr Linney. I'll not only use my own brain, I'll use yours too.'

'Everyone calls me Raife. I don't like being called Mr Linney, never have. It reminds me of my father an' he were as sour a fellow as you could ever meet.'

She walked thoughtfully back to Throstle Lane. She couldn't imagine how they'd go on living at Linney's. Still, it was more promising than she'd expected and she really liked old Raife. Kindliness shone from his face.

Carrie waited until all the others came home from work that evening, though she had to stop Robbie from grabbing a piece of bread and going straight out to the pub by telling him they were moving to a new house and needed to talk about it.

When she explained exactly what had happened

that day, and what their mother had done, there was dead silence for a moment then Marjorie began to sob.

Robbie looked angrily across the table. 'Well, *I'm* not going to live with Linney. He's not having all my wages. What was she *thinking* of to marry him?'

'You know what she's like,' Carrie said quietly. 'She can't manage without a man. I don't suppose it'll be too bad. His father lives there too and he's really nice, and the house is lovely. There's even a piano and Raife is going to play it to us.'

Robbie's expression was challenging. 'Does that mean you're going to live there and do as he tells you? I thought better of you, Carrie Preston.'

'I don't have much choice.' She looked round at the younger ones. 'I have to make sure the children are all right.'

'That's Mam's job.'

Carrie just looked at him and he didn't say anything else except, 'I suppose I can have my tea now?'

She watched him grab a piece of bread and cheese and go out, chewing as he walked. She knew he'd be straight down to the Dragon. Well, there was no way she could stop him. She wondered if he would go with them to the new house or whether he'd find himself lodgings. He hadn't been a lot of help lately, seemed constantly angry at what was going on at work, but she hated to see the family split up further.

She looked down at her cracked old plate, comparing it with the pretty one she'd eaten off at Linney's. Already she was eating better, with cheese twice today. She tried to take comfort from the sight of everyone filling their bellies and tell herself it augured well that Nev had sent round cheese as well as bread, but for some reason she couldn't fathom, she couldn't shake off a sense of foreboding about the changes that were to take place.

Where would they all lead?

Jane came round the following afternoon soon after Carrie had finished work. 'Nev sent me for the money.' She plonked a big sacking bag on the table and flopped down on the nearest stool, waving one hand at the bag. 'That's the food for tonight an' tomorrow morning. Eh, it's grand not to have to worry about what to eat, isn't it? Well?' She held out one hand.

With a sigh Carrie handed over her two shillings. 'You'll not spend it on the way back, will you?'

Jane shuddered at the mere thought. 'Oh, no. Nev's a bit strict about money. He deals with all that. He's not at all like your father.' She looked over her shoulder then lowered her voice as if she expected him to be eavesdropping. 'I don't think it's fair not to give me anything when he got all that money for the twins.'

'How much did he get?'

'A hundred pound . . . fifty each.' Jane clapped a hand over her mouth. 'Oh, dear, I shouldn't have said that. He told me not to tell anyone how much. You won't let him know I told you, will you, Carrie? He'd be that angry.'

'No, of course I won't. He hasn't been hitting you, has he? You seem a bit afraid of him.'

Jane's face relaxed. 'No, he'd not hurt me, an' he's a comfortable man in bed, too. I like that. It's just that he gets a look on his face if something upsets him, an' then – well, I'm more frightened of him when he *looks* at me like that than I ever were when your Dad threatened to thump me.'

Carrie couldn't help asking, 'Why did you do it, Mam?'

'Do what?'

'Sell the twins.'

Jane shrugged. 'Nev said it were best for 'em an' I daresay he's right. It were because of the money that he were happy to marry me. He's a clever fellow an' I know I'm not, but I do know how to keep a man happy.' She stared at Carrie. 'That's something you'll have to learn, my girl. You're far too independent. Men don't like women to go against them. You'll see, once you're wed.'

'I keep telling you I'm never going to get wed, an' I mean it. But I was talking about the twins. Don't change the subject. I still can't believe you'd give them away. Don't you miss them?'

For a moment or two Jane's face puckered up, then she sniffed and knuckled away a tear. 'I do an' I don't. They were bonny little things, but I used to get that tired. Now . . . well, there's Nev looking after me and life's going to be so much easier.' She smiled. 'You'll see. Best thing I ever did for all of us, marryin' him. You wouldn't believe how comfortable our bed is. It's got a proper feather mattress. I've never slept so well for years. Or eaten so well either.' She beamed at her daughter.

It was so easy to keep her mother happy, Carrie thought. If she had a man to tell her what to do, food and somewhere to sleep with that man, then Jane was satisfied. Carrie wished she herself could take life more easily and not worry about the future. No, she didn't. She didn't want to drift along and let someone else point the way.

Marjorie took after their mother. She would be plump if she could eat well, was soft by nature and easily influenced. Carrie's other sisters were happy-go-lucky creatures, too young and working too hard to worry about anything as long as they had food, clothes and a chance to stand on street corners with their friends, laughing and chatting to lads. Dora, at least, was starting to eye lads with real interest.

But if Nev tried to get rid of any more of her brothers and sisters – for whatever reason! – Carrie would stop him somehow. A family should be together, look after one another, that above all. She was still angry at Robbie for saying he wasn't coming with them.

# 12

Eli got up early, rubbing his hands together to warm them. The mornings were nippy now, but they'd done the donkey work on the music room and were about to start fixing up the walls so that they could work on the interior. He went outside to check that everything was all right and to see if any of the workmen had arrived yet.

Joanna joined him, cradling a cup in her hands. 'There's a pot of tea in the kitchen if you want some.'

He nodded, his thoughts still on exactly how they were going to organise the next stage. He'd drawn it out several ways to try to get some idea of what it'd all look like, but still couldn't decide which design would be best.

His cousin came to stand beside him. 'You do this every morning.'

'What?'

'You come out to inspect your little kingdom.'

He grinned. 'Well, it's as good a way as any to start the day.'

Joanna shivered and moved back towards the side door of the pub. 'I'll be glad when we've got the place enclosed. That wind's cutting right through me.'

Eli followed her, accepting a cup of tea, drinking it quickly and then holding his cup out for a second one. 'Uncle Frank not up yet?'

'No. Dad's not feeling so well. I told him to have an extra hour in bed. Now we've got you, he doesn't have to get up at the crack of dawn, if only he'll believe it.' She stirred some sugar into her second cup, wondering what was wrong with her father who hadn't looked at all well lately. Was it just old age or something worse? He and she never showed their feelings to one another, unlike her mother who had spoken of her love to her daughter every day. But nonetheless, if she lost her father, Joanna knew she'd miss him. He wasn't easy to love but still he was her father, had been there all her life.

'I can't decide on how that stage should be placed,' Eli said abruptly.

There was the sound of a door banging in the pub and someone called, 'It's only me.' Carrie appeared in the kitchen doorway a minute later, her face rosy from her brisk walk down the hill. 'Shall I get started, Miss Beckett?'

'Have a cup of tea first. Bram will be here soon with Bonny, then we'll all get going.' Joanna took another cup off the shelf and got out a loaf, cutting two slices and sticking them into the wire contraption that you could hold out to the fire to toast them in. 'Here, Eli, make yourself useful and toast these.'

He took the gadget without a word and held it in front of the glowing coals in the centre of the stove.

Carrie sipped her tea, relishing a moment's rest

before the day's work started. 'What's happening out in the music room today? I love to see it changing.'

Eli grimaced. 'Clearing up, filling in the gaps in the walls, then starting work on the inside. I'm still trying to decide on the design for the stage. Here, take a look.' He turned and with his free hand shoved three pieces of paper across the table, all of which bore sketches.

'Did you draw these?'

He nodded. 'Do you want me to explain them?'

'No, I can see what you mean.' Carrie stared at them, understanding at once how each might fit in at the end of the music room. But there was something not quite right. She frowned, trying to work it out. 'Could you—' She broke off, suddenly embarrassed at the thought of voicing her suggestion. What did she know about anything?

'Could we what?' Eli smiled at her. 'Go on. Everyone's entitled to an opinion.'

'Well, the music saloon we went to in Manchester had a little stage here,' she touched the sketch, 'for the Chairman to sit on. And since our music room is going to be quite narrow, if the Chairman sits on the stage like in this drawing, he'll take up too much room. Doesn't he need to be to one side?'

Eli pulled out the sketch underneath. 'I tried that, but that puts him between the audience and the performers. We do need a Chairman, but we don't want him blocking the view.' He said it then, though he'd not told anyone yet. 'I'm going to be the Chairman here. I reckon I can do it.'

'Watch out for the toast burning!' Joanna called out.

Eli pulled the metal frame hastily away from the fire, but was more interested in watching Carrie frown at the two sketches than he was in turning the toaster round. He liked the way her brow furrowed and the way she absent-mindedly brushed away wisps of hair. Lovely hair she had, and her hands would be pretty too if they weren't so reddened by scrubbing.

Carrie looked from one to the other. 'Couldn't you—' She broke off again, still nervous of offering ideas.

'If you've any idea, however small, share it with me,' begged Eli. 'I'm fair stumped at the moment.'

She turned to Joanna. 'Can I go and see what's down there?' She pointed to the narrow passageway that led behind the kitchen to the scullery and various amenities like the coal hole, a large one because they used so much coal keeping the pub warm, with two fireplaces in the big room and the smaller one in the snug, as well as the kitchen fire.

'Yes.' Joanna exchanged puzzled glances with Eli.

Carrie walked down the passageway, then came back, counting her steps aloud. 'I need to check outside as well before I know if it'll work.'

As she vanished outside, Eli dumped the toaster on the table and they both followed her, intrigued.

Again Carrie counted her steps. When she was at the far end of the music room she turned and gestured to the wall. 'There's only the coal hole behind here. Couldn't you store the coal somewhere else, knock down the wall, and give the Chairman a set-back space here?'

Dead silence greeted her words, then Eli gave a shout of triumph and ran to catch her in his arms, swinging her round and round, laughing triumphantly. 'That's it! That's it!'

Joanna watched them from the doorway, smiling at his exuberance.

When he stopped twirling Carrie round, he turned to his cousin. 'It was staring us in the face all the time. I've been working on those designs for weeks and she solves the problem in a few minutes flat. Carrie lass, you're a genius!'

She blushed at this compliment. Her heart was still pounding from being picked up like that – picked up by Eli of all people. She'd loved the feeling of being in his arms, loved the joyful laughter that had echoed in her ears. 'Oh, well, it just seemed obvious. I'm glad I've helped you.'

'Come in and finish your breakfast now, Eli,' Joanna said.

Inside the kitchen Carrie hesitated, feeling embarrassed, not knowing what to do next.

'Sit down again, lass,' he said. 'I want you to look at my other drawings for the entrance and back of the music room after you've finished work. If you can see problems as easily as that, I'd like your opinions on the rest.'

'It was just chance,' she muttered, embarrassed. 'Listen, there's Bonny. I'd better start work.'

When she'd gone he looked at Joanna. 'It may be

pure chance, or it may be a gift she has, to see how spaces fit together. I can't believe she solved my problem so easily. It's worth seeing if she can improve on the rest.'

He forgot his toast and went to pace out the scullery and corridor as Carrie had done, then to look outside at the back of the pub and work out where to build another coal store in the rear yard. It was all coming together, he thought triumphantly. He was well on the way to getting his music room. And they hadn't laughed when he'd said he was going to be the Chairman.

Eli and Joanna brought Carrie back into the kitchen after she'd finished her work, spreading out the sketches again and asking her to think about them.

But this time she was conscious of Frank watching her sourly and couldn't seem to get her thoughts together. 'Can I think about it, Mr Beckett? I've a lot on my mind today, I'm afraid. We're moving tomorrow, if you remember.'

When she'd gone, Frank grumbled about them bringing the girl into his kitchen. 'She's a scrubbing woman, that's all. What does she know about building music rooms? What do *you* know, come to that? I should never have let you start. It'll be the ruin of me.'

Joanna intervened before Eli could say anything, asking if her father wanted some fried ham with his dinner that night, and the moment passed.

Afterwards she took her cousin aside. 'You'll have to get used to him carping, Eli. That's what he's like.

He never does anything happily, especially if it means change of some sort. And *don't* tell him about knocking down the coal hole. Not yet.'

'He gets on my nerves sometimes. How the hell have you put up with him all these years?'

Joanna shrugged. 'Oh, he wasn't always this bad. Some men seem to get grumpier as they grow older. I've seen it with our customers.' But she too was getting tired of her father's carping and criticising, tired of having to gentle him along. Only what choice did she have but to go on putting up with it?

As Robbie gathered his things together on the last evening, Carrie and Marjorie sat by the fire, exhausted after all their work cleaning the house, brushing down the walls, washing the windows and scrubbing every floor.

'You should be coming with us,' Carrie said abruptly.

Her brother turned from his small pile of possessions. 'I can't face it. And I'm not giving Nev Linney my money.'

'So you're leaving everything to me?'

'It's Mam's responsibility, not yours. You should go and live in at the Dragon. You'd be better off there. Happier.'

'When did Mam ever stand firm about anything? If I'm not there, Nev will do what he pleases with the children, and I'm not risking him ill-treating them.'

Marjorie went to stand behind Carrie's chair, her hands on her sister's shoulders. 'You won't be alone.

I'm not as strong or as clever as you, but I'll do the best I can.' She too looked accusingly at Robbie. 'You should have come with us, at least at first, till we know what he's like.'

He shook his head, jaw jutting out stubbornly. 'I'm *not* changing my mind.'

'You won't have much money left for drinking by the time you've paid for your lodgings,' Carrie said.

'I'd have nowt left if I went to live with *him*.' Robbie stopped fiddling with his things and looked at them. 'But if I can ever help you in any way, you know I will.' He looked at them as if expecting an answer, then shrugged and went upstairs, his boots echoing on the bare boards above their heads.

'Come to bed, love,' Marjorie said softly. 'You've done all you can.'

'Have I?'

'Yes.'

Carrie stood up and stretched, feeling exhausted.

Marjorie gave her a little push towards the front room. 'I'll see to the fire. You get off to bed.'

Instead, Carrie turned and gave her sister a hug. 'Thanks. I don't know what I'd have done without you this past week.'

'It makes you think, doesn't it? Life can change just like that.' Marjorie snapped her fingers and the faint sound echoed in the bare room. 'And there's nothing you can do to prevent it.'

'You just have to do your best and keep going,' Carrie said with a sigh.

Marjorie gave her a loving glance. 'I've left too

much to you. From now on I'll try to stand more firm, like you do.'

Carrie struck a stiff pose and Marjorie gave her another shove towards the door, laughing. In the bedroom, with muffled giggles, they rolled the sleeping Dora to the far side of their mattress and snuggled down beside her.

You just have to do your best, Carrie thought again as she drifted towards sleep. Well, she'd done that all right. But would it be enough? Would the children be happy in their new life?

And what were her baby sisters doing tonight?

Carrie woke with a start when the knocker-up started banging on the upper windows of the house opposite. She lay still for a minute, then as sleepy sounds showed that her sisters were starting to surface, threw back the covers and put on her outer clothes. It was the last time she'd do that here.

In the kitchen she got the fire going, relieved that some embers were still glowing and she didn't have to go next door to beg a burning coal. She shivered in the cold air as she waited for the small pieces of kindling to catch fire, and for a minute or two stood there, watching the glow spread. Realising suddenly that she was wasting time and the others would be up in a minute, she lit a candle and began to slice up the loaf. She must give Nev Linney his due. He'd made sure they had food every day, with enough for the following morning and some left over to take to work for dinner in the middle of the day. Exactly enough, not a crumb too much. Plain food, but better by far than anything they'd had during the past few years.

But she didn't like Nev doling things out, didn't feel right without even a penny of her own in her pocket. At least her half-sovereign and the other coins were safe with Essie, so he wouldn't be able to take them off her. That thought was a great comfort.

One by one the others left the house for the last time, exclaiming and wondering what it'd be like at Linney's. None of them had been inside yet. Her mother had said Nev didn't want them tramping mud in with such rainy weather, and it'd be time enough to show them the house when they moved in.

Robbie was the first to leave. He took his mattress, blanket and bundle next door, where he'd pick them up after work, then came back and stood looking at Carrie. He hesitated before coming across to hug her. 'I'll visit you.'

'If he lets you.'

'Don't be daft. Why should he stop me?'

Carrie felt sad as she heard the door bang behind him. She couldn't remember a time when Robbie hadn't been part of her life, tormenting her when he was a lad, but sticking up for her too against other groups of kids. He'd been a tall lanky creature till he turned nineteen, then he'd filled out a bit. She wondered how he'd manage his money now.

Ted was the last to leave. He waved Grace and Lily out, saying he'd catch up with them, then said to Carrie in a rush, 'I've got a few pence saved, but if

I take them with me, *he'll* have them off me, I know he will, like he takes your wages. What am I going to do with them?'

'Take them to Essie at Dr Latimer's, tell her you're my brother and ask her to keep them safe with mine.'

Ted stared at her, then grinned. 'You've got a bit put by too?'

'Yes. I'm surprised you have, though.'

He began tracing the pattern of the wood on the well-scrubbed kitchen table, avoiding her eyes. 'It was earning some money ourselves from selling the wood that did it. I spent it on food at first, then after we had more to eat I saved my pennies. I thought it might come in useful one day to have something because . . . Carrie . . .'

'Yes?'

'Can you ask him, Mr Linney I mean, if he'll let me work with Sammy's dad when I leave school? He says he'll teach me about carpentry, and if I seem likely he'll let me do a proper apprenticeship with him, though we'd have to find the money to pay for that. I didn't think we could, but Mr Linney's got plenty of money, hasn't he? Tell him I'll pay him back, make him things out of wood and . . . well, you will help me persuade him, won't you?'

Ted looked at her hopefully but she didn't feel optimistic about getting him what he wanted, not from a man who had a reputation for making every penny count twice. 'I'll do my best. We'll wait a bit to ask Nev, though, see how we all settle in together first. How soon do you need to know?'

'Not for a year or so. But I do want to work with wood, an' do it *properly*. I love making things.' His hands drew shapes in the air and his smile was blissful. After a minute it faded and he added gruffly, 'I don't want to work in Stott's. Some of the fellows there are rotten to the young 'uns, torment 'em and hit 'em. I'll run away if anyone tries to make me work there.'

Carrie sighed as she watched him go, then thought about his money. Elevenpence. That wouldn't go far. But it must seem like a fortune to Ted after having nothing all his life.

By the time the cart came she had everything ready. As the men carried their possessions out to it, the women from the street who didn't go out to work appeared on their doorsteps, their eyes assessing every item. One or two didn't bother to hide their scorn. Well, it was a pitiful collection, Carrie knew. Not much to show for a family as big as theirs. She'd let Robbie take his mattress and blanket. They all needed new mattresses now. She'd been going to make them in a week or two. Would Mr Linney let them buy some straw and make new ones?

Sending the men off with the cart, she turned round and started scrubbing the kitchen floor, working her way out to the front door just as the rent man turned up.

'You've taken your stuff out, then?' he said.

'Yes.'

'And left everything clean?'

'Yes. Hold on! I've just scrubbed the kitchen and passage.'

He peered inside then frowned down at his boots.

'Is it satisfactory? Mr Linney said it had to be satisfactory before I could leave.'

He studied her damp apron and sweaty face, and his gaze softened. 'Aye, lass. It'll do just fine.'

They stood there for a moment, she wringing out the floor cloth, he chewing the inside of his cheek.

'So you're going to live at Linney's, are you?' he said at last.

'Yes.'

'I don't envy you that.'

He turned and walked off down the street.

With a sigh Carrie gathered her things and did the same.

Carrie walked slowly down the hill, feeling utterly exhausted now, both from the extra work and from the strain and worry of the past week. She concentrated on placing one foot in front of the other, wishing she could have a break before she got to Linney's.

When someone lifted the bucket out of her hand, she jerked round, sagging in relief when she saw it was Bram.

'I'll lug this for you, love. What have you got in it? Rocks?'

She smiled. 'I have actually. Donkey stones.' Other women in the street used the soft creamy stones to colour the pavement near their front doors. She'd never been able to afford them before, but had given the babies' old clouts to the rag and bone man in exchange for a couple of donkey stones. It was another small step up the ladder of respectability. 'I had to leave the house clean and tidy,' she said by way of explanation and began walking again and he fell in beside her.

'Are you feeling all right?' he asked after they'd gone a few yards. 'Because I'm telling you, you don't look all right.'

'Just feeling a bit tired.'

'Robbie told me what a week you've had. I found him those lodgings. He'll be all right there, so that's one worry out of your hair.'

She stopped walking and raised her eyes to meet his, feeling tears well up at this unexpected support and sympathy. 'I feel as if he's deserted us.'

'I reckon it's better for him to be on his own. About time he learned to fend for himself, don't you think?'

'He'd be better if he didn't drink so much. Do you have to take him to the pub so often?'

'He'd go with or without me. At least I keep an eye on him an' stop him getting blind drunk. Besides, he won't be able to afford to drink as much from now on once he's paid for his lodgings. That'll be good for him.'

She dashed her hand quickly across her eyes, hating anyone to see her weeping.

'You'll be all right at Linney's. He's a fusspot, but he isn't a bad chap.'

'You're the only one who's got a good word for him.'

'A lot of folk are jealous because he's done well for himself.'

When they reached her destination, Carrie held out her hand for the bucket. 'Thanks.' She stood for a minute, watching Bram stride away, then took a deep breath and made her way round to the side entrance. When she got there she didn't know whether to knock or go straight in, so knocked then opened the door and called, 'It's me, Carrie.'

Raife came out of the kitchen to greet her, wiping his hands on a piece of rag. 'Nice to see you, lass. The men brought your things a while back. I'll leave everything for you and your mam to sort out. She and Nev have gone out to buy the day's food. They'll be back soon.'

Carrie stood there, numb with tiredness, not sure what to do first.

'Come and have a cup of tea before you start.' When she didn't move he took her arm and guided her to the table, removed the bucket from her grasp and pushed her gently down in one of the wooden chairs. He sat down next to her and put one arm round her shoulders. 'What's wrong, love?'

'I feel lost. For years I've been the one who had to sort everything out and now—'

'Now Nev will be in charge. He's not bad if you manage him right.' Raife winked at her and leaned forward to whisper conspiratorially, 'And he likes being flattered as much as the next man.'

Carrie was betrayed into a gurgle of laughter and he squeezed her shoulder then sat back. 'That's better. You look bonny when you smile. Oh, and one other thing. If you want something from Nev, find a way to make it show a profit for him, and you'll be more likely to get it.'

She looked at him wonderingly. 'Why are you telling me this? He's your son. Shouldn't you be on his side?'

'I'm on the side of making life as happy and easy as possible. When he was younger, Nev and I didn't get on very well. My fault as well as his, but mostly his mother was to blame. Now I'm a bit wiser, and though I'm dependent on him, I can usually manage to get what I want. It pays him to have me here, you see, because then he doesn't need to hire a woman to keep the place tidy and cook, just has to get someone in to scrub the floors and do the washing. My knees aren't up to scrubbing and I never could get the hang of washing.' Another wink. 'I shrank his underdrawers the first time I tried it, so he brought back the wash-erwoman.'

She chuckled.

'And I play the piano for him in the evenings some-times. He loves a bit of music, Nev does. Runs in the family. Can you sing?'

She shook her head. 'No. I sound like a sick frog when I try.'

He gave another of his rusty little chuckles. 'Then don't. He won't thank you for spoiling his music. Now, let me brew that tea.'

The back door opened and a voice called, 'Dad? Where are you?'

Raife stood up. 'There you are, Nev. Just in time for a cup of tea. Let me get it for you.'

Jane went to sit at the kitchen table, looking tired

herself. She glanced across at her daughter with a sort of shame-faced triumph, then down at herself.

'Goodness, you've got new clothes!' Carrie said at once. 'How nice you look! Has Mr Linney bought you them?'

'Yes. He's so kind to me, my Nev is.'

Carrie looked across at him, saw her step-father preening himself, and added, 'I'm glad my mother married you, Mr Linney. I know you'll look after her. And we're all grateful to you for giving us a home. We'll work hard and try not to be a nuisance.'

He nodded, a smug expression on his face.

Behind him, Raife winked at her.

Suddenly the burdens on Carrie's shoulders felt lighter, they really did.

After she'd eaten, she automatically helped Raife clear the table, then looked at her step-father. 'Shall I go and sort out our bedroom now or do you want me to do something else?'

'No, I don't need you for anything today.'

She went into the room at the very back of the building. It had a row of coffin-like stalls down each of the long sides, making sixteen 'beds' in all, each about two feet wide. She hated the idea of sleeping in one of those, and anyway the girls had only got two big mattresses, though Ted's narrow mattress fitted neatly into one of the boxes. She hesitated. If she'd been at home, she'd have sorted it out herself, but here . . . She sighed and took Raife's advice, going to look for Nev. She found him in the little room near the kitchen, counting out coins into piles and setting them ready.

He looked up as she knocked on the half-open door. 'Come in.'

She stared at the coins, wondering what he was doing with them.

He followed her gaze. 'There are some lodgers who say they've not got the right change and will pay in the morning when they've changed their money. Then they try to sneak away without paying. Folk call it "going on the mizzle", but I call it stealing. I make sure I always have enough change and no one comes in who doesn't pay me first.'

'They keep plenty of change in the Dragon, too,' she volunteered.

'Yes, they'd have to. Did you want something? Time is money, you know. I don't usually waste my time chatting.'

She explained her problem.

He frowned, then heaved himself to his feet. 'You'll have to go to the livery stables and get a couple of bales of straw delivered. We have a roll of mattress ticking waiting for the winter, so you and your mother can spend the afternoon making new mattress covers.'

It was out before she could stop herself. 'Mam can't sew. She can't see well enough.'

'Hmm. Then you can start the job, and your sisters can help you finish it when they come home from work. Tell the man at the stables to send the bill to me.' Then Nev's face brightened. 'This year I won't have to pay anyone to sew up the mattresses. You and your sisters can do it.'

'Marjorie's the best sewer. She's really good at sewing.'

'Good at mending too?'

Carrie nodded.

'Very convenient.' He waved one hand in dismissal and she went out, happy to get some fresh air while the weather was fine enough.

When she got back from the livery stables, Carrie went to ask Raife where the mattress ticking was stored and he took her up to the attics. She couldn't believe how much space there was up there, little of it being used except for one area full of boxes and bundles.

Raife gave her one of his enigmatic looks. 'That far side is warmest because it's over the kitchens, and if you had partitions put in between the posts, you could easy make bedrooms for yourselves.'

'What would Nev say to that?'

'Depends how you ask him. But remember, if you lot are using the back room, there'll be fewer beds for paying lodgers. You should remind him of that.'

Carrie had never had anyone help her like this and was speechless for a moment, then looked at him with tears in her eyes. 'Thank you.'

'What for?'

'Being so kind.' Her voice came out choked.

'It's my pleasure. I'll leave you to bring the mattress ticking down and I'll go and set the tea to cooking. There are needles and thread in the left-hand dresser drawer when you need them.'

When she was alone, Carrie walked up and down the attic, mentally creating bedrooms for them all. Was Raife right? Would she be able to manage Nev Linney? She didn't know, but she could at least try.

She was sewing up the third mattress when the children got back from school. Nev had looked in twice, grunted and gone away again. Did he think she'd be sitting around doing nothing? Carrie had never had much chance to be idle, not since she was old enough to carry a baby about. This was easy work and someone else was getting tea ready.

Ted, Grace and Lily were the first to arrive home. They'd waited for one another after school and were in an unusually subdued mood, even Ted.

Raife brought them through to the back room and Carrie set them to stuffing the new mattress covers with straw.

Nev looked in again and crooked one finger at Ted.

Grace and Lily stopped what they were doing to look apprehensively at Carrie.

'He's probably got a job for Ted. He doesn't like to see folk sitting around idle.'

It was dark by the time Marjorie and Dora came home. Edith was late, which meant the shop must be busy.

By the time Raife summoned them to the kitchen to eat, the mattresses were all sewn up and the girls had tried them out.

'I don't like the thought of sleeping like this,' Lily grumbled to Carrie. 'It'll be cold without Grace an' Edith to cuddle up to.'

'Don't complain. We'll see how we go, eh?'

Tea was stew, cooked by Raife, with more meat in it than Carrie had ever seen in a stew before. Big chunks of potatoes and pieces of carrot floated in a lovely gravy, and there was bread on the table as well.

When they all sat down, everyone looked instinctively at Nev, who had the pan of stew in front of him, standing on a trivet to protect the table. Raife brought a pile of dishes and he ladled out the stew. Jane put a piece of bread on each dish as it passed her.

Ted picked up his spoon but Raife hissed a warning and shook his head at him, so the lad put it down again, puzzled.

Nev filled his own dish last, piling it higher than the others and with more pieces of meat in it, but that was only to be expected. The man of the house always got the best food.

'We'll begin now,' he said.

Raife picked up his spoon and nudged Ted to do the same, then there was silence as everyone began eating.

'What did you learn at school today, young fellow?' Nev fired at Ted, who choked and had to be patted on his back before he could answer.

The meal was filled with awkward silences as everyone tried to eat quietly, or to answer the questions shot across the table at them. No one dared start a conversation of their own, not even Ted, and Lily couldn't be persuaded to speak at all, even when Nev asked her something. When all the dishes had been cleared of food, Nev refilled his own, looked into the pan and stared down the table at Ted. 'You look like a hungry young man.'

The boy goggled at him, not sure what to make of this.

'Pass me your dish. There's a bit left. Men need more food than women.'

When they'd all finished, Jane said, 'You and Dora can clear up, Marjorie, then do the dishes.'

They got up to obey her orders.

Carrie caught Raife winking at her and then looking meaningfully at Nev. Guessing what he was hinting, she cleared her throat. 'That was a lovely meal, Mr Linney. Lovely. We all thank you.'

He smirked at her. 'No one goes hungry under *my* roof.' When the table was cleared, he said to his father, 'We'll have a bit of music tonight, eh?'

'That'll be champion,' said Raife.

Nev led the way into the parlour, turned to frown at his new family and said abruptly, 'No one is to sit down till I get back.' He brought some sheets and spread them across the furniture. 'We shall have to do something about your children's clothes, Jane. They're dressed in rags, and dirty rags at that.'

'Sorry, Nev.'

When they were sitting down, Raife went to the piano. 'What shall I start with, son?'

Nev reeled off several song titles, then sat back with a pleased smile on his face.

Raife began to play, his fingers nimble on the keys, his face taking on a happy expression.

The one thing Carrie hadn't expected in their new home was an evening like this. Good food, followed by music. Tears of delight came into her eyes.

Nev's voice cut through the music and his father stopped playing at once. 'What's the matter, Carrie! Why are you crying?'

She explained and he began to smile at her. 'You've moved up in the world living with me, my girl.'

She nodded. It was true. And she might not be able to sing herself, but she loved listening to music, loved the way faces relaxed and bodies swayed as people joined in.

An hour later, Nev pulled out a big watch. 'Time for bed. Raife will show you how I like my hot milk, Carrie, then it'll be your job to prepare it at night for everyone.

'Hot milk?' she asked, astounded. 'We're to have hot milk as well?'

She found it hard to reconcile this generous side of Nev with the public opinion of him. Could life in his house really be as good as this?

# 13

The following Sunday was fine and Athol Stott decided to take a stroll around town after church. He sent his family back home and ambled down the main street, letting out a small 'Aaah' when he saw ahead of him a young woman he'd noticed several times in church. He'd made it his business to learn her name and been surprised to find she was Beckett's daughter and worked in the Dragon. A useful place, that pub. Drinking kept his workmen poor and therefore in need of every penny they could earn, in whatever condition he cared to keep his business.

Joanna Beckett wasn't pretty exactly, but then he'd found the pretty ones didn't always live up to their physical promise. This woman looked intelligent and he was tired of dull women, of whom his wife was surely the dullest. Also, Joanna had a beautiful voice, as he'd discovered one week when he'd been late for the service and had slipped into a rear pew. He enjoyed singing, was quite proud of his own voice too. But Joanna Beckett took care to conceal that beautiful voice of hers by singing in a subdued manner. He wouldn't have known about it if he hadn't been sitting right behind her. She wasn't in the choir either, which surprised him. There was a whole gaggle of hopeful spinsters in the choir, and she looked like a confirmed spinster.

Probably they wouldn't have her because she wasn't exactly respectable, working in a pub, was she? And her father hadn't been seen in church since he buried his wife, from what Athol's wife said.

All in all, he was intrigued by this young woman and had decided to pay her a bit of attention. He needed a new interest.

Speeding up, he soon overtook her then tipped his hat and slowed down to walk by her side. 'Miss Beckett, isn't it? I've seen you in church. Athol Stott, at your service.'

She looked at him in shock, as if she didn't know what to say, then muttered something and hurried on.

He speeded up and stayed beside her, amused by this. Playing hard to get, eh? Well, he didn't mind humouring her as long as these silly games didn't go on for too long. She must realise how flattering it was to be singled out by him for attention. 'I couldn't help noticing what a beautiful voice you have and wondering why you don't join the choir?'

Joanna scowled at him. 'I've no time for that sort of thing. I've my living to earn.'

'Working in the Dragon? Surely your father doesn't need to involve you in that sort of menial toil? It must be a little goldmine, that place.'

She stopped dead in her tracks. 'I don't know why you've chosen to accost me, sir, but I'd be grateful if you'd return to your wife and family and leave me alone!' The man was well known in the town for preying on young women, usually ones who dared not refuse him. Surely he didn't think she was one of them? A quick glance at his thin, smiling face made her shiver. There was something predatory and fox-like about him. He had a thin jutting chin, a nose that was too pointed, a mouth full of over-large teeth. His hair was a faded reddish-brown, receding rapidly, and that made his face look even more elongated and, well . . . fox-like.

When she set off walking again he remained by her side and a quick sideways glance showed her that he was smiling, no doubt enjoying her annoyance. Joanna was quite sure that if she started running, he'd run beside her. Well, she'd simply ignore him and get home as quickly as she could, but she hated people seeing them together, absolutely hated it.

Bram was strolling down the street, enjoying the sunshine. He'd had his usual Sunday quarrel with his mother about not attending mass and since it was a fine day had decided to leave the house and get some peace. When he saw Joanna walking towards him accompanied by Athol Stott he was puzzled. He wouldn't have expected her to keep company with that randy devil. Then he saw her stop and say something, noticed her heightened colour and the way her whole body was radiating anger, and moved forward to intercept them.

'Miss Beckett!'

'Mr Heegan.'

Her smile was warmly welcoming and he could sense her relief, so took a risk, nodding to the man beside her, 'Mr Stott,' then turning back to her. 'My dear Miss Beckett, I'm sorry I was late meeting you after church. I was unavoidably delayed.' When he offered her his arm, Joanna took it and clutched it far too tightly, almost pulling him away.

Stott tipped his hat again and stayed where he was.

When they were out of earshot, Bram asked, 'Was that sod bothering you?'

'Yes.'

'What did he do?'

'He didn't *do* anything I could complain about, but he walked beside me and made me feel – as if I had no clothes on.' She blushed at what she had just said, but it was the literal truth.

Bram could feel a shudder run through the arm that lay on his. 'He's a womaniser.'

It was out before Joanna could stop it. 'They say that of you, too.'

He stopped walking to stare earnestly into her eyes. 'The difference is, I keep company with women who're willing. He doesn't mind if they're unwilling, in fact some folk reckon he prefers it.'

She began moving forward again. 'So I've heard. I can't think why he picked on me. I'm not pretty, and surely I don't seem to be of loose morals?'

'You work in your father's pub. He probably thinks that means you're . . .' He hesitated, not knowing how to phrase it without offending her.

'Free with my favours,' she finished for him.

'It's only because he doesn't know you.' Bram grinned. 'I'll tell him you're ferociously respectable, if you like. You've that reputation among those who know you.'

She smiled, but it was an effort.

'Ah, he's probably bored. Likes variety. And his wife is the most colourless woman I've ever seen.'

'You don't think he might – pester me again?'

Bram shrugged. 'He might. If it amuses him to see you squirm. I could escort you to church and back for a few weeks, if that helps, though I warn you now, you'll not get me inside one of those places.' He chuckled. 'At least it'll stop me having the usual Sunday morning row with Mam when I refuse to go to mass with her.'

Joanna smiled and relaxed a little. 'Is that what happens?'

'Every single week. She's not giving up on me and sets the priest on to nag me, too. But *he* knows when he's beaten, at least, and makes no more than a token effort, which is more than I can say for Mam.'

They had reached the Dragon now and Joanna stopped, smiling at him, feeling more at ease with him than ever before. 'Thank you for your offer. I would appreciate your company on Sundays, Mr Heegan, if it's not too much trouble? Just for a few weeks.' She didn't want to ask Eli or it'd start her father hoping for a match between them again.

'I told you when we went to Manchester, my name's Bram to my friends.'

'Bram, then.'

'Does that mean we're friends?'

She looked flustered and he changed the subject quickly. She clearly wasn't used to banter. 'Before you go in, how about showing me round the new music room? They've made a lot of progress on it this week, I hear.'

'All right.' She led the way round the left side of the pub, walking along the narrow path that twisted through the piles of rubble waiting to be carted away. When she reached the open space she stopped but Bram went past her, right to the far end.

'Is this where the stage will be?'

'Yes.'

'Then let me christen it for you.' Quite unselfconsciously, he began to sing 'The Last Rose of Summer', his voice carrying clearly to where she was standing. It was one of her favourite songs. Without realising it Joanna began to move forward, unable to resist joining in.

When the song ended, he grinned and said, 'Let's sing it again. I'll do the harmony this time, if you'll hold the tune.'

They were singing before she could think about it and when the song ended they were both smiling at one another.

'Sure, I love singing,' he said, his voice more Irish-sounding than usual. 'Do you know, "Drink To Me Only"?'

She nodded and followed him into that song. Their voices matched so beautifully it sent a shiver of delight down her spine. She didn't know the harmonies as he did, only the melodies, because she'd never sung with anyone before.

She realised that the pleasure of singing had wiped away the dirty feeling Athol Stott had left her with and followed Bram willingly into 'The Ash Grove'.

When they'd finished there was applause from the kitchen doorway and she spun round to see Eli standing there, grinning as he clapped.

'Oh, dear.'

Joanna sounded so upset that Bram asked softly, 'What's the matter?'

'I don't usually sing round the pub because Dad hates it. My mother loved singing but he stopped her once they were married, I never found out why. He used to slap me if I sang after she died, though she and I would often have little sing-songs when he wasn't around or when we went for walks on the moors.' Maybe that was why he'd been so against the music room? Maybe it'd reminded him of her mother? Oh, who knew why her father did things? Joanna sometimes wondered if he simply enjoyed being contrary.

'I can't imagine why anyone would want to stop you using that beautiful voice of yours,' Bram said. 'I've not enjoyed myself so much for a long time.'

Their eyes met and she flushed. Then she suddenly caught sight of a figure standing in the street looking down towards the music room. Athol Stott again. He took his hat off and bowed, then put it on again and mimed applause. 'Let's go inside,' she said hurriedly, not even waiting for Bram's agreement. 'I need a cup of tea, and I'm sure you won't refuse one.'

In the doorway Eli stopped Bram for a minute. 'What's that bugger doing?' He jerked his head in the direction of Stott.

'He tried to escort Joanna home from church and wouldn't take no for an answer, so I walked back with her.'

'I'll take her to church myself next week. I'm not having *him* pestering my cousin.'

'No need. I've already arranged to escort her there and back.'

Eli looked at him in surprise. 'Have you, now? I'm not sure—'

Bram scowled. 'She'll be quite safe with me, I promise. I've a great deal of respect for your cousin.'

'She'd better be safe with you.'

'Didn't I just tell you she would?' Bram pushed past him and went into the kitchen where Mr Beckett was sitting in his shirt sleeves. He scowled at the visitor, but Joanna smiled and gestured to a chair. 'I was just telling Dad how you saved me from Mr Stott and that the least I could do was reward you with a cup of tea.'

Frank scowled at them. 'Why were you caterwauling out there? On a Sunday too. They'll have you up for disturbing the peace.' He picked up the previous day's newspaper, shaking it out noisily and holding it in a way that prevented anyone from sitting next to him.

'How do you like your tea, Mr Heegan?'

Bram was amused at how nervous Joanna seemed.

She must be five and twenty at least. Had she never walked home with a man before? He answered his own question. No, of course she hadn't. She was not only a spinster, but known in the town for being bad-tempered. Only she wasn't like that with him. He'd better be careful, though. She was the sort you married, not the sort you fooled around with, and although his mother was pestering him about finding a wife, she'd throw seven fits if he brought a Protestant lass home.

Still, he did enjoy Joanna's company. And he absolutely loved singing with her. Music was something so special, so important to him . . . Bram wondered if he could persuade her to sing with him again. He had sheet music at home, which he'd been collecting ever since he bought a load of old papers and found that the ones with lines and squiggles on were music. He'd kept them on a whim and later paid a piano teacher to show him how to read the music. He smiled at that thought. He could read the music more easily than he could read the words, if truth be told. He wasn't one for book learning.

Eli didn't join them and Bram wondered briefly where he was, then concentrated on behaving himself and not upsetting old Mr Beckett further. Although he chatted easily with Joanna, he was glad when he could get away from the miserable old sod. No wonder she was so grumpy. It'd make anyone grumpy, living with Frank Beckett.

When she came to the pub door with him, smiling at Carrie and Bonny who were just finishing off their quick Sunday clear-up, Bram said, 'If it's fine next week, would you consider giving church a miss and coming walking on the moors with me instead?'

Joanna's mouth fell open in shock.

'I know a place where no one can hear us and we can sing to our hearts' content. I have lots of song sheets.' He could see a refusal coming in the way she opened her mouth and added quickly, 'I love singing, but I can't find anyone to sing with – well, no one who's good enough to make it a joy.'

'I don't think . . .'

'You'll be safe with me, Joanna, I give you my word. I'm not Athol Stott. And I really do love singing.'

'So do I, though I could never do it in public like you do.'

As the silence lengthened he asked quietly, 'Well, then? Will you sing with me, Joanna?'

'I'll think about it.'

Bram waited till his aunt had put her cleaning materials away then walked home with her. He knew better than to push Joanna into agreement now, but felt confident she'd come walking with him. He'd seen the joy on her face when they'd sung together.

When the other two had gone inside, Eli couldn't resist walking round the half-built music room, looking up at the old beams with the rags of cobwebs still hanging from them. They could be brushed clean the very next day. There were piles of rubble near the entrance and the last pile of wood was ready for Carrie and her little brother to take away. To his relief the flagstoned floor ran most of the way through the building, except for where the horses' stalls had been. The floor needed repairing in places and he'd have to order some new flagstones, but the old ones could be cleaned up.

He sighed. That would have to do for the time being. His uncle would never be persuaded to spend money on a proper wooden floor. Still, the space itself was quite large and the ceiling nice and high. That was important if the sound was to carry and resonate properly. He wished he knew more about that sort of thing, but he didn't, so he'd just have to hope it'd all work. Then he smiled as he remembered how his cousin's singing had rung out. Maybe the sounds made here would echo in the right way.

He hadn't realised Joanna had such a lovely voice. And Bram too. They sounded grand together. Would she agree to sing in the music room? He thought of the way she kept herself to herself and didn't feel optimistic about that. Maybe Bram would be able to persuade her. He was already popular in the free and easy sessions.

Eli walked back, counting the paces. They could fit two or three rows of long tables in, plus some smaller tables for the better folk nearer the stage, and . . .

The sound of footsteps made Eli spin round quickly to find that Athol Stott had had the gall to come inside.

'I didn't realise you had so much space here, Beckett.'

'Didn't you?'

'We've been looking for storage space. This would be perfect, just down the hill from the engineering works.'

'Sorry. We need the space ourselves.'

'What on earth for? You already have the largest pub in town.'

'This is going to be a music room.'

Athol screwed up his mouth, his narrow face taking on a calculating expression. 'I think I could make it more worth your while to rent out the space to us, or even sell it.'

'I'm afraid we're quite set on having a music room.' Eli turned and began to walk back towards the entrance. 'I must get this boarded up. We don't want people walking in off the street, do we?'

His unwelcome visitor scowled at this, stopped again in the entrance, still looking thoughtful, then walked off without a word.

Eli watched till the fellow was out of sight then went back into the pub because it'd soon be time to open up again. But he couldn't get the avid expression on Stott's face out of his mind. That man was used to getting his own way. Eli had better make sure work on the music room proceeded as quickly as possible. He didn't want his uncle being tempted to sell this land.

No, surely even Frank Beckett wouldn't do that, when he'd given his promise and his own daughter was eager to have a music room?

But Eli's father had warned him not to trust his uncle and Eli wished suddenly that Athol Stott hadn't come here today. He dismissed the thought as he looked at the side wall where they'd knock through into the old coal hole once a new coal store had been built. Well, they needed extra coal space anyway if they were to heat the music room properly. The gas lights he planned to install – he hadn't told his uncle about those yet – would partly warm things up, but in winter they'd need huge fires in here as well.

So much still to plan. Eli had several lists of things to attend to, so would keep out of his uncle's way in his bedroom.

As he pushed open the kitchen door, he wondered yet again how Carrie had known so quickly how to make a space for the Chairman? He was still intrigued by that. Hell, he was intrigued by *her*, kept telling himself he couldn't afford to get involved, and yet would still catch himself making time for a friendly word with her most days.

The memory of Joanna's beautiful voice threaded through Bram's week and even invaded his dreams. He found himself counting the days till Sunday and praying it wouldn't rain.

Even his mother noticed his absent-mindedness.

'Have you found yourself a girl, son?' she asked suddenly one evening when he brought Bonny back. 'You're acting like a young man in love.'

'I am not!'

She snorted and tossed her head in that way that said she didn't believe him. Well, she could think what she liked. He wasn't in love.

Then the memory of Joanna's rapt expression as she was singing with him blurred the room around him and shock kept him rigid for a few moments. He wasn't in love, surely not?

He couldn't be, wouldn't let himself be. Definitely not! Bram had only to see his brother Declan's miserable marriage and his brother Michael's poverty since he'd got married to know that kind of a life wasn't for him.

But for all his firm determination, he still kept hearing Joanna's voice in his dreams.

# 14

Carrie set off for work early, relieved to get out of the house. For all they were treated well at their new home, she felt on edge all the time because of the way Nev seemed to notice everything they did. Even the children were quieter than usual, as if they'd sensed it was wisest. Ted had been scolded a couple of times, and cuffed lightly about the ears once, but he'd deserved it so she wasn't worried about that.

The best thing was that the food continued to be good, with enough for them all to eat every single day. You could tell people who were long-time hungry. She'd seen it often in the Lanes, that gaunt, hollow-eyed look; seen it in her own brothers and sisters too. But not recently. They'd all grown rosier these days and that gladdened her heart.

Well, with the money he'd got selling her baby sisters, Nev could afford to be generous. She still resented that, thought it a dreadful thing to do, and missed the babies. Which was stupid, really, when she'd been upset to see them born.

It suddenly occurred to her that her mother might have another baby, even now – Nev's baby. No, surely not? She was too old and something had gone wrong last time, so that the doctor had said it was unlikely Jane would have any more.

Carrie was glad when she arrived at work. It seemed much colder this morning and her shawl wasn't thick enough to keep her warm. Autumn was moving towards winter and, like most people she knew, she didn't look forward to the colder months. She'd have to find something warmer to wear then. Her heart sank. That meant she'd have to ask Nev for the money to buy it.

She pushed open the front door of the Dragon, calling, 'Good morning, Miss Beckett. Shall I get started?'

She went to the far corner of the big room and began giving the tables their first rough wipe then stacking the stools and chairs on them so that she could sweep the floor.

When the door opened she looked up to see Bonny come in, followed by Bram. Joanna moved across to them and after a minute Bonny put on a sacking apron and came across to help with the tables. Joanna stayed by the door talking to Bram, and it seemed to Carrie that she was more animated than usual, smiling at him, talking and gesticulating.

Anyone would think she fancied him!

Carrie smiled to herself. She couldn't imagine Joanna Beckett getting fond of a man in that way, somehow. 'Right, Bonny, let's get these tables stacked for sweeping.'

But her companion was looking over towards the door. 'I like Miss Beckett. Bram likes her too,' she confided, in her slow, slurred voice. 'He allus smiles when he sees her.'

It was true, Carrie thought. In fact, the pair by the door were both smiling and when Bram had left, Miss Beckett stood there for ages with a dreamy expression on her face before she started working again.

Halfway through the morning, while Beckett was out shopping, the big double doors of the Dragon were flung open and Mr Athol Stott walked in. He looked round with his usual sneer and crooked one finger at Bonny. 'You! Come here.'

But poor Bonny looked at him in terror, uttered a strangled squeak, then ran and hid in the snug.

Reluctantly Carrie stepped forward, not going too close because Mr Stott was famous for taking liberties with you and touching you in places he shouldn't. 'Can I help you, sir?' You always had to say *sir* when you spoke to him or he'd explode with rage

'I want to see Mr Beckett.'

'Mr Eli or the older Mr Beckett, sir?'

'The older one.'

'I'll go and see if I can find him, sir.' Carrie hurried away, looking over her shoulder to see him following her across the room. To her relief Mr Beckett was sitting in the kitchen, adding up some figures. He looked up and scowled at her when she knocked on the door. 'What is it? Can't you see I'm busy?'

'It's Mr Stott, Mr Athol Stott. He's come to see you.'

Frank pushed the papers aside and waved one

hand at her. 'Go and fetch him in, then. What are you standing there like an idiot for?'

She went out to find Mr Stott standing by the bar now, looking round as if he owned the place. 'Mr Beckett's through here, sir.' She took care to leave herself space to back away. Sure enough, Mr Stott's hand stretched out towards her breasts. He laughed as if it was all a big joke when she skipped backwards and he missed, but Carrie didn't think it was funny. She hated men who tried to make free with her body. That was one reason why she'd never work in the pub in the evenings.

Mr Beckett called out, 'Shut the door, girl!' so she did that, then went to persuade Bonny to come out of the snug and start work again. They continued scrubbing the floor, which they did in sections on different days, sweeping up the dirty sawdust and laying fresh after the wood had dried. Other days they wiped down the wooden panelling that came partway up the walls or bottomed the snug.

Joanna Beckett liked things kept clean and men who drank were often dirty in their habits, so it was hard to keep the place fresh. But men didn't behave as badly in the Dragon as they did in some other pubs because they were afraid of Miss Beckett, who'd come and shout at them if she saw them spitting on her clean floor.

Carrie wondered briefly why Mr Stott had come to see Mr Beckett instead of sending for him, but soon forgot about it as she pushed on with her work.

★

Inside the kitchen Frank stood up to greet his visitor. 'Please take a seat, sir.' He watched the other man inspect the chair for dust before he sat down. As if Joanna would let things get dusty! If anything, she was too fussy about keeping the house clean. 'How can I help you, Mr Stott?'

'It's rather that I think we can help one another.'

'Oh?' Frank might feel intimidated by this man, but he was a shrewd enough businessman to wait and let the other state his reason for being here.

'The piece of land to the side of your pub . . . I'm interested in buying it.'

'It's not for sale,' Frank said immediately, but something inside him jumped at the thought of making money from it instead of throwing it away on Eli's schemes.

'I think if the price were right, you might perhaps be tempted.'

'I'm afraid not, Mr Stott. We're opening a music room there. We'll make a lot of money from it. They're the coming thing. Music saloons they call them in Manchester.'

'You could make a lot more money by selling the land to me, and make it now. A man of your age wants cash in hand, not dribbling in slowly for years, surely?'

Frank scowled at him. He hated folk pointing out how old he was getting, hated the way he was feeling his age lately and having to depend on others so much.

'What would you say to a thousand pounds? It

wouldn't affect this place, but you'd have extra money to do what you wanted, even stop working if that's your fancy.'

'That land is worth far more,' Frank said automatically. 'It's near the centre of town. There's no other plot of that size to be had near the centre now.'

Athol felt triumph swell within him. If Beckett was willing to discuss prices, the fellow might be tempted into selling. But he didn't intend to seem too eager. He rose to his feet. 'I'm sure we can come to an agreement that benefits us both, but I'm not the man to do the negotiating.'

Frank stood up as well. 'I don't think I want to sell. It'd spoil my trade to have an engineering works next door. Lot of smoke, smelly sort of business, dirt everywhere.'

'Oh, didn't I say?' Athol waited but Frank didn't fall into his trap as people usually did, displaying their interest. After a few moments of silence he added, 'I want it for a warehouse. Storage. We're getting some good orders in, but we're short of space to store the machinery till we've made enough to fill an order.'

'Hmm.'

Athol judged that he'd planted the seeds and pretended to leave, turning back to add as if on an afterthought, 'Go and see my lawyer, at least discuss it. He'll deal with you on my behalf.'

'I don't really want to sell,' Frank repeated. 'Still, I suppose it never hurts to find out what's on offer. But there again, I'm a busy man. I'll give it some thought.'

Which was rather different from a blunt 'Not for sale', Athol decided as he walked towards the door. This time he didn't notice the lass scrubbing the floor but he did see the older woman with the idiot's moon face jerk back behind a table when she saw him coming. As if he'd be interested in *her!*

When he got outside, he went to peer down the side of the pub before making his way back to his works. This place would be ideal. Absolutely ideal.

Eli found out about Athol Stott's visit when he stopped to pass the time of day with the grocer along the road, a friendly fellow who spent a lot of time at his shop door chatting, leaving serving behind the counter to his wife and son.

After they'd commented on the weather and how business was, James Marker nudged Eli in the ribs. 'My goodness, you're keeping high company these days at the Dragon.'

'What do you mean by that?'

'Mr Stott himself visiting yesterday morning. And he stayed quite a while, too.'

'Stott? Which one?'

'Athol, the older one.' Marker pulled a face. 'Mind you, I'd just as soon he kept away from me, that one. There's always trouble follows him.' He glanced quickly round, realising he'd been indiscreet, relaxing when he saw that no one was near enough to have overheard.

'Thanks for letting me know. Look, would you tell me if you see him visiting again when I'm out?'

The grocer raised his eyebrows, then nodded.

Eli, who'd only stopped to pass the time of day, judged it wise to purchase something and chose a poke of best humbugs. He was very thoughtful as he walked back and lost no time in taking Joanna aside to ask if she knew about Stott's visit.

'No, I don't. When was this?'

'Yesterday morning, and he stayed quite a while, according to Marker down the road.'

'Dad didn't say a word.' She frowned then added slowly, 'He must be up to something, though I can't think what.'

'We'd better ask him then.'

'If he is up to something, he won't tell us until he's good and ready.'

'And if we ask him, he'll know we suspect something.'

'Yes, I suppose so.'

'Still, we can't let him think we don't know.'

She nodded. 'All right. I'll do it, though.'

They waited until Frank had eaten his dinner and was sipping the glass of beer with which he always finished off his midday meal. Joanna leaned forward and asked him bluntly, 'What was Athol Stott doing here yesterday?'

Frank choked and beer foam sputtered over his chin. As he wiped it he said in an aggrieved tone, 'Do you have to take me by surprise when I'm enjoying a drink?'

'What did he want, Dad?'

'To talk about trouble-makers. Wanted me to report

any who were sounding off about their work. Says he's getting rid of anyone who doesn't toe the line. But I told him I don't go out on the pub floor nowadays. I leave that to you young 'uns. But you could tell me if you hear owt and I'd send word to him.'

Joanna studied the bland expression on her father's face. He wasn't telling the truth, she was sure of that. He always looked as if he hadn't a care in the world when he was telling a pack of lies. But she didn't challenge him because it'd do no good.

Afterwards she went out to where Eli stood talking to Jem Harding about the next stage of construction. The two men were smiling and gesticulating.

Eli turned as she approached. 'We're getting on nicely. They'll take all the rubble away in the next couple of days, then fill in the new frontage so that no one can get in from the street.'

But the following day there was no sign of Jem, and when Eli went round to see him and find out why they hadn't started, the builder looked at him in surprise. 'Your uncle sent word not to do anything until next week, said he was sick of the noise and wanted a bit of peace. And since he's the one who's paying, I've no choice but to do as he asks. Sorry, Eli lad. He always did hate paying out money, old Frank.'

'I'll speak to him.'

Eli went storming back to confront his uncle and the two of them had a loud row, which brought Joanna in from the snug.

'I've paid out enough for one month,' Frank

insisted. 'And the noise *is* getting me down. What's wrong with waiting a few days?'

'There's no *need* for it. The longer we wait, the longer it'll take before the music room starts paying for itself.'

Frank thumped the flat of his hand down on the table and shouted, 'It's me as is boss here an' don't you forget it! If I say I want a rest from the noise, then we'll have a rest. I'm not made of brass, you know. I don't want to break into my capital, so we'll wait till next month to continue the work.'

'*Next month!*'

'Aye. An' that's my final word.'

Neither Eli nor Joanna could budge him from that stance, though they both tried several times.

By Friday Joanna was sick of quarrels and living in an atmosphere full of anger and tension. She was feeling more and more tempted to go walking with Bram Heegan on Sunday, but kept worrying about what people would think. She had to conclude that they'd think she was giving herself to him, because of his reputation. So it simply wasn't possible. Unfortunately.

When he came to pick up his aunt after work that day, Joanna marched across to intercept him while Bonny was putting the cleaning things away. She cut Bram's easy flow of conversation short and said curtly, 'I can't possibly come walking with you on Sunday, so if you'd rather not escort me to church, I'll get Eli to do it.'

'What's made you change your mind?'

'The thought of what people will say if they see us

walking out together. *You* normally only go with women for one reason.'

He opened his mouth, then shut it again. 'Hmm.'

'Is that all you can say?'

'I'm thinking.'

'Well, I've got work to do, so I'll leave you to your thinking.'

He grabbed her arm and swung her round.

'Let go of me this minute!' He did but Joanna didn't move away, just stood rubbing her arm, pretending he'd hurt her.

'Why don't we take Bonny with us, then? Will that make it all right?'

It was Joanna's turn to think, then she shook her head. 'No, I'm afraid it won't.'

Carrie came up to them just then. 'I'll be off now, Miss Beckett.'

Bram grinned at Joanna. 'We *do* have another chaperone, one we've used before.'

They both turned to stare at her.

Joanna was very tempted. After all, Carrie had gone with them into Manchester. She looked at Bram then turned back to her employee. 'Would you like to earn some extra money on Sunday morning?'

'Yes, of course.'

'I want to go walking on the moors with Bram after we've cleaned up this place, but people will think badly of me if I'm alone with him. If you come with us, as you came into Manchester, it'll look better. I'll pay you two shillings extra.'

'All right.'

When she'd gone, Bram smiled at Joanna, a danger-ously lazy smile. 'You don't hesitate when you want something.'

'I want a bit of peace, that's all. It's been a nasty sort of week.'

Even as she was speaking, voices could be heard from the back, raised in a quarrel.

Bram raised one eyebrow, and Joanna explained what had happened.

'If Stott is involved it won't be for any good reason. I'll see if I can find anything out, if you like. You hear all sorts of scraps of information down at the markets.'

'Thank you.'

Eli came storming out of the office and across to the door, not even bothering to greet Bram, he was so angry. 'He's told me to stop working on the music room, even in my own time. Says it's a waste.'

'A waste?'

'Aye.'

There was silence.

Joanna's scowl was as black as Eli's. 'I think he's going to stop us having a music room. If he does, I'm leaving here. I've had enough of his nasty, selfish ways. He never thinks what sort of life *I* want.' She hadn't, either, till Eli had come along with his ideas. Had just done the best she could with the life her father had set up for her.

'I'll see what I can find out,' Bram promised. 'And I'll pick you and Carrie up on Sunday at nine o'clock.'

'What's all that about?' Eli asked as soon as Bram and Bonny had left.

Joanna flushed slightly. 'I'm going walking with him on Sunday – and no, it's not what you think. He's got some sheet music and knows a place where we can sing together.' Her flush deepened. 'I love singing. I can't do it here, and I have to keep my voice down in church or people will notice – they won't like a woman from a pub making a spectacle of herself, believe me. Sometimes I think I'll burst with keeping it inside me.'

'You've a lovely voice, lass. It's a shame your father doesn't like to hear it. And when you and Bram sing together, it's a rare treat to listen to you.' Eli looked towards the office then back at her. 'I wouldn't mind getting out for an hour or two myself. Mind if I join you? Me and Carrie will walk on, if you like, then you won't feel so nervous about singing.'

Joanna hesitated, but couldn't resist his offer. 'That'd be lovely. Let's hope it doesn't rain.'

Frank walked slowly along Market Street, going to put his takings in the bank, which was the only thing which ever took him out of his pub these days. He nodded to acquaintances but didn't stop to chat to anyone until he'd paid the money into the safety of the bank and had checked the current total.

He smiled as he stood still for a minute in the doorway, contemplating his healthy financial state. Joanna and Eli would stare if they knew how much he was worth. But you didn't build up your money unless you knew when to spend and when to save, when to buy and when to sell.

On that thought he left the bank, took a quick glance in both directions, and since there was no sign of Eli or Joanna, hurried across the road to see Stott's lawyer. He didn't even glance at the highly polished brass sign that read 'Hordle and Sons', but pushed the door open and went straight inside.

It was the very speed of his movements that attracted attention to him. James Marker stopped in astonishment at the sight of his neighbour actually hurrying. James himself was out for a brisk stroll along Market Street, something he did at quiet times because he had a new young wife and wanted to keep himself in trim for her. Now, he stopped and chatted to another shopkeeper, then went inside the iron-monger's and asked his friend who owned it if he could stay there and just keep an eye on something across the road.

It was fifteen minutes by James Marker's sturdy pocket watch before Frank Beckett came out again, and the man had a smile on his face.

What was Beckett doing visiting a lawyer and coming out smiling? Never mind Eli wanting to know what was going on, James did too now. Beckett could be selling his business, which was the only reason James could think of for his seeing a lawyer, though why he'd go to Hordle and Sons puzzled James. They didn't usually deal with small traders. And James himself had a friend who'd be interested in buying the old pub, had offered to do so a couple of times in fact but been turned down flat by Beckett.

He let Frank get out of sight, then walked slowly

back to his own shop. After some consideration, he sent his errand boy to find Eli Beckett, giving the lad strict instructions not to pass the message on if Frank Beckett was anywhere nearby. Mr Marker's compliments and he'd like to see Mr Eli Beckett at his earliest convenience. He made the boy repeat it twice to make sure he had the message correct, then helped his wife attend to a few customers while waiting.

Eli came into the shop half an hour later.

James finished serving his customer then jerked his head to indicate that Eli should follow him into the back room.

'Your uncle went into Hordle and Sons after he'd paid the takings into the bank today. I happened to be passing and saw him hurry across the road and whisk inside as if he didn't want to be seen.' Marker let out a grunt of amusement. 'I'd not have noticed him if he hadn't been moving so fast. Not like Frank to hurry, I thought. What's up? So I stopped to watch.'

'He went into Hordle and Sons?'

'Aye. Top lawyers in town they are. Work for Stott's and some of the county folk who live out of town. Don't deal with little folk like us normally.'

Eli stood thinking furiously, remembering Athol Stott's interest in the old stable area.

'Know what Frank's up to? If he's selling the pub, I've a friend who'd be interested in buying it.'

Could his uncle be selling the pub? Surely not? Frank loved the old place, no one could doubt that. 'I don't know what's going on, but I intend to find out.' Eli shook James Marker's hand. 'I'm grateful to you for telling me what you saw. Very grateful. I won't forget this. When the music room opens, you and your family will come as my guests.'

James nodded and watched him go. His smile faded and was replaced by a thoughtful look. He too intended to find out what was going on. He usually did. You heard a lot when you ran a busy grocery store. If customers didn't tell you things, they told each other, and not always in a whisper.

When Carrie got home, she decided to tell Nev about the Sunday outing. She hated this feeling of having to report to him before every breath she took, but felt she had no choice if she was to keep on his good side.

He and her mother were in their favourite place, the kitchen, sitting over one of their endless pots of tea with Raife pottering about behind them. It was he who smiled a greeting at her, not her mother, who was busy whispering in Nev's ear.

'Pour yourself a cup, lass,' Raife said. 'It's not long been brewed.'

She did so and sat down, explaining about Sunday between sips.

'Why should they take you with them?' Jane wanted to know. 'If they're walking out with each other they won't want someone else around.'

'Miss Beckett doesn't want folk thinking she's letting him – you know, make free with her.' With Nev's unwinking gaze on her Carrie found it embarrassing to talk about this. 'I can't say no to her, not when she's my employer, can I? Anyway, it's a bit more money earned.'

Nev nodded approvingly. 'No, you can't refuse good money. Jane love, church-going folk have to be very careful of their reputation. That's why she's taking your Carrie with her. Pity you can't take some of the children with you as well. They're a right noisy lot on Sundays. I shall have to find them some work to do if they've got that much energy.' Nev fixed his step-daughter with another of his intense gazes. 'You'll have to tell us what they do on this walk.'

'I expect they'll just talk.'

'Then you'll tell us what they talk about.'

She nodded, but resolved not to tell him anything too personal.

'I think we'll open the winter room next week,' he said. 'You and your sisters had better put your spare clothes and such in the store room. We don't want folk pinching them.'

Carrie moistened her lips. 'I've been wondering about that. I don't like to think of us stopping you earning good money.'

'There's nothing much we can do about that.' He sighed. 'You have to have somewhere to sleep.'

'I did wonder about the attics . . .'

Nev stared at her. 'The attics?'

'Yes. I was having a look round when I went up to fetch down some of those new blankets for Raife, and I did wonder whether we couldn't make a bedroom for ourselves up there? It wouldn't take much to put up a partition or two, and we'd soon make it up with the extra money from the winter lodgers. You said you charged a halfpenny a night more for the winter room.'

'I thought the roof was too low in the attics. Mind you, I haven't been up there for a while. My knees are bad and I don't like climbing stairs unless I have to.'

Nev didn't hesitate to send his father up, though, Carrie thought indignantly. 'Well, I thought you could make a room over the kitchen. The roof's a bit higher there and we'd be warmer, too.'

'It sounds to me like you've done more than just look round once, young lady.'

Carrie could feel herself blushing. 'Well, I did go back and plan it out in my head. Mr Eli says I'm good at working out spaces and how things fit into them. I helped him with his music saloon, too, thought how to fit the Chairman's table in. He was very pleased about that.'

'He should have paid you extra for it, then.'

'They're good to me. They give me and Bonny cups of tea and a piece of cake sometimes in the mornings.'

'They work you hard enough.'

'Miss Beckett works as hard as anyone. It's old Mr Beckett who just sits there.'

Nev sat for a minute, his eyes out of focus, and she reckoned he was doing some calculations in his head. 'Come and show me what you mean,' he said after a minute or two. 'I can't see things in my head like you can.'

He puffed his way up the stairs and Carrie explained what she'd worked out, drawing lines with her feet in the dust on the floor to help him understand.

'I'll have to cost it,' was Nev's only comment.

She followed him downstairs again, worried that he wasn't going to let them sleep up here. It was bad enough trying to get dressed decently with Ted around. She hated the thought of sleeping in a room full of strange men and women, different ones every night, absolutely hated it.

# 15

Athol Stott raised his glass, holding it up against the glow from the fire to admire the rich ruby colour of the port before he sipped it. He looked across at his cousin, who seemed to be lost in thought this evening. 'Beckett went to see Charles Hordle yesterday.' He sighed and rolled his eyes as his cousin didn't seem to grasp the import of that. 'Have you forgotten already? I told you I'm going to buy some land from Beckett.'

'Oh, yes. For storing things. Good, good.'

Athol could see that Edmund's mind wasn't on the subject and asked impatiently, 'What's the matter with you tonight? You were quiet all through dinner, no company at all.'

'It's the steam engine. The seals are bleeding steam. As I keep telling you, the whole apparatus is old and worn. Athol, we really do need to replace it, and soon.'

'You're supposed to be an engineer. Repair it.'

'I've done everything I can think of. We had to stop work only a few months ago because the governor wasn't working properly, if you remember, and at this rate it'll be happening again. If the governor goes wrong, the safety valve can't open and steam could build up dangerously.'

Athol scowled at him. 'Nonsense! There wasn't an explosion last time, though we lost good money because *you* insisted on shutting things down to do the repairs. You'd better make sure that doesn't happen again. Just adjust the governor. I'm not sending the men home again. You're far too cautious about that damned engine.'

'Better we lose good money than good men, don't you think?'

'No, I don't! Men are ten a penny. Steam engines of that size cost a great deal, which would cut right into our profits, not to mention us having to shut down the works while they install a new engine.'

'An explosion could do more than cut into profits. It could destroy half the building.'

'You always were a worrier.'

'With very good reason this time.'

Athol leaned forward. 'Well, I'm *not* buying a new steam engine till the year after next at the soonest, and even then only if trade continues good. So I'd appreciate it if you'd stop pestering me about it. We've only just recovered from a slump. I'm not made of money.'

From his side of the fireplace Edmund looked at his cousin with disgust. Not made of money! Athol was rich, and getting richer all the time. Even Edmund's minor inheritance from his uncle gave him enough to live on in modest comfort for the rest of his life without doing a day's work.

Containing his anger, he closed his book and stood up. 'I think I'll go out and get a bit of fresh air.'

He knew Athol understood exactly what he intended to do which was to visit his mistress. He didn't like the way his cousin talked about Faith, as if she was nothing. She wasn't. Edmund was very fond of her, enjoying not only her company in bed, but also simply being with her. Life would be so much more pleasant if he could live openly with her. But when they'd met, his uncle had still been alive and Edmund had known he'd be cut off without a penny if he married a smallholder's daughter, whereas he'd been applauded for taking her as his mistress and even offered one of the mill houses for her to live in. Now it'd create a public scandal if he married her or even lived openly with her.

He hadn't been fair to her, but Faith seemed happy – well, most of the time. Except when she saw her family in the street and they passed her as if she was a stranger. That always upset her.

A walk in the chill air cleared his head and Edmund began to think more clearly. He loved these clear frosty evenings when the stars seemed brighter than usual. His sister-in-law kept the house too warm for his liking, with huge fires in all the rooms in the evenings because Athol preferred it that way, but Edmund hated it.

Faith was sitting in the front room, sewing. She tried to hide what she was doing when he came in, not running to fling herself into his arms as she usually did.

'What's the matter?' he asked at once. 'Faith love, tell me?'

As he drew closer he saw the dampness on her

cheeks. He went and sat beside her, putting his arm around her shoulders. 'Why have you been crying?'

She bowed her head then leaned against his shoulder as a sob escaped her. 'Promise me you won't be angry!'

'You know I won't, love. I'm never angry with you.'

'I'm expecting a baby.'

He was so shocked he couldn't speak for a moment. They'd been together for three years now and there'd been no sign of a child, so he'd assumed either that she was barren or that he was unable to father a child.

She began to sob again. 'You *are* angry, I can tell. Oh, Edmund, don't leave me or turn me out. Please! I love you so.'

'Whatever made you think I'd turn you out?'

'My mother. She s-said when I came to live with you that you'd th-throw me out as soon as my belly started to swell.'

'Your mother is—' He broke off. No need to tell Faith about her mother. She was a deeply religious woman who saw no joy in this life and had made her daughter's life a misery for years. No wonder Faith had been ready to live with him, even out of wedlock. Edmund put an arm round her and tried to come to terms with the prospect of a child. The more he thought about it, the more he hated the idea that any child of his would be born a bastard, tormented by other children, called after in the streets. Hated even more the way people would treat Faith – even worse than they treated her now – for bearing a child. People could be so cruel.

'Edmund? Are you – very angry?'

'Dearest Faith, it takes two people to make a child, so if I were to get angry with anyone, I'd have to get angry with myself as well.' He took her hand in his and raised it to his lips. 'I'm not angry, only surprised. And actually, I find I'm rather excited at the prospect of becoming a father.'

She began crying again, more softly this time, tears of relief. 'I'll try not to let it be a nuisance.'

'I shall *want* it to be a nuisance. Did you think I wouldn't want to see my own child? Hold it, love it, play with it?'

'I don't know what the gentry want. My father never played with us.'

'I keep telling you: I'm not gentry, I'm a working engineer. And my family may have a lot of money now – or rather, Athol does – but our grandfather was only a common weaver who liked to build looms and other bits of equipment, so I'm not all that different from you.' He weighed the idea for a minute or two longer then said, 'Faith love, I think we'd better get married, don't you?'

She stared at him in shock, her eyes wide open, her mouth gaping. '*Married!* But, Edmund love, people like you don't marry girls like me!'

'They do if they want to.'

'Mr Stott won't let you.'

'Athol's my cousin, not my keeper.'

'He'll still stop us from getting wed, you know he will.'

Edmund was silent for a moment or two, then

nodded. 'You're right. I think he will try to stop us, so we'll have to get married secretly and not tell anyone until you're Mrs Edmund Stott. I'll get a special licence and we'll do it before anyone knows. We're both over twenty-one, after all.'

'Oh, Edmund, do you really mean it?'

'Of course I do, silly. I love you and I was wrong not to marry you before.'

'I love you, too.'

Her eyes were glowing with such joy he felt almost dazzled by it. But then, her capacity for happiness was what had attracted him to Faith in the first place. Strange how she'd retained that, even with a sour-natured mother like hers. He'd met her out on the moors, where he was walking to clear his head of fumes from the works and she was gathering bilberries. How quickly they'd fallen in love!

He hadn't wanted anyone else in all the time they'd been together, didn't want to marry anyone else either. This was definitely the right thing to do.

'We'll have to find somewhere else to live,' he said when she had calmed down. 'There's not much going in the town, but I'll ask around and see if there are any houses available to rent or to buy. Do you mind where we live? I rather fancy one of the outlying villages.'

'I'll be happy anywhere as long as you're there. Oh, Edmund! To think of you being with me all the time. It'll be heaven.'

When he walked home in the small hours of the morning, he felt himself to be brimming over with happiness. Only when he unlocked the back door did that joyous feeling dim. It was as if you could sense the unhappiness in this house, as if it waited there like a living creature. The servants didn't dare open their mouths, poor Maria rarely said more than 'Yes, Athol' or 'No, Athol', and the children were terrified of their father. Even the governess was a nervous woman, who kept her eyes lowered and her charges silent whenever their father was around.

Edmund wanted more than that for his children, much more. He wanted a house full of laughter and happiness, children who shouted and ran. And he intended to get it, too.

Sunday was fine but cold. When Joanna came downstairs at the time she would normally be setting off for church, she was dressed in stout shoes and her warm everyday clothes. She saw her father study her with narrowed eyes.

'Where are *you* off to?'

'I'm going for a walk.'

'You never go for walks on Sundays.'

'Well, I am today. It's such a lovely day.'

'Who with?'

She turned to Eli, her eyes pleading.

'Me,' he said at once, but realised they'd be seen so amended it to, 'Well, me an' some others. We're off for a tramp across the tops.'

'Which others?'

'None of your business.'

Frank spluttered in indignation. 'What do you

mean, none of my business? You're living under my roof, aren't you? Owt you do here is my business.'

'Maybe I'll not be living here much longer. If there's not to be a music room, there's no point in me staying.'

'You keep saying that, but you'll stay all right because you know which side your bread is buttered on.'

Eli looked at him, wondering yet again if he'd guessed correctly about what his uncle was up to. But he wasn't going to worry about that at the moment. The weather was sunny and clear if cold, and he intended to enjoy his morning away from the pub. He'd enjoy Carrie's company as well. To hell with caution! You were only young once.

Carrie felt excited as she rushed home from cleaning to get ready for her outing. When she went into the kitchen, Nev was waiting. She might have known! He had to be involved in every single thing she did.

'Let me look at you.' He studied her critically. 'Not smart enough. You'd better borrow your mother's new coat. It hangs loose at the back so it won't matter if it's a bit too big. And you'd better wear that new bonnet of hers as well.'

Jane at once protested that she didn't want to lend anyone her coat and bonnet, but was overridden with an impatient wave of her husband's hand, so contented herself with scowling at her daughter.

Carrie stared at herself in the hall mirror when she was ready. Her rough red hands were hidden by her mother's gloves and she looked quite smart, she thought. She hurried through the streets to the pub and found Miss Beckett waiting for her just inside the door, Mr Eli too.

'Oh, there you are, Carrie. Don't you look nice!'

Carrie could feel Mr Eli's eyes on her, see the admiration in them. 'My mother lent me her new coat.'

'It suits you.' Joanna glanced at her cousin, who hadn't spoken. 'Eli's coming with us as well. We both feel like getting out in the fresh air. We're just waiting for Bram and then—'

There was a knock on the door and he poked his head in. 'Everyone ready?' Bram was carrying a roll of songsheets and had a long scarlet muffler wound round his neck, something most men would have refused to wear. When he saw Joanna staring at it, he grinned. 'My Auntie Bonny knitted it for me. She loves bright colours. I can't hurt her feelings by refusing to wear it, now can I? And besides, it's such a pretty colour it cheers me up in the dark days of winter.'

Joanna smiled. 'I didn't know she could knit.'

'She's good at it. There are no dropped stitches here, it's all even. See.'

Before she knew it she was standing close to him and examining the muffler, which was indeed beautifully crafted. 'Lovely,' was all she could think of to say because his closeness was having its usual effect on her. She stepped back abruptly and took Carrie's arm. 'Come on. Let's not waste another minute. I don't want my father finding an excuse to call me back.'

They set off through the streets, going up the hill past Stott's, in the opposite direction from the groups of churchgoers. Joanna set such a brisk pace that they had soon left the town behind.

As they were climbing over a stile, the group somehow rearranged itself and Carrie found herself walking next to Eli, with Bram and Joanna leading the way now. Even as she watched, Bram took hold of Joanna's hand and she made a half-hearted effort to pull away then let it stay in his. Carrie glanced sideways and saw that Eli had noticed it too. He winked at her and took *her* hand. She didn't know what to do about that but couldn't bring herself to pull away either.

Ten minutes brought them to an old shepherd's hut and Bram opened the door with a flourish. 'Here you are. I brought some wood up last time I was driving over the moors, so we can be quite cosy as we sing. I've even got some congreves to light it with.'

Eli noted Joanna's slight embarrassment and turned to Carrie. 'I think these two will be better left on their own, don't you?' He grinned at his cousin and spoke more loudly. 'Us two will tramp on a bit, then come back in, say, an hour. All right, Joanna?'

She nodded gratefully. She got embarrassed, singing in front of people.

Carrie followed Eli outside again and stood staring around. 'Isn't it lovely up here? All this space and no people. It's so peaceful. I've only been up on the moors a few times when I was about ten. Mum wasn't so tired then and Dad wasn't drinking as heavily, so

he took me and Robbie and Marjorie out walking
sometimes in the summer.'

'Haven't you been since?'

She shook her head and grimaced. 'Too many
babies.'

'It must have been hard.'

'We managed. Do you have brothers and sisters,
Mr Beckett?'

'Eli.'

She met his eyes and flushed. 'Are you sure it's all
right to call you that?'

'I'm very sure. I call you Carrie, don't I? And we're
not at work now.' He could see that she was still a
little shy, so went on cheerfully, 'As to brothers and
sisters, I have one of each, both older than me. My
parents have a small pub, only a beerhouse, and my
brother Thomas will take that over one day. It isn't
big enough to give us both a living, and anyway we're
too different to work together.'

'And your sister?'

'Oh, Izzie married a farmer years ago and they've
four children now. It's a hard life, because it isn't a
big farm, but she's happy enough.'

'I can't imagine having only one brother and sister.'

'There are ten of you, aren't there?' He saw tears
fill her eyes and stopped walking. 'What have I said
to upset you?'

He could see her struggling to keep the tears back
and it seemed only natural to take her into his arms.

'She sold them!' Carrie sobbed. 'The babies. My
mother sold them!'

Eli let her weep out her sad little tale, and held her as she cried.

'I'm sorry,' she said after a minute or two. 'I've nearly cried a few times, only I held it back.' She began hunting in her pockets, seeming distressed not to find what she was looking for.

Eli pulled out his handkerchief. 'Is this any use?'

'Thank you.' Carrie wiped her eyes and blew her nose, so that the handkerchief was soon a crumpled mess. She looked from it to him in dismay. 'I ought to wash this for you, but I daren't take it back with me or *he* will want to know why I needed to borrow your handkerchief.'

Eli chuckled and took it from her. 'I'll just put it in the wash. No one will notice a thing. There's a washerwoman comes in every fortnight.' He hesitated then took her hand and pulled her forward. 'Come on. There's a nice view at the top. We've just got time to get there and back in an hour.'

By the time they reached the summit of the small hill Carrie was breathless, her face full of colour and her eyes sparkling. When she stumbled he caught her, held her close, had to kiss her.

As they drew apart Eli didn't know what to say. The kiss had taken him by surprise. Her, too, from the expression on her face. 'I shouldn't have done that. I know you're not free with your favours.'

Carrie took a step back, the happiness fading from her face. 'It's all right. But please – don't do it again. I'm definitely not that sort of girl. And anyway, you should be kissing girls of your own sort.'

'I don't want to kiss anyone else. I enjoyed kissing *you*. But this isn't the time to – to start anything. I'm too busy with the music room. Well, I hope I am.' And somehow Eli found himself telling her about his fears that his uncle might be up to something with the owner of the engineering works.

'I don't like Mr Stott. No one who works there does, Robbie says. Mr Stott is allus touching the lasses where he shouldn't. Even tried to touch me when he came to see your uncle.'

Eli found himself filled with anger at the mere idea of that. 'If I see him pestering you, I'll say something.'

Carrie smiled, but sadly. 'Better not. It'd make an enemy for you and for me as well. Besides, I'm not likely to be near enough for him to hurt me, especially as we're not living in one of his houses now.' She stared into the distance, changing the subject firmly. 'It's nice looking down on Hedderby from here. Perhaps I'll bring the children up on the tops one day for a walk.'

On the way back Eli caught hold of her hand again. And she let him go on holding it.

So much for good resolutions.

In the hut, Bram brought out the music and words to some well-known songs and they tried them out. Here, where she wasn't afraid of anyone overhearing, Joanna had no hesitation in letting her voice soar.

'I hadn't realised what a powerful voice you had!' he exclaimed when the last notes had died away. 'And it's beautiful, a little richer than most sopranos. You could earn your living on the stage, you know, with a voice like that.'

Joanna blushed bright red. 'I'm not that good.'

'Yes, you are.'

'Let's just – get on and sing. While we can.'

After a trial run-through of the melody they began again, with Bram harmonising with her. Joanna felt as if she were in heaven. His voice seemed made to go with hers.

The second song they tried was 'The Last Rose of Summer' which they'd sung before, but now they had all the words. It was so wonderful to sing it with him and the richness of the harmonies brought tears to her eyes.

'Are you all right?' he asked anxiously, stretching out one finger to brush away a tear from the corner of her eye.

His touch made Joanna's breath catch in her throat. 'Yes. It was just – so beautiful it made me want to weep.'

'It does that to me sometimes . . . music.' Bram smiled. 'Though only when it's sung or played properly. It hurts me inside my head when someone sings flat or plays the wrong chord on the piano.'

'You too?'

'Aye. I try not to let on, though. Folk'd laugh at me.'

'Yes. I try not to show my feelings at all.'

'Is that why you always seem so bad-tempered?' The minute the words were out he wished he hadn't said them.

Joanna looked down. 'Not seem. I often *feel* bad-tempered. I get so frustrated with Dad. And I have to keep folk away from me in the pub, so it helps if they think I'm nowty.'

'You're not bad-tempered with me, though.'

'No. I feel comfortable with you. Especially when we're on our own.'

'Would you feel comfortable if I took you in my arms?' He didn't wait but suited the action to the words, then kissed her.

For a minute she was so startled she tried to push away from him, but Bram held her close and suddenly she could hold back no longer. She slid her arms round his neck and returned his kiss, feeling mesmerised by the softness of his lips, by the warmth that was flowing through her. When he pulled away, just an inch or two, she stayed where she was, looking at him, wanting something more, not knowing what.

'Sure, it's like magic, the change in you,' he teased, and kissed her again.

'We shouldn't,' she murmured against his cheek when he stopped.

'Why shouldn't we?'

'Because – it's dangerous. I daren't . . .'

He knew what she meant. And suddenly he had to face it, the fact that he wanted her but didn't want to hurt her. Joanna wasn't a woman who gave her affections lightly, and he wasn't a man who had so far given his affections to any woman. Oh, he liked women. He liked a lot of people. But love, that was what it'd have to be with Joanna. And he wasn't sure he could love someone in that single-minded way.

'I've never loved a woman,' he confessed, then hesitated as if unsure of himself.

She hardly recognised this side of genial Bram Heegan. His expression was serious, without the old easy smile.

'I don't know if what I feel for you is love, Joanna, but I think it may be. And that frightens me.' He gave her a wry half-smile. 'I think you're the same. Am I right?'

She nodded.

'So we both need time, don't you think? Time to get to know one another, to find out if this is real, because there would be – problems. My family are strongly Catholic.'

'And you?'

'I'm not sure I'm strongly anything, but I don't want to hurt the Mammy.'

'There'd be problems on both sides, I think. My father – isn't easy.'

He nodded. 'But if this is love . . . well, I won't let that stop me.'

'No. I won't, either.'

He drew her towards him, just to hold her close for a minute or two. And it felt good. Too good. Then he took a deep breath and pushed her to arm's length. 'I think we'd better start singing again.'

'Yes.' But she'd rather have stayed in his arms.

Only when Joanna was in bed that night did she dare think about Bram again. He'd been honest with her, seemed as surprised by their feelings as she was. She valued his honesty much more than she'd value flowery declarations of love, because all her life her father had said one thing while doing another. There in the darkness she admitted to herself that she hoped it was love between her and Bram, that it might lead somewhere, in spite of the difficulties. She seemed to have been alone for such a long time, ever since her mother had died, and though she didn't feel as angry these days, not since Eli had come and given her hope for a better future, she still felt the need for someone to love, someone of her own.

A shiver ran through her and she snuggled down under the soft blankets. She was afraid and yet hopeful, too. Kissing him had been wonderful. Being held by him . . . Oh, she didn't know what she felt, only that she wanted things to work out between her and Bram Heegan.

# 16

A few days later, Frank Beckett got ready to go out. He put on a clean shirt and his best clothes. Joanna stared at him, noticing at once that he had shaved, something he rarely did except on Fridays and Mondays. She couldn't help asking, 'Where are you going, dressed like that?'

'None of your business.' Her father pushed past her and was out before she could say anything else. She followed him to the door and stood watching him walk along the street, half inclined to go after him.

Carrie came up beside her. 'I've never seen Mr Beckett dress up like that.'

'No, I haven't either. Well, not for years.' Joanna took a sudden decision. 'Carrie, could you follow him and see where he goes? Only . . . try not to let him see you.'

'If you want me to.'

'I do. I need to find out what he's doing. If he sees you, tell him I sent you to buy some more butter, then go into Marker's and get a pound of best to prove it. Mr Marker will put it on our account. But if Dad doesn't see you, keep watching. Here, give me that apron.'

Joanna watched Carrie hurry off along the street, then forced herself to go indoors and carry on with the cleaning. If nothing else, it'd take her mind off things.

Carrie had no difficulty following Mr Beckett because he never walked fast. He stopped to have a word with Mr Marker, so she turned into Crookit Walk and stayed at the end, leaning against the wall, earning herself a few curious glances as she peered along the street.

When Mr Beckett moved on, she waited a minute or two then followed him, sauntering now but even so having to stop and look in shop windows to prevent herself from catching up with him because he walked so slowly. He didn't look back, not once.

She was surprised when he went into Hordle's. She strolled on past the lawyer's shiny front door and the polished brass sign on the wall, heading towards the Town Hall. Before she got there, she turned and went to stand on the bridge, pretending to stare at the river bubbling along beneath her. From here she could just see the front door of Hordle's.

A gentleman came strolling along the street, and some of the people who saw him coming found a reason to cross to the other side. No one wanted to get in Mr Athol Stott's way. He raised his top hat to two ladies then turned into the lawyer's office.

It couldn't be chance that had sent these two men into Hordle's at the same time, surely? Not when you knew, as Carrie did, that Mr Stott had visited Mr Beckett at the Dragon only a few days ago.

She debated whether to wait and see how long the two men were in there, but decided after a moment or two's thought that she might as well go back to the Dragon now. That way Mr Beckett wouldn't know she'd been out.

When she slipped back into the pub Joanna dropped her wet cloth into the bucket and hurried across to her.

'Well?'

'Your father went into Hordle's. A minute or two later Mr Athol Stott went in as well.' Carrie could see that this news had upset Miss Beckett. 'Should I have stayed to see how long he was there? I thought it'd be better if he didn't know I'd been following him.'

'You were right to come back.' Joanna took off the sacking apron and handed it back to Carrie. 'You continue with the work. I'll go and finish off in the snug.'

But she didn't do anything except sit down and wish Eli was there to discuss it with her. And that day the room got the skimpiest cleaning it'd ever had, because Joanna kept listening for her father's return, worried that he was taking so long.

Frank sat down in a comfortable leather chair in Mr Hordle's room and waited for the lawyer to speak.

'Have you come to any decision, Mr Beckett?'

Frank knew the other man was trying to get him to speak his agreement to sell, but he knew more about the law than Mr Hordle realised because he'd already been to see his own lawyer. Jack Burtell dealt with local shopkeepers and tradesmen, not the gentry, but he was a shrewd young man for all that, and had immediately grasped what Frank needed and given him some careful advice. You hadn't to say you'd agreed to anything till you were ready to sign the contract, it seemed, or you could be tied to it by a verbal agreement.

Well, Frank intended to sell that land and make a nice fat profit from it, but there were one or two things he wanted to sort out first and it wouldn't do to let them think they'd got it from him too easily. Besides, he wanted to show Mr Burtell the contract before he signed it – and even then he'd prefer to chew things over before taking the final step. That was how he'd always taken major decisions in his life. Slowly. Carefully. And this was a very big decision.

There was the sound of someone arriving and the clerk's voice fussing over him. Frank didn't even turn his head. He knew that voice. Mr Athol bloody Stott! Well, well, so the man was deigning to deal with him in person today. He must really want that piece of land.

The clerk ushered the important client in and not until he was settled in the most comfortable chair did Athol so much as look at Frank.

'Well?'

He waited a minute then said, 'I may be interested, but I'm not sure. There are one or two details that still need to be sorted out before I can consider it seriously. And even then, I'll want to take the contract home to study it and make sure everything's to my satisfaction before I agree to sell.'

Athol breathed deeply. One day he'd teach this oaf a lesson about how to deal with the gentry! Who did he think he was, holding up the project like this? It'd be that nephew of his who was behind this shilly-shallying. The fool probably still thought he could get his music room. As if common scum needed entertainment in the evenings, apart from a drink or two! But he contained his impatience and let Hordle lead the conversation round to a price.

And even so, all Beckett would say was, '*If* I agree to sell – and I'm still not sure about it – that price might be acceptable.'

Athol was certain then that the other man had been to see Burtell, a jumped-up newcomer to the town. 'Then we'd better get Hordle to draw up the contract, so that you can check it.'

Frank nodded. 'Mmm. That'd be the way to go.'

'But you will sell?' Mr Hordle asked again.

'I'll think seriously about it, but I'm not sure yet.'

'There's just one condition,' Athol said, taking a sudden decision.

Frank looked at him in surprise. 'Oh? What?'

'I want that nephew of yours out *now*. Send him back to wherever he came from.'

Both the other men stared at him in patent surprise.

'What's Eli got to do with it?' Frank asked.

'I'm sure he'll try to persuade you not to sell. So as an earnest of your goodwill, I want him out.'

'But I need him in the pub.'

'Hire someone else. I don't like his face.'

There was silence, then Frank said in the mild voice he always used for business negotiations, 'I'll get rid of him then, but not for any reasons of good-will because I haven't made my final decision yet. No, I'll get rid of him because he's annoying *me* lately, always wanting something. Time he went back to his own family. It hasn't worked out, having him here.' Anyway, Bram Heegan could do the job now.

Athol Stott leaned back. Well, he hadn't managed to draw any sort of promise from Beckett, but if he got rid of the young man who'd been so insolent to him, that'd please him greatly. He nodded to Hordle.

'I think that's as much as we can do for today,' Charles Hordle said smoothly. 'Let me show you out now, Mr Beckett.'

Athol listened to his lawyer escorting the old sod out, as if he needed to extend the courtesy to a fellow like that, and when he came back, asked the question dearest to his heart. 'Have we got enough out of him to constitute a verbal agreement to sell?'

'I'm afraid not.'

'But if we both swore he'd agreed . . .'

Charles Hordle looked at him and his tone turned frosty. 'I'm afraid I couldn't do that. I take my prac-tice of the law very seriously, Mr Stott. I would never perjure myself.'

Athol bit off a protest. 'Well, he's going to sell anyway, you can see that he's happy with the price now. Draw up the damned contract and send him a copy. He'll no doubt take it to that Burtell fellow, and *he* will make a fuss about some of the wording, just to show he's earning his money, but we'll get there in the end.' He stood up. 'No need to show me out.'

Hordle listened to his receding footsteps and made no attempt to summon his clerk. Stott's father had been an honest man, at least, if rather opportunistic. But the more Charles dealt with the son, the more he wished he didn't have to. The trouble was, in a small town you couldn't afford to offend one of the richest men, especially one known for avenging anything he saw as an insult.

With a sigh, he went to summon his clerk and began work on the contract.

Frank walked slowly back to the pub, feeling tired now, as if each step was a huge effort. He often felt tired lately. He scowled. He didn't really want to get rid of Eli who was a big help in the pub and knew his stuff, but he didn't want to jeopardise the sale or offend Stott, who could make a very nasty enemy. Why the hell had the man taken against his nephew?

Edmund went to see the new lawyer, Jack Burtell, and took him into his confidence about his forthcoming marriage.

'Will you manage the legal side of my affairs? I want to withdraw them from Hordle because he also deals with my cousin and I want to make sure my lawyer is on my side. Oh, and I'll need to make a will so that if anything happens to me, Faith's safe. In fact, could you draw up a simple one immediately, leaving everything to her? I'll come in and sign it tomorrow.'

Burtell looked surprised but nodded.

'My most pressing need is to find somewhere for us to live. That's not easy in a town where a few rich men own most of the houses.'

'Well, as it happens, I may be able to help you there. A client of mine has just died – Miss Spindler – and her nephew wants me to sell her house. He's happy living in the South, doesn't want anything to do with Hedderby these days.'

Edmund beamed at him. 'I think I know the house you mean. It's in the village of Out Rawby, isn't it? How soon can I go and look at it?'

'As soon as you like.'

'I don't want my cousin finding out until everything's *fait accompli*, both the house and my marriage. If you can give me a key, I'll take Faith out walking and we'll drop in to inspect it. She's a great walker, my lass is.'

They went to see the house the very next day, which was a Saturday and fortunately fine. Edmund set off as soon as the works closed, leaving Turner and the stoker to bed the engine down, claiming that he needed a breath of fresh air and was going walking with a 'friend'. His cousin was preoccupied with something and hardly bothered to listen to his plans, but clearly realised whom he meant by his 'friend' and gave him one of those knowing smiles that irritated Edmund lately for some reason.

He called for Faith and they walked out of town

together, chatting in a companionable way, never at a loss for something to say.

Out Rawby was a pretty hamlet of only about thirty dwellings. Miss Spindler's house was in the centre of it, with a long, narrow garden at the back, the lawyer said.

'Let's go inside,' Edmund said when they got there.

'Just a minute.' Faith moved a step away from him and studied the house. 'It looks friendly, don't you think?'

A man walking up the street wished them good day, then went on to chat with a woman standing at her doorway. There was a small church at one end of the street and a pub at the other, with a shop next to it and a sort of barn next to that.

Edmund studied the nearby properties in satisfaction. Cottages and houses, each with a garden, not terraces of cramped dwellings opening directly on to the street. 'I've always thought Out Rawby a very pretty place.' He opened the gate. 'Come on. You can't stand in the street all day.'

But Faith stood for a minute longer, taking it all in. 'I've missed having a garden!' she said softly.

She had missed all sorts of things to be with him, he knew, including her sisters. She'd been called names in the street and snubbed by shopkeepers for living in sin. Well, now he was going to make it up to her as far as he possibly could. He hoped some people at least would be forgiving once she was married.

Edmund liked the property very much. It was three storeys high and situated in the very centre of the village. Miss Spindler had kept house there for an unmarried brother until his death and had elected to stay on afterwards in the place she loved, living there with one maid and a man who did some gardening, the lawyer had said.

They did a quick tour of the rooms to get a feel for the place, then went round again more slowly.

'Do you like it?' asked Edmund as they went back into the kitchen and gravitated towards the rear window with its view across the moors.

'I love it.' Faith turned to look at him, her gaze troubled now.

'What is it, love?'

'I feel I'm forcing you to marry me!'

'You're not. All you're forcing me to do is stop shilly-shallying.' He hesitated then added, 'I think Athol will throw me out of my job when he finds out we're married, though.'

'Edmund, no!'

'I'm afraid so. But it's about time I left. I don't enjoy the way he treats his men, don't enjoy the way he treats his wife come to that. I know he's my cousin and just about my only relative but I was never particularly fond of him, and since he inherited he's grown so cruel and arrogant that I've come to detest him.'

'What shall you do if he dismisses you?'

'Live on my uncle's money – I inherited enough to keep us in modest comfort whether I work or not – and maybe set up a small workshop at the end of the garden. Who knows? I haven't had time to think about that yet.' He took hold of her hands and raised first one then the other to his lips. 'Faith, I haven't felt this happy since before my parents died, certainly not since I came to live with my uncle. Getting married, starting a new life together . . . that's the right thing for us to do, I'm quite sure of it.'

She put one arm round him and leaned against him. They stood there for a while, staring out at the beautiful view, happy simply to be together, not even needing to put that into words.

As they walked back to town, Edmund raised the question of servants and found her reluctant.

'You must have at least one maid. As my wife, you can't be seen scrubbing floors any more. Besides,' he smiled down at her, 'I want to cherish you and that child of mine.'

'Do what you think best, then, but I don't know how I'll deal with a maid.'

The next day Edmund went to see Mr Burtell to discuss purchasing the house.

'Would you be interested in taking on Miss Spindler's maid?' the lawyer asked him. 'Grania is one of the Heegans. She's living with her brother and his wife at the moment, and I know she's looking for work. She's sharp-tongued but I've always had a soft spot for her, and she's unhappy about having no job, even though Miss Spindler left her twenty pounds a year.'

'Would she be interested in working for us? You know our situation. There are some people who'll never forgive us for living together out of wedlock.'

'I could ask her, if you like?'

'I'll only employ her if she and Faith get on with one another.'

'I'll mention that. I could send her round to see your good lady, if you like.'

'Yes. Please do that.'

There was only one more thing to do now, arrange his marriage, so Edmund went straight round to the church. The minister was frosty about the need for a special licence and a secret wedding, but agreed not to say anything.

'I'm not sure you're doing the right thing, though, Mr Stott.'

'And I'm sure I am. My Faith's never been with another man and I should have married her years ago. I'm more sorry than you'll ever understand that I let my uncle's wishes stop me.'

The minister watched him go. He was tempted to let Mr Athol Stott know what was going on, but in the end decided that what had been said in confidence must be kept confidential. Pity to see a good man marry below him, though, and Mr Stott would be very annoyed.

There was a knock on the front door and Faith took a quick glance out of the window before answering it. She was feeling nervous about getting married and was worried sick that Athol Stott would find some way of preventing it. But her visitor was a woman of uncertain years, dressed all in black and with a severely respectable look to her.

Faith opened the door. 'Yes?'

The woman studied her, then gave a little nod as if she approved of something. 'Mr Burtell sent me round to see you. I was maid to Miss Spindler at Out Rawby, and I'm looking for another position. He thought you might wish to consider me.'

'Oh, yes. Do come in. Won't you sit down?'

'My name's Grania Heegan,' she announced, and took a good look round the front room where Faith liked to sit in the daytime. Another of those nods, then she looked at Faith herself. 'Do you not want to ask me any questions?'

'I shouldn't know what to ask you.'

What might have been a shadow of a smile passed across Grania's stern face, then she said, 'Well, we'll not worry about that then. I'll tell you to your face, it sticks in my gullet that you've been living in sin. But on the other hand, we're all human and you *are* getting married, so that's good enough for me.'

'Oh. Yes,' Faith said faintly.

'When is the baby due?'

'In about six months. How did you know about it? I haven't told anyone except Edmund.'

'You've the look on you some women get when they're expecting.'

Faith chewed her lip, wondering what to say, then decided on total honesty. 'I haven't the faintest idea of a maid's duties, and it'd be silly to pretend otherwise. Edmund says we must have a maid and it *is* a big house. But if you come to work for us, I'd be most grateful if you'd help me learn how to manage things when I'm married to a gentleman like Edmund. I don't want to let him down, you see.'

Grania blinked, then nodded again. 'Does that mean I have the job?'

Faith nodded.

'Then I think I should go out and get the place ready for you.'

'We're not telling anyone we're going there until after we're married. Edmund's cousin may be – difficult.'

'I can keep my mouth shut as tight as you like. Wages?'

'Whatever is usual.'

Grania relaxed visibly. 'I think we'll do well together. You keep this place very clean. I'd not have worked for you if you'd been slovenly in your ways.'

Faith blinked in surprise at this.

Grania stood up. 'I'll be off then. Tell your man I'll need some money to get food in. I'll let myself out now.'

Faith waited until her new maid's footsteps had vanished into the distance, then allowed herself to smile. It wasn't the way ladies usually dealt with their maids, she was sure, but she never could pretend. And it seemed that Grania too preferred to speak honestly about things.

And to her delight, Edmund approved of what she had done and said he'd send their maid some money. Then he kissed her and Faith forgot everything else for a while.

★

When Frank got back all he wanted was to sit down and have a rest, even a nap. But as he walked into the pub, which was clean now, he found that the two scrubbing women had left and Joanna and Eli were waiting for him in the kitchen, neither of them looking happy.

'Is the kettle hot?' he asked. 'I'm parched.'

Joanna pushed it to the hottest part of the hob without a word.

Frank turned to his nephew. 'Haven't you got any work to do? I don't pay you to sit around all day guzzling tea.'

It was Joanna who spoke first. 'We want to speak to you, Dad.'

'Well, I don't want to speak to you. It's a poor lookout if a man can't have a minute to himself before the pub gets busy.'

'It's a poor lookout if a father doesn't tell his daughter what he's doing.' Joanna sat down, folded her arms on the table and leaned forward on them. 'I know you're up to something, Dad. I can always tell. And I want to know what.'

'I'll tell you when I'm good and ready, not until.'

Eli intervened then. 'I reckon you're dealing with Athol Stott, and I already know he wants to buy the old stable space.'

Frank didn't know what to say to that, so turned to look at the stove. 'That kettle's boiling.'

Joanna paid no attention to it. 'Dad, you're not selling the land to that man, are you?'

He scowled at her. 'You leave business matters to me, my girl.'

'But you promised us we could have a music room there!'

'It's mine to do with as I please. If something better turns up, I'd be a fool to ignore it.'

'You *are* selling it, then,' Eli said bitterly. 'You've broken your word, just as my father said you would.'

They both looked at Frank in silence for a minute and he didn't like the expressions on their faces. Ganging up on him, that's what they were. In his own house too. Athol Stott was right. He should get rid of his nephew then Joanna would stop being so troublesome.

'How much has he offered you, Dad?'

'A tidy sum.'

'*How much?*'

'None of your business. You won't be getting your hands on any of it till I'm dead.' He took a deep breath and looked across the table at Eli. 'And while we're on about all this, I don't need you any more. You'd better pack your things. I'll give you till tomorrow to leave.'

The only noise in the kitchen was the sound of the kettle steaming furiously. Joanna got up automatically and moved it but made no attempt to brew a pot of tea. 'Dad, you can't mean that! After all Eli's done here. No one could have worked harder. No one!'

Frank shrugged, feeling a bit ashamed because she was right there and Eli had been a good support to him. 'I'll give you a month's wages as a bonus,' he said, his guilt lessened immediately by the thought of his own generosity.

'Why?' Eli asked.

'What do you mean, why?'

'You know you can't manage the pub now without help, so why are you getting rid of me?'

Frank shrugged.

Eli folded his arms. 'I'm not moving till you tell me why.'

Joanna folded hers. 'Neither am I.'

Incensed to see them ganging up on him again, Frank shouted, 'Because that's a condition of the sale. Stott wants you out of town. You've upset him. I don't know what you've done, but he wants you out.'

There was dead silence in the room.

'I'm disgusted that you'd treat your own kin like that,' Joanna said, 'absolutely disgusted. And what's more, if Eli goes and you insist on selling the stables, then I'm leaving too.'

Her father laughed at that. 'What, abandon your inheritance? Not you.'

'I shan't care about it if I can't have that music room,' she said, then the words poured out of her, the words she'd held back for years. 'Do you think I *like* working in this shabby pub? Well, I don't, I hate it! It's full of drunken fools, and it stinks of tobacco and stale ale. It turns my stomach in the morning when I start cleaning, and it makes me feel as if I'm choking at night when the air is blue with smoke. We could have improved it, but *you* wouldn't. You won't even let me sell food here. So if my inheritance is only this pub and not a music room, I reckon it's not worth hanging around waiting for it. I don't think it'll be *worth* waiting for because, knowing you, there'll even be something tricky about the will.'

A dull flush stained Frank's face.

'There! You've put some conditions in the will, I knew you would. I've been a fool to stay here so long, but I'll not do so any longer. Come on, Eli. Let's pack.' Joanna thrust herself to her feet and walked towards the stairs.

'Wait! Come back!' her father called, half rising in his seat.

But she didn't even turn her head and her feet drummed on the wooden stairs in a way that showed how very angry she was.

'She'll come round,' Frank muttered.

Eli stood up and followed his cousin, turning at the door to ask, 'How will you manage without us both, do you think?'

Frank scowled at him. 'I won't have to. My Joanna will soon be back. She's no money – well, no more than a pound or two – she'll not last long out there.' He waved his arm in the direction of the street.

'But *I* have some money saved and I'll be happy to help her.' Eli ignored his uncle's angry mutter and ran lightly up the stairs to tap on his cousin's door. When she didn't answer, he pushed it open.

She was standing by the window, staring blindly down Market Street.

'Joanna?'

She turned to him, her face tight with misery. 'I *am* leaving, Eli. Don't try to persuade me to stay.'

'I won't. I came to ask if you'd like us to go some-where together?'

She gave him a faint smile. 'That'd be nice. I was just trying to think where to go, what to do.'

'Have you got any money? You father doesn't think you have.'

'I've more than he realises. I'm not stupid, I've been saving money out of the housekeeping for years, just in case. I've got enough in the bank to tide me over till I find something to do, for a year or two if necessary, or to set myself up in a small shop.' She looked at him, her eyes filled with tears. 'I'm sorry, Eli. He's broken his word to you as well. And all at the bidding of *that man.*' She remembered the way Stott had followed her home from church one Sunday and how she'd hated even being near him. 'Dad won't be able to manage without help, you know. He's slowed down a lot lately.'

'He'll probably sell the whole place and spend the rest of his life in idleness.'

'Maybe. But he likes the pub, likes gossiping with some of the regulars and having a pot of beer any time he fancies one. No, I can't see him selling it, only the land.'

She sighed, looking so unhappy he went across to give her a hug. 'Where shall we go then?'

'I don't know, Eli. We'll have to find some lodgings for the time being, I suppose, but I can't think where. All the lodging houses I know of in Hedderby are in houses belonging to the big employers, and the lodgings are for people who work for them. Stott's has one for its single men, and the cotton mill has two, one for men and one for women. I can't see Stott letting us stay in his lodging house, and I wouldn't want to anyway.' She shuddered at the mere thought of being in that man's power in any way.

'There's Linney's.'

'A common lodging house! Do you really fancy spending your nights in a room full of other people, near paupers? I don't.'

'No, I don't. But we have to find somewhere. Though I don't like to think of you giving up your inheritance because of me.'

Joanna gave him a sad smile. 'It's not because of you, not really. Why do you think I used to be so bad-tempered? Because I was unhappy, could see no improvement in the future, either. But the idea of the music room – well, that gave me hope. You can't imagine how much I enjoyed our outing to Manchester, how I could see us doing something like that in a smaller way, how I wanted to have music in my life openly.' She stared blindly out of the window, then said softly, 'My father's as stubborn as a mule, and blind to everything but money and what *he* wants.'

Eli looked thoughtful. 'I wonder if they've any spare bedrooms at Linney's – in the house part, I mean. I could nip down and ask Carrie, if you like.'

She shrugged. 'I doubt they have, but it wouldn't hurt to ask. I'll start my packing. We can always go to a hotel in Manchester for a night or two. Oh, and when you go down, could you give Carrie and Bonny their money, please? Tell them Dad'll be in charge after today.' She handed over four shillings.

When Eli went downstairs, he avoided going near

his uncle, who was still sitting in the kitchen, sipping a pot of ale now. The big room was clean, but not yet set to rights. No customers would be allowed in for another half-hour. Carrie was in the far corner, starting to pull down the chairs and stools from the table tops. Bonny wasn't in sight, was probably throwing out the dirty water. He knew their routines as well as his own.

Carrie looked at him uncertainly as he came over to join her. 'I heard shouting . . .' She let the words trail away, worried that he might think she was poking her nose in where she had no right.

'There's a problem come up for me and my cousin. Mr Beckett is selling the land next to the pub to Mr Stott, breaking his promise to let us have a music room there. So we're leaving. Trouble is, we've nowhere to stay. Does your step-father have any rooms besides the common lodging house? Rooms he'd let us have? There's nowhere else in town that I know of for us to stay.'

Carrie stared at him in surprise, then said slowly, 'That's why Mr Stott came to see him, then, the other day? I'm sorry about your music room. I know how much you wanted one.'

'I was taking a risk, but we'd got so far I thought it was certain. Shows what a fool I was. Frank Beckett isn't known for keeping his word.' Eli pulled a wry face. 'I'll get my music room somehow, one day. But in the meantime Joanna and I need somewhere to sleep for a few nights in the faint hope that our moving out will make my uncle change his mind. If it doesn't, we'll move on somewhere else, Manchester perhaps.'

Carrie thought rapidly. 'There are two bedrooms not being used. We'd need to turn them out, but . . .' She thought furiously, then nodded. 'If it means more money, Nev will probably let you have them, though he never allows the common lodgers inside the house and doesn't want the children sleeping near him and my mother.' She knew why. They all knew why. It was embarrassing the way he and Jane were carrying on.

'I'll go and pack, then Joanna and I can walk back with you. Oh, I nearly forgot, she sent you this money. You'll have to deal with Mr Beckett about the cleaning from now on.'

Carrie pulled a face, then looked across to see Bonny come back in. 'We can't leave till Bram comes for his aunt.'

Eli looked at the clock on the wall behind the bar. 'All right.' He wanted to be out before customers started arriving, though the place was never full early on.

When he and Joanna carried their bags down the stairs, Frank came to the door of the kitchen to stare at them. He didn't say a word. Joanna looked at him and, since he didn't speak, she kept quiet too. What was there to say? He thought they were bluffing. She knew they weren't, but she'd have to prove that to him.

Bram insisted on walking back to Linney's with them, helping Joanna with her bags. 'Shall I keep Bonny at home tomorrow?'

She shook her head. 'No. She might as well continue working there. She knows her job. They'll be a bit pushed without me to help, but that's *his* lookout now.'

'He may ask me to help him, take Eli's place. There's no one else. Shall I turn him down if he does?'

She looked at Bram in surprise. 'Would you do that?'

'For you I would.'

'You're – um – very kind.'

'Aren't I?' he teased, winning a faint smile from her. 'Well, shall I?'

'No. If you're there, you can keep an eye on what he's doing. But tell him you can't do any more nights than you're doing now. That'll leave him short of help.'

'Right you are.' Bonny was tugging at Bram's arm, so he turned to explain to her what was happening.

She looked near to tears once she understood what it meant for her. 'I don't like Mr Beckett. He shouts at me. If Miss Beckett isn't there, I don't want to work there any more.'

'Carrie will be there. She'll look after you. And I'll still be picking you up. You'll be all right, love.'

Bonny looked at the couple in front of them but didn't seem fully convinced.

Eli walked ahead of the others with Carrie. 'Strange how things turn out,' he said, turning to glance back at the pub.

'I still can't believe Mr Beckett will let you two go. His nephew and his own daughter!'

'He's very fond of money – and still thinks Joanna

will come back. We don't know whether he's signed an agreement to sell yet or not, but he obviously intends to. He wouldn't tell us any details.'

'But you've lost your dream. I'm so sorry for that, Eli.'

'It's only postponed.' He looked straight ahead, grim determination in every line of his body. 'I'll achieve it one day – or die trying. That's the sort of stubborn fool I am.'

'I envy you.'

'What for?'

'Having such a splendid dream in the first place.'

'Don't you have any dreams? Most girls want to get married. Don't you?'

Carrie pulled a wry face. 'No, not really. Nev's house is nice and we have enough to eat there and can keep ourselves clean. Those were my dreams once. I just wish he didn't take all the money we earn. It doesn't seem fair.'

'Why don't you want to marry? I thought that was every lass's dream.'

'Because I don't want to be like Mam, have so many children I can't feed them. She gave up trying, stopped looking after us properly, stopped keeping herself clean even. It'd tear me apart here,' she thumped her chest, 'to have children and give them away like she has. I still miss the twins. Silly, isn't it, when I didn't want them at first?'

'Poor Carrie. You've had a hard start in life yet you've kept going, and it's *you* who've looked after your brothers and sisters. I admire that.'

'Admire me!' She laughed. 'Well, that's the first time anyone's ever said that to me.'

'I meant it.'

She fell silent, but there was a warm feeling inside her at the compliment and there was an equally warm look in Eli's eyes. She was quite sure she wasn't mistaken about that. Eh, she felt so comfortable with him. Only – where could it all lead? Nowhere, and she had to remember that, had to hold her feelings back. Ambitious men like him didn't marry rag-poor lasses like her. But if it had been possible with him, she'd have changed her mind about marriage. She admitted that to herself, at least.

When they got near Linney's, she stopped and said, 'Let me go in and speak to Nev first.'

So the others waited on the street corner with their luggage, attracting curious stares from passers-by.


Carrie hurried round the back of the house, relieved to find Nev in. 'Can I have a word?'

'Something wrong?'

She remembered Raife's advice. 'No. But I saw a way for you to earn some money.' She explained the situation.

He began to look thoughtful. 'Will they be staying long, do you think?'

'Could be only one night, but most likely it'll be a few. They're determined to leave Hedderby if Mr Beckett sells that land to Mr Stott, you see.'

Nev's expression had grown ugly. 'Stott doesn't care who he treads on if he wants something.'

She'd heard him speak scathingly of the owner of the engineering works before, though he'd never said why he didn't like the man. Carrie waited, letting him come to a decision.

After a minute or so he punched one hand into the other. 'I'll do it, if only for the pleasure of being on the opposite side to Stott. They can have my two back bedrooms. Ten shillings a week for each room and linen, another ten if they want feeding, which I've no doubt they will.'

'I'll go and tell them.'

'Give me this morning's wages first.'

She might have known he'd not forget that.

# 17

Edmund feigned illness on the morning of his marriage, lying in bed and telling the maid he just wanted to be left alone to sleep. He'd never felt less like sleep, had been awake several times during the night, in fact, worrying that something might go wrong today.

He heard Athol leave for work at eight o'clock sharp and tiptoed to the window to watch his cousin stride down the hill.

Even then he waited till after nine before he started packing his clothes, working swiftly and methodically as he did everything, laying them in the sheets he'd bought in town a few days previously and tying these up to make bundles. Luckily the household was used to seeing him come in with parcels of books, papers, all sorts of strange objects, and nowadays no one ever asked what he'd brought back. It was ridiculous that he had to go to such lengths to leave home, but he knew that if he tried to bring his trunk down from the attic, Maria would send word to her husband that he was leaving and then Athol would come rushing home to find out why. He didn't want any quarrels, and most of all didn't want anything to prevent the main business of the day which was for him to get married.

When his sister-in-law went out to call on her friends, Edmund breathed a sigh of relief. He'd been counting on the fact that Maria did this every Wednesday.

Soon after that he saw Bram Heegan drive up to the house and stride around to knock on the back door. A couple of minutes later there was a knock on Edmund's bedroom door and he opened it to see the downstairs maid.

'If you please, Mr Edmund, there's a man to see you. Says he's come to collect something.'

'Yes. I have the things ready.'

'Are you feeling better, sir?'

'Yes, thank you. I shan't be in for dinner tonight.' He picked up one of the bundles.

'Can I help you carry them down, sir?'

'No, thank you, but tell the man to come round to the front door, will you, please? It'll be easier for me to give these to him there.'

'Yes, sir.'

Edmund carried his three unwieldy bundles down the front stairs without seeing any of the servants. 'You'll keep them somewhere safe?'

Bram nodded and smiled. 'Yes, of course.'

'I'll see you in about half an hour at the church, then. It's still all right for you to act as our witness, isn't it? And you'll bring someone else with you as you promised?' It wasn't until this had happened that Edmund had realised he didn't have any close friends in Hedderby. Oh, he had plenty of acquaintances, though they were mostly family acquaintances, not real friends as he'd had when he was pupil to an engineer in Edinburgh. He still wrote to one of the other men who'd been a lad with him there, sharing problems and ideas with his old friend.

Since he'd come back to Hedderby he'd been wrapped up in his work, and the rest of the time he'd spent with Faith who was a friend as well as a lover.

As Bram drove off, whistling cheerfully, Edmund went back upstairs, checked his appearance in the mirror for a final time and put on his hat and coat.

He stood for a moment at the bottom of the stairs, looking round at this house in which he had spent over half his life. It hadn't felt like home since his uncle died and Athol and his family moved in. But still, it felt strange to leave it, to know he'd never live here again.

Bram went to look for his brother Michael, who'd agreed to act as the second witness to the marriage, only to find he'd forgotten and gone off to collect some bits and pieces to sell at the market.

'Damnation!'

As he was walking towards the church, he met Eli and grabbed his arm. 'Will you do me a favour?'

'Yes, of course.'

'A fellow I know who's getting married needs a witness. My brother Michael was going to do it, but he forgot and has gone to pick up some stuff. There isn't time to bring him back so . . .' He cocked one eyebrow questioningly at Eli.

'I'll be happy to oblige. Who's getting married?'

Bram looked round to make sure no one was close enough to overhear. 'Edmund Stott. He's marrying his mistress and his cousin won't be pleased, so he's doing it quietly. Doesn't want anyone trying to stop him.'

'How could anyone do that? He's a grown man.'

'I can tell you're a newcomer to the town. Athol Stott doesn't hesitate to use violence or any other nasty trick to get his own way, and I'd not put it past him to kidnap the bride if he heard what was going on.' Bram's voice became mocking. 'A Stott marry a common lass? Unheard of.'

'Then you're risking your own safety by helping him?'

Bram grinned. 'Not me. I've a network of Irish fellows who'd help me if I were in trouble, and I can handle myself in a fight. Should Stott lay one finger on me or mine, or rather pay someone else to do it, he'd stir up more trouble than it's worth for himself and he knows it. But his cousin Edmund's different. He's a good man, and a good engineer, too, the men who work with him all say so. He's well thought of by everyone, but until now has seemed to be under his cousin's thumb. Who'll be protecting *his* back against Athol's anger, that's what worries me?'

As they began walking Bram added in a thoughtful voice, 'You know, Athol Stott doesn't realise, or perhaps doesn't care, how many enemies he's made in this town. Ordinary folk don't like the way he pesters their womenfolk. The men who work for him hate him because he treats them like dirt, and the bad feeling against him has grown even worse since he's cut their wages.'

'I've heard them talking about him in the pub. I didn't realise he was quite so dangerous, though.'

'He is, believe me. Never underestimate him.'

They reached the church. As he led the way in, Bram chuckled.

'What's so amusing?'

'The Mammy would go mad if she could see me coming in here. *She* would never set foot in a church that isn't Catholic, that's for sure.' He looked towards the front where a woman was sitting on her own and went to join her. 'Good morning, ma'am. I'm Bram Heegan. Is the bridegroom not here yet?'

'Edmund went to find the minister.'

Faith looked pale and nervous, Bram noticed. 'I wish you well on this happy day. This is my friend Eli Beckett, who's going to be the other witness.' He chatted easily with her until Edmund came back accompanied by the minister, who was looking very disapproving.

The service was as short as possible and when the minister had said, 'I now declare you man and wife,' it was a minute before Edmund realised it was over. He turned to beam at Faith, who now wore that starry-eyed look he loved so much.

He said it without considering who was listening, because it was important to tell her, 'I love you, Faith.'

'I love you too, Edmund.'

Eli and Bram exchanged quick smiles.

The minister looked as if he'd swallowed something nasty. 'If you'll come through with your witnesses and sign the register, I'll not keep you any longer,' he said coldly.

That was soon done, then they walked back to the main door of the church where they were partly hidden from the road by a tall hedge. Eli shook hands with the groom, wished him happiness and claimed the privilege of kissing the bride's cheek, then left. Bram also kissed the bride then went to retrieve his cart and drive it round to Faith's house, as agreed. There, he loaded her personal possessions, promising to come back for her furniture later.

Faith and Edmund walked out of the town centre to their new home arm-in-arm, not saying much, just enjoying the thought that they were now married and Athol couldn't do anything about it.

Early in the evening Edmund looked at Faith. 'I can't put it off any longer. My cousin will be home from the works now. I need to go and tell him what's happened.'

'I wish you'd just written him a letter.'

'That'd be the coward's way. Besides, he might surprise me and accept the fact that we're married, if only because he needs an engineer.'

She gave him one of her clear-eyed looks. 'We both know he won't do that.'

'Then I'll be out of a job, and as I've told you, I won't mind too much.'

Edmund admitted to himself that he felt nervous as he walked into town because his cousin could be very nasty when upset about something. But apart from dismissing Edmund from his post as engineer at the mill and probably never associating with him again, there was little Athol could do. Edmund would miss the children, but he wouldn't care if he never saw his cousin again.

He opened the front door, took a deep breath and went inside, finding his cousin in the small parlour drinking a glass of wine. It occurred to Edmund that Athol was drinking more heavily these days. When had that started?

Athol greeted him with, 'Where the hell have you been all day? First you were ill, then you vanished. Maria's been worried and I could have done with you at the mill today. That damned engine's been playing up again. Turner had to weight the governor arms to keep it running.'

Edmund forgot his own troubles for a moment. 'Don't you realise how dangerous that is with an old engine like ours?'

Athol waved one hand dismissively. 'Nothing went wrong. You worry too much. Anyway, where were you?'

Edmund took another deep breath. 'Getting married.'

Athol's hand jerked, sending wine splashing on to his trousers. He put the glass down hastily and started dabbing at himself. 'I don't think that's funny.'

'Neither do I. Faith and I were married this morning.'

'*What?* You can't mean you've married your mistress? The scheming little slut! How did she persuade you?'

Edmund kept control of himself only with diffi- culty, telling himself he'd known how Athol would react. 'I'll thank you not to speak about my wife like that again.'

'I shall speak of her how I like! She's a clever little bitch, must spread her legs nicely, but I never thought you'd—'

His words were cut off abruptly as Edmund punched him in the face. Athol fell backwards, drop- ping the glass which spilled wine all over the carpet. Cursing, he struggled quickly to his feet and dived at Edmund. The two men rolled to and fro, trying to thump one another, sending furniture flying and ornaments smashing. The noise brought the rest of the family to the doorway.

Maria was the first to arrive and stood with one hand pressed against her mouth. After a minute or two she realised the children were also watching and sent them away.

As the uneven battle continued, she could see that her husband was gaining the upper hand, his face a snarling mask of exultation as if he was enjoying himself, while Edmund's lip was cut and he was desperately trying to avoid further blows. She ran into the next room and dragged the heavy chenille table cover off, sending a bowl flying. Rushing back into the parlour, she waited for her opportunity then cast the heavy cloth over the two men.

As they struggled from underneath its heavy folds, she screamed, 'Stop it! Stop it this minute!'

They stood up, eyeing one another warily.

'How dare you behave like this in my house?' Maria demanded.

Edmund stepped backwards, brushing the back of one hand across his lower lip which was bleeding. He still half expected his cousin to rush him again, but Athol merely stood there breathing rapidly and glaring at him.

'I do apologise, my dear,' he said. 'We both forgot where we were.'

'I'm sorry, Maria,' Edmund added.

'What on earth caused this?' she demanded.

'He's married his mistress.'

She gaped at Edmund. 'You haven't!'

'Why should I not? I love her and she's expecting my child.'

Athol began laughing. 'Oldest trick in the book. In a month or so you'll find she's not expecting or else she'll "lose" the baby. But you'll be stuck with her. You're a fool!'

'I'm very happy to have married Faith, should have done it years ago, in fact. I've bought the old Spindler house in Out Rawby and have moved most of my things there.'

'Then you can move them out of the works, too. I'll not have you there any more.'

'Very well, I'll come and collect them tomorrow morning.'

'Make sure you don't speak to anyone while you're there.'

'If I'm not employed by you, then I'm not obliged to obey your orders any more, for which I'll be devoutly grateful.'

'Then let me put it this way: if you speak to anyone, that person will be dismissed. Come at ten o'clock and don't be late, or your things will be thrown away.'

Edmund inclined his head, then moved towards the door. 'I'm sorry for the mess, Maria.'

She didn't reply, having regained her usual wooden expression.

He strode out of the house and into the fresh air. It was starting to rain and he held up his face as he walked, glad of the cold moisture on his stinging cuts and bruises. If Maria hadn't intervened, he suspected his cousin would have half killed him – and enjoyed doing so.

When Edmund got home, Faith took one look at him and burst into tears, but soon pulled herself together and took him into the cosy kitchen where she and Grania could tend his injuries.

While the maid was getting some hot water, he said, 'I'm going to the works tomorrow, to collect my things.'

'Don't. He'll have some nasty trick ready to play on you.'

Edmund suspected his wife was right. 'I'll ask Bram Heegan to find me a strong man who can protect me if necessary. As you can see, I'm not very good at protecting myself.' He put his arms round her as she stood beside the chair he was sitting on and leaned his head against the soft fullness of her breasts. 'Not the nicest thing to happen on your wedding night. Sorry, love.'

'As long as you're all right. That's what matters most.' Faith stood for a moment then added softly, 'Perhaps we should move away and not tell him where we're going? I'm really afraid of him, Edmund.'

'No. Hedderby is my home and I'm not going to be chased away – by anyone.'

Carrie felt nervous going into work the next morning, knowing Miss Beckett wouldn't be there. There was no sign of old Mr Beckett when she arrived, so she went to get out the brooms and buckets. He came in while she was doing that.

'Ah, there you are, girl. Get on with your work and don't expect any cups of tea or pieces of cake today. Things are going to be different round here from now on.'

'Yes, Mr Beckett.'

'Has the idiot arrived yet?'

Carrie wanted to cry out hotly at this unkind description of Bonny, but bit back the words. It seemed to her that she could best help Eli and Joanna (who had told her last night to stop calling her Miss Beckett) by staying on here and keeping an eye on what old Mr Beckett did.

Bonny came in through the front doors just then, looking nervous, so Carrie went to chat to her as they started cleaning the tables, trying to set her at ease. She was only partly successful because every time Mr Beckett came out to watch what they were doing, poor Bonny started dropping things and fumbling.

In the end Carrie went across to him. 'Excuse me for saying so, Mr Beckett, but Bonny works better when you're not scowling at her. She knows her job, none better, but she's very timid and she's frightened of you. I can manage her and we won't cheat you, I promise.'

He looked at her, lower lip jutting, then nodded. 'All right. You *were* working without my having to tell you this morning, I'll give you that. You see that idiot keeps hard at it, then.'

'We shan't be able to do as much as usual with only two of us, I'm afraid. Miss Beckett usually helps out.'

'Then don't try to do as much. Just keep the big room looking all right. I never did see the need to mop things so often.'

Carrie sighed and went back to her tasks, speaking gently to Bonny while trying to work more quickly than usual.

When they'd finished, Mr Beckett came out of the back room and beckoned to her. 'You've not done the snug.'

'I haven't had time, Mr Beckett.' She glanced at the clock behind the bar. 'And I usually finish now.'

'Can you stay on another hour and give the snug a quick lick over? I'll give you another sixpence.'

She nodded and went back to tell Bonny it was time to finish and she should wait for someone from her family to pick her up.

Nev would be pleased about the extra money, Carrie thought as she sorted out the snug, but she didn't like being here on her own, felt as if the place was dangerous somehow.

Oh, don't be so stupid! she told herself, but the strange fancy persisted.

At Linney's Eli and Joanna had breakfast with the family, noticing how well behaved the children all were, though they said little. Jane made rambling conversation until her husband told her to be quiet, but he told her gently, in quite a different tone of voice from that he used towards the children.

When they'd all left for work or school, Nev looked at his guests. 'What are you intending to do today? I don't usually allow lodgers to stay in the building after nine o'clock.'

Eli leaned forward and said firmly, 'Well, we're not your usual sort of lodger, and since we're paying you well for the rooms and meals, I think we should be allowed to come or go as we please.'

'Hmm, I suppose so. But don't make a mess or expect waiting on.'

They went upstairs and by mutual consent went into Eli's room, which was at the front.

'Better leave the door open,' Joanna said. 'It looks better.'

He went to stare out of the window. 'What the hell are we going to do with ourselves all day?'

'I'm going to sew. I shall buy some material and make myself a new dress.'

'I'll go with you as far as the shops, then I think I'll go for a walk on the tops. It's a long time since I've had a really long tramp.'

They looked at one another.

'I don't think Dad will give in on this,' Joanna said with a sigh. 'But I'd rather wait for a few days, in case something happens, just to give him a chance.'

Edmund went round to ask for Bram's help in removing his things from the engineering works. It seemed he was always seeking his help lately.

'I'll go with you myself,' Bram said at once.

'I think it'll be better if it's someone Athol doesn't know, actually. He doesn't think well of you and I don't want to make matters worse.'

Bram grinned. 'He hates me because he can't order me around.'

Edmund nodded. 'Yes. But if it's someone else who goes with me, maybe we'll get through it all without trouble. I can say I need help carrying my things, and I do. I have quite a few tools and other things that don't belong to the works. They're heavy so we'll need a handcart. You have one, haven't you?'

'I've got all sorts of equipment, me being a man with a few irons in the fire. And what I lack, someone else in my family is sure to have.'

Edmund smiled back. 'If I ever start a small works, I'll come to you for help in setting it up.'

'Were you thinking of doing that?'

'Possibly. There are some smaller pieces, equipment for the railways and such like, that would be easy enough to manufacture in a modest workshop. Things Stott's doesn't produce.'

'If you do that, let me help you choose the men who work for you. We wouldn't want people put in to keep an eye on you and cause trouble, would we?'

'I hadn't even thought of that.' Edmund sighed.

'You should make sure you watch your back from now on.'

'I hate having to think like that.'

Bram patted his shoulder. 'Better to do so than risk your new wife and home.' He waited a minute then added in another tone of voice, 'I'll see if Michael's around, then. But I'll be waiting outside for you.'

Punctually at ten o'clock Edmund arrived at the works, accompanied by Michael, who was almost as big as his brother Bram but looked less forceful somehow.

He was kept waiting at the gate while Mr Stott was told he was there, a gratuitous insult that warned him to expect the worst. It was a full fifteen minutes before his cousin sauntered across the yard.

'You'd better come in, I suppose.'

Michael stepped out from behind Edmund.

'Just you.'

'I need help carrying my things.'

'You're not taking anything that belongs to me.'

'I wouldn't do that, but I'm not leaving behind anything that belongs to me, either. Some of the tools are my personal possessions. It's easy to spot which because they're engraved with my initials.'

'They were bought for you by *my* father.'

'And given to me when I was in pupillage to learn my trade. I can prove they're mine in a court of law, if necessary.'

Athol turned without a word and led the way into the main workshop, walking along one side of it to the engine room and the small chamber just off it which Edmund had used as his office.

Men's heads turned as he passed.

'It's true, then,' one whispered to another. 'He is leaving.'

'Aye. An' Turner is boasting about getting more work out of the old engine. Mr Edmund told *me* it needed replacing last year.'

It took over an hour to locate all Edmund's tools because Turner was using some of them. During that time Edmund realised that the humidity had risen in the engine room. The seals must be leaking even more. Damnation! Why would his cousin not take his warnings seriously?

When Edmund removed one of his tools from Turner's hand, the man turned to Athol. 'How am I to work without the right tools, sir?'

'You'll need to furnish me with a list of essentials and I'll buy you more.'

'But I need some of them now, sir.'

Athol turned to Edmund and snapped, 'We'd appreciate a loan of the tools. *You* won't be needing them, after all.'

He hesitated then shook his head. 'I never trust my tools to anyone else.' Especially Turner. He'd always had to keep an eye on the fellow who'd been appointed by his cousin against Edmund's wishes on one of those days when Athol was in a particularly bad mood and wished to prove who was master. Turner knew a fair amount about engineering but was inclined to skimp on anything he could get away with, and even in the day and a bit since Edmund had gone, he'd left some of the tools dirty instead of cleaning them before they were put away.

'Then I'll buy them off you.'

'I don't want to sell them. Some of them were 'specially made for me.'

'Are you deliberately trying to annoy me?' Athol asked in a tight, angry voice, the veins at his temples throbbing visibly.

'No. I simply don't want to sell or lend my tools.'

'You'd better not try to set up in opposition to me.'

'There are other sorts of engineering work I can do.'

Athol looked at him through narrowed eyes. 'I'm not having you set up a business of any sort in this town.'

'You can't stop me.'

His cousin merely smiled.

Edmund felt a shiver run through him at that look, but tried to conceal his fear. He turned to Michael. 'Will you carry that box out for me, please? I'll bring the other one.' Before he left the engine room, he stopped to look at the engine, then raised his voice to say, 'It's dangerous to run this with weights on the governor, Turner. You're risking men's lives here.'

Athol shoved him out of the door. 'What we're doing is none of your business now.'

'Then I just hope the men stay away from that steam engine as much as possible,' Edmund said, still speaking loudly so that some of them at least would hear him. 'I wouldn't like to be in there if something went wrong. You can be scalded to death by steam, you know.'

Athol grabbed him by the arm and swung him round. 'If you don't shut your damned mouth, and right *now*, I'll shut it for you!'

A few steps away Michael paused, looking from one brother to the other. Every eye in the place was on them.

Edmund shook his cousin's hand off his arm, nearly dropping his box as he did so. 'I'm worrying about the men . . . something *you* should be doing.'

Athol moved close to him so that no one could overhear them. 'I was willing to overlook the fact that you'd deserted your post if you behaved as you should. But I'm angry that you'll not lend us those tools till we can get new ones. And I'm warning you now: if you try to set up on your own in Hedderby *doing anything*, I'll see no one deals with you, make sure they know you were dismissed for incompetence.'

A threat like that didn't worry Edmund. This time his smile was genuine. 'I think you'll find that my good name will stand on its own merit in the circles I frequent. *You* deal only with the money side of things. *I* know every engineer in a twenty-mile radius – and they know me. I'll not try to compete with Stott's because I couldn't. But I'll do what I choose other-wise.'

'You'd be better leaving this town.'

'It's my home and I'm staying.'

He started moving forward, not wanting to continue quarrelling so openly, and was relieved when Athol didn't follow him.

Michael waited for him to walk past, then followed him to the handcart. Edmund dumped his box on it and said, 'Let's go.' He was glad when his companion stayed silent because he was seething with anger, an unusual state for him.

He was so lost in his own thoughts that when three men stepped out from behind some trees on a little-used lane near the outskirts of town he didn't see them until they blocked his way.

Michael dropped the handles of his little cart and quickly put his fingers in his mouth, blowing a piercing whistle just as one of the men reached him.

For the second time in two days Edmund found he had to defend himself, and proved once again how little he knew about fighting. Within a few seconds one of his attackers had landed a punch on his jaw that rocked him on his heels and, when he stumbled, another man came in from the side to kick him on the shins with an iron-tipped clog. Letting out a cry of pain, he felt himself falling backwards and knew in despair that they'd make short work of beating him up.

If that was all they intended.

But as he tried to roll out of the way of the foot that was swinging towards him again, someone jumped between him and his attackers. It took him a minute or two to pull his swimming senses together again, by which time Bram had disposed of one man and was laughing at the other, who was standing in a semi-crouching position, as if unsure whether or not to continue the fight.

As Edmund struggled to his feet, he saw that Michael had now laid his attacker low and was standing over him, waiting for his brother to dispose of the third man. But the fellow turned tail and fled.

As the one on the ground tried to scramble to his feet, Bram grabbed him by the shoulders and slammed him against a nearby tree trunk. Although the two men were of a similar size and build, Bram seemed so much stronger and fiercer that the other man shrank back.

'I know you,' Bram said. 'But I don't know who's paid you to do this. If you tell me, I'll not hand you over to the constable as you deserve.'

There was a minute of complete silence, then the man shook his head. 'I daren't.'

'Let yours go, Michael lad,' Bram said in a conversational tone. 'I'm going to beat this one senseless.'

Michael stepped back and his former assailant moved quickly out of the way and ran off.

Then Bram smiled at the remaining man. 'You'll tell me who sent you or I'll beat it out of you.'

'*He* would do worse to me.'

'He'll not know.'

There was a minute's hesitation, then the man looked at Edmund, who was now leaning against another tree. 'It was *his* cousin. And that's all I'm saying.'

'No, my lad. There's one more thing I need to know. Were you supposed to kill him?'

'No, just hurt him bad.' Bram let go of him then and the man ran off, looking back over his shoulder as if afraid of being pursued.

Bram turned to Edmund. 'Nice cousin you've got.'

'Do you think that fellow was telling the truth?'

'I'm sure of it.'

'Hell, what am I to do?'

'Nothing for the moment. After all, you have a new wife to look after and you need to recover from your injuries. But don't walk into town alone again.'

Edmund sighed. 'I never was much good at fighting.'

'Then you'll have to protect yourself by being clever. Your cousin will play other dirty tricks on you, I'm sure.'

'He told me to leave town.'

'And shall you?'

Edmund shook his head. 'No.'

'It might be the wisest thing to do.'

'I'll not leave. But thank you for coming to my aid just now.'

'Your cousin's upset me and mine a few times. It's a real pleasure to upset him in return.'

# 18

Carrie kept a close eye on Mr Beckett the next day. Although he did the cellar work necessary to look after the beer, he seemed to her to be moving slowly and to spend a lot of time sitting down in between tasks. When she looked into the kitchen to ask if she should do extra work on the snug today, it took him a minute to realise she'd spoken and then she had to repeat what she'd said.

'Aye, you do that. Can you do it every day till I get things sorted out a bit? I'm sure my daughter will be back soon. Give her a few days an' she'll realise how silly she's been.'

Carrie could have told him differently. She felt Joanna was growing angrier each day, and clearly had no intention of going back to the Dragon unless her father changed his mind about selling that piece of land. She looked at the mess in the kitchen. 'Do you want me to tidy up in here as well, Mr Beckett?'

He stared round, then shook his head. 'No. Not today. I'll send out for something to eat. But you could bring me in another scuttle of coal, if you would.'

★

The following day Carrie started work on the snug as soon as Bonny left, then heard the outer door bang. She couldn't resist peeping out to see who it was.

A prim-looking elderly man came in, looked scornfully round the big room and went across to the bar, calling, 'Hello? Mr Beckett?'

'Through here.'

Carrie hesitated, then tiptoed to the rear door of the snug, which led into the living quarters, and stood listening, making sure she couldn't be seen.

'I've brought the contract from Mr Hordle for you to look at,' the man said.

'Aye, well, leave it with me and I'll get back to your master after I've read it. I'm still not sure I want to sell.'

The man left and Carrie tiptoed back to the snug, feeling worried.

When she got home, she told Joanna what she'd heard and saw her friend's shoulders slump.

'He must be going ahead with it. I'll tell Eli when he comes back. Maybe we'd better start looking for new jobs in Manchester.'

'Mr Beckett told the man he wasn't sure about selling.'

'He always says that when he's pushing for a good bargain. No, he's planning to sell or he wouldn't have wasted his time looking at a contract.'

'Will you go back to him after he's sold? He seems to think you will.'

'No. Definitely not.'

★

That evening Carrie suggested to Nev that they invite their lodgers to come and listen to Raife play the piano, thinking it might cheer them up for an hour or two. They all went into the parlour after they'd eaten and washed up.

The old man settled himself at the piano and began to play.

After a while Eli turned to his cousin and asked, 'Why don't you sing to us, Joanna?'

'I'm not in the mood.'

'Go on. You're letting yourself brood.'

'I can play owt you like,' Raife said, 'though I don't have any music to sing by.'

Joanna hesitated for a moment then stood up feeling nervous even among friends. 'Very well. Do you know "The Minstrel Boy"?'

'Aye.'

When she sang it everyone except Carrie and Eli stared in amazement. Jane was nodding her head in time to the music, Nev beating time on his thigh with one plump hand, and it was obvious that the whole family was enjoying the singing. Carrie caught sight of Marjorie's rapt face and thought she'd not seen her sister look so happy for a long time. Unlike her, Marjorie could hold a tune, had quite a nice voice actually, but not powerful like Joanna's.

After a few songs, Joanna glanced round. 'Can't anyone else sing? We should have a little sing-song.'

They all looked instinctively to Nev for permission.

'Why not?' he said, and led them without embarrassment, because although he didn't have a particularly strong voice, he knew he could carry a tune better than most.

It was nearly ten o'clock before anyone realised it, then they had to clear up quickly and get ready for bed. People who started work at six o'clock in the morning couldn't afford to stay up too late.

'That was beautiful, Miss Beckett,' Nev said. 'I didn't realise you could sing like that.'

'My father doesn't like me "making a spectacle of myself", as he calls it.'

Eli went to stand by the piano. 'If we were still going to open the music room, we'd be offering you a permanent job there,' he told Raife.

'Is my father that good a pianist?' Nev asked in surprise.

'Yes. Definitely.'

'It's a shame you're not getting that music room then. Me an' Jane would have liked going out of an evening.'

Carrie watched them, still feeling surprised at the way Nev had changed since he'd married her mother. They'd had some enjoyable evenings since they'd been living here, she thought as she got into bed, but this had been the best of all. And to think she'd dreaded coming here.

Eli was fretting at the inactivity of his present life, something he had never experienced before and devoutly hoped he wouldn't experience again. He'd tried to continue sketching his ideas for the interior of the music room, but couldn't concentrate because he couldn't persuade himself there was any hope of achieving his dream. He woke early and went down to the kitchen to cadge a cup of tea from Carrie and her mother, who were preparing breakfast and packing lunch for everyone.

Marjorie and Dora were sitting yawning at the table, eating their bread and butter quickly. They nodded a greeting but continued gulping their food down, keeping an eye on the clock because anyone arriving late at the mill was fined. The minute they'd finished they grabbed their parcels of food for eating at noon and went clattering off down the street in the clogs everyone wore for working in the mill. Eli smiled at Edith and she smiled back. She always ate her food neatly. Well, everything about her was neat. When she'd finished, she too left for work. Everyone had a job, it seemed, except him, Eli thought gloomily.

'There you are.' He looked up and realised Carrie had placed a plate of bread and ham in front of him.

'Thanks.' He looked beyond her at her mother, who should have been doing this but who was staring into space instead, her hands held out to the warmth of the fire. 'Aren't you going to get your own breakfast?'

Carrie nodded, took a plate and sat down opposite him. But she only had bread and butter, he saw.

'Don't you get ham?'

'No.' She smiled. 'Ham is for paying lodgers and Nev. But we get good bread and butter every single day, and cheese sometimes, so I'm happy enough. What are you going to do today?'

He shrugged. 'Go for a walk round town. I'll see if Joanna wants to come.'

'She said she'd be sewing. That's going to be such a pretty dress. She's teaching Marjorie how to sew better. My hands are too rough.' Carrie took another bite and chewed thoughtfully. 'I'm sorry Mr Beckett hasn't changed his mind.'

'Yes. Me too.' Eli smiled at her and went on with his own breakfast. When he'd finished, he pushed his plate aside and looked out of the window. 'That was good. Since it's fine I'll go out and get a breath of fresh air.'

Carrie heard him run lightly up the stairs, then come back down with his cap and coat, a muffler tossed carelessly round his neck. 'Have a nice walk,' she called.

'Yes. Thanks.'

But Eli didn't really look at her and still seemed lost in his own thoughts. She was worried that he'd be leaving town soon and then she'd never see him again. But she had no right to care about him. Hadn't he told her plainly this wasn't the time for him to be thinking of courting?

'I'll just go and – um – check the parlour.' But that was only an excuse to watch Eli walk down the street. He had such a vigorous, energetic stride – both in real life and in her dreams. With a sigh for her own foolishness, Carrie went back into the kitchen and finished wiping the dishes.

'He's not for such as you,' her mother said abruptly.

'What?'

'Eli Beckett. He's not for such as you, so it's no use mooning after him.'

'I'm not!' But Carrie could feel herself blushing.

Nev came into the kitchen then. 'Who is she mooning after?' he asked his wife.

'Eli Beckett.'

'I am not!' Carrie hung the damp cloth on the airing rail of the big stove and snatched her shawl off the hook, avoiding their eyes. 'I'll be late for work if I don't hurry.'

They watched her go, then Nev cocked one eyebrow at his wife.

'She *is* mooning after him,' Jane repeated. 'But it'll do her no good. Now, what do you want for breakfast, love? Oh, and do any of *them* want owt to eat?' She jerked her head in the direction of the common lodging room at the rear of the kitchen.

'Six of them have paid for bread and dripping. Here, let me cut up the loaf. You make the slices too thick. I reckon we get a penny less profit a loaf when you cut it up.' As he picked up the bread knife Nev added, 'I've a fancy for a fried egg or two, and maybe a bit of ham.'

Since this was what he ate most mornings Jane wasn't surprised and soon had them ready. If she'd learned one thing in this splendid new marriage of hers it was to make sure her husband was well fed. And this morning it was particularly important to keep him in a good mood. After they'd got the children off to school and cleared the common lodgers out, and Miss Beckett had finished her breakfast, she needed to speak to Nev privately.

Once her early-morning tasks were done, Jane gathered her courage together. 'I have something to tell you, Nev love.'

'Oh, can't it wait? I have to order more supplies in. You know I like to do my shopping early.'

'I think we should talk first.'

That got his attention. 'Something wrong?'

'Not wrong, exactly, but – well, unexpected.' She was finding it difficult to force the words out, so in the end just said baldly, 'I'm expecting.'

He stared at her in shock, opening and shutting his mouth, then scowling as anger took over. '*Expecting!* But you said you couldn't have any more children.'

'I never.'

'Oh, yes, you did! Just after you lost your husband you said that.'

She tried to think what had given him such an idea but couldn't. 'The doctor said it wasn't *likely*, not at my age, but I allus did fall easy.'

He sat down with a thump, scowling at her. 'But I don't *want* any children, you know I don't. I want *you*, a bit of comfort in my bed, someone to talk to, but I don't want a baby to raise, not at my age.'

'We could sell it,' she offered.

'Sell my own child! I'd never do that.'

Jane started to cry. 'You sold mine!'

'That was different. You had others and you were too tired to look after the twins.' He shoved his chair back. 'I can't talk about this now, but I'm very disappointed, very. I'm going into town. See that you finish clearing this place up properly. You haven't mopped the floor yet, and you didn't mop it at all yesterday. I like things kept clean.' He stormed out.

When the door had slammed behind his son, Raife came into the kitchen and found Jane still weeping. She explained why and he too looked at her in shock.

'Didn't think my Nev had it in him,' he said.

'Well, he does. He likes his bed play, your son does. Only he doesn't want the baby.' She began to sob again. 'What am I going to do? He'll throw me out, I know he will.'

'Not he. And you don't need to do owt. He's got no choice about the baby, has he, now it's happened?' He put an arm round her shoulders. 'Ah, he'll come round once he's used to the idea.'

But Jane wasn't sure about that. Nev liked everything to be just so. He'd hate the mess little children made, and she was already feeling tired, sickly in the mornings, sleepy in the evenings. 'It's not fair,' she muttered. 'I've had enough childer. Other women my age stop having 'em, why can't I?'

In the middle of the morning Frank announced that he was going out. 'I know I can trust you to keep an eye on this place, Carrie.'

'Yes, Mr Beckett.'

'And make sure the idiot works hard. Here.' He tipped two shillings into her hand. 'In case I'm late back, you can pay her. I'll be home in time to pay you.'

As soon as he was out of hearing she muttered, 'Bonny's *not* an idiot. She's a lovely woman.'

Carrie was on her own working in the snug when Mr Beckett got back. She popped her head out of the door to let him know she was still there, but he didn't seem to notice her. He looked exhausted and was carrying the papers the man had brought round yesterday. They were rolled up in his hand and he was hitting his free hand with the roll, tapping away as if upset about something.

He stopped behind the bar to draw himself a pot of beer and took it through into the back room, still without speaking.

When Carrie went in for some hot water, he had the papers spread out across the table and an ink bottle open beside them. He looked up at her. 'See this!'

'What is it, Mr Beckett?'

He tapped the papers. 'This is the contract. Once I sign it, I'll have sold that bit of land for twenty times what I paid for it.' He noticed her expression. 'Ha! Joanna's been getting at you – or was it Eli? Well, they won't change my mind. You can't beat cash in hand. Them two wanted to spend all my money. Hard earned that was. Took me years to get where I am. I didn't *want* to spend it.'

He seemed to need an audience, so Carrie stood listening as he rambled on. She couldn't help noticing the greyish tinge to his face and that he seemed slightly breathless, though he'd had a sit down since his walk.

'I'm supposed to go down to Hordle's to sign this, but I'm tired today and I'm not walking into town again.' He stared down at the papers again, then up at her. 'I know, you can witness my signature, then you can take the contract to Hordle's for me.'

'I don't think . . .'

'Watch this!' He dipped the pen into the bottle of ink and signed his name at the bottom of one of the four pieces of paper, underlining it with a flourish. 'There! That's done. My lawyer said to sell quickly at such a good price and sign this as soon as I could. Here, come and write your name under mine, then you can take it into town. I want it all settled, then Joanna will come back.'

Carrie looked at him in horror and took an involuntary step backwards. She couldn't do this. It'd feel like betraying Eli and Joanna. 'I'd rather not, Mr Beckett.'

He glared at her and his face slowly turned a dull red colour. He patted his chest and tried to burp, but couldn't, muttering, 'Damned indigestion! And as for you, Carrie Preston, you'll do as I say or you'll be out of a job. The cheek of it, refusing me!'

Suddenly he clapped his hand to his chest again. 'Hurts,' he muttered, pressing hard and leaning forward. Then he fell sideways, so slowly Carrie thought at first he was still moving about to try to ease his indigestion. He'd had this pain before, she knew. He ate too much and ate too fast, she always thought. No wonder he got indigestion.

But he continued to fall and tumbled right off his chair, landing with a dull thud on the rug in front of the stove. And he didn't move, just lay as he'd fallen.

For a moment she could only stare at him in shock, then she rushed to kneel by him. But she knew what she'd find. Frank Beckett's eyes were open, but he wasn't seeing anything, never would again.

*He'd just dropped down dead!*

She jumped to her feet, thinking to run for help, then caught sight of the contract, with his signature in big black sprawling letters at the bottom. If only he'd not signed it. If only this had happened five minutes earlier. All Eli's and Joanna's hopes would be for nothing now. It wasn't fair! If Mr Beckett had to die, it'd have been better for everyone if he'd died five minutes sooner.

And that was when the idea came to her. She stood stock still for a minute, then moved towards the table and picked up the contract. Should she, dare she . . . Yes, she'd burn it. Then she frowned. People knew he had the contract: his own lawyer, Mr Stott's lawyer who'd written it. She couldn't just burn it and get away with it.

Still undecided, she stood there, frantically trying to think what to do. Then she had an idea. Suppose Mr Beckett had been standing in front of the fire, reading the contract through when he died? Suppose the papers had fallen into the flames when he dropped dead and only a few fragments had been left?

She looked down at him. If he'd been standing next to the fire, he wouldn't have fallen like that. She'd have to move him. It was hard because he was so much heavier than she was, but Carrie managed to heave his body into a different position, muttering

'Sorry' as she did so. She stood back, head on one side, looking at him, then moved his legs again. When she studied him that time he looked right to her so she left him as he was. Then she picked up the four pages of the contract, dropped three of them into the fire, snatching one out again almost immediately, then the next a second later, watching as the flames consumed the black signature at the bottom of the final page and only pulling it out once that part was gone completely. Then she scattered the papers on the rug, and felt that fate was on her side when the draught caused by her movements made some burned black fragments float down more slowly to join the larger pieces.

Carrie looked round. She had to think, to do this carefully. But her heart was beating so fast she couldn't seem to work out what to do next. She pressed her hand to her chest, willing her heart to slow down. She'd better go for help now.

As she turned round, she heard the front door of the pub open and ran out to see Eli standing there. She let out a little moan of relief. 'Come quickly! It's Mr Beckett.'

Eli came running across the room and she stepped back, happy to let someone else take charge now.

He bent over his uncle, kneeling beside him, but straightened up almost immediately, shaking his head. 'He's dead.'

'I thought he was. I was just going to fetch help when you came in. He said he had a pain in his chest, then he fell over.' That at least was true.

Eli bent to close the staring eyes and noticed the fragments of paper. 'What are these?'

'He said it was the contract for selling the land next door.'

He looked at the writing materials on the table, the pen which had obviously been used. 'He'd signed it, hadn't he? Did *you* burn this?'

In the middle of the night there was the sound of breaking glass and Edmund jerked upright in bed.

'What was that?' Faith whispered.

'A window breaking. I'll have to go downstairs, see if we have an intruder.' He got out of bed, and when he made for the door could see that she had got up as well, her white nightdress showing clearly in the moonlight. 'What are you doing?'

'If you're going downstairs, so am I.'

'I'd prefer you to stay here.'

'I'll not do it. There may be someone in the house and, if so, two of us are better than one.' She picked up the nearest candlestick. 'I'll hit him with this.'

'Please stay here, Faith. Think of the baby.' He moved towards the door, opened it quietly and closed it again.

She waited a minute then followed him downstairs, standing on the bottom step, waiting for she knew not what. Within a minute, Grania had joined her.

Edmund went noiselessly on bare feet from one room to the other, noticing his wife, relieved that she remained at the bottom of the stairs, thankful Grania was with her. He might have known Faith wouldn't stay tamely in bed.

There was no sign of an intruder and when he found the broken window, it was easy to see that the hole was too small for anyone to have entered that way. So he went into the kitchen, stuck a spill into the embers and got himself a light.

When he went back into the small sitting room he saw the smooth riverstone on the floor and wrapped round it, tied tightly with string, a piece of paper, presumably a message. He had to take it into the kitchen to cut the string with a knife before he could see what it said. He wasn't surprised to read, '*Get out of Hedderby if you value your wife's safety.*'

Faith came up beside him, Grania behind her. 'What does it say?'

Edmund tried to screw it up, but she took it out of his hand and smoothed it out holding it near the candle and reading it slowly, then passing it to Grania and looking at her husband sternly. 'I hope you're not going to let *him* drive us away?'

No need to ask who she meant by *him*. They both knew who had sent this message, even if he hadn't thrown the stone himself. 'I don't know what I'm going to do.' He looked down at her belly. 'I have two of you to consider now.'

'I think we'd better get a dog, sir,' Grania said. 'A big fierce one. And I think you should hire someone to keep watch at night. When things settle down your cousin will grow used to the situation surely?'

'You know who's behind this, then?'

'My nephew told me, warned me to take care. Bram's not stupid.'

'I think I'll take your advice about a dog.'

'I've friends in Out Rawby. I'll tell them, ask round for help. We look after our own here.' The maid left them and went upstairs again.

Edmund held out his arms and Faith stepped into them. It felt so right to hold her. 'I think I'd die if anything happened to you.'

'We won't let it.' She was silent for a moment or two then added, 'I'm glad now that I've got Grania here for the daytime.'

Eli repeated quietly, 'He had signed it, hadn't he?'

Carrie stared at him in horror. He'd guessed at once what had happened and others would probably do the same. It just showed she wasn't clever enough to do this, but she had so wanted to help Eli. She couldn't force a sound from her throat, which suddenly felt dry, so she nodded.

'And you burned it so that Joanna and I could have our music room?'

She nodded again, then found enough of a voice to say, 'It wasn't fair to take it away from you when he'd promised.'

Eli stared down at the dead man. 'No, it wasn't.'

'And he won't care now, will he?' Carrie held back further words, waiting for him to decide what to do.

He pulled her into his arms and gave her a quick hug, then held her away from him, looking at her in such a strange way she didn't realise what he was going to do until his lips touched hers. It was the briefest of kisses, but it was sweet, so very sweet. 'No time for this now,' Eli said quietly. 'Let's sort things out before someone else comes.'

Turning to the table, he pulled out his handkerchief and carefully wiped the pen, then put the top back on the ink bottle.

Hope surged through her.

'Put these away quickly, Carrie love.'

She picked them up and put them back in the cupboard while he bent over the body, rearranging it slightly. He stood up and gave her a quick smile. 'Now, let's have a look round to see if anything else could give us away.'

She turned slowly in a circle, studying the kitchen. 'Would it look better if there was food on the table?'

'Yes. Good idea.'

She got out the loaf and a knife, setting them on the bread board.

Just then there was the sound of the door opening in the pub.

'Right, then,' Eli said grimly, 'let's spread the news.' He peered out into the big room to see one of the potmen walking towards the bar, rubbing his hands together to warm them up. He went rushing out to meet the man. 'Carrie's just found Mr Beckett dead. Can you go and fetch Dr Latimer?'

The man goggled. 'Dead? He's dead?'

'Yes. It looks like he just dropped dead of a seizure but the doctor had best examine him.' When the man had hurried away, Eli turned to Carrie. 'Will you stay with the body while I fetch Joanna?'

'Yes, of course.' But she felt uneasy sitting next to

Mr Beckett after what she'd done so went to stand in the doorway. It seemed a very long time before Eli got back with Joanna.

Carrie drew aside to let the other woman see the body. For a minute or two there was silence in the kitchen, then Joanna sighed and looked around. Noticing the fragments of paper, she picked one up. 'Was this the contract?'

'I don't know what it was,' Carrie said. 'He'd been into town to see his own lawyer and came back with those papers. He told me he had to go and see Mr Hordle this afternoon to sign them.' The lie flowed smoothly from her lips, but she didn't dare look at Eli as she said it.

'He was going to sell the place then?'

Eli moved to put his arm round his cousin's shoulders. 'He can't now though, can he?'

Joanna looked at him and closed her eyes, letting out a long, shuddering breath. 'No, he can't. Just think how close we came to losing everything.' She made as if to throw the pieces of paper in the fire, but he stayed her hand. 'Better leave everything as it was, eh?'

Dr Latimer was there within the half-hour. He examined the body and questioned Carrie. 'Mr Beckett probably died of heart failure if he'd had pains in his chest before he fell. I'll leave you to make all the necessary arrangements.'

When he'd gone Joanna looked at her father and her mouth trembled. 'I wish he hadn't died with anger between us.' Then she straightened her shoulders and said firmly, 'Let's get him up to his bed. It's not right to leave him lying here.'

'Eli and I'll carry him,' Carrie said quickly. 'You go and get the bed ready.'

When Joanna had gone Eli looked at Carrie very solemnly. 'Thank you.'

She looked back at him, equally solemnly. 'It was only fair.'

'You're a brave lass!'

She carried the compliment home with her like sunshine in her heart.

Mr Hordle heard the news about Frank Beckett. He sent his clerk to make enquiries and found out the man had died before he'd signed the contract, so sent word to his client.

Athol went home early from the works in a towering rage, leaving Turner to close up. He'd been so close! Surely there was still some way of getting what he wanted?

Maria was quieter than ever that evening, continuing with her everlasting embroidery and saying nothing unless he spoke to her. He stood up and went to refill his glass with port from the decanter.

'Why the hell do you do that stuff?' he flung at her. 'It's no use to man or beast.'

She looked at him in surprise. 'I like to keep my hands occupied.'

'Well, it's getting on my nerves. Put it away and don't get it out again in my presence. Have a glass of port with me instead.'

She folded her embroidery and put it carefully into the basket, but shook her head. 'You know I don't like strong drink.'

'You don't like anything, especially not me in your bed.'

She flushed and tears came into her eyes.

When she said nothing, he asked, 'What shall we do with ourselves now that I haven't got Edmund to keep the conversation going and you've not got your embroidery to hide behind?'

She hesitated then went to sit in the armchair opposite him, the one his cousin had used, folding her hands primly and sitting very still. 'Whatever you wish.'

He leaned back and took a gulp as he contemplated her – plump, plain and virtuous. 'I should follow Edmund's example and take a mistress. I wonder if his new wife has any time to spare?'

Maria cast a horrified glance in her husband's direction but said nothing.

He stood up and went to refill his glass. 'Ah, get yourself to bed. The sight of you sickens me. The only use I have for you now is to keep this house and rear my children. If you'd been a better woman you'd have given me more than two, and if that damned doctor hadn't been so certain another would kill you, I'd bed you again in spite of your ugly face.'

Maria walked out of the room, spine very erect, shoulders stiff. Only when she got to her own bedroom did she lean against the door and allow herself to shudder. What was she going to do in the evenings now that Edmund wasn't there to prevent Athol from openly taunting and humiliating her?

More to the point, what was Athol going to do? He got bored so easily, couldn't be bothered to read anything, pestered women . . .

Downstairs her husband took the decanter back across to the small table beside his chair and sat staring into the fire. He wasn't going to let his cousin get away with bringing disgrace to the family name by marrying that whore.

*Thou shalt not kill*, the Bible said. But it didn't say anything about not teaching your cousin a sharp lesson. He'd drive Edmund and his wife out of Hedderby, that at least he'd do. He wasn't having that low creature flaunting herself as Mrs Stott in the town where *he* was one of the leading citizens.

And as for Beckett dying on him, just when he'd been about to sign, he was going to find a way around that, too. He wasn't letting anyone get the better of Athol Stott.

# 19

Carrie felt sad when Joanna and Eli moved out of Linney's and back to the Dragon. She'd miss their company and Joanna's beautiful voice in the evening sing-songs, though at least she'd see the two of them at work every day. And best of all, Eli wouldn't have to leave Hedderby now.

She was so preoccupied with going over what had happened today in her own mind that she didn't notice until she was finishing her bread and butter that something had upset Nev or that her mother was wearing her anxious expression.

When they'd gone to sit in the parlour and Carrie was helping clear up after the meal, she asked Raife what was upsetting his son, since he always seemed to know what was going on before anyone else did.

He hesitated then said, 'You might as well know then you won't say summat to make things worse: your mother is expecting and Nev's not best pleased about it. He thought she was past all that.'

'She's expecting *again!*'

'Shh! Keep your voice down.'

'Is she going to give this one away as well?'

'Nay, lass, don't be bitter. Them twins will have a

better life than she could ever have given them.'

Carrie looked at the kindly old man. 'I can't help feeling upset. I looked after those babies and grew to love them. She didn't even give me a chance to say goodbye to them.' Her voice cracked on the last words and she had to sniff away the tears that threatened.

Raife put his arm round her. 'It's like when someone dies. However much you're hurting, you have to carry on with your own life. That's all you can do. It doesn't help anyone to dwell on the past.' He nudged her in the ribs. 'Let's think about pleasanter things, eh? Your young man will get his music room now that old Mr Beckett is dead, won't he? That's turned out for the best, at least.'

She nodded. 'Yes, I suppose so. But Eli isn't my young man. He's just a friend.'

Raife made a scornful, disbelieving sound.

'He *is* just a friend!' she protested, because she didn't dare let herself hope. 'I can't see someone like him ever marrying a girl like me. And anyway, I don't want to get married.'

'Of course you do if it's to the right man. I've seen the way Eli looks at you. If that lad isn't fond of you, I'll eat my hat.'

Carrie couldn't help asking, 'Does he really look at me like that?'

'Aye. I wouldn't pretend about something so important, Carrie love. Mind you, I don't reckon he'll make an easy husband, not with his mind set on music rooms and such. If you want a fellow who fusses over you, don't set your heart on Eli Beckett.'

'Don't talk any more about marriage,' she pleaded, not wanting to tempt providence. But she kept remembering what Raife had said, couldn't get it out of her mind. Was it really possible that a lovely man like Eli could think of her in that way?

A short time later there was a knock on the back door and Carrie opened it to see Robbie standing there with a bundle in his arms, clearly upset. 'What's wrong?'

'I've been turned off,' he said. 'Mr Stott says I'm a trouble-maker an' he's not having me working there any more. He won't even pay me for the days I've worked this week, so I've no money for lodgings. Do you think Nev will let me stay here?'

She pulled him inside and gave him a big hug. 'Of course he will, I'll make sure of it. Put your bundle down and we'll go and see him now.'

Carrie linked her arm in his and took him through to the parlour where Jane immediately engulfed her eldest son in hugs, asking many questions but not allowing him time to answer any of them.

Nev put a hand on her shoulder. 'Quiet now, love. Let the lad speak.'

She stopped talking at once, but still smiled at her son.

Robbie looked at his sister pleadingly, so Carrie told them what had happened. The way she put it was that Robbie had come straight to seek his step-father's advice. Her brother didn't contradict her.

'That man,' Nev said, 'will go too far one day.' He studied Robbie. '*Were* you a trouble-maker?'

'No, I wasn't. I was working for Mr Edmund till he left, and *he* said I was good at my job. He was teaching me all sorts of things. I reckon that's why I've been turned off. Mr Stott doesn't let people even say Mr Edmund's name. He's got Turner looking after the steam engine now and we're all afeared it'll explode. No one likes going near it.' He hesitated, then added, 'My landlady didn't want me to stay. Let alone I can't afford to pay her now, she's frit of Mr Stott. I didn't know where else to go.'

'Hmm. You can sleep in the attic here. I'm *not* afraid of Stott. If he ever upsets me, I could tell a few things about what he got up to when he was a lad . . .' Nev broke off. 'Well, that's as may be. We'll have to look round for another job for you.'

'Mr Stott told me to get out of town or I'd regret it.'

'It's a good thing you're friendly with Bram Heegan then,' Nev said at once. 'He'll help you, and his lads will keep an eye out for you. Carrie, will you go and make up a bed for your brother? Show him where to stay. Mind you,' he detained Robbie with one raised finger, 'same conditions apply. Anyone as lives under my roof hands over his money to me.'

Robbie nodded. What did that matter? He wasn't earning any now.

Carrie took him up to the attics, chatting about this and that because she could see he was upset. He'd set a lot of store on what he did at Stott's, Robbie had, and been proud to be singled out by Mr Edmund. Now he had nothing except a bundle of clothes. 'Here you are, love. You can sleep in here with Ted, like you used to. Us girls are over there.'

'It's a big house. People mock Nev, say he's a miser, but he's done well for himself, hasn't he?'

She nodded. 'And if you'll take my advice, you'll listen to him. He does like to control the money, but he sees us all right. He isn't miserly with us. We've eaten good food every single meal since we've come here.' She hesitated. 'There's just one thing you ought to know: Mam's expecting again.'

Robbie rolled his eyes and made a growling noise in his throat.

'Nev's not best pleased. He thought she was past all that. Don't mention it unless he does, but it's better you know what's going on.'

The funeral of Frank Beckett was well attended, with nearby shops pulling down their blinds as the black horses clopped past drawing the hearse. Eli kept an eye on his cousin who'd been very quiet since her father's death. Joanna looked pale and strained today, and he was glad she didn't have the added burden of knowing her father had actually signed the contract to sell the land.

Afterwards they opened the snug to invited mourners and offered them a drink and a bite to eat, as was only right.

An hour later, when the gathering looked like turning into a party and Joanna was drooping visibly, Eli stood on a chair and used his powerful voice. 'We thank you all for coming today, but now it's time for you to go home. My cousin is exhausted and needs to rest, and we still have the pub to open.'

There was a buzz of surprise at this, but Eli nodded to the potman serving drinks to stop then escorted Joanna to the outer door of the snug, so that everyone could pay their respects as they left.

Bram was the last to go. He took Joanna's hand and looked at her in concern. 'You all right?'

She swallowed hard and gave a tiny shake of the head. He couldn't help putting his arms round her.

Eli watched in surprise as Joanna leaned against him, closing her eyes and sighing audibly. He'd known those two were attracted to one another, but not that it'd got to the stage of her letting Bram put his arms round her in public. 'I'll just go and check on the big room,' he said diplomatically, and walked out past them. They didn't move and he wasn't sure they'd even heard him.

'Oh, Bram, I thought people would never leave,' Joanna murmured. 'You'd think it was a party not a funeral, the way some of them were laughing and talking.'

'Will you miss him?'

'Yes. He was a surly old devil, but he was always *there*. Part of my life.'

'Like the Mammy. Heart of our family she is, though she does nothing except scold me these days. Will we sit down a minute and be quiet?'

She let him guide her to one of the hard wooden chairs and sank down on it with another weary sigh.

Bram pulled a chair closer for himself and sat

facing her, taking hold of her hands. 'What will you do now?'

'It depends on what Dad's put in the will. I know there's some condition or other about my inheriting, because he let it slip one day, but I don't know what it is.'

He raised one of her hands to his lips. 'You know if you need anything, you've only to ask – whatever it is.'

'Yes, Bram. I do know that.'

They sat on a little longer, not saying anything, just being together, each enjoying the peaceful interlude.

Then one of Joanna's favourite customers put her head round the door. 'Is the snug open again now, love?'

She pulled herself upright. 'Yes, Mrs Betts. I'll come and serve you in a minute.'

'Sorry for your loss, love.'

'Thank you.' Joanna pulled a wry face at Bram. 'I'll have to get back to work now.'

He smiled at her. 'Will I see you tomorrow?'

She felt suddenly shy. 'Yes. In the afternoon, if you want.'

'I do. You know that.'

Late the following morning Eli and Joanna left the two women to finish cleaning the pub and walked into town together to see her father's lawyer, Mr Burtell. They sat in his office and he took out Frank's will.

'It's very short, Miss Beckett, but it's – um – a little unusual.'

Her heart sank. 'In what way?'

'To sum up, he left everything he owned to you two, to be shared equally between you, on condition that you both get married within a month of my reading this will to you.'

The lethargy that had gripped Joanna since her father's death vanished abruptly. '*What?* Oh, the old devil! I knew he'd do something like this, I just knew it! Well, I won't marry my cousin Eli, even if it means losing everything.' She couldn't possibly consider marrying one man when she loved another.

Jack Burtell frowned at her. 'Miss Beckett, if you'll just—'

'How could you let him write such a condition? You should have told him it wasn't legal.'

'I did try to persuade him not to, but he—'

She turned to Eli. 'Did *you* know about this?'

'No, of course I didn't. And with all due respect, I don't intend to marry you either.' He couldn't marry his cousin when he loved Carrie. That thought made Eli blink because it was the first time he'd let himself face the full extent of his feelings. Hell, he did love her! How had that happened?

'Mr Beckett, please—'

Neither of them was paying any attention so Jack Burtell thumped on his desk and roared, 'Will you two please let me finish!'

Joanna blushed and stared down at her lap. Eli muttered something and stared out of the window.

'Although the will stipulates that you must both marry within the month, it doesn't say *who* you must marry.'

The silence seemed to hum around them and the lawyer had their fullest attention now.

'I'm afraid I practised a little deceit when I drew up that condition for Mr Beckett. He was so insistent on having the clause about you both marrying that in the end I couldn't refuse to include it. But I did manage to couch it in terms which don't stipulate that you need marry *one another*. He – um – didn't notice that.'

Eli threw back his head and roared with laughter. 'You're a man after my own heart, Mr Burtell.' He turned to look at his cousin, but she was frowning. 'What's wrong, Joanna?'

'Within the month is . . . well, it's rushing things.'

'Considering the way you were cuddling up to Bram Heegan yesterday, that shouldn't worry you,' Eli teased.

She looked down. 'They were . . . special circumstances. But we're only just starting to get to know one another . . . I can't expect him to . . .' Her voice trailed away.

Eli reached out to pat her hand. 'We'll sort it all out, love.' He turned back to the lawyer. 'We're both grateful to you for making things easier for us, Mr Burtell, and I assure you that we'll comply with the condition. What's more, I for one will be happy to give my future business to you.'

It wasn't till they were halfway home that Joanna thought to ask, 'Who are *you* going to marry then?'

'Carrie Preston, of course.'

'If she agrees.'

'Oh, she'll not turn me down.' Eli walked on another few paces then asked, 'Do you want me to sound out Bram for you, explain to him about the will?'

'*No!* I'll tell him myself, thank you very much!'

'Tell or ask?' he teased, but Joanna refused to smile so he went back to practicalities. 'We'd better act quickly. If we have to be married within the month, there'll be a lot to plan. I'm going to ask Carrie today.'

'So soon?'

'Why waste time?'

It was all right for a man, she thought resentfully. They expected to be the ones to propose to a woman. It was going to be a lot harder for her.

And would Bram agree? He'd joked about his mother, but Joanna was sure his family would be very upset if he married someone who wasn't a Roman Catholic. He cared very deeply for them. Did he care enough for her to go against their wishes?

Eli went round to Linney's and knocked on the front door. He wondered suddenly whether he needed to ask permission to marry Carrie, then dismissed the thought. She had turned twenty-three. She didn't need anyone's permission.

Raife opened the door to him. 'Hello, lad. Come in.'

'I need to see Carrie.'

'She's helping her mother finish the washing. It's all got a bit too much for Jane.'

'Well, this is very important. Can't Carrie leave the washing to her for just a few minutes?' Eli hesitated then added in a low voice, 'I want to ask her to marry me.'

Raife looked at him in surprise. 'Can't that wait? She won't want to remember being all hot and sweaty when you asked her.'

'I need to see her today. There's a reason I need to marry quickly.'

'I'll see what they're doing. If they're in the middle of the starching, you won't get her to stop till they're done.'

He came back a minute later followed by Carrie who wiped her hands on her apron then smoothed it down. 'Take him into the parlour, lass.'

'Nev won't like that.'

'Oh, I think he will this time.'

She cast Raife a puzzled glance then led the way in. 'I'm sorry but I can't stay long, Eli, not in the middle of doing the washing. Do you need me to work some extra hours?'

He took hold of her hand and pulled her down on the sofa. 'No. This isn't to do with work. It's – something else.' Suddenly he found himself fumbling for words. It had all seemed so easy when he was talking to his cousin, but now, sitting beside Carrie, he couldn't find the right way to start. 'You and I, we've been – um – attracted to one another, haven't we?'

She looked surprised, then blushed and nodded.

'But I told you I was trying to make my way in the world, couldn't think of marriage yet because my future was so uncertain. Only now . . .' He broke off and let go of her to wave his hands in the air, ending up by shrugging and letting them drop. 'There's no easy way to say this, Carrie, but I want to make sure you understand that it's *because* I'm attracted to you that I'm asking you.'

'Asking me what, Eli?'

'If you'll marry me?'

She gaped at him, unable to believe she'd heard correctly.

When she didn't answer, he prompted, 'Well, will you?'

'Why have you changed your mind? You still have your way to make, don't you? You'll get your music room now, but you can't be sure it'll be a success.'

He took her hand again, playing with her fingers as he explained, 'It's my uncle's will. He left everything to me and Joanna, but on condition we get married within the month.'

Carrie jerked her hand away as disappointment seared through her. 'Then why are you asking *me* to marry you?'

He explained about the lawyer's trick, which at least gave him a choice of bride. 'So I came straight round to see you, to ask you . . .'

'Oh.'

He watched her anxiously.

She waited, hoping he'd say he loved her. If he did, she'd jump at his offer. But if he was only asking her because he needed a wife to get his inheritance, she wasn't at all sure she wanted that. Marriage was hard enough anyway but if your husband didn't care about you, it'd surely be a lot harder?

'You'd have a better life than you have here,' Eli said tentatively.

'Yes.' *Say it!* she pleaded inside her head. *Please say it!* But he didn't.

'Is something wrong? Have I misread your feelings? Don't you feel the attraction when we're together?'

'I do feel – something. But this is all very sudden and we – we don't really know one another.' And though she loved him, had done for a while, did she want to marry a man who didn't love her in return? Carrie wasn't sure she did. 'I'll have to think about it, Eli.'

It was his turn to say, 'Oh.'

She stood up. 'I can't stay. It's a bad time for you to have called. Mam should have finished the washing this morning, only she didn't and Nev hates having wet washing around, so we have to get on with it.'

She went to the door and looked round to see that he hadn't moved. 'We can talk about it again tomorrow when I come to work.' She opened the front door for him. Eli stood on the doorstep looking at her, his face showing puzzlement rather than anything else. He'd expected her to jump at his offer, she could see. That thought only made her more determined to make him wait, to think about it carefully.

'I don't know what I'll do if you say no, Carrie.'

She tried to smile, but her face wouldn't obey her. 'I'll see you tomorrow,' she repeated.

Only when she'd closed the door on him did she cover her eyes with her hands and let the tears fall. He needed to marry so he could get his music room! That was the only reason he'd asked her.

She felt a hand on her shoulder and turned to see Raife looking at her anxiously.

'What's wrong, lass? I thought you'd be the happiest young woman in Hedderby after you'd seen Eli. Here, come back in the parlour and tell me what's wrong.'

So for the second time Carrie sat on the sofa, but this time with a man who took her in his arms and let her weep on his chest, a man who patted her shoulders and made soothing noises, who flapped his hand in dismissal when her mother tried to come in.

When she had finished sobbing out her tale, Raife sat there with her head on his shoulder. 'I definitely think he's fond of you.'

'Is he? I think he's fonder of the money.' She wiped her eyes with her apron, but more tears continued to flow. 'I've never really wanted to get wed, Raife, not till I met Eli anyway. It seems as if all women get out of being wed is hard work and babies. It's the men who get the best part of the bargain. So I'd decided I didn't want that. I thought I'd be like Essie and live my own life. As soon as Mam stopped having babies, I was going to leave home and go into lodgings or into service – or *something*. I didn't want a life like hers, like that of most women I know.'

He sighed and patted her hand again. 'I don't know what to advise you. You'd be bettering yourself by marrying Eli Beckett, that's for sure, so it wouldn't be like your mother's life. And I doubt Eli will turn into a boozer, like your dad did.'

Carrie sat silent for a minute or two then looked at the clock. 'I think I'll go and talk to Essie. She always makes sense of things for me, and she's not as busy at this time of day. I can't go back to the washing, Raife. Mam will just have to manage on her own for once.'

'I'll give her a hand. You go and see your friend.' He shook his head as Carrie went slowly and heavily up the stairs, moving like a woman with a load on her mind. This wasn't how he'd expected her to react to a proposal from the man she loved. But then, Carrie had surprised him quite a few times since she'd been living here. She was a clear thinker, for all her lack of education, could see a problem quickly, work out practical solutions, even had Nev eating out of her hand because what she said made sense.

But Raife hoped she would see fit to marry Eli. She deserved more out of life than she'd had as her mother's unpaid slave. And he was sure the young man was genuinely fond of her. Why the hell hadn't he told her so?

Carrie went up to the attic to change out of her damp clothes. She'd been lifting heavy pieces of wet washing, which had been soaking overnight, into and out of the boiler for two hours, ever since she'd got home from the Dragon, rinsing them in the big tub, then getting the water out of them in the box mangle. Nev had such good laundry equipment here that she didn't understand why her mother made such a fuss about washing day. It was a pleasure to have clean clothes, and if you were careful how you put them into the box mangle, most things didn't need ironing afterwards.

But then, when had her mother ever been careful about anything?

Carrie coiled her hair up more tidily, checked her face in the tiny mirror to make sure she hadn't any smuts on it, then got out the bonnet and jacket Mrs Latimer had given her. This occasion seemed too special for her just to wrap a shawl round her head.

As she walked slowly round to the doctor's house she wondered what she really wanted her friend to say.

Essie opened the door and beamed at her. 'Haven't seen you for ages, love. Come in.'

'I need your advice, Essie.'

'Is something wrong?'

'Not wrong exactly. I'm just – I can't make up my mind what to do.' Carrie sat down and explained her problem.

Essie let her talk herself out, then said slowly and thoughtfully, 'You love him, don't you?'

Carrie nodded.

'Then what's stopping you saying yes?'

'He's not said a word about loving *me*. I'm being silly, I know, but if I do get married I want it to be to someone who cares for me. Otherwise I'd rather be like you and manage my own life.'

Essie was silent for a minute or two, then said gently,

'I'd rather have got wed, love, than be living like this. Even to a man I didn't love. I always wanted children, always.'

Carrie stared at her in surprise.

'I don't usually talk about it but when I was a lass I had a young man and we were walking out, only he died of a fever. Very sudden it was. Just like blowing out a candle.' Essie took a deep breath because it hurt to talk about her Johnny, even now. 'By the time I'd got over him, all the young fellows I knew seemed to be married and no one else ever showed an interest in me. If they had, I'd have said yes, love or no love.' She let that sink in, then asked, 'Is he a decent fellow? Will he treat you right?'

Carrie sat there, staring blindly into the red heart of the fire. 'Yes. He was really kind to me the first time I met him, even when he didn't know me. He's always kind and fair with folk.'

'And do you like him touching you . . . kissing you?'

Carrie's cheeks felt hot suddenly as she nodded.

'Then you should say yes. Don't end up like me. I won't have much to look forward to in my old age, so I save all my money and hope it'll be enough to see me through when I get too old to work. I'll kill myself before I go into the poorhouse.' Essie gave a grim smile. 'That's surprised you, hasn't it?'

Carrie nodded. 'I wasn't sure what you'd say. Not this, though.'

'You'll do what you think best, of course. But don't ask for the moon, love. I don't know anyone who's managed to get that.'

Carrie was very thoughtful as she walked home. Not only had Essie's advice surprised her but her own reaction to Eli's proposal had too. What on earth was she hesitating for? He was probably the best chance she'd ever have of a comfortable life.

But would that be enough to make her happy?

A boy delivered an urgent message from Mr Burtell to the Dragon at seven o'clock that evening, asking Eli and Joanna to go and see him first thing in the morning. Sadly, something had cropped up which put their inheritance in doubt. He couldn't see them this evening, because he had an important engagement he was unable to break, but he would be in his office early, at eight o'clock sharp, if they could be there then.

They stared at one another in consternation.

'What can it be?' Joanna worried. 'What can possibly have put our inheritance in doubt?'

'I don't know.' Eli thumped the flat of his hand on the table. 'Damnation! Will nothing go smoothly for us?'

He'd already told her about his interview with Carrie.

Joanna looked at him. 'I was going to speak to Bram tonight, but I'll put it off until I know what's upset Mr Burtell.'

The evening seemed endless but when at last they'd got the customers out and the beer pots washed, they sat on in the kitchen, both too worried to feel sleepy.

'We can't do anything now,' Eli said at last. 'Come on, let's get to bed.'

# 20

Carrie went to work at seven o'clock the next morning, feeling very nervous about giving her answer to Eli. But when she got there he was nowhere to be seen and Joanna seemed to have something on her mind. Carrie felt aggrieved. She'd expected him to be waiting for her, eager for an answer.

It was quite a while before he came up from the cellar. When he saw her, he hesitated then came towards her. Why had he hesitated? Was he regretting proposing to her? She couldn't bear it if he was, so asked him straight out, 'Are you regretting what you asked me yesterday? If so, we can just forget it.'

Eli stared at her in surprise. 'No, I'm not regretting it. Carrie, you surely don't think I'd change my mind?'

'Oh. Well, you weren't here when I arrived, and you didn't look pleased to see me just now . . .'

'I didn't want to talk about such an important thing in public.'

He drew her outside into the old stable area, keeping his arm round her waist. That made her feel better. She loved the warm strength of that arm.

He swung her round to face him. 'You won't say

no to me, Carrie, will you? I do want to marry you – whatever happens today.'

'What do you mean?'

'We had a message yesterday evening from Mr Burtell saying another problem had cropped up about our inheritance.'

She pulled away. 'Well, hadn't you better settle that first before you think of marriage?'

He drew her back. 'No. I want to marry you whatever the problem is – only, if Joanna and I don't inherit, you and I might have to wait a bit, that's all.'

Carrie could feel herself softening. 'You *are* sure about it, then?'

'Of course I am.' He looked at her with the smile that always made her heart do a little skip. 'Well? Will you marry me, Miss Carrie Preston?'

So she gave in to temptation and said it. 'Yes, Mr Eli Beckett. I will.'

'That's wonderful!' He pulled her into an embrace, his lips meeting hers, their warmth and softness as overwhelming as his strength had been a minute earlier.

Everything blurred around her and Carrie was conscious only of him and the feelings that flowed through her body, making her want to press herself against him. When he drew away she let herself lean against him, sighing with happiness.

'Eli! Are you . . . ? Oh.'

They both turned round as Joanna's voice came from nearby.

'Sorry to interrupt, but it's time to go and see Mr Burtell.'

He took Carrie's hand. 'Before we do, you can be the first to congratulate us. Carrie's just agreed to become my wife.'

Joanna's worried expression turned into a smile and she gave Carrie a quick hug. 'I'm so pleased for you and hope you'll both be very happy. But we have to leave now, I'm afraid.'

Carrie could see the worry settle back on both their faces so forced herself to move away from Eli. 'I'll get on with the cleaning then.' She watched them walk away, hoping the news wasn't bad. What sort of threat could there be to their inheritance? Had someone found out what she'd done? No, Eli would have told her if they had.

She still didn't feel guilty about that, because it wouldn't have been fair for Eli and Joanna to lose their music room. She looked round, seeing this place in her mind's eye, full of people, light, singing, laughter. She still thought about her visit to Manchester, which had shown her exactly what they were aiming at, made her want it for them – and for the people of Hedderby. Maybe if there was somewhere else to go at night, men wouldn't get so drunk.

But if that horrible man Stott was set on having this place, to what lengths would he go to get it? He had so much money and power that she was worried for Eli. So much greed too, you could see it in Stott's face. She didn't think a man like that would give up easily.

Mr Burtell looked across his desk at Eli and Joanna. 'I'm very sorry to have to tell you this but Mr Stott has been to see me. He informed me that Mr Hordle sent his clerk round to Mr Beckett with the contract to sell the land next to the pub, and Mr Beckett agreed verbally that he was going to sign it. I think Mr Stott intends to go to court on this basis and claim that the land is morally his – unless you wish to honour the agreement and sell to him, in which case you'll receive the payment, of course.'

'Dad wouldn't have said that,' Joanna said at once. 'I've watched him buy and sell things many a time and he never admits anything till the final moment. He's pushed up the price of things he's been selling that way, and pushed down the price of things he's been buying.' She shook her head and repeated, 'No, he definitely wouldn't have done that.'

'Mr Hordle's clerk, James Copeland, who is very well respected, is prepared to swear in a court of law that your father did say he was going to sell. And Mr Stott is prepared to go to court for what he regards as *his* property. I must say, I wouldn't normally question Copeland's word.'

Both his clients were silent, trying to come to terms with this.

'What do you want me to do about it?' Mr Burtell asked after a while.

Joanna said immediately, 'Deny this claim. We'll go to court.' She looked sideways at her cousin and he nodded.

'You'd get a decent sum of money for the land, whereas if you go to court, the case could drag on for a long time and cost you a great deal.'

'But we don't want to sell,' Eli insisted. 'And it's our word against this Copeland fellow's.'

'Very well. But I can promise you nothing, I'm afraid. In cases like these it very much depends on the judge.' He hesitated, then felt obliged to add, 'I should inform you that Mr Stott's lawyer, Mr Hordle, is well thought of in legal circles. And Mr Stott is a wealthy man. That makes a difference, I'm afraid.'

'I'm not giving that land away,' Joanna said. 'I'm not. Especially to *him*.'

Eli nodded agreement.

'Very well. I'll inform them of your decision.'

They walked back slowly along Market Street.

'Did we do the right thing?' Joanna asked.

'Who knows? We did what we wanted to, at least.' Eli sighed. 'I was going to see Jem Harding today about finishing off the music room. I'd better wait.'

'Dad could never do anything straightforwardly. I'm absolutely certain he wouldn't have said that to the clerk, though.'

His uncle *had* signed the contract, though, as Eli very well knew. Only he wasn't going to tell her that. It would remain a secret between him and Carrie, whom he trusted absolutely. She was a grand lass.

When they got back they found her scrubbing the floor. She looked up as they came in, saw their expressions and got to her feet, tossing the scrubbing brush into the bucket of water and wiping her hands on her apron as she came hurrying across to join them. 'What is it? What did Mr Burtell tell you?'

They took her into the kitchen and explained.

'Mr Beckett definitely didn't tell the clerk he was going to sell,' she said instantly. 'I was in the snug, listening. I wanted to know what was going on, in case I could help you.'

They looked at her in shock then Eli asked hesitantly, 'Are you sure of that?'

'Yes, of course.' Carrie looked a bit embarrassed as she added, 'I shouldn't have been eavesdropping, I know, but I was worried about you two, and you weren't here to help yourselves.' She closed her eyes for a moment, trying to remember what she'd heard. 'Mr Beckett said, "I'm still not sure I want to sell." Yes, those are exactly the words he used.'

'Will you come with me to the lawyer and explain that?' Eli asked.

'Yes. I'll have to finish the floor first, but—'

'To hell with the scrubbing! We've got to settle this once and for all.'

'I'll nip up and change, then carry on with the cleaning,' Joanna said. 'You go with Eli.'

So Carrie walked along Market Street with him, feeling ashamed to be seen in her damp and dirty working skirt. She felt even more embarrassed when shown into Mr Burtell's beautiful office and tried to hide her reddened hands under the apron.

He questioned her closely, nodded from time to time, then said, 'You'll have to make a deposition about this in front of the magistrate. I'll send word to him now and ask if he's free. Can you wait a few moments? Good. In a small town we can usually clear these matters up quite quickly.'

So they sat there and made laboured conversation with Mr Burtell, or rather Eli did until his junior clerk came back to say that Mr Hull would see them now. They had only to walk across the road to do this.

Carrie didn't let herself be overwhelmed by facing the magistrate, because she knew what she'd heard, but she was glad when it was all over and they could stroll back to the Dragon, leaving Mr Burtell to inform Mr Stott's lawyer of the new development.

Outside the pub Eli stopped to ask in a low voice, 'Did my uncle really say that? Or are you rescuing us again?'

'He really said it.'

'That's even better.' He gave her a hug, and when two ladies walking past stopped to stare at them, said, 'She's just agreed to marry me.' Which took the disapproving looks off their faces and made them smile.

Only after they'd gone did Eli realise one of them had been Mrs Stott. She'd looked strained, had aged a lot lately. Well, she might be rich but he didn't envy her, being married to a man like that. It'd age anyone.

Bram came into the pub that night to help keep order. The men from Stott's were in a foul mood muttering to one another, though they took care not to say anything aloud that people outside their group of friends could overhear.

Robbie came in as well, looking ill at ease.

'What's up, lad?' Bram asked.

'Mr Stott turned me off yesterday.'

'What on earth for?'

'Nowt as I could see, though I reckon it was because Mr Edmund thought well of me.'

'That fellow is doing nothing but upset folk lately.' Bram jerked his head towards three tables packed solid with Stott's men, none of them looking happy. 'If the steam engine is as dangerous as they're saying, you're well out of that place.'

'It's all right for you to say that, but how will I live if I've no job? I had to go and ask Nev Linney to take me in. How do you think I felt about that?'

'And did he?'

'What? Oh, yes. He never hesitated, I'll give him that.'

'I think Nev's a bit of a dark horse.'

'He hates Stott, says he could tell a few tales and Stott daren't touch him because of what he knows.'

'I wouldn't be so sure of that. I hear Tom Parker's been taken on at Stott's. Special duties. He attacked your Mr Edmund on his way to Out Rawby after he'd picked up his tools and stuff from the works. Luckily, I was nearby.'

'He attacked Mr Edmund? Nay, I can't believe it.'

'I was there, saw it myself.'

'Tom's a mean sod. He carries a knife and boasts he's killed with it. He's not liked.' Robbie sighed. 'I'd better get back. I just wanted to let you know what had happened.'

'I'll buy you one beer to cheer you up. You'll have to stop drinking so much now, my lad. Keep a clear head on you and watch your step. If Stott wants you out of town, make sure you're not out alone in the

Lanes after dark. I'll get Michael to walk home with you tonight.'

'I can look after myself.'

'No one can look after himself in every situation. Not even me.' He patted Robbie on the shoulder then walked across to join Joanna.

'I need to talk to you,' she said abruptly.

'Any time you like.'

'Tomorrow? About three in the afternoon.'

'I'll be there. What's it about?'

'I can't tell you here.'

A little later he joined Eli and said, 'I hear congratulations are in order.'

'What? Oh, yes. Me and Carrie.'

'It's very sudden.'

Eli shrugged. 'Condition of my dear uncle's will that we marry within the month if we want the money.'

'Joanna too?'

'Yes. Look, if she speaks to you . . .'

'That'll be between me and her. Look at that eejit!' Bram was off to stop a drunken man trying to balance a pot of beer on his forehead. He took care not to go near Eli for the rest of the evening. He didn't want the other man telling him any more. It was up to Joanna to do that.

Bram walked home slowly after the pub closed. He had a lot to consider now that he had some idea why Joanna wanted to see him. It was hard to go against your family and upbringing, which he'd have to do if he married her, hardest of all to hurt the Mammy. But he'd grown to love Joanna, who was more vulnerable than people realised, and he couldn't imagine life without her now.

Oh, hell, things were never simple! Why did he expect them to be? He let out a snort of laughter. Who'd have thought he'd fall for a woman like her? He'd always gone for plump, accommodating women before. Joanna wouldn't make a meek wife, and probably not a comfortable one, either. But she was the one Bram wanted.

It was only thoughts of his family which held him back, really. He chuckled suddenly. And waiting for Joanna to propose. Having to do that would make her *really* grumpy.

That evening Athol was in such a rage that Maria hardly dared open her mouth. He never stopped talking the whole time, so at least she only had to nod, say yes or no, and provide him with an audience. But she felt constantly on edge.

'I'll stop them!' he threatened several times. 'You see if I don't find a way.'

'Yes, dear.'

'Can you say nothing but that? Have you no opinions of your own, woman?'

She hesitated.

'Well?'

'Wouldn't it be better for you to buy a bigger piece of land, even if it is further out of town?'

'No, it damned well wouldn't. That piece is just along the road from the railway, and just down the hill from our works. It's really convenient. We can get our stuff to the freight yard easily from there, what-ever the weather.'

He sat staring into the fire for a few minutes, smiling the sort of smile he wore when he was plotting to hurt someone, Maria thought with a shiver. She knew all his expressions by now, had to watch him carefully in self-defence. But it was a struggle to keep a calm, interested look on her face and she wished desper-ately that he hadn't forbidden her to sit and embroider, not because she loved the work so much but because doing it meant she didn't have to look at him.

Athol's smile grew even more wolfish. 'Besides, the Dragon itself stands on a nice big plot right next to the land. One has to look to the future. The way Stott's is expanding, it would only be sensible to have more land available next door for later use.'

Maria was startled into saying, 'But there's a busy pub on that piece of land! Would you just knock it down?'

'If necessary.'

'Where would the men drink?'

'Who cares?'

Later he asked, 'Well, what's the latest gossip from town?'

She knew he liked her to bring back every piece of news, however small, and racked her brain, but could only think of one thing. 'The young man who now owns the Dragon has just got engaged.'

'Has he? To whom?'

'I don't know her name. But she was very shab-bily dressed and had red hands, like a scrubbing woman. She was pretty, though, dark-haired and quite tall.' Maria could see that she'd caught his attention and he was much more pleasant to her after that. But still, the evening seemed very long.

The following day Mr Burtell sent another message to the pub, asking all three of them to go and see him again later that day. A further problem had occurred, it seemed.

'What the hell's Stott done now?' Eli exclaimed. 'What other problem can there possibly be?' He paced up and down for a minute or two, then said abruptly, 'I'm going into town for some more nails. I can't settle to anything till I know what's up.'

On the way back he stopped to talk to Mr Marker.

'I'm glad you didn't let Stott have that piece of land,' the grocer said. 'He'd make an uneasy neighbour and none of us wants him down here. I reckon he'd soon have been wanting the Dragon as well.'

'You're right. And expecting to get it. Eh, life must be easy if you're rich.'

'Some make it easier than others. And you say there's another problem?'

'Yes. I don't know what yet. We're going in to see Mr Burtell later.'

At the hour suggested, Joanna, Eli and Carrie went into town again.

The lawyer looked at Eli. 'You didn't tell me you were engaged to Miss Preston.'

'What has that to do with anything?'

'Mr Stott is claiming Miss Preston is lying to help

you, and I'm afraid the magistrate will take into account the close relationship.'

'But I heard Mr Beckett say it!' Carrie protested.

'We have only your word for that.'

'And only the clerk's word that my uncle said he intended to sell,' Eli snapped. There was silence, then he said, quietly and firmly, 'We're *not* giving him that land. He'll have to force it from us.'

Joanna nodded.

'If you go to court it'll take some time, and may I remind you that by the terms of the will, you still have to marry within the month to inherit. Mr Stott seems to know about that, too, though how he found out, I don't know. Once Miss Preston is your wife, her credibility as a witness will be even lower, I'm afraid.'

'We're still not giving in,' Joanna insisted.

But they were all three very subdued as they walked back.

Mr Marker was standing in the doorway of his shop. He took one look at them and stepped forward. 'What's happened now?'

They told him.

His face brightened. 'If that's all, I can corroborate Miss Preston's story. Mr Beckett told me himself, only an hour or so before he died, that he wasn't sure he wanted to sell. Now, who was in the shop with me at the time? Ah, yes. Mrs Lorringham. She would have heard him as well. And *she* isn't afraid of anyone, not with the money she inherited.' He started undoing his apron. 'I'll go and see her at once, then we'll speak to that lawyer of yours.'

'Why are you doing this?' Joanna asked.

'Because I don't want Stott as a neighbour, and because I know what I heard. They say the truth will out. Well, I'll be the one bringing it out this time.'

Carrie hesitated then spoke up. 'Why don't you go and see Mr Burtell on your own and let him send someone to fetch Mrs Lorringham? That way, no one can say you and she have worked this out together.'

All three of them stared at her in amazement.

'That's a good idea,' Mr Marker allowed. 'A very good idea.' He nodded to Eli. 'You've got yourself a smart one there. It never hurts to have a clever wife. I don't know what I'd do in the shop without my dear Sarah.'

When they got back to the pub, it was to see Mr Stott's carriage outside and find him pacing up and down the music room area.

'Don't make him angry!' Joanna said quickly as Eli took a hasty step forward. 'It won't do any good.'

So he walked down the side to find Mr Stott and a stranger there, pacing out the space. 'You're trespassing,' he said, which was as polite as he could get.

Stott turned round with that sneering smile on his face. 'Oh, I don't think so. Unless you've got someone else to swear black's white.'

'I'd appreciate it if you'd leave. You don't own this land and I see no need for you to measure it up.'

'Time's money. I want to start building my warehouse as soon as the paperwork is done. I don't understand why you're making such a fuss. You'll be paid plenty for it, after all.'

'We don't want money, we want this space.'

They stood there scowling at one another.

In the end, the stranger moved towards the street again. 'We have enough to be going on with, Mr Stott.' He began walking away.

But Athol sauntered up to the far end of the space and stood there, one hand on his hip, surveying it with an air of ownership. Only then did he amble back to his carriage.

'Why someone hasn't killed that man before now, I'll never know,' Eli muttered as he watched the glossy black carriage pull away.

Edmund was enjoying having his own home, and Grania and Faith seemed to be getting on well together. When he asked around in the village about getting help in the garden, he found it easily. He had considered using the old wooden shed at the end of the garden as a workshop, but then discovered there was an empty stone-built barn next to the village shop that was no longer used and had come to an agreement with its owner to rent it.

There had been another stone thrown through his front window. To his delight and relief, several of the villagers came round the next day to discuss the incident and offer him suggestions.

'I'm more grateful than I can say for your concern,' Edmund told them.

'You've brought jobs into the village and your wife buys things from our shop,' the old man who was Church Warden told him. 'We look after our own here. Now, Tam, what about that dog of yours? Could you lend it to Mr Stott for a week or two?'

'Happy to, for as long as he feeds it.' Tam gave Edmund a toothless grin. 'It was my son's and it's eating me out of house and home.' His expression grew sad. 'He died a few months ago, poor lad. Only thirty, too. Left a wife and children. They have a struggle to make ends meet, I help them out a bit.'

Edmund told Faith about this and found out later that she'd already been round to see Tam's daughter-in-law at Grania's suggestion, offering her work helping with the washing.

'You don't mind, do you?' she asked anxiously. 'Only I have so much now that I feel I should share it with those who're in trouble.'

'Of course I don't mind. You'd not be my Faith if you didn't care about other people.'

As he was getting ready for bed that night, Edmund realised that if he didn't have the shadow of his cousin looming over him, he'd be the happiest man on earth.

Now all that remained was to find himself an assistant to help in his workshop, but that wouldn't be as easy because he needed someone skilled, not a mere labourer.

Athol walked up and down the big workshop, checking what the men were doing. When he got to the end, he stood and listened. Did that steam engine sound a bit different today? No, it was probably his imagination. But still, it didn't hurt to check, so he popped his head round the door, gestured towards the metal monster that powered his machinery and lathes, and asked Turner, 'How's it going?'

'It's coping. But I still need those tools, sir, if I'm to nurse it along. I can't tighten some things properly without them.'

'I'll see what I can do.' Furious at his cousin for having the necessary tools sitting around doing nothing when Stott's needed them, Athol sent for the man who'd helped him out before and gave him strict instructions as to what to do.

A few minutes after that there was a knock on the door of his office and a message was brought in from Mr Hordle, stating he would like to see Athol at his earliest convenience as another problem had occurred in connection with the Dragon.

One thing after another, Athol thought angrily as he got ready to leave. Hordle might be the best lawyer in town, but he was an old fusspot and was taking far too long to settle this sale. If he'd only been prepared to swear that old Beckett had agreed to sell, there'd be no need for all this delay.

Putting on his overcoat and top hat, he marched out of the works, yelling at the foreman to make sure he kept the men hard at work. That was another thing. He'd have to find and appoint an assistant manager now his damned cousin had left. Turner might be a competent engineer, but he had no idea how to control the men. It was strange how well they'd worked for a weak sod like Edmund. It just showed, you never could tell.

Charles Hordle watched his client sit down and

wished once again that he didn't have to deal with Athol Stott. He was quite sure the man never hesitated to lie, saying only what would further his own wishes. Well, no use trying to break this news gently. 'Two other witnesses have made depositions to say that they heard Frank Beckett say he wasn't sure about selling only an hour before he died. While he was on his way home, in fact.'

Athol made a scornful sound in his throat. 'Friends of young Beckett, no doubt. Who are they? We'll soon put paid to that.'

Charles drew himself up. 'Might I ask what you mean by "put paid to that"?'

'I mean, I'll go and question them myself and they'll soon cave in.'

'I wouldn't advise you to do that.'

'I'll do as I damned well choose.'

'One of the two is Mrs Lorringham.'

Athol stared at him. 'I don't believe you! She wouldn't.'

Charles Hordle stiffened. 'I resent that remark, sir. I never lie to my clients. Unless you withdraw that accusation, our association will end here and now.'

The client in question let out an aggrieved sigh and forced himself to say a few conciliatory words. 'Sorry. Been a trying day. Apologise. Who's the other person?'

'Mr Marker, the grocer. The incident apparently took place in his shop. Since his story and Mrs Lorringham's are identical, he's not likely to be making it up.'

'No chance she could have been mistaken?'

'No chance whatsoever. In fact, Mr Marker went to see Mr Burtell, who took the matter to the magistrate, and Mr Hull himself called on Mrs Lorringham to question her. He was quite satisfied that she'd spoken to no one else about this, and that no one had spoken to her. After that Mr Hull decided there was no case to answer and declined to pursue the matter further. My advice to you therefore is to accept that you've not succeeded in purchasing the land and look elsewhere to satisfy your needs.' He stood up. 'And now, I'm keeping another client waiting. I'll wish you good day, sir.'

Athol sat for a moment, chewing the corner of his lip, then stood up, inclined his head to the older man and left.

When he'd gone, Charles Hordle called in his clerk and dismissed him for lying on behalf of Mr Stott.

James Copeland stared at him in dismay. 'Please, sir, give me another chance!'

'How can I? A lawyer and his staff must be above reproach.'

His clerk began to sob. 'I didn't want to do it, but Mr Stott threatened my family if I didn't say what he wished. My wife's in a delicate state of health and I've got six children, sir, all depending on me. I was terrified.'

Mr Hordle stared at him in shock. 'He threatened you!'

'Yes, sir.'

The trouble was, he believed the man. 'What if he threatens you again? How can I trust you?'

'I'll never, ever do anything wrong again, sir. I promise you. Whatever anyone says or threatens. Please!' He covered his face with his hands and went on sobbing, quite beside himself.

Charles Hordle couldn't bring himself to be too harsh. Until this incident Copeland had been a highly satisfactory employee. 'Very well, I'll give you one more chance. But make sure you don't let me down. And if Mr Stott threatens you again, come straight to me.'

It was a while before his clerk was calm enough to go back to his work. The sight of an ageing man sobbing, his life almost destroyed by that unscrupulous rogue, only added to Hordle's determination to have nothing more to do with Athol Stott.

When the clerk had gone back to work, he pulled a piece of paper towards him, opened the lid of the inkwell and wrote a brief note, saying that in future Mr Stott should find himself another lawyer. Out of consideration for his clerk, he didn't state the reason. Then he pulled out the boxes containing all documents relevant to Athol Stott and his engineering works and sent their contents, together with the note, to Mr Stott's residence.

He then went to call on his colleague, Jack Burtell, to let him know he no longer represented Athol Stott and that the sale of the land next to the Dragon could be considered null and void.

# 21

That same night, Edmund and his neighbours were woken by a furious barking, with the borrowed dog doing its duty with great enthusiasm. The dog next door also raised a protest, and from down the street other animals contributed to the chorus.

'Don't go outside,' Faith whispered. 'The dog will warn them away.'

'I need to show that I'm alert as well, dearest. Stay there. I won't be long.' Edmund slipped his bare feet into his shoes, pulled his overcoat round him over his nightshirt and went downstairs. In the kitchen he lit a walking lantern and took the latter outside, shining its one-sided beam down the garden and from side to side.

The dog skidded to a halt beside him, panting and wagging its tail. From over the fence his neighbour called out to ask if Edmund was all right.

'Yes, I'm fine. If there was someone here, I dare say he's been driven away.'

'And he'd better stay away, too. We don't need burglars in Out Rawby,' Mr Olworth bellowed in the over-loud voice of one who was partly deaf.

The dog sat down beside Edmund, looking pleased

with itself, but showed no inclination to bark or invest-
igate anything else, so he gave it a pat and a word of
praise and went back inside.

In the morning as soon as it was light he went to
check the rear garden and found marks in the soft
earth where someone had climbed over the end wall,
and where they had climbed back again in clumsy
haste, chased by the dog, judging by the muddle of
footprints pointing away from the house.

Mr Olworth, an inveterate early riser, came out to
join him and stared across at the rear wall. 'You can
see there was someone here.'

'Yes.'

'Can't beat a good watchdog.'

As Edmund turned to go back to the house he
noticed that the door of the shed at the bottom end
was partly open and the footprints led to and from
there. Why would anyone want to burgle a shed? It
only contained the gardening tools and equipment.

*Tools!* He knew one person who definitely wanted
his tools, but surely Athol wouldn't stoop to robbing
his own cousin?

But he was a bully and had always taken whatever
he wanted without thought for other people's wishes
and needs. This was partly the reason his uncle had
sent Edmund out to pupillage to learn engineering,
and he'd spent most of his youth in a happier envir-
onment, living mostly with the man training him. But
even his uncle hadn't realised how bad Athol was.
That had only been revealed since the old man's death.

After an early breakfast Edmund went into the

village and opened up his new workshop. Since his neighbours there had heard the noise of the dogs barking the previous night they came round to find out what had happened.

'I think I'll have to get a night watchman here,' Edmund said as he finished telling his tale all over again. 'I don't want to lose my tools and equipment.'

'Pay old Bert to do it. If you give him a chair and a bell, he'll keep watch for you happily and ring if he needs help,' the shopkeeper who owned the barn suggested. 'He never did sleep much, and he worries his daughter wandering round his cottage at night. He could use some extra money, poor soul. He needs new clothes and doesn't eat all that well, though his lass gives him what she can.'

So Edmund found himself employing another of the citizens of Out Rawby and overheard the shop-keeper telling one of his customers that it had been a good day when Mr Edmund Stott moved into the village. Edmund couldn't hear the woman's reply, but the shopkeeper's response made his mouth tighten with annoyance.

'I take people as I find them, Mrs Doughty. And all I know is that Mrs Stott is married now, helps those less fortunate than herself and is as nicely spoken as you'd wish. What's more, Grania Heegan's well satisfied with her new employers, and you know *she* wouldn't put up with loose behaviour.'

Edmund continued to feel deeply guilty for what he'd done to Faith and only hoped enough people would be forgiving so that she could enjoy her life from now on. He'd not even pass the time of day with anyone who slighted her.

Robbie went out to see Mr Edmund because Nev said he'd need a reference from someone if he was to get himself another job. He enjoyed the walk to Out Rawby, had forgotten how much he used to relish a tramp round the countryside when he was a lad. It occurred to him suddenly that Carrie had rarely been able to do this and he felt a bit guilty that being a boy meant he'd had an easy time compared to her and his other sisters.

He asked an old man where Mr Edmund Stott lived and was told that his house was further along the one and only street, but that the gentleman was in his workshop at the moment.

When Robbie knocked on the door of the building the old man had pointed out, a voice called out for him to come in and he found himself inside a much larger space than he'd expected because the building went back quite a long way. It looked nothing like a workshop, though, just a big open rectangle with no ceiling, only the roof beams showing under the slate tiles.

Mr Edmund was just putting up a rack for his tools and having difficulty holding it in place while he marked where to drill holes, so Robbie hurried over to hold it for him. They worked together, as they had done many times before because Mr Edmund had never minded getting his hands dirty, then he turned round and realised who was helping him.

'What are you doing out here on a workday, Robbie Preston?'

'Mr Stott turned me off.'

'Was there a reason?'

Robbie shrugged. 'He just did it one day. I think it's because I'd worked closely with you.'

'Well, that's good news for me because I'm in need of an assistant here.'

'You are?'

'Yes. Interested in the job?'

Robbie closed his eyes for a moment, then opened them again, a bit ashamed to realise they were full of tears of sheer relief. He nodded.

'Good. Now I want you to live out here because you'll be safer than if you have to walk back into Hedderby after dark. And actually, it'd be best of all if you lodged in my house. There's a servants' wing at the back with only Grania Heegan occupying it at present, so we've room. My cousin sent someone to burgle my house last night so you might be called upon to help me defend it.'

Robbie gaped at him. 'He attacked *you?*'

Edmund shrugged. 'Who else could it be? He was annoyed about my marriage and my refusal to sell him my tools. I don't want you to discuss that with anyone, but you need to know because you'll be in danger too if you work for me.'

'It's the men at Stott's who're in most danger, I reckon. That steam engine sounds really rough now. You'd not notice it unless you knew the normal sound, but *I* can tell the difference. I kept telling Turner . . .'

Robbie broke off and stared around, then exclaimed. '*That's* why he got rid of me. Well, it won't stop the other lads worrying. They're not stupid. It was a sad day when Stott's lost you, sir.'

'It was bound to happen. My cousin and I don't agree on many things.' Edmund looked sternly at Robbie as he added, 'Oh, and one more thing! I'm not having you getting drunk. I want you clear-headed, morning and night. Is that understood?'

'Yes, Mr Edmund.'

'But if you prove yourself, after the first year we'll put you in training and make a proper engineer of you. You've an aptitude for the work. Now let's see if you can apply yourself properly.'

The tears did overflow then, so Robbie went across to the workbench, pretending to examine the tools. When he could turn back again without shaming himself, he said in a husky voice, 'You'll not regret it, sir, I promise you.'

'Right then. Go back to Hedderby and fetch your things.'

Robbie felt as if he was floating on air as he walked back into town. He burst into the kitchen at Linney's without knocking and announced, 'I'm found mysen a job! I'm going to be working with Mr Edmund in his workshop at Out Rawby. What do you think of that, our Carrie?' Then he realised his mother, Nev and Raife were there as well. 'Oh, sorry. I was just so excited.'

Carrie rushed to fling her arms round him. 'I'm right pleased for you. You didn't like working at Stott's after the old man died.'

'I didn't hate the work, only Mr Athol's ways, and lately that Turner's been picking on me.' Her brother hesitated then added bashfully, 'If I work hard, Mr Edmund says he'll train me properly as an engineer.'

'There!' Jane said with satisfaction. 'Haven't I got clever childer?' She looked at Nev and her mouth trembled as if she was about to cry.

'Well done, lad,' Raife said.

Nev nodded. 'I'm pleased for you. I like to see young folk make something of themselves. Here's Carrie doing well for herself, wedding Eli Beckett, and you're doing your mother and myself proud too.' He looked at Jane, sighed and put his arm round her. 'Me and your mother have a bit of news. She's expecting. It's taken me by surprise, I will admit, but if the child turns out to be as clever as you two, then I shan't be unhappy about it.'

'Oh, Nev!' Jane flung her arms round him and began sobbing noisily.

'I'll help you pack your things, Robbie,' Carrie nudged him and signalled to leave Nev and Jane alone. 'You'll be finding lodgings out there, I suppose?'

Robbie followed her out. 'I'll be staying at Mr Edmund's house.' He looked over his shoulder to make sure no one could overhear. 'Someone's already tried to burgle it. Mr Stott wants Mr Edmund's tools, but they belong to him not the firm. He was allus very careful of them tools. I reckon Mr Stott won't be happy to see his cousin setting up in business, either.

He's bound to do well, Mr Edmund is, because he's clever with machinery, big or small. Never met anyone like him.'

'You'd better make sure you don't let him see you drunk and silly then.'

'He said that, too,' Robbie confessed.

'Don't turn out like Dad.'

'I won't, love, not now I've got a chance to make summat of mysen. I've learned a few sharp lessons lately.'

It didn't take long to bundle up his things, then he gave Carrie a hug, went to say goodbye to his mother and strode off, whistling cheerfully.

As he walked through the town he saw Bram ahead of him and caught up with his friend to explain what he was going to be doing.

Bram clapped him on the back and wished him well, then went off to find Joanna.

'You're late,' Joanna snapped as soon as Bram walked in.

'I ran into Robbie Preston. He's going to work for Mr Edmund at Out Rawby and wanted to tell me about it. Would you have had me ignore him?' His eyes challenged her.

He knows what I want, she thought, so she said it. 'You know, don't you?'

'Why you want to see me?'

Joanna nodded.

'I've a fair idea.'

'Well? Will you do it?'

He grinned and folded his arms. 'Oh, no, my girl. You don't get away as easily as that. I want to be asked properly.'

'You're just being awkward.'

'Maybe I am, but you'll have to put up with that, won't you?' He sat down at the kitchen table and pulled a nearby chair out with one foot. 'Sit down and get it over with.'

Joanna sat, but couldn't seem to find the words or even look him in the eyes. She was angry at him for making her say it, angry at herself too for being such a coward. And she couldn't, just couldn't, find the words to ask him to marry her. Her eyes filled suddenly with tears of embarrassment and one rolled down her cheek. She turned her head slightly, hoping Bram hadn't seen it.

But he had. 'Oh, Joanna love!' His voice was soft and he caught hold of her hand, not allowing her to pull away. 'I didn't realise you'd be so embarrassed. I was only teasing you.'

She buried her head in his chest and her words came out muffled. 'I thought I could do it, but . . .' Her voice trailed away.

He cradled her against him. He'd bet he was the only person who'd seen this vulnerable side of her, or ever would. 'Eli told me about your father's will, how you both have to marry within the month.'

'Yes.'

'And he's going to marry Carrie.'

'Yes.'

'She's a nice lass, got a good head on her shoulders.'

He lifted Joanna's chin and looked into her eyes, smiling. 'Dare I hope you'd like to marry me?'

She nodded. 'I'm not usually so – tearful. I don't know why it seems so awful to ask you like this, but it does.'

'Instead of my asking you to marry me because I love you. Which I do. Don't you love me?'

Her expression softened and the faintest of blushes coloured her cheeks. 'You know I do.'

'Then that makes it easy. Will you marry me, Joanna? Not because of the money, but because we both want to?'

'Yes. Oh, Bram, yes!'

And then she was both sobbing and laughing till he put a stop to that by pulling her on to his lap and kissing her so thoroughly she grew soft as warm candle wax in his arms.

'How shall we manage it?' she asked after a while, still sitting on his knee with one arm round his neck and the other holding his hand. She had no desire to move away because she felt so safe and happy there. 'You're a Roman Catholic, aren't you?'

'Only half-hearted.' Bram's expression grew sad. 'It'll upset the Mammy that I'm marrying a heathen, though.'

'I'm not a *heathen*!'

'You are in her eyes. She'll set the priest on me again and create a big fuss, but in the end she'll forgive me – and you – because she loves me. But we'll have to be married in your church, if you don't mind. Will your priest mind that?'

'I don't think he'll be pleased, but he'll do it. Oh, Bram! It's been such a dreadful few days. Mr Stott tried every way he could to stop us keeping the land, but now I think we've won.'

Bram was unable to picture that man giving up so easily, though. 'It'll pay us keep a good watch on things. I don't think you've heard the last of him.'

'I'm afraid of that, too.'

'Shall I move in here when we're wed? It'd be safer for you. And there ought to be room enough.'

'Yes, of course. And you'll help with the pub all the time now, won't you? It'll be half yours after we marry, after all.'

'Not just the pub. If you'll let me, I want to be part of this music room. In fact, I want to sing there.' He smiled at her.

'I hoped you would. You have such a lovely voice.'

'So have you. We could maybe sing together?'

'Oh, no! I couldn't possibly sing in public. Don't ever ask me to do that!'

Eli came in just then, saw how they were sitting and stopped short, saying with mock severity, 'I think I should demand an explanation of why my cousin's sitting on your lap, Bram Heegan.'

She tried to get up but Bram wouldn't let her.

'Your cousin and I have decided to get married, and so that you realise I'm not marrying her just for the money, I'll tell you both now that I've a couple of hundred pounds saved up in the bank myself. I've always been a careful man with money.'

'I'd not care if you had nothing,' she muttered.

'I would,' he said. 'And I was telling Joanna that I'd like to sing in this music room of yours.'

Eli stuck his hand out. 'Good. I'm starting to think of how we'll find people to perform. Welcome to the family.'

Bram turned up at the Dragon that evening looking angry and bringing a pile of boxes, bags and bundles on his hand cart. He left Michael outside guarding it while he went in to see Joanna.

'Can I move in here tonight?'

She stared at him, then understanding flared in her eyes like a warm flame. 'Oh, no! Surely your mother didn't turn you out?'

'Yes, she did.' He gave her a wry smile. 'And she did call you a heathen.'

Joanna linked her arm with his and laid her head on his shoulder. 'I don't know what to say.'

He swung her round to face him. 'You don't have to say anything, love. This was bound to happen one day because I'm not, and never will be, religious. I can never be the sort of son the Mammy wants. She'll come round in time. I'm sorry about the row, of course I am, but I've always made my own life and I'm certainly going to choose my own wife.' He drew her closer. 'Now, doesn't a man who's feeling sad get a kiss to help him through the evening?'

'Yes, of course.'

Bram was breathing deeply when he drew back. 'We'd better go no further. Have you a bed for me?'

'Of course. There are several unused bedrooms

upstairs.' Joanna smiled. 'We need Carrie to tell us how to divide the house part up for the two families.'

'These two will be living here as well?'

'Of course.'

Eli came in. 'I hear you're moving in tonight?'

'Who told you that?'

'Your Michael. He's worried about you. Why don't you and he bring your things round to the side door, then we'll carry them upstairs? You'll be all right managing the pub for a while, Joanna?'

'Yes, of course.'

But she wasn't all right. There was a group of men who were talking too loudly, not drinking as much as some but acting as if they were roaring drunk. Suddenly the area around them erupted into a fight, with men rolling to and fro on the floor and furniture flying. She ran to yell up the stairs for Eli and he came clattering down followed by Bram.

It was Eli's voice which made the first difference, that amazingly loud voice he could summon up which carried across a room full of men drinking, or as now standing back and watching a few others fight. Some were egging them on, but most were muttering in annoyance at having their evening spoiled.

'*Stop that this minute!*' Eli yelled again. He began to push his way towards the centre of the disturbance, followed by Bram and Michael. '*Stop it, damn you!*'

Men who saw them coming got out of their way. Others, who'd been hovering nearby as if tempted to join in the fighting, were pulled backwards and when they saw who it was, made no protest. Finally there

was just a small group, rolling about and yelling. Even
as Eli watched, one of the ringleaders deliberately
grabbed a bystander's legs and dragged him down so
that he had to struggle to save himself from being
bashed. Another of the fighters did the same to a
second man.

'They're doing it deliberately,' Eli said. '*Get away
to the front of the room!*' he yelled at the top of his
voice, gesturing to the bystanders, and such was his
presence that men did as he asked, shuffling past him,
some with regretful glances back over their shoulders.

He picked up a stool and moved forward. Then as
one of the ringleaders rolled towards him and grabbed
his leg, brought it down on the man's head. 'Someone
keep an eye on this one, don't let him leave!' he shouted
to the bystanders. 'There'll be free beer for the ones
who help me.'

Two men stepped forward with alacrity and
dragged the semi-conscious man aside, but even as
they did so, one of the other trouble-makers surged
to his feet, glaring at Eli, then launched himself towards
him.

Bram, who'd been circling the group, put out a
foot and tripped him, then left him to Eli and grabbed
another of the fighters by the collar, hauling him off
his victim. Although the man was big, Bram dealt
with him easily, punching him on the jaw and sending
him flying, yelling, 'Someone keep hold of him!'

Within minutes all was quiet, with the group who'd
caused the trouble struggling against enthusiastic
captors eager to earn free beer, while other customers

who'd joined in the fighting stood sheepishly to one side.

Eli looked round. 'Who saw what happened?'

No one seemed eager to step forward and explain how the fight had begun. Men avoided his eyes, shuffled their feet and edged away. He looked at the four men who were struggling, seeing the small burn marks on their skin that you got in the engineering works in certain jobs.

Bram went to another man who looked familiar. 'Jez Verley! Older and uglier than ever. When did you come back to Hedderby?'

Jez glowered at him.

'And who paid you to do this?'

Jez crossed his arms and shut his mouth firmly.

Eli looked at Bram. 'I can guess who caused this, can't you?' Then he turned to the bystanders who'd got involved. 'If you ever let yourselves get dragged into a fight in here again, I'll ban you from this pub.'

'We won't!' one said hastily. 'It just sort of happened.'

'No, it didn't. Someone set it up deliberately, wanted to cause a disturbance.'

There was a voice by the door and he turned to see the new constable making his way across the room.

'Complaint about a disturbance, sir.' He looked round in puzzlement. 'They said the whole pub was in an uproar.'

'We don't allow uproars in here,' Eli said. 'As you can see, we stopped it before it had got beyond a few men. These four are the ones who started it, if you want to arrest anyone.'

The young constable's face lit up. 'The sergeant said to make an example. Is there someone who can give evidence in court about these?'

But no one stepped forward, and when his gaze fell on them men shook their heads and shuffled back into the crowd.

'I'm afraid I wasn't here when it began,' Eli said. 'Though I saw them deliberately dragging bystanders into the fight.'

The constable looked disappointed. 'I think it'll just have to be a warning, then. Names, please.'

None of the men spoke.

'This one's Jez Verley,' Bram said. 'He doesn't usually live in Hedderby these days and he fights for a living. He's not going to be allowed inside this pub again, nor are the others. Right, Eli?'

'Right.'

The constable nodded approval. 'And who are these three?'

A voice from the back, disguised, supplied one of the names, then another high falsetto voice added, 'Pearing works at Stott's.'

With the help of the bystanders, Eli and Bram frog-marched the four of them to the door.

'Tell Mr Stott I'll be on the watch from now on,' Eli said quietly in Pearing's ear.

'Don't know what you mean.'

'Oh, I think you do.'

He went back in to find Bram talking easily to the

constable while the drinkers helped the potmen tidy up the tables and chairs that had been sent flying. When the constable had left, Eli raised his voice and called, 'I want to thank those who came forward to help and offer them a drink or two.' He looked scornfully at a man who hadn't.

The man bowed his head and turned away, but later made a chance to talk quietly to Eli and explain, 'Mr Stott sent them four to cause trouble, I'd swear to it, but I daren't speak out if I want to keep my job.'

'Go back and lick his boots, then. What if he tells you to kill someone? Will you do that, too?'

'Nay, he'd never. And I wouldn't.'

'Don't be too sure. Next time, at least send me a warning.' Eli walked away. He sympathised with the man, who no doubt had a wife and children depending on his wage, but he wasn't having the Dragon's licence put at risk.

'We haven't seen the last of this,' he said to Bram later as they were closing the pub.

'No. I'd better send out word to the lads that I may need help. I think you and I should plan on spending some money to keep this place well guarded.'

'Damn Stott!'

All three of them went to bed worried about what the man was going to try next. They had no doubt Athol Stott wouldn't give in easily, even though the law was on their side.

Carrie came in next morning to be greeted by Eli

with a smacking kiss that made Bonny cackle with laughter and point one pudgy finger at her.

'You'll need to get home early and change into something better than this, my girl. We have to see the parson this afternoon about getting married.'

'Oh.'

'Aren't you pleased?'

'About getting married, yes, but not about seeing the parson. He always looks down his nose at folk like me.'

'I promise not to let him eat you. What is it? There's something else worrying you?'

'It's the clothes for getting married in. Nev takes my money and – well, I don't have any nice enough clothes.'

'I'll buy you some then.'

She shook her head. 'No.'

'If we're going to be married anyway—'

She shook her head even more vigorously. 'No. You're not buying my wedding clothes. I'll think of something.' She had the money with Essie, but if she used that, Nev would know she'd kept it back – unless she said it had been provided by Eli.

She hurried home and managed to catch Nev before he had his afternoon nap. Well, he and her mother called it a nap, but everyone knew what they were doing. 'Me and Eli are seeing the parson this afternoon,' she said breathlessly. 'So I have to change my clothes.' She put the two shillings down on the table. 'And I have a problem, need your advice.'

'Oh?' Nev pocketed the money then looked at her, seeing her hesitating. 'Well, come on, what is it?'

'I need something better than this to get married in.' She spread her hands and stared down at herself.

There was silence. Raife winked at her but said nothing. Nev scowled down at the table, then across at his wife.

'Eli won't mind what you're wearing,' Jane said comfortably. 'Then after you're wed, he can buy you some new clothes. He's got plenty of money.'

Nev bristled with indignation. 'I'm not having him thinking I can't afford to clothe my family!'

Behind his son's back Raife put a finger to his lips in a shushing gesture and Carrie kept quiet.

Nev let out an aggrieved sigh. 'We'll have to find you something. Put your best things on for this afternoon. They'll have to do. If you're back before I let the lodgers in, we can go and buy you some clothes later. If not, we'll go tomorrow.' He scowled at his wife. '*Your* family is costing me a fortune.'

Raife said mildly, 'But they do help out here, so you don't have to bring anyone in to clean and cook for you.'

'There is that,' Nev allowed.

'And they're a nice bunch,' his father added. 'A pleasure to have around.'

Jane beamed at him.

Carrie had a sudden idea. 'Mrs Latimer's got some clothes in her attic. She gives them to poor people. She's got a blue skirt and jacket that fitted me lovely, but weren't hard-wearing enough for every day. Maybe she'd let me buy them and give her some money for the poor? She likes helping people. I could ask Essie.'

Nev nodded. 'Good idea.'

Three hours later Carrie came bursting into the house with a huge bundle. 'I went round to Mrs Latimer's after we'd been to see the parson. I got the blue skirt and all sorts of other things, and she says a guinea will pay for it all.' She looked at Nev.

He winced but said nothing except, 'I'm not paying out till I see what I'm buying.'

Carrie spread out the clothes, blushing a little at having the underclothing arranged for his inspection.

He fingered each and every item, his lips moving, then smiled at her. 'You did well there. Couldn't have bought this lot for a guinea at old Heegan's second-hand clothes shop, even if he'd had such nice stuff in.'

Everyone relaxed.

Funny, Carrie thought. She'd not expected Nev Linney to be like this. It was almost as if he really was their father, the way he behaved. And she suspected that he liked having them living there because he'd been lonely before. Who'd ever have thought it of a man with his reputation for meanness and keeping himself to himself?

She was still smiling as she went to bed that night. Her sisters had tried on her clothes and then they'd had a sing-song with Raife playing as usual. She'd miss that when she was married, miss her sisters too, even miss Ted, who wasn't such a pest when he wasn't hungry all the time.

If only she could be sure Eli really wanted to marry her, wasn't just doing it to get the money.

# 22

The parson looked at the two couples before him and sighed. He didn't refuse to marry anyone, whether they were a regular attender or not, on the principle that it was better to marry them than to let them live in sin, but really, Miss Beckett should have known better than to marry an Irishman. The parson had no time for the Irish, none at all, and always ignored that priest of theirs when he passed him in the street.

As for the other couple, *she* had hands like a washerwoman, and her mother, who had come with her, was pregnant. A woman of that age! It was shocking. In his opinion women should keep to the house when they were in that condition, but no, this one was flaunting her big belly in the street, seemed to have no shame about it at all. And the woman's husband didn't seem to see anything amiss. Well, what could you expect of a man who kept a common lodging house?

Just as he was about to begin the marriage ceremony the door at the back of the church opened and a small woman with white hair crept in, looking around her as if terrified. Not a parishioner. By her side was another hefty young fellow who closely resembled this Abraham Heegan whom he was about to join in matrimony to Miss Beckett.

Bram turned round, saw his mother hesitating at the back next to Michael, and left Joanna's side to hurry over and take her hands. 'Mam!'

'I still don't approve of this,' she threw at him, crossing herself with another nervous glance round. 'But I'll not have it said I abandoned you, son.'

He bent to plant a smacking big kiss on her cheek. 'You've made my day brighter.' He turned to Michael. 'Thanks for bringing her. Come and sit at the front and we'll get started.'

He led them forward and introduced them to Joanna, ignoring the parson's furious expression. Then he saw them into a pew, took his place beside Joanna, who squeezed his hand sympathetically, and nodded to the sour-faced old cleric to continue.

The man gabbled through the marriage ceremony so quickly it was over before they could blink, and Joanna and Bram suddenly found themselves husband and wife. Then the clergyman summoned Carrie and Eli out to the front and repeated the procedure just as quickly, after which he hurried them through to sign the register. When given his fees, he counted the money as if he expected to be short changed before vanishing back into the vestry without a further word.

It was left to Eli to smile round and say, 'Well, he didn't waste time, did he?' Still smiling, he led the way outside, let Bram introduce him to his mother and said, 'We've got a bite to eat at the Dragon, if you'll join us there?' He saw her hesitate and added,

'It's in a private room, Mrs Heegan, not in the pub itself. Please come.' Before she could refuse he set off with Carrie on his arm.

The two of them got there before everyone else because Jane couldn't walk quickly. Eli was able to swing his bride into his arms and kiss her soundly. Carrie sagged against him in a way that said she wasn't unaffected by his touch and he smiled at her. He was looking forward to tonight. He just wished she was looking a bit happier. 'Are you all right?'

'Yes. Yes, of course I am.' But the speed of the ceremony and the parson's unfriendliness had upset her. It seemed like an omen somehow. Only she didn't want to talk about that now.

When they went into the snug, she busied herself taking the damp cloths off the pies and cakes, and Eli went to draw beers for the gentlemen while she made tea for the ladies.

It was surely the strangest collection of wedding guests ever assembled, he thought as he sat everyone down and called for silence. 'I want to propose a toast,' he announced, 'so if you'll raise your glasses or teacups . . .'

Raife stood up. 'Nay, lad! It's not for a bridegroom to do that. I'm Carrie's step-grandfather, and it's my privilege.' He turned to the guests, 'I'd like you all to drink the health of the two couples and wish them long and happy married lives.' When he raised his glass of beer, everyone followed suit.

Nev smiled and nodded, but didn't say much. He took the opportunity to have a good look round the snug, though, and even peeped into the kitchen, pleased to see how big this place was.

The guests didn't stay long, but Bram was able to escort his mother to the door and have a quiet word with her. 'You'll never know how much it meant to me that you came today, Mam. And once you get to know Joanna, you'll like her, I know.'

She reached up to pat his cheek. 'I'm not giving up trying to bring you back into the fold, mind. And for a heathen, your wife seems a decent enough woman, though she's a bit old for you. You'd better start having children straight away because she's five and twenty if she's a day.'

He could only smile at that left-handed compliment. 'Yes, Mam.' He watched her and Michael walk away and felt a suspicious moisture in his eyes. When he felt someone slip an arm through his, he turned to Joanna. 'How are you feeling, love?'

'Surprised. It's all happened so quickly.'

'Well, for a heathen, you're doing all right.' He smiled at her expression then put on a thick Irish accent and added, 'Though she did admit you seem "daicent enough" for a heathen.'

Joanna chuckled.

As they turned to go back inside, he murmured in her ear, 'I could do without the pub to run tonight. Make sure you're not too tired when we get to bed.' And laughed at the bright colour that flooded her cheeks.

As they went into the snug, Eli bent over Carrie to whisper something similar and another bride blushed a fiery red.

★

It seemed a very long evening to Carrie. To her delight, her sisters came to the side door of the pub to wish her happiness, and she took them into the kitchen.

'I wish I could have been there,' Marjorie said, 'but I'd have lost my job if I'd tried to take any more time off.'

'Aren't you going to show us your room?' Dora asked. 'I've never been upstairs in a pub before.'

'It's only rooms, same as anywhere else.' Carrie led the way upstairs. 'There. This is where Eli and I'll be sleeping.'

But it was a big bedroom compared to what they'd known when they lived in Throstle Lane, and it had proper furniture, a bed, chest of drawers and big wardrobe.

Then they tramped downstairs again and she gave them all a piece of cake to celebrate her wedding. It didn't make it seem any more real, though, she thought as she waved them goodbye. She ought to feel different, surely, now she was a married woman? Or was that only after you were bedded? She wasn't looking forward to that, for all her mother said it was the best part of being married, because she didn't want any children yet. She wished she and Eli had had time to talk about such things, but they'd been so busy they'd hardly said a word to one another since she agreed to marry him.

At last the pub closed and they cleared up quickly. Joanna and Bram went up to bed first, leaving Eli to see the potmen out. He came back yawning. 'You all right, love?' he asked Carrie.

She nodded. 'A bit tired.'

'Me too.'

When they were in the bedroom she was suddenly paralysed with nerves and couldn't move, let alone take off her clothes.

He looked at her shrewdly. 'I'm not going to hurt you.'

'I know. But I feel – a bit strange.'

His face crinkled into a smile. 'Come here and give me a hug, woman. After all, we've been married for several hours now.'

But he had to walk across the room and take her in his arms because she only stood there, staring at him, her eyes huge and frightened-looking. 'Eh, what am I going to do with you? You're shaking.'

'It's all happened so quickly.'

He wanted her very much, but it seemed to him that she wasn't ready, so he kissed her on the cheek and gave her a little push towards the bed. 'I'm just nipping down for a drink of water. You get yourself to bed. I won't be long.'

In another bedroom at the far end of the upper floor, Bram twirled Joanna round and smiled at her. 'At last! I thought the evening would never end.' He drew her into his arms and began to kiss her, confidently but gently.

She put her arms round his neck and gave herself up to this mystery of how a man loved a woman. Oh, she knew more or less what to expect, of course she did, but she didn't know what it'd feel like or whether she'd do it right.

'You're as stiff as a board!' he said, holding her at arm's length. 'Get yourself undressed and we'll have a bit of a cuddle first. I like to hold a woman in my arms and kiss her before I love her. He saw her hesitate and added, 'I'll take a walk downstairs, shall I, while you get ready for bed?'

She smiled at him shyly. 'Thank you, Bram.'

He met Eli in the kitchen and pulled a wry face. 'Is yours undressing too?'

'Yes.'

'Happened in a bit of a rush, didn't it?' He looked at the clock. 'I'll give her two more minutes then I'm upstairs again.'

Eli followed him soon after.

When Bram went into the bedroom this time he found Joanna sitting up in bed brushing her hair. He smiled across at her. 'You've lovely hair. Why do you screw it into a knot like that?'

'To keep the customers away from me.'

He went across and picked up a strand, running it through his fingers, seeing her shiver at his touch. Hiding a smile, he took off his clothes, blew out the candle and got into bed.

'I'm a bit nervous,' she whispered.

'I'm not, darlin'. You're not my first woman, but you'll be my last, and I'll make sure you enjoy it too.' Using every ounce of skill he'd learned over the years, he began to caress her, rejoicing at her rapid response to his touch.

Afterwards she lay in his arms and said wonderingly, 'I didn't expect to enjoy it.'

'You'll enjoy it even more next time, I promise.'

'Good.' She snuggled against him and was soon asleep.

He lay there a little longer then let himself slide into sleep, comforted by the knowledge that Declan and one of his cousins were keeping watch outside. He and Eli intended to make sure Stott didn't interrupt their wedding night.

When Eli went back to the bedroom, Carrie was lying there with the covers pulled up to her chin, still looking rigid and ill at ease. He blew out the candle and slipped out of his clothes, putting on a nightshirt before getting into bed beside her.

'Look, love, we can wait a day or two, if you like? We're both tired tonight and we've got years ahead of us for bed play.' She lay there quiet and still, not answering, so he asked again, 'Carrie, love?'

She turned to him in the darkness. 'Can we really wait a day or two? Won't you mind? My dad didn't like to wait even an hour when he wanted Mam. It was embarrassing sometimes.'

Not for the first time, Eli mentally cursed her father. 'Well, I do want you, Carrie, but I can wait till you feel right about this too.'

She let out such a sigh of relief he felt sure he was doing the right thing. It was damned hard on a man, though, and he knew he'd not sleep well with her soft body beside his in the bed and affecting him physically. 'You get to sleep, love.'

In only a minute or two she was breathing deeply

beside him. Eli smiled wryly in the darkness then tried to get comfortable without touching her.

It took him a long time to fall asleep.

In the large house behind the engineering works, Athol Stott drank his way steadily through the evening. It was about midnight when someone tapped on the window of his library, which was a room where some books were kept but were never opened. More important, it was here he kept a supply of port and brandy for times like tonight. He opened the window and looked out at the man he'd employed to upset the newly-weds.

'Well, did you do as I asked?'

'Couldn't, sir. They'd got men on watch.'

'Damn!' Athol hurled the glass into the hearth, watching it splinter into shards and fragments. He looked at his bully boy. 'We'll leave them for a while, lull them into thinking I've given up. Then I'll surprise them.' He took out some coins and pressed them into the outstretched hand, then closed the window.

The man went to rejoin his companion. 'He didn't blow up, at least. Sounded like he'd been drinking, voice all slurred.'

'I don't like doing this.'

'Neither do I. But if we don't do as he asks, we'll lose our jobs. I'd like that even less.'

The following day Jem Harding brought his men back to work on the music room and to Eli's relief the weather was clement enough for them to finish the new frontage. With Bram beside him and the two women doing most of the work in the pub, he found they were able to get far more done than when his uncle had been alive.

The main change Eli insisted on was that Carrie wasn't to scrub out the pub any more. He found another woman to work with Bonny, and left Carrie and Joanna to divide the housework and other chores as they saw fit.

It was a week before Eli tried to woo Carrie again, but by then she had her monthly courses. No sooner had she recovered from that than he developed a head cold, something that was unusual for him. As he admitted to himself, a sneezing man who spent half the night blowing his nose was not going to be an attractive bed partner.

It seemed as if fate was against their consummating the marriage. And Carrie still stiffened in alarm if he so much as put an arm round her. Eli wasn't the sort to force himself upon a woman, whether she was his wife or not.

It was a puzzle to him how to deal with this, but he had the pub and everyone's safety to worry about so couldn't take the time to sort things out yet. But he would, he definitely would.

# 23

A month passed, an uneasy period for the occupants of the Dragon. A rainy spell proved that the roof and walls of the music room were watertight, which was a good thing because the weather was getting really cold now, ice rimming puddles in the early morning, breath steaming in the chill air, and those who entered the pub making straight for the fires to stretch out their chilled hands to the blaze.

Eli breathed a sigh of relief that they'd made so much progress and watched with satisfaction as Jem Harding's men worked on the inside of the new room.

'Surely Stott's given up hope of getting this place now?' he said one day to Bram as they were standing outside inspecting the day's progress. 'I heard he's negotiating with a farmer up beyond the engineering works to buy a field.'

'Where did you hear that?'

'Two men who work at Stott's were talking about it in the pub last night.'

Bram frowned. 'Very convenient they should talk about it in front of you, don't you think?'

Eli shrugged. 'They didn't know I was standing

behind them. Look, I'm not going to act carelessly, but Stott hasn't actually done anything to us, has he?'

'Even if he has to give up trying to buy this place, that man won't give up on getting his revenge.'

'It sounds like a melodrama I saw in London once. Madman seeking his revenge.'

'That's not so far from the truth,' Bram insisted.

'Surely he has better things to do than chase after us?'

'Look, you've only been in the town a few months. I've lived here most of my life. No one holds a grudge like Athol Stott. Everyone knows of folk who've left town because they got on the wrong side of him, even before his father died. I think we should continue to pay two watchmen at night.'

'Perhaps only one?'

'If you get rid of one, I'll hire a second myself.'

Eli stared at him, then pursed his lips and shrugged. 'We'll go on as we are, then, for the time being.'

But no attempts were made to damage the place, and indeed the whole town seemed quieter than usual. They were not the only ones to comment on that. James Marker remarked upon it several times but his view was that 'summat's brewing'.

Then Bonny, usually so sunny-natured, turned up at work looking unhappy. Carrie, who was very fond of her, saw her stop a few times to frown, as if something was worrying her, and went across to ask if everything was all right.

Bonny hesitated then pulled her aside. 'There was a man standing outside our house last night. And other nights. I didn't like him. He saw me looking out of the window and waved a knife at me. I fetched my sister, but he'd gone by then an' she said I was imagining it. But I wasn't. I wasn't.'

'Does Bram know about this?'

'No. She said not to tell anyone.'

After some consideration Carrie went to tell him what Bonny had said.

Bram's face grew grim. 'If anyone lays so much as one fingertip on my aunt, I'll kill him.'

Later he passed news of this on to Eli, who was inclined to make light of it.

'She could have been mistaken.'

'My aunt doesn't make mistakes about things like that. She's learned to keep her eyes open, because some folk like to torment her. I think I'll nip round to my mother's before it gets busy tonight to check that my family are keeping their eyes open and their doors locked.'

When he didn't come back Joanna began to worry, but they were so busy she could do nothing about it, and anyway, Bram could usually take care of himself.

Then, just before closing time, two men came into the Dragon, supporting Bram between them. His head was bleeding and he seemed dazed.

Joanna dropped her wiping rag on the counter and ran across. 'What happened?'

'Someone hit him with a bloody great rock, missus,' one of the men said. 'If we hadn't happened round the corner just then, who knows what they'd have done? They ran off.'

'Did you see who they were?'

The men avoided her eyes and one said loudly, 'No, couldn't tell who they were. Too dark to see 'em properly.'

'Bring him through to the kitchen.' She led the way, pushing a couple of men aside in her impatience to tend her husband.

As they lowered him on to a chair, Bram opened his eyes, suddenly seeming fully aware. He looked at his rescuers and said quietly, 'You must have seen something, lads.'

They exchanged glances, then one muttered, 'It were them two new men Stott's set on. But don't tell anyone we said that.'

'No, I won't. Thanks.'

Joanna spoke briskly, 'Tell the potmen to give you a couple of drinks. I'm really grateful for your help.'

'Glad we come along in time, missus.'

She poured hot water into a bowl and began to clean Bram's head, asking quietly, 'Were you dazed when you came in?'

'No. I was pretending to be worse than I really was.'

'Why?'

'To make them think I'm out of action.'

She stared at him in dismay.

'Don't worry about me, love. I've a hard head. Ouch!' He winced as she cleaned up the ragged cut and when she'd finished took hold of her hand and looked at her very seriously. 'Stott won't give up, so we have to catch him out.'

Eli poked his head through the door. 'How is he?'

Bram smiled. 'I'll live.'

'Seems like you were right.'

'I wish I weren't. I'm sure this is just the start. Eli . . .'

'Yes?'

'If we pretend I'm worse hurt than I am, it'll give me a bit of freedom to get out and about after dark.'

Eli stood thinking about this, head on one side. 'Better get Dr Latimer in if you're going to do that, then they'll be convinced. I'm sure he'll not give you away if you explain. Carrie can go round to his house in the morning and ask him to call in.'

The following morning Joanna sent word to the police that her husband had been attacked. When the young constable came to find out the details, he found the doctor just leaving and Bram lying in bed, head heavily bandaged.

After listening to a description of what had happened, the constable screwed up his face in deep concentration. 'Does anyone have a grudge against you?'

'Aye. Athol Stott.'

The young man sighed. 'Do you have proof of this?'

'Of course I don't.'

'Then you'd best not make accusations.'

'Everyone in town knows who's behind it.'

The constable moved a step closer and lowered his voice. 'I'll mention it to the sergeant and he'll bear it in mind. That's all we can do without proof, sir. Got powerful friends, Mr Stott has. The sergeant says we're always to tread carefully with him.'

Once the man left, Joanna looked at her husband. 'I'm worried about you.'

He held out his arms and she went to sit on the edge of the bed and nestle up to him.

Eli walked in then backed out again hurriedly. He felt jealous of how close the other two were. Carrie looked at him so apprehensively each night that he still hadn't had the heart to insist they make love, but maybe he'd talk to her tonight, try to coax her a little.

But just as they were getting ready for bed there was the sound of glass breaking downstairs and, with a muttered curse, he dragged his trousers up again and ran downstairs.

He and Bram found one of the watchmen unconscious with a big bump on the back of his head.

'Looks like the storm is about to break,' Eli said, his expression tight and angry.

The following afternoon Bram received a visit from his brother Michael. When he'd left, Bram went down to find Eli, speaking to him from the stairs so that he'd not be seen from the pub. 'There's more bad news. You know Jack Casterby?'

Eli looked at him in puzzlement. 'The man who was drowned in the mill reservoir last week?'

'Word is he didn't fall in, but was pushed and held under. The magistrate said it was an accident because there were no marks of violence on the body. But what if Jack was drugged first and was unconscious when he went into the water?'

'You can't mean that?'

'I do. Jack Casterby punched Stott in the face once for ravishing his daughter. Old Mr Stott paid out good money to hush that up, but after his father died Athol used to smile in that nasty way he has every time he passed Casterby in the street.'

Eli thumped one hand into the other. 'How does the fellow get away with it? This is 1845 not 1545. We've got a new police force in Hedderby, for heaven's sake. What are they doing except parading around in their fancy uniforms and ignoring what's going on under their noses?'

Carrie came into the kitchen just then, whisking through the door as if someone was chasing her and shutting it behind her with a bang. She stood with her back against it, panting as if she'd been running.

Eli hurried across to her. 'What's the matter?'

She let him take her in his arms. 'I met Mr Stott in the street and he said –' she shuddered and broke off for a moment, then continued, her voice muffled by his chest '– to enjoy my marriage while I could, because it wouldn't be much fun being a widow.'

'Did anyone else hear him?'

'No one was close enough. He came out of Crookit Walk and strolled past me. He didn't stop or look at me, just spoke quietly as he passed.' She shivered. 'He frightens me, Eli. And if anything happens to you . . .'

He looked across at Bram. 'We're letting him do this, waiting for him to act. It's more than time we

did something about him. I don't know what exactly
yet, but I'm not sitting around and letting him think
he's got the upper hand.'

Neither of them had ever heard Eli speak in quite
that tone, or seen such a grim look on his face. They
were both silent for a minute or two, then Bram said,
'Well, we're together on that, at least.'

When Edmund heard about Jack Casterby, he knew
with sick certainty that his cousin was responsible for
the man's death. He'd also heard about the minor
troubles afflicting the Dragon and its inhabitants and
feared for their safety, too.

'There's nothing you can do,' Faith said.

'There has to be. We can't let this go on. And
there's another thing needs dealing with, and perhaps
more urgently. I met one of the men from the works
tramping across the tops on Sunday morning. He
says the steam engine is sounding really rough and
Turner's had to put more weights on the governor to
keep it working.'

'But—'

Edmund began pacing up and down. 'It's no use
trying to talk to Athol. He won't listen to me.' He
frowned in thought. 'I know! I'll walk into town and
listen to the engine from outside the back of the works.
I'll be able to get some idea of how bad a state it's in
by that. I know better than anyone how it should sound.'

'Edmund, no! Don't go. *Please!*'

He kissed her gently on the forehead. 'I have to,
love. Men's lives are at stake. I can't sit by and do

nothing. But I will take Robbie with me.'

The two men went the very next morning, planning to arrive around eleven o'clock, when the steam engine would be flat out and the lane at the back of the works most likely deserted.

'It seems strange to come here again,' Robbie said.

Edmund put his forefinger to his lips in warning, then closed his eyes and stood listening. He knew every thump and hiss of that old engine and could tell at once that it was ailing badly. 'Turner's thrashing it to death. That engine won't last much longer at this rate.'

'If you've finished, we'd better move on,' Robbie said.

'What? Oh, yes. Let's go into town and take a stroll round before we go back. I'll buy Faith some bonbons. She's got a craving for sweet things.'

'Could I call in and see my sister Carrie?' Robbie asked. 'Just for a minute or two.'

'Of course.'

When they got to the Dragon, Edmund went to Marker's for the bonbons, then strolled down Market Street, lost in thought.

Athol came out of a building there, saw his cousin and stepped backwards again, his face slipping into that predator's smile.

Edmund was a fool to come into town on his own. He'd regret that.

As soon as his cousin had walked on, Athol left the building and slipped up through the back streets to return to the works.

★

Carrie heard footsteps and looked up to see Robbie standing in the kitchen doorway. Beaming, she went to hug him, then stood back to study his face. 'You look really well.'

'I've cut down on the drinking and I'm eating better than I ever have in my life before. I'm enjoying what I'm doing, too. Mr Edmund is teaching me so much.' He studied her in turn. 'You look well yourself. Married life must suit you.'

She felt heat rise in her cheeks and hoped he hadn't noticed. Everything about her new life suited her except what happened in their bedroom. Or rather what didn't happen. She wasn't certain what she wanted, but the distance that had grown between her and Eli worried her. She longed to talk to him, really talk, but they were both so tired at night and she knew she was still very stiff and unwelcoming in the bedroom. Every day she vowed to smile at him, make him feel more welcome, reach out and cuddle him even. But she couldn't bring herself to do it. Or else he delayed coming to bed and she fell asleep waiting for him.

Robbie stayed chatting to her for a few minutes, telling her about his new life, then said he must be going. Outside he found Mr Edmund chatting to Eli, who was gesturing widely and had a bright, alive expression on his face as he talked about his music room, which was nearly ready for the furniture to be moved in.

Edmund smiled at his employee. 'Ah, there you are. How's your sister?'

'She's looking well.'

They set off walking back to Out Rawby. It was looking like rain so they moved briskly to keep warm.

When they were nearly there, two men with their faces covered by mufflers jumped out from behind a wall and attacked them. The two didn't say a word but lashed out at them with fists and feet, and although Robbie was able to defend himself, as usual Edmund fared badly at the hands of his assailant.

Seeing his master knocked to the ground, Robbie redoubled his efforts and managed to punch his opponent so hard the man swayed dizzily. Clouting him again as hard as he could, Robbie leaped forward to drag the other man away from Edmund, yelling to his master to get up and run away. The man he'd knocked down grabbed him by his legs from behind and he felt himself falling, then grunted in pain as a heavy boot made contact with his ribs. As he hit the muddy ground he rolled desperately to one side but the foot swung towards him again.

At that moment a large dog leaped over the wall and started barking furiously, the sort of dog used to herd sheep. Through a haze of pain Robbie heard a man's voice yelling orders at the dog, which seized one attacker's arm and would not let go.

By the time the owner of the dog had vaulted over the wall, the first man had set off running back towards Hedderby and the second was trying to follow him, but was unable to shake off the dog. In the scuffle, his muffler had fallen down and Robbie recognised him as one of the new men Athol Stott had brought into the works.

'Let go, boy!' roared their saviour and the dog backed off, still barking a warning.

The man hared down the rutted lane after his companion and was soon hidden from view.

'Thanks,' Robbie panted, pushing himself to his feet and going to help Mr Edmund up.

'What's the world coming to?' the shepherd asked, patting his dog. 'Good boy! I never thought to see folk attacked out here. What were them rogues after?'

'Giving us a beating,' Edmund said. 'I'd stake my life that my cousin set them on to us. Well, I recognised one of the men. He works at Stott's.'

'I saw him too,' Robbie agreed. 'Deversall, they call him.'

The shepherd told his dog to get back to the sheep and the animal leaped the wall and was to be seen rounding them up again. 'Best not use this lane again, sir. It was only chance that I was nearby and saw what was happening.'

Edmund grimaced. 'I need to go into Hedderby sometimes. Dammit, I can't let Athol keep me a prisoner in the village.'

'I'll show you a short cut,' the shepherd offered. 'It goes through two farms, but as long as you keep to the path and shut the gates after you, no one will mind you using it. We don't tell outsiders about it.' He walked with them to the end of the lane and mounted the bank of earth, standing leaning on the dry-stone wall, pointing out the alternative route they could take.

Afterwards the two men limped into the village and

endured Faith's gentle scolding as she and Grania bathed their cuts and bruises.

'I doubt there's anything we can do about that steam engine,' Robbie said as he spooned up a large bowl of hot broth at the kitchen table, sitting next to his master who was applying himself with enthusiasm to another equally large bowl.

'I mentioned it to Eli Beckett. He said he'd spread the word in the pub about how dangerous it now is. I'm also going to send a letter to the magistrate, setting out my fears formally. But if no one does anything, I'll have to take action. I can't bear to think what'll happen if one of the seams goes.'

'Do you think that's wise, sir? Isn't the magistrate a friend of Mr Stott's?'

'Not a friend, no. But they do see one another socially.' He looked at Robbie. 'I can't let men be maimed and injured without trying to do something, I just can't.'

Athol scowled at the two men who had returned to confess that they hadn't managed to harm Edmund seriously. 'Can you do nothing right? My cousin's a weakling. It should have been easy to beat him senseless.'

'Robbie Preston was with him. He knows how to handle hissen, that one does.'

'Damn the man! I'm not having *him* staying in this town, either. Did he recognise you, do you think?'

They hesitated, then one said, 'My muffler come undone when that bloody dog attacked me. Preston knew me.'

'Then you're no further use to me. You're dismissed. I'll give you a couple of pounds to set you on your way. Make sure you get out of town quickly and don't show your face round here again.'

The man threw him a resentful look but said nothing, picking up the coins from the floor, where Athol had contemptuously thrown them.

His companion got back to work without a word, but he was in a foul mood for the rest of the day.

The other men at the works had noticed the two leave and then come back, all during working hours. Mr Stott had sent them off to do something no doubt, but what?

That evening Athol said hardly a word to his wife. While she picked at her food, he ate a hearty dinner in silence, downing a bottle of wine with it. Afterwards he paced up and down the parlour for a few minutes, then with a muttered exclamation went into his library, slamming the door behind him. Pouring himself a glass of port, he began to make plans. He'd had enough of this shilly-shallying. Eli Beckett was going to pay for refusing to sell that land, and pay dearly.

And his cousin was going to be glad to leave Hedderby, him and his whore of a wife. Athol felt furious every time he thought of that woman bearing the same name as himself.

## 24

Carrie walked Bonny home, keeping a careful watch for Mr Stott or any of the men from his works, most of whom she knew by sight. She went on to visit her mother at Linney's and found Jane sitting in the kitchen, looking puffy and pale, with Raife fussing over her.

'She just had a fainting fit,' he explained. 'I tried to send for Dr Latimer but she doesn't want any fuss made.'

Jane scowled at him. 'I've borne ten living children without a doctor's help, an' I'll have this one the same way, thank you very much. Granny Gates is good enough for me.'

Nev came in whistling tunelessly, the sound cutting off instantly when he saw his wife. 'Have you fainted again?' he demanded.

'*Again?*' Carrie asked.

'Yes, she keeps fainting. So that's it!' He glared at Jane. 'We're having the doctor and we're having him now. Carrie lass, will you run round to his house and then stay with her while he examines her? I want to hear exactly what he says.'

'Yes, of course.' She hurried round to Dr Latimer's

house and managed to have a quick word with Essie while she was waiting for him, then stayed with her mother while the doctor examined her.

'I told you not to have any more children, Mrs Linney.' He stood back from the bed and studied her, head on one side, eyes narrowed.

Jane looked up at him mutinously. 'How can you help having childer when you've a husband?'

'By stopping the bed play.'

She gave a scornful sniff. 'What's married life without that?'

'Well, it's too late to be sensible this time, so you'll have to stay in bed from now on. Your heart won't take much activity. It's weakened by all the childbearing.'

'Stay in bed! I'll not do it.'

'You'll do it or die, and the child with you.'

There was silence, then she pleaded, 'At least let me go and sit in the kitchen. I'll go mad on my own up here.'

'I'll discuss it with your husband.'

Jane burst into tears and it took Carrie a long time to calm her.

By the time she went downstairs the doctor had left and Nev and his father were reorganising the parlour as a bedroom for Jane. Carrie couldn't believe how much they'd misjudged Nev Linney or how lucky her mother was to have married him.

If only her own marriage would work out as well! But there felt to be an invisible wall between her and Eli, and events seemed to be conspiring to keep them apart.

★

The following day was Saturday and in the afternoon a lad of about ten slouched into the village asking for Mr Edmund Stott.

Someone pointed to the stone barn. 'He's in there, son.'

The lad knocked on the door, looking round as if terrified of someone following him.

Even after Robbie opened the door and brought him inside, he looked no less scared, his breath coming fast, as if he'd been running, and his eyes darting here and there.

'Got a message for Mr Edmund Stott,' he said.

'He's over there.'

The lad hurried across the room. 'Me dad said to tell you the engine's getten worse. He says they're all feared for their lives an' they beg you to help 'em afore someone gets killed.'

'Who's your father?' Robbie asked.

'Bill Magsey.'

'Did he send you?'

The lad avoided their eyes, nodding as he began to edge towards the door.

'What are you so frightened of?' Edmund asked gently, following him and laying one hand on his shoulder to stop him leaving.

'I'm afraid of Mr Stott catching me. Please, sir, can I go now?'

'Tell me the message again.'

The lad repeated it word for word.

'Did your father say nothing else?'

'No, sir.' The lad suddenly ran for the door and

was out of it before they could stop him.

The two men looked at one another.

'Do you know Bill Magsey and his family?'

Robbie shrugged. 'Not well. He allus kept himself to himself at work. Surly devil, but he did his work properly, at least.' He looked at his master. Are you thinking what I'm thinking?'

Edmund pursed his lips, then said slowly, 'That lad repeated that message word for word, as if he'd learned it by heart. And surely a lad that age wouldn't be quite so terrified of Athol unless . . . ?'

Robbie finished the sentence for him. 'Unless it's a trick. Unless it was Stott who sent him, not his father. Look, why don't you let me go into town later and ask about Bill Magsey and this lad? What I can't understand is why the men from the works would send *his* son with a message.'

'It feels cowardly to let you go alone.'

'If I don't set off till dusk and I stay off Market Street, I reckon I'm not risking much. If there's trouble I can always nip into Linney's or the Dragon. But I think it'd be better if you went home from here before I left, sir, and . . . well, made sure you had a gun handy.'

'Are we jumping at shadows?' But Edmund shook his head and answered his own question. 'No, I don't think we are. Heaven help me, but I believe the worst of Athol now. This could be a trick.'

Two hours later Robbie set off, leaving by the back door of the house, relieved there was a moon just rising to guide him along the short cut through the fields. When he reached Hedderby he went round to a friend's house first and had a quiet chat to him. He left, as he had come, by the back door, slipping down the alley at the rear.

If he'd used the front door and the street he'd have seen nothing, because of the row of houses in between him and the engineering works, but the alley led round to the back of the works, the very place where he and Mr Edmund had listened to the engine.

To his surprise there were lights on in the works and he frowned, wondering what was going on. Everything was usually damped down by this time and locked up for the night.

Robbie hesitated then decided to go and see another friend nearby first. Maybe he would know why someone was there so late. But whatever his friend said, Robbie intended to check the works before he returned to Out Rawby because Mr Edmund would want to know what was going on there. At a guess, it'd be Turner, working on the engine. Even Mr Edmund had had to work late sometimes, because it was a contrary old devil.

But what if it wasn't the engine? What else could be happening there?

In the Dragon, at the busiest time of the evening when everyone was singing along with Raife, a woman came up to the counter and tugged at Carrie's sleeve. 'Your mam's been took badly, love. She's calling out for you. The doctor doesn't think she'll live through the night. Can you come?'

Carrie stared at her in shock, unable to speak for

a moment or two, then stammered, 'Yes. Give me a minute to tell my husband.'

Frantic with worry for her mother, she looked round for Eli, but couldn't see him for the crowd who were enjoying the free and easy session. She could hear Raife begin another tune on the piano, and with a cheer the crowd began singing it. Not daring to wait any longer, she turned to the potman. 'Tell Eli when he comes for a break that I've had to go round to my mother's. She's been taken ill, isn't expected to live.'

'I'm right sorry to hear that, Mrs Beckett.' He nodded, picked up his tray and hurried back into the thirsty crowd.

Carrie followed the woman outside. 'Are you one of her new neighbours?'

'Aye, love. We live just along the road. I help the doctor out sometimes when folk are poorly.'

Just as they were turning up the hill, the woman stepped quickly sideways into a doorway and when the door shut behind her, Carrie guessed instantly that she'd been tricked. She started screaming even before the two men grabbed her. Fighting furiously with nails and feet, she struggled to escape but they threw her to the ground and managed to tie her arms behind her then put a gag into her mouth.

'Stupid bitch!' one of them said. He hauled her to her feet and tried to make her walk, but she let herself drop to the ground again and rolled sideways. The man clouted her across the side of the head, but Carrie still refused to walk, so they picked her up between them and staggered along with her bucking and squirming against them.

Robbie had just returned to check out the back of the engineering works when the men arrived and carried their captive inside. Clouds were passing across the face of the moon so he couldn't see who the woman was, but he could see that she was bound and gagged. He hesitated. No use his going in alone after her. Two men had carried her inside and there were obviously others there as well. He had to go and get help.

Bram!

No longer trying to stay hidden in the shadows, Robbie ran down the hill towards the Dragon, pushing his way inside the brightly lit room and shouting, 'Bram! Where's Bram Heegan?'

Men not involved in the free and easy gaped at him, then someone gestured to where a row of people standing up blocked the view to the music session. 'He's in there, wi' them as can afford an extra three-pence.'

Robbie pushed towards the rope barrier and shoved his way through crowds who complained good-naturedly as they let him pass. He was lucky to find Bram standing nearby with his brothers and explained breathlessly what he'd seen.

Bram told Michael to stay there and Declan to come with them. 'You're sure she was tied up?' he asked as they pushed their way out again.

'Certain.'

'We'd better go and see what they're doing. If Stott is tampering with unwilling lasses again . . .'

'Had we better call the police?' Robbie wondered aloud.

'Not till we see what's going on. Because if I get a chance to punch that sod first, I'm going to take it. He's set men on to threaten my parents *and* he's frightened my Aunt Bonny. I'm not having that.'

During the next interval in the singing, the potman passed on the message to Eli that his wife had been called out to see her mother, who was dying.

Eli stared at him in puzzlement. 'I saw Mrs Linney today and she looked well enough to me.'

'Woman who brought a message said she'd been took bad and Mrs Beckett went out with her. Looked right upset, she did.'

Eli nodded his thanks and stood for a minute, frowning. As Raife came towards them, also taking a break, he waited for the old man and asked, 'When did Jane take ill? Why didn't you tell us?'

'Jane? She's not ill. She were sitting in the kitchen with her feet up eating a piece of cake and laughing about something with our Nev when I left to come here.'

Fear skittered through Eli. 'Some woman brought a message to Carrie that her mother had been taken ill and was dying.'

'Nay, why should anyone do that?'

The two men stared at one another.

'To get hold of my wife and threaten me.' Eli looked round for Bram, knowing he needed help in searching for Carrie. He couldn't see him, so went across to ask Michael where his brother had gone.

Just as Michael had finished explaining, a lad came in with a note for Eli. He tried to slip away through the crowd when he'd handed it to him, but Eli yelled, 'Free beer to the one who stops that lad,' and he was soon brought back, struggling and begging to be let go.

Eli read the note which said only, *'If you value your wife's life, leave the pub on your own and you'll be taken to her.'*

He closed his eyes for a moment, feeling sick with anxiety for Carrie. It had to be Stott. Who else in Hedderby held a grudge against him and wanted something he had? If he went on his own he knew he'd stand no chance of defending her, yet if he took men with him, whoever it was might kill her. He couldn't bear even to think of that.

He became suddenly aware that someone was tugging at his arm and turned to see Joanna.

'What is it?' she asked. 'What's happened?'

He held out the note and she read it quickly, her mouth falling open in shock. 'What are you going to do?'

'Question the lad first.' He went across to the group of men who were holding him. 'Can a couple of you bring him into the kitchen and make sure he doesn't get away?'

As he led the way, the noise increased again behind him, but it wasn't the full-throated joyful sound it had been. Those who had seen Eli Beckett's face as he read the note turned to their companions and began to speculate about what it could have contained, instead of joining in the singing.

In the kitchen Eli asked sternly, 'Who gave you this?'

The lad wriggled in his captors' hands but couldn't get away.

Eli picked up the poker and slammed it into the heart of the fire. 'If you don't tell me, I'll get this poker red hot and burn what I want to know out of you.' He winked at one of the men, but made sure the lad didn't see this. He could no more have carried out his threat than flown to the moon, but he was desperate for information and thought it'd be quickest to frighten it out of the lad.

Eyes goggling, the lad looked from him to the poker. For a minute longer fear of the man who'd sent him held him quiet, then as Eli took hold of the end of the poker, he whimpered.

'Let's see if it's hot enough.'

The lad pulled back against his captors' hands. 'Don't touch me! I'll tell.'

'Go on then. Who gave you the note?'

'It were one of them new men who've come to work for Mr Stott. He told me I were to give it you then run away quick. Said if I let on who'd sent me they'd break my neck.'

One of the men holding him asked, 'What's in the note, Mr Beckett?'

'Read it to him, Joanna,' Eli said. He pulled the poker out and studied its glowing end. 'I think it's hot enough.'

'But I've told you all I know,' the lad wailed. 'I don't know any more.'

'There are other things I want to know yet. Is this the only errand Mr Stott's sent you on?' He waved the hot poker around in front of the boy's face.

'No. He sent me out with a message for Mr Edmund.'

'Another note?'

'No. A message. I had to learn it, an' he hit me when I didn't get it right at first.'

'Tell me.'

The lad gabbled the message again. 'Me dad said to tell you the engine's getten worse. He says they're all feared for their lives an' they beg you to help 'em afore someone gets killed.'

'That engine's no worse than it was a day or two ago,' one of the men holding the lad protested. 'Though it's not in good heart, anyone can tell that. Turner's thrashing it, forcing it to work when it should be repaired, and we all know it can't last much longer. Why should he have sent that message to Mr Edmund?'

'I don't know, but I mean to find out.' Eli put the poker down and went into the pantry, coming out with a coiled clothes line. 'Tie him up with this. Joanna, you keep an eye on him till I get back.'

'Where are you going?' she asked. 'You can't go out on your own, Eli.'

'I have to, for Carrie's sake.' He looked across at the men. 'But I'm hoping you and some of your friends will come after me.'

'Aye. We'll do that all reet,' one said at once. 'I know a few as are sick to death of what's going on at Stott's.

And when they find out he's tekken Carrie Beckett, as nice a lass as you'd find anywhere, they'll not hesitate to come an' help you rescue her.'

'Thank you. Send a man to follow me and find out where they take me, but I bet it'll be to Stott's. It'll be nice and quiet at the works now.' Eli turned and left the kitchen, walking through the crowd without his usual banter, his face grim, worry for Carrie's safety sitting heavily in his guts. Stott had had her for over an hour. What had he done to her in that time?

If he'd hurt her in any way, Eli would make him regret it.

Robbie, Bram and Declan moved carefully through the shadows, taking the back alleys they all knew so well and even then walking as quietly as they could. There was no light showing at the front of the works, but as Robbie led the way round to the back they could see light shining from the engine-room windows. He pushed open the little gate at the rear and found it unlocked, so they went inside.

As they drew nearer to the side door they heard men's voices from inside. Then the back gate creaked behind them and they were trapped between two groups. Robbie glanced quickly round and dragged his companions to one side, shoving them behind a pair of huge water butts that collected the run-off from the roof and himself crouching behind a pile of iron parts.

The man who'd just arrived walked purposefully

towards the rear door of the works. As he passed them his shadow played along the butts like a monster in a child's tale come to catch naughty children.

When he'd entered the building, Robbie stepped out of his hiding place and began to follow him. Before Bram and Declan could join him, there was a yell and two men ran from the direction of the gate to hurl themselves on Robbie. The noise brought Stott back to the door so Bram dragged his brother back into the shadows.

Robbie was soon overpowered and dragged inside.

'We need more men,' Bram whispered. 'Go back to the Dragon and fetch help.'

'What about you?' Declan whispered.

'I'll keep an eye on what they're doing. Take care how you go out, and hurry back!'

'All right.'

Declan made more noise leaving than Bram liked but luckily had gone out of earshot down the back alley before the two men came out again and went to stand near the gate, clearly keeping watch.

When the men took Carrie into a building they set her on her feet, laughing as she tried to kick them.

'She's a fierce little devil, isn't she?' one commented admiringly. 'I'd like to have the taming of her.'

'He said not to touch her,' the other reminded him.

'I can look, can't I?'

Turner poked his head out of the engine room. 'I need one of you to help me in here.'

'Haven't you got that damned engine fixed yet? You've been working on it all day.'

'It's fiddly work and the engine's old.' Turner scowled at it. He knew, everyone knew, that if he didn't fix it, Mr Stott would bring in someone else to do the job and he'd be out of work. But the way Turner was feeling at the moment he wasn't sure he cared. His hand was still stinging from where a sudden spurt of steam had caught and scalded him earlier, so that the flesh looked raw and blistered. And he didn't really know what to do next, was just trying things.

Each of the two men looked at the other.

'He'll help you,' one said quickly. 'I'll keep an eye on the woman.'

Turner looked at him. 'Bring her in here with you. I might need two of you. Her hands are tied. If you rope her to one of those bars in the wall, she won't be able to get away.'

Carrie fought every inch of the way across the room, managing to make one man curse as she scraped her shoe down the front of his shin. He raised his hand to clout her and the other man grabbed it and held him back.

'He said she wasn't to be damaged.'

'She deserves damaging, that bitch does. Shall I put the gag back?'

'Only if she makes a noise.' He looked at her. 'Up to you, lass. Keep quiet or we'll stuff a rag into your mouth again.'

Carrie kept quiet. She was roped to a bar in the

wall that held spare metal rods and other pieces of equipment safely upright and could only stand there helplessly, watching what they were doing. It was hot and the air felt damp. Soon sweat was trickling down her face. She didn't like the feel of this place or the expression on the face of the man tinkering with the engine, but most of all she didn't like the metal monster that was hissing and thumping in a ragged rhythm at the other side of the room.

When Mr Stott walked in she hoped for a minute he'd come to release her, to berate his men for capturing her, but he smiled when he saw her. He took two steps towards her but the noise of shouting outside made him turn and stride out through the door. When he came back again he was followed by two men dragging her brother Robbie with them. He looked dazed and his upper lip was cut and swelling fast. She tugged against the ropes holding her, feeling helpless. Robbie didn't seem fully aware of what was happening around him.

'What the hell was *he* doing here? He must have followed her.' Athol turned on the two men who'd brought Carrie. 'Didn't I tell you to make sure you weren't followed?'

'We did. No one come up the hill behind us, I swear. He must have been near the place already. Maybe he'd come to damage it out of spite. Should be had up for that, don't you think, sir? Easy to tell the magistrate we caught him breaking a window.'

Stott stared at Robbie through narrowed eyes. 'Tie him up for now. I'll decide what to do with him later.

Now, you two go back on watch outside and make sure no one else gets into the yard without you seeing them. When Beckett arrives, bring him straight to me.'

He flung himself down on a chair and watched Turner for a minute or two. 'Haven't you got that damned engine fixed yet?'

'It takes time, sir, and I don't have all the tools, keep having to improvise. But it sounds better, don't you think?'

'How the hell should I know how it sounds? I'm not an engineer.'

All four men were now ignoring Carrie and Robbie, but when she risked asking him how he was, the nearest man turned round and snapped, 'Shut up, unless you want us to gag you again.'

She fell silent, worrying not only about her brother but about her husband. If they expected Eli, they must be using her to force him to come here. Why? What did Stott want from him?

Well, that was easy. The land next to the pub.

They could use her to force Eli to do as they wished. But how would they persuade Joanna to sign away her half?

That was explained a few minutes later when another pair of men dragged in a terrified Bonny, who was moaning and weeping.

'Shut the idiot up!' Stott snapped.

One man back-handed Bonny across the face and yelled at her to be quiet. After a loud scream of shock and pain, she managed to hold back her weeping to snuffles and whimpers.

'We'll have quite a row of them soon,' Stott remarked with another smug smile.

There was the sound of the outer door opening again. Everyone turned round to see who it was.

# 25

Edmund fidgeted about the house, then sighed and admitted to himself he simply couldn't stay at home and let Robbie run all the risks. He insisted on Faith and Grania going next door while he was away, and his gruff old neighbour immediately got out his blunderbuss and vowed to 'pepper' anyone who tried to get into his house. Mr Olworth insisted on sending his 'lad' with Edmund to show him the short cut. The lad in question was fifty if he was a day but seemed quite happy to tramp into town on a chilly winter's evening.

Edmund wasn't sure whether he'd be able to help much, but if the steam engine really were malfunctioning he was certain Turner wouldn't be able to cope. The fellow didn't seem able to work things out for himself, only follow procedures he'd already been shown. Robbie Preston had far more promise as an engineer, though how Edmund could train him properly in such a small and ill-equipped workshop was a worry.

When they got near Hedderby, Edmund called a halt and sent his guide back. He stood looking down at the town from above the engineering works, noticing at once that there were lights on in the engine house and that a thick plume of smoke was pouring from the chimney. Why the hell were they running the engine flat out at this time of night?

When he started walking along the lane that led into the huddle of streets, he heard other footsteps and someone grabbed hold of him.

'I've cotched one of 'em!' a voice yelled.

A man came closer, shone a lantern in Edmund's face and laughed. 'Tha's cotched Mr Edmund, tha bloody great fool! What're you doing here, sir? We've just sent two lads out to fetch you.'

'I've come to see what's going on in that engine house. I heard the engine wasn't running properly.'

'It isn't. But we can't do owt to it till we get young Mrs Beckett away safe. Your cousin's took her and is threatening to hurt her unless Mr Beckett does as he wants.'

Edmund gaped at him for a moment, then his eyes went back to the smoke that shouldn't be coming out of the chimney at night. 'Any reason for them firing up the engine?'

'They've not bedded it down, more like. Turner's been working on it since they closed this afternoon. There's summat wrong, Mr Edmund, any of us old hands can tell that. Only *you* could fettle that old engine.'

'As soon as you've got Mrs Beckett out, I'd better find out what's wrong with it.'

As they stood waiting, Edmund couldn't keep his thoughts off the steam engine. If Turner was adjusting the governor again, he'd have to keep the boiler going full tilt. And should it explode, the people inside the engine house would be killed and afterwards dozens of men would be out of work.

What the hell was the fool playing at? And why could his cousin not see the danger?

Once Eli was away from the pub, a man came up to him and said, 'Follow me.' He wasn't in the least surprised to be taken to the rear yard of Stott's. There two men moved out of the shadows to bar his way.

'He said you'd come,' one remarked.

The other gave a snort of laughter. 'I'd come too with a pretty young wife like that in Mr Stott's hands.'

'Shut up, you fool! What if *he* heard you?' the first one warned, then turned back to Eli. 'Mr Stott's waiting for you, but first we've to check you for weapons.'

'I'm not armed.' Eli forced himself to stand still as they patted his clothing to assure themselves he was telling the truth, then when one prodded him forward, he began walking, pretending to stumble. 'Shouldn't have had so much to drink,' he muttered, trying to slur his words.

The garrulous one let out another snort of laughter. 'Fine rescuer this one is. He's drunk.'

'*Will* you shut up and get him inside!'

They led Eli into the engine room. He pretended to trip and cast a quick glance round as he righted himself. Carrie was tied to one of the wall bars, with Robbie and Bonny beside her. Anger welled in him, not only at the sight of his wife being treated like that but at Bonny's tear-stained, bewildered face. But he held the red-hot rage back and let his mouth hang half open. He couldn't rescue her on his own, had to delay matters till the others came, which he had no doubt they would do.

'He's drunk,' one of his guards announced.

Carrie looked at him in surprise, then quickly lowered her eyes.

With a sneering expression on his face, Stott sauntered across. 'Not too drunk to listen to my terms, I hope?'

Eli stared at him in that wide-eyed, slack way he'd seen drunks look at the world so many times, letting himself sway slightly.

'Tonight your wife will be taken from here and kept safely somewhere else, together with that idiot aunt of Heegan's, until you and your cousin have signed a contract to sell the land and pub to me. Once you've done that they'll be released.' Stott turned to look towards his prisoners and added, 'But if you value your wife's safety, you'll keep her brother from making a nuisance of himself in the meantime.'

'You didn't want the pub before,' Eli said. 'Jus' the land next to it.'

'I've changed my mind. I'm going to need all of it eventually and don't want more trouble from you later. I want you and your cousin out of Hedderby, and the sooner the better. I do hope you're not going to give me any trouble or else . . .' He turned to stare meaningfully towards Carrie and then looked questioningly back to Eli. 'We'll start by having you sign a memorandum of agreement to sell.' He fumbled inside his overcoat and brought out a folded paper.

Eli forced a belch and said, 'Got to be sick!'

Athol stepped quickly sideways, wincing as he bumped into a hot pipe and shouting, 'Take him outside, you fools, but make sure he doesn't get away.'

Eli made the appropriate noises of a man about to vomit, a trick he'd developed as a young lad, and let his guards hurry him outside.

Carrie watched in puzzlement, knowing Eli never drank much, let alone enough to make him sick. Bonny continued to sniff dolefully and Robbie seized the moment when all eyes were on Eli to tug at his bonds, which had been fastened carelessly because he'd been pretending to be dazed and had sagged against them. He tried to wriggle his wrists out and felt the rope give a little, but not enough. Someone turned to look at him and he became still.

Outside Eli stumbled towards the water butts as if about to vomit beneath them and gasped as he saw two men in the shadows between them.

'Get them across here,' Bram whispered.

Eli pretended to heave then made a staggering run across the yard towards the gate, upon which his captors rushed across to grab him, thinking he was trying to escape.

As they passed the water butts, Bram and Declan hit them with some pieces of wood they'd picked up, making sure both men were unconscious.

'Stott's got Carrie, her brother and Bonny tied up

in there,' Eli said in a low voice. 'I'm expecting some men to join us from Hedderby, but if not, we'll have to go in and rescue them ourselves.'

But even as he spoke there were footsteps in the back alley and men slipped quietly into the yard, standing patiently and looking to Eli for instructions. He explained what had happened and there was a low rumble of anger from the newcomers.

'Let's go in and get the bastard,' one man whispered. 'I've a score of my own to settle with him, been waiting years.'

'No!' Eli stuck out his hand to bar the way. 'We have to plan this. If he's got a weapon, he could hurt my wife.'

'There's another door leading outside from the store cupboard,' one man said. 'It's not much used and I doubt Mr Stott even knows about it, but Mr Edmund allus kept it unlocked. He said if the engine ever blew, it was another way out. If that's still open, we could get inside through there as well as through the main door to the engine house.'

'Good. Send someone to check it.'

A man ran off.

'They're tied up. Has anyone got a knife?' Eli asked.

Declan and another man produced knives, the blades shining in the moonlight.

'What are you doing out there?' a voice yelled. 'Hasn't he finished puking yet?'

'Just.'

The man who'd gone round the side came back. 'It's unlocked,' he whispered.

'Good. Now I've got to go back in,' Eli said. 'Get round the other side, some of you, and the rest wait out here.' A few men slipped round the corner of the building. 'Two of you act as if you're holding me up. Keep your heads down and with a bit of luck he won't notice you're not his men until we're inside.' Eli took a deep breath and tried to make his features go slack, moistening his chin with spit.

Two men moved to hold him up and they edged quickly into the room.

Stott had put the piece of paper on a shelf with an ink pot next to it. He beckoned to Eli, 'Come and sign this, then we'll—' He broke off abruptly as he noticed that these weren't his men and shoved his hand in his pocket, starting to move backwards as he pulled something out.

Behind him, Robbie writhed desperately, tugging at his bonds. But it was Carrie who stuck out her foot and tripped Stott. As the man stumbled, desperation lent Robbie extra strength and he wriggled his hands free, diving at Stott just as he aimed the pistol at Eli.

While this was going on Bram had slipped into the engine room from the store cupboard, his eyes scanning the room rapidly. He left Robbie to struggle with Stott for possession of the gun and ran to cut the ropes that bound Carrie and his aunt, shoving them towards the men who'd entered with him and yelling, 'Get them to safety!'

While this was going on, Edmund appeared in the doorway, staring in horror at the governor of the steam engine. The gadget's arms were heavily weighted down or they would have swung up to activate the safety valve. Turner was cowering in one corner while men were struggling against the wall and steam was hissing out of several joins in pipes. But worst of all was the ominous rumbling sound coming from the boiler. There was nothing he could do now.

'It's only a matter of minutes before it blows,' he shouted. 'Get everyone out of here! *Quickly!*'

Even as he spoke Athol managed to pull the gun's trigger and the bullet ricocheted round the room. Robbie punched him hard on the jaw and he fell back on the floor, banging his head on a piece of metal and dropping the pistol.

Eli kicked the weapon out of the way, grabbed Robbie's jacket and hauled him to his feet. 'Come on! We have to get out.'

Men were rushing out of both doors, and since he knew his wife had already left through the storeroom, Eli tugged Robbie towards the other door.

Stott pushed himself to his feet and began to stumble after them, dizzy and slow, holding his head.

As the boiler began making loud noises and shaking, Turner looked round in panic and with a yell of terror ran round the room towards the main door, seeming to have forgotten about the store-room exit in his panic. Before he could get there the boiler exploded in a flash of brilliant whitelight, sending scalding steam pouring into the room in a rapidly expanding cloud. The explosion caught him and threw him to the floor.

The last of the rescuers, who had only just left

through the doorway, yelled in pain as vapour burst from it behind him, hitting the back of his neck. But the others were already halfway across the yard, running to escape the clouds of super-heated steam.

A man screamed inside, but no one else came out of the door. The screams went on and on, so filled with pain that those who heard them shuddered. Then they cut off suddenly.

Eli stepped forward as if to go back inside and try to rescue the sufferer, but Edmund grabbed hold of him. 'There's nothing you can do till the steam clears and things settle.'

The ensuing silence seemed to echo round the yard.

'There was only Stott and Turner left in there and I hope they're both dead,' one man said.

'No one could survive that.' Edmund found that he was shaking suddenly and couldn't seem to stop.

Eli let out a deep shuddering breath and looked for his wife. His heart pounding with fear that she'd been injured, he ran round the side of the building. There he found a group of people huddled against the wall, rescuers and villains mingled, all deeply shocked by the accident.

In the middle of them were the two women.

'Carrie!' he called at the top of his powerful voice.

She raised her head, let go of Bonny and lurched forward stiffly, as if her legs weren't working properly.

With a sob of sheer relief Eli gathered her into his arms. 'My darling, tell me you're not hurt.' He rained kisses on her face then pulled her close again.

'I'm not hurt. What did you just call me?'

'My darling. When I thought Stott was going to hurt you, I wanted to kill him but all I could do was act the fool. I wasn't drunk. I wasn't being a coward. I was waiting for the others to arrive.'

'I guessed that.' Carrie put her arms round him and held on to him tightly. 'You had everyone fooled, but I know you better.' She felt moisture on his cheeks and raised one fingertip to check that it was what she thought. 'Why are you weeping?'

'Because you're safe. If I'd lost you—' Eli couldn't finish the sentence but hugged her close, his throat thick with emotion. He kissed her hair and her forehead, caressing her cheek then bringing her hand to his lips. 'I couldn't bear to lose you now, Carrie darling.'

'Nor I you.'

Oblivious to what was going on around them, they kissed one another deeply, pressing against one another and sighing with the need to touch, to caress, above all to be sure that the other really was safe.

Not until someone cleared his throat loudly next to them did they break apart, realising where they were. Bram was smiling at them, one arm round his aunt's shoulders.

'They're kissing each other,' Bonny announced, her tear-stained face breaking into one of her wide smiles. 'That's good.' She patted them and for a moment clung to Carrie's hand then leaned against her nephew again. 'All safe now.'

'Yes,' Carrie agreed huskily. 'All safe.'

'I can see you two have important things to – er – discuss,' Bram said. 'Why don't you go home and leave me to sort things out here? Tell Joanna I'm all right and I'll be back as soon as I can.'

Just then a voice yelled, 'Everyone stay where you are!' and the new police sergeant came striding into the yard, flanked by his two constables.

Bram gave Eli a push. 'Slip round the side or you'll be here half the night answering questions.'

Bonny watched them go then looked at her nephew. 'I was frightened, but I'm not frightened now.'

'I know. We've stopped Stott and you won't need to be frightened of him ever again. Now, let's go and tell the sergeant what happened.'

Eli and Carrie slipped out of the works unchallenged because so many people were rushing towards it to see what had caused the explosion, calling to one another excitedly, their eyes on the big cloud of steam hanging above the area, brightly lit by the moonlight.

When Eli and Carrie got back to the pub, it was almost empty because even the potmen had abandoned their posts to go and see what had caused the explosion.

Joanna was clearing up the pots but set her tray down the minute she saw them and came running across the room. 'Bram?' she asked in a voice that trembled. 'I didn't dare go after him in case I missed him in the crowds.'

'He's fine. He stayed behind to help the police.'

Joanna closed her eyes and shuddered. 'Thank goodness. Come and tell us what happened.'

Raife had been sitting behind the bar sipping a beer, but set it down and waited for them to join him.

'We'll go into the kitchen,' Joanna said. 'You'll want a hot drink, I'm sure. Raife, you'll join us, won't you?'

He nodded and gave Carrie a big hug. 'I'm too old to rush out and gape at accidents, but I were afraid for you, lass, when we heard the explosion. Eh, it were that loud! Everyone shut up, then someone ran in and told us it were at Stott's. Before we knew it they had all rushed out to see it.'

'Including the potmen,' Joanna said. 'I'll have a few things to say to them tomorrow.' She too gave Carrie a hug. 'Are you sure you're all right?'

'I'm fine. Eli and the others rescued me in time.'

They explained what had happened, their account punctuated by Raife's soft exclamations and Joanna's louder and more indignant ones.

'So he's dead, Mr Stott?' Raife asked when they'd finished their tale.

Eli nodded. 'He must be. No one could have survived in there.'

'He were bad through and through, that one. You'd only to see that sneering face of his to know it. Deserved all he got, I reckon.' The old man smiled at the two of them. 'But I think this night's brought you two closer together, eh? And about time too.'

They exchanged quick smiles.

Raife looked round the room and grimaced. 'A right old mess they've left the place in, haven't they? I'll leave you folk to close up. Nev will want to know what's happened.'

Eli walked across to the entrance with him, going out into the street to stare in the direction of Stott's. The sky was brightly lit now, as if something was burning. With a shake of his head, he locked the front doors then went back to the kitchen. Carrie was no longer there.

'She's gone up to bed,' Joanna said softly. 'Why don't you go and join her and leave me to wait up for Bram? I think you two need to be together. Have you made up your differences?'

'I hope so.' Had it been so obvious? Eli wondered as he walked up the stairs. He was feeling weary now and worried that the minute he got into the bedroom, Carrie would freeze up again.

When he pushed the door open he found her sitting on the bed, looking exhausted, but she gave him a shy smile and held out her arms.

'Come and hold me, Eli. I can't believe it's all over and we're safe. I need you to hold me close.'

He sat down beside her and pulled her in his arms. 'I've been wanting to hold you close ever since we got married, love.'

'I know. And I've been afraid.'

'Of loving me?'

She nestled against him. 'Afraid of all sorts of things. Of you not really loving me but wanting to marry me to get the pub. Of being like my mother and having so many children.' Her voice dropped to a low whisper as she added, 'Most of all of not being able to please you in bed. I'm older than most lasses when they wed and I've never walked out with lads. I just felt – bad about myself.'

'It all happened too quickly between us, that's why. And we were so busy.' He cradled her against him. 'But from now on, I'll make time to be with you, I promise.'

She couldn't hold back a gurgle of laughter.

'What have I said that's funny?'

'The minute there's a crisis with the music room you'll forget everything else, me included. An' you'll always be busy. I'm getting to know you, you can't sit still for a minute.'

Eli looked at her, shame-faced, and admitted, 'Well, I'm a bit like that when I'm doing something, I will admit, and I reckon I always will be. But if I tell you now that I love you, that I want you beside me whatever we do, will you hold tight to that and put up with my ways?'

'As long as you prove you love me.' Carrie looked at him shyly. 'It's more than time, isn't it?'

He kissed the soft cheek that was so close to his. 'I'll go and lock the bedroom door. The devil himself can knock and I'll not open it tonight.'

As he walked back he began shrugging out of his jacket and unbuttoning his shirt.

She raised her hands to her own clothes but he stopped her. 'No. I want to undress you tonight, love. Slowly and tenderly. I want to show you how wonderful love can be between us.'

He swung her into his arms before she'd realised

what he was doing and laid her down on the bed, smiling at her as he leaned across to blow out the candle.

And she found that in his arms she wasn't afraid any more, that his love and tenderness made every touch a pleasure, every sigh an expression of joy . . .

Carrie and Eli woke late and when they went downstairs found Joanna and Bram in the kitchen, looking tired. Out in the big room there were sounds of people working. Here there was a glowing fire and friends to share the news.

'The police sergeant wants to see you two today,' Bram said. 'We kept him from disturbing you last night, though, said Carrie was too upset by it all.'

She blushed. She'd completely forgotten the accident once Eli started making love to her.

'What's happened?' Eli asked.

'The bad news is that the works will have to be closed down till they can rebuild the engine house and get a new steam engine.'

'It'll be hard for the men out of work,' Carrie said at once. 'Eh, what'll they do to put bread on the table?'

'The other bad news,' Bram said, 'is that Athol Stott is still alive.'

They stared at him in amazement. 'He can't be!' Eli said. 'No one could survive in there.'

'Apparently he was near enough the door to miss the worst and his fine clothes helped protect him. But he's so badly burned they don't know if he'll survive.

If he does, he'll be a cripple because a burning beam fell on one of his legs and crushed it. Dr Latimer had to amputate it.'

'It makes me so angry that an evil creature like him should survive,' Joanna exclaimed. 'After all the trouble he's caused!'

'He may not survive,' Bram said. 'Dr Latimer says it'll be touch and go for a while.'

'Well, then,' said Eli. 'Let's get something to eat and set about our own concerns. We've a music room to finish and a pub to run. We'll go and see the sergeant this afternoon and we'd better look in on your mother too, Carrie.'

Joanna nodded. 'Nev's already called round today to ask if you're all right. I refused to wake you up.' She chuckled. 'Even Bram's mother came to see us, to make sure he wasn't hurt. She spoke to me quite civilly, too.'

'That's because she doesn't know you yet and is being polite,' he said. 'You wait. She'll soon be telling you how to run your house and bring up your children, not to mention trying to convert you. She never gives up.'

'She loves you, though. It shines in her eyes.'

'I love her too. She's a grand mother, for all her sharp tongue.'

There was a loud voice outside and Bram rolled his eyes. 'The sergeant hasn't waited for you to go to him.'

And from then on the day was filled with a procession of people, wanting to see that they were all right and to hear first-hand what had happened, until Carrie and Eli took refuge in their bedroom again and made Joanna tell people they were feeling poorly.

And once more she found joy in his arms, pleasure beyond her wildest dreams, and another sort of pleasure that she hadn't expected in lying there afterwards, cuddled up close, talking quietly.

Two days after the accident, Maria Stott sent a message asking Edmund to go and see her.

She received him in the parlour and indicated a chair. 'Thank you for coming. It's very generous of you, given the circumstances.'

'How are you, Maria?'

'I'm quite well.'

'And Athol?'

'In great pain. They keep him asleep as much as possible or he screams out.' She shuddered. 'He'll be badly scarred on one side of his face.'

'Is there anything I can do to help you?'

'Yes. That's why I asked you to come. Could you possibly take charge at the works? Get the repairs started, buy a new steam engine and get things going again as quickly as possible? Families will be going hungry till Stott's reopens.'

'What will Athol say to my being involved?'

'He'll be in no position to say anything for some time yet. It's me who's asking your help. We can't let the business dwindle to nothing, for the sake of me and my children as well as the men who work there.'

'If I agree, I'll want to do things my way,' Edmund warned.

'I'd prefer that. I know Athol can be very harsh with the men.'

Her face was pale but determined and it seemed to Edmund that Maria had come out of hiding, was showing her real personality for once.

'I'll not do it unless you accept my wife socially,' he said. 'I'm sorry, but I have to think of her and my child, as well as you and yours.'

'You must bring her to tea as soon as we know whether Athol will live or not.' Maria waited, looking at him questioningly.

'Very well. I'll take charge for the moment. But it'll cost a lot of money to set the works to rights. There are some jobs we can do without the old engine, and maybe we can find a small one to use temporarily while we have another one fitted and a new engine house built.' His voice grew enthusiastic. 'They're making much better engines now. We'll be able to do so much more with it.'

'That's good. When Athol's conscious, I'll get him to approve everything.'

'I don't envy you if he recovers.'

She shrugged slightly. 'Your cousin has never been easy to live with, but I took him for better for worse, he's the father of my children, and I'll honour my vows.'

Which was more than Athol had ever done to her, Edmund knew.

He left soon afterwards, to go round to the works

and make a start on organising men to clear the site. That would keep some of them in work, and perhaps he could find other tasks for them.

During the next two days Athol Stott hovered between life and death. His wife made sure he received the best of care. When Edmund visited her again Maria agreed to everything he suggested. When he'd gone she took out her embroidery and sat quietly in the parlour, listening to footsteps upstairs as those caring for the injured man moved to and fro.

Later she visited her children in the schoolroom and they prayed for their father and her husband together. It was, she thought, a very strange time, with everything she knew suspended and life feeling unreal.

When Edmund sent to ask whether she wished to visit the engineering works, she agreed, having a sudden fancy to get out of the house, but first she visited Mr Hordle.

'I'm no longer acting for your husband,' he told her.

Maria looked at him with her usual quiet composure. 'I know. But I thought, until he recovers, I might persuade you to help me? He's unconscious and I must take charge for the moment. I need to draw up a document giving Cousin Edmund complete authority to manage the works until such date as my husband is once again fit to run things, and to make sure the bank pays the cost of everything.'

Hordle suppressed a sigh. 'Very well, I'll help *you*. But I must make it plain that I shan't continue to act as your husband's legal adviser once he takes over again.'

She nodded.

When she got to the works, she found Edmund labouring with the men, as dirty as them and somehow one of them, as Athol had never been. He walked round with her, showing how he was keeping as many employed as possible by restarting the old water wheel that he'd insisted on maintaining against Athol's wishes. They could still use that to turn some of the smaller machinery.

'I've arranged for you to have complete authority to run things,' Maria said as they stood by her carriage. She passed him the necessary papers. 'The bank manager will remit whatever monies you need. You should consult him before finalising the purchase of a new steam engine.'

'How is Athol today?'

'Delirious. In great pain. They keep him sedated with laudanum.'

'I wondered whether Stott's could provide some food for the families in want?'

'Yes, of course, Edmund. How can we arrange that?'

'My wife and our maid will see to it. You'll have enough to do already.'

Two days after the explosion Eli woke up full of energy and enthusiasm. 'I've worked out what to do next,' he announced over breakfast. 'We can finish the music room quite quickly, enough to use it anyway. And we'll put on a gala the first evening, with the proceeds going to help the men who've been put out of work by the explosion. That'll bring folk in from all round. We'll pay the performers as our contribution, but the audience will have to buy their own drinks, so we won't lose much.'

He went outside with a piece of toast uneaten in his hand, pacing the big, airy room, muttering to himself and eventually casting the toast aside.

Carrie watched him through the window with an indulgent smile then turned to Joanna. 'I doubt he'll do more than pop in for food every now and then until that room's finished.'

'He's obsessed by it.'

'It's a long-held dream. I admire that. Did he tell you what he's going to call it?'

Joanna nodded. 'The Pride of Lancashire.'

'It's a wonderful name, isn't it? And Eli says it's only the first step. He wants to own a proper music hall one day, like the ones they're starting to build in London. He's going to take me there and show me.' Carrie's eyes strayed to the window again.

'He's lucky he's married to someone like you,' Joanna said suddenly.

'Why do you say that?'

'Because it'll take a strong woman to love Eli. He's not going to make an easy husband.'

'I know.' Carrie grinned. 'But I could say the same about Bram.'

They both smiled and started on their day's work.

A week later Maria Stott was called in to her husband's room by the nurse. 'He wants to speak to you, ma'am.'

Athol was lying in bed looking at her, sweat pearling his brow, his hands clenched on the bedcovers with the effort needed to control the pain of his injuries for long enough to speak to her.

'How are you feeling?' she asked, moving to stand at the bedside.

'How the hell do you think? In pain.' He groaned but forced himself to speak. 'Before they give me that damned laudanum again, I want to know what's happened to the works.'

'I asked Edmund to take over and he's working very hard to replace the steam engine and get things running properly again.'

'He always was a fool! If I was him, I'd not do it.'

She thought for a minute that Athol had lost consciousness but he opened his eyes again and stared at her. 'I'll not see him. I'll not see anyone. I'm not having them gloating at this.' One wave of his left hand indicated his ravaged, twisted face and claw-like right hand.

'No one would gloat, least of all Edmund.'

Athol closed his eyes and said in a savagely controlled voice, 'Give me some more of that stuff now.'

The nurse came forward with the glass and helped him drink.

Athol lay back. 'One day I'll make them sorry for what they've done,' he muttered.

Maria said calmly and clearly, 'No one did this to you, Athol. It was an accident.'

He gave no sign of having heard her and after a

moment she left the room. He didn't refer to the matter again and spent most of his time in a haze of laudanum. The stump of his leg picked up a slight infection and for days they feared for his life, but gradually he recovered.

Maria didn't know whether she was glad or sorry about that. And she couldn't get his threat of revenge out of her mind. But since he told her to get out every time she went into his bedroom from then on, she had no further opportunity to talk to him for a few weeks.

## 26

# THE PRIDE OF LANCASHIRE

Hedderby's brand new music room will open on

## Saturday January 10th

with a Gala Performance in aid of the
workers from Stott's and their families.

************************************************************

*Featuring:*   **The Manchester Songbird**
               **Jimmy Sadler, comic songs**
               **Carring Brothers, acrobats**
               **Our own Bram Heegan**
               **The Barrett Sisters, songs and dance**
               **. . . . . and more**

**The evening will end with a musical sing-song of
old favourites, led by Bram Heegan, musical
accompaniment by Raife Linney**

*Tickets may be purchased in advance from the*

## Dragon Public House

*6d per head for seating on the main floor,
1/- for the front tables*

Four weeks after the explosion posters went up all over Hedderby and the surrounding villages, advertising the opening of the new music room.

Inside the stage was finished, with an alcove just below it on the right for the Chairman's table, where the old coal place had been. There was a fireplace at the rear of the long room and one to the left. The floor was still flagged, but Eli had found rugs to put under the best tables and chairs, which were set out nearest the stage. Those paying only sixpence were seated on benches at the three long rows of tables set further back at right angles to the stage.

Eli and Joanna made frequent trips into Manchester to buy supplies of all sorts, but had to be careful because the money they'd inherited wasn't unlimited.

'We're taking a risk,' she said abruptly one day in the train on the way back. 'I lie awake at night sometimes, worrying about it. Don't you?'

He shook his head. 'I'm too tired.'

'You're working far too hard.'

'Aren't we all? My Carrie's been a tower of strength.'

Joanna watched how his face softened as he said his wife's name. She was so pleased to see them happy with one another.

'It'll be worth it,' Eli insisted. 'We'll be rich one day, you and I, but we'll never feel such a thrill as we do now, starting off, making our money stretch, using our wits.'

When the opening night came the four owners all got ready early. Eli, who would be Chairman of the proceedings, was wearing black trousers and tailcoat with a brocade waistcoat underneath in a dusky rose colour. Bram was similarly clad, with a green waistcoat. He had laughed at the idea of dressing up to ape the gentry but had nonetheless succumbed to Joanna's coaxing because he was one of the acts.

Carrie was wearing the most beautiful dress she'd ever owned, a brand new one that had been made 'specially for her. The dark green velvet suited her colouring and the skirt was so full it seemed to have a life of its own and swayed to and fro as she walked. The separate bodice was pointed and boned so that she couldn't bend easily and the sleeves were long and tightly fitted. She wouldn't like to wear a dress like this to do her daily work. Joanna was wearing a dress in a similar style, but in blue, with lace at neck and wrists.

The two women had done each other's hair, pinning it up and adding ornaments of ribbon and lace which Joanna had purchased for them in Manchester.

Eli checked the pub, which wasn't as full as usual because everyone who could scrape the money together had bought a ticket for the gala. 'Your brother Declan has everything under control,' he told Bram when he rejoined them.

Joanna, who had been checking the dressing rooms behind the stage, came through and said, 'Everything seems all right. The artistes aren't used to arriving early and waiting, when they usually do two or three shows in a night, but they're in a good mood because it's an easier night for them.'

'They should be happy,' Eli grumbled, 'the amount we're paying them.'

'They all accepted less for tonight because it's a good cause,' Bram said easily. 'Stop worrying about the money. We'll do well here, I know it.'

'I can't believe this is happening,' Carrie said as they went through to the foyer, checking that everything was ready. Here they had waiters not potmen, two of the three being men who had worked in Stott's before the explosion. They had been trained by Joanna, then provided with dark trousers and waistcoats, with long black aprons round their waists.

The whole town was trying to give the men who'd lost their jobs employment until the works were fully operational again.

Soon the first members of the audience arrived, Mr Marker and his family who had been invited to come at Eli's expense but had declined, saying they'd prefer to pay and support the families who were in difficulties. They sat beaming with anticipation at one of the front tables.

It seemed from then onwards that a stream of people poured through the doors till surely the Pride could hold no more. The more affluent customers were well dressed, but even the poorer ones had made a special effort for this gala night.

Bram kept an eye on the audience, to make sure they behaved themselves, but people were in a mood for pleasure, talking, laughing and cramming in somehow. Nev Linney had brought along all Carrie's sisters and even young Ted, though Grace and Lily were in the kitchen with their mother whose all too obvious condition kept her from appearing in public. Jane had been brought to the pub earlier in a horse-drawn cab, and would be able to hear the singing while sitting with her feet up, so was perfectly happy.

Dr Latimer and his wife were there at the front tables, and Essie was sitting at one of the long ones with her friend who was housekeeper to Mr Hordle. Edmund Stott and his sweet-faced young wife were there too. In fact, anyone who could spare the money was crammed into the big room, even the owner of the cotton mill.

But in spite of the fact that the gala was in aid of his men, Athol Stott's family was not there, though Edmund had invited Maria to join him and Faith. Even Athol's servants hadn't dared come, having been threatened with dismissal if they did.

When it was time for the show to begin, Eli turned to Carrie. 'I've never been nervous before,' he confessed suddenly. 'But I'm nervous tonight.'

'You'll be wonderful,' she said. 'You know how to do it after all that practising.' She kissed him quickly then gave him a little push, standing quietly at the back of the room and watching with enormous pride as he walked forward to take his place at the front. People went quiet as Eli passed, nudging one another and making shushing noises. As he raised his gavel excitement seemed to buzz round the room, affecting everyone.

'Ladies and gentlemen,' he boomed, his voice carrying clearly to every corner, 'I bid you welcome to the opening night of Hedderby's own music room – the Pride of Lancashire.'

Applause and cheers forced him to wait a minute, smiling, then use his gavel again. 'If you don't let me continue, my friends, we'll never get this show started. Now, let's all put our hands together for our musicians!'

Beaming at everyone, Raife led out his drummer and fiddler and they took their seats on the smaller, lower platform to the left of the main stage. He played a series of crashing chords on the piano, then nodded his head to tell Eli to continue.

'Our first act tonight is Jimmy Sadler, well known in Manchester for his comic songs. No one can sing them as well as Jimmy, so let's give him a warm Lancashire welcome . . .'

One act followed another. The audience sang the choruses, 'oohed' and 'aahed' at the acrobats, used the short breaks to order more drinks or visit the necessary, and generally enjoyed themselves hugely.

The loudest applause was for Bram who gave them three sentimental songs that had some people wiping their eyes, then held up his hand for their attention. 'Mr Raife Linney has written a song 'specially for tonight. It's called "The Pride of Lancashire".' Cheers rang out. 'If you listen carefully, you'll soon learn the chorus and be able to join in.' He nodded to Raife and sang the song, which had a simple but lilting melody and an easy chorus of: *'She's the pride of Lancashire, boys, she's the pride of Lancashire'*.

Soon they were all joining in, swaying to and fro

as they echoed the simple words, feeling a sense of pride because it was *their* town's song and *their* county they were singing about.

Finally The Manchester Songbird came on stage, and everyone fell silent. She might be ageing now, but her voice had a rare beauty that made everyone listen intently and stay silent for several seconds after she'd finished. Then they all seemed to recover at once and roar into applause, shouting for more, so that she deigned to give them not just one encore, but two.

With that the evening was over, but it was some time before the audience dispersed because everyone wanted to speak to Eli, Bram and Joanna, who were standing near the big double doors. Carrie had refused to play so public a part and was waiting by the side door that led into the kitchen, tired but still buoyed up by excitement. She was so proud of Eli. This was all due to his grand dream, and together they'd made it come true.

After he'd locked the doors, he led the way back into the music room, put one arm round his wife's waist and looked at Joanna and Bram, who were standing nearby holding hands.

'We did it,' Eli said at last, and blew his nose vigorously.

'Hard work, but it's all paid off,' Joanna agreed. 'Do you want to count the takings tonight or tomorrow?'

'Tomorrow.'

'There'll be more hard work tomorrow, cleaning up,' Bram said with a grimace.

'We'll train the staff to do it afterwards,' Eli said.

'But for tonight I didn't want them lingering. Come on! I left the stage lights on deliberately. We're going in to have our own final chorus.'

'You know I can't sing,' Carrie protested.

'You're not being left out,' he said firmly, and led the way on to the stage.

'What shall we sing?' Joanna asked.

'"The Pride of Lancashire", of course.'

Joanna went to play a chord on the piano and Bram led them into the song, the music echoing round the room.

When they'd finished, Eli wiped one hand across his eyes and said in a thickened voice, 'Eh, look at me, skriking like a baby.'

But they all had tears in their eyes.

'I'll never forget this night as long as I live,' Carrie said, her voice warm and soft with satisfaction. 'You've made us dream with you, Eli, and now the dreams have come true.'

He laughed. 'I've other dreams waiting in the wings. I want a real music hall one day, with top acts coming to Hedderby, and a wife who doesn't have to work so hard.' He gave Carrie a loving glance.

'I don't mind hard work, you can dream more dreams if you want,' she said. 'But let's enjoy the music room as it is for a while.'

Eli put his arm round her waist again and the four of them left the stage. He extinguished the big gas lights and the room was suddenly dark and mysterious, except for the light shining from the open kitchen door.

Joanna and Bram disappeared through it and Eli stopped in his tracks for a minute. 'If it wasn't for you, we wouldn't have this,' he said. 'I love you, Carrie Beckett. I couldn't have found a better wife.'

'I love you, too.'

As they went slowly up to bed she smiled. Eli didn't say those words often, but she was quite sure now that he meant them.

His music room might be the Pride of Lancashire, but Eli was her pride and joy. She'd never even dreamed of being so happy. With a sigh of bliss, she began to undress then turned into his loving arms.

# ABOUT THE AUTHOR

Anna Jacobs grew up in Lancashire and emigrated to Australia a while ago, but still visits the UK regularly to see her family and do research, something she loves. She has two grown-up daughters and lives with her husband in a spacious waterfront home. Often, as she writes, dolphins frolic outside her office. Inside, the house is crammed with thousands of books.

# Contact Anna

Anna Jacobs is always delighted to hear from readers and can be contacted:

**BY MAIL**
PO Box 628
Mandurah
Western Australia 6210

If you'd like a reply, please enclose a self-addressed, business size envelope, stamped (from inside Australia) or an international reply coupon (from outside Australia).

**VIA THE INTERNET**
Anna has her own web domain, with details of her books, latest news and excerpts to read. Come and visit her site at http://www.annajacobs.com

Anna can be contacted by email at anna@annajacobs.com

If you'd like to receive an email newsletter about Anna and her books every month or two, you are cordially invited to join her announcements list. Just email her and ask to be added to the list, or follow the link from her web page.

**READERS' DISCUSSION LIST**
A reader has created a web site where readers can meet and discuss Anna's novels. Anna is not involved in the discussions at all, nor is she a member of that list – she's too busy writing new stories. If you're interested in joining, it's at http://groups.msn.com/AnnaJacobsFanClub